Charming A Grim

Book Two of the Draxmere Academy of Conjuring Series

M.N. Lash

Charming A Grim

M.N. Lash

Table of Contents

Before you even begin to flip through the pages of this book—read this list. This is a dark fantasy/romance and has several dark elements involved. Those include:

—Lack of emotions/feeling/dissociation (The character believes herself to be monstrous/bad because of these issues, but I am NOT trying to portray people with these issues as such)

—Graphic death (murder, accidental, in-the-process-of-dying)

—Graphic violence/gore (torture/body mutilation)

—Mentions of dead parents/family

—Mentions of divorce

—Self-harm/suicidal thoughts

—Mentions of infertility issues (including miscarriages/ectopic pregnancy)

—Sexual activities (explicit content)

—Substance abuse (including alcohol and drugs)

—Stalking/obsessive behaviors

—Content that may or may not make you cry (in a good way, maybe?)

—Also, I kept the Florida jabs to a minimum, but I did add some general Southern state jabs as well. You know, to be inclusive and all.

Playlist

CHARMING A GRIM

Conjuring Ability Identifiers

WEREWOLVES
VAMPIRES
SHIFTERS
SIRENS

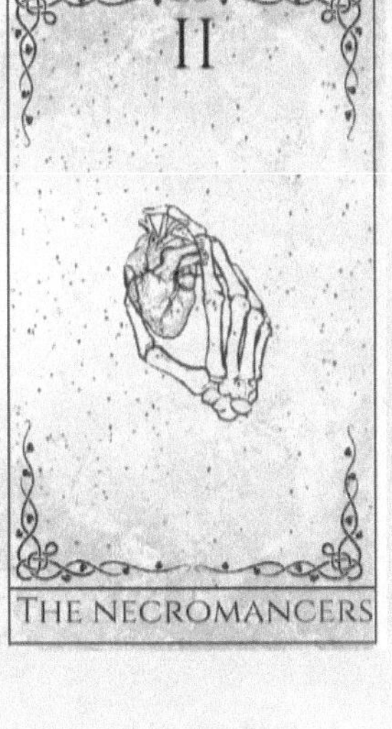

Conjuring Ability Identifier

AIR
FIRE
EARTH
WATER

LIGHT
SHADOWS

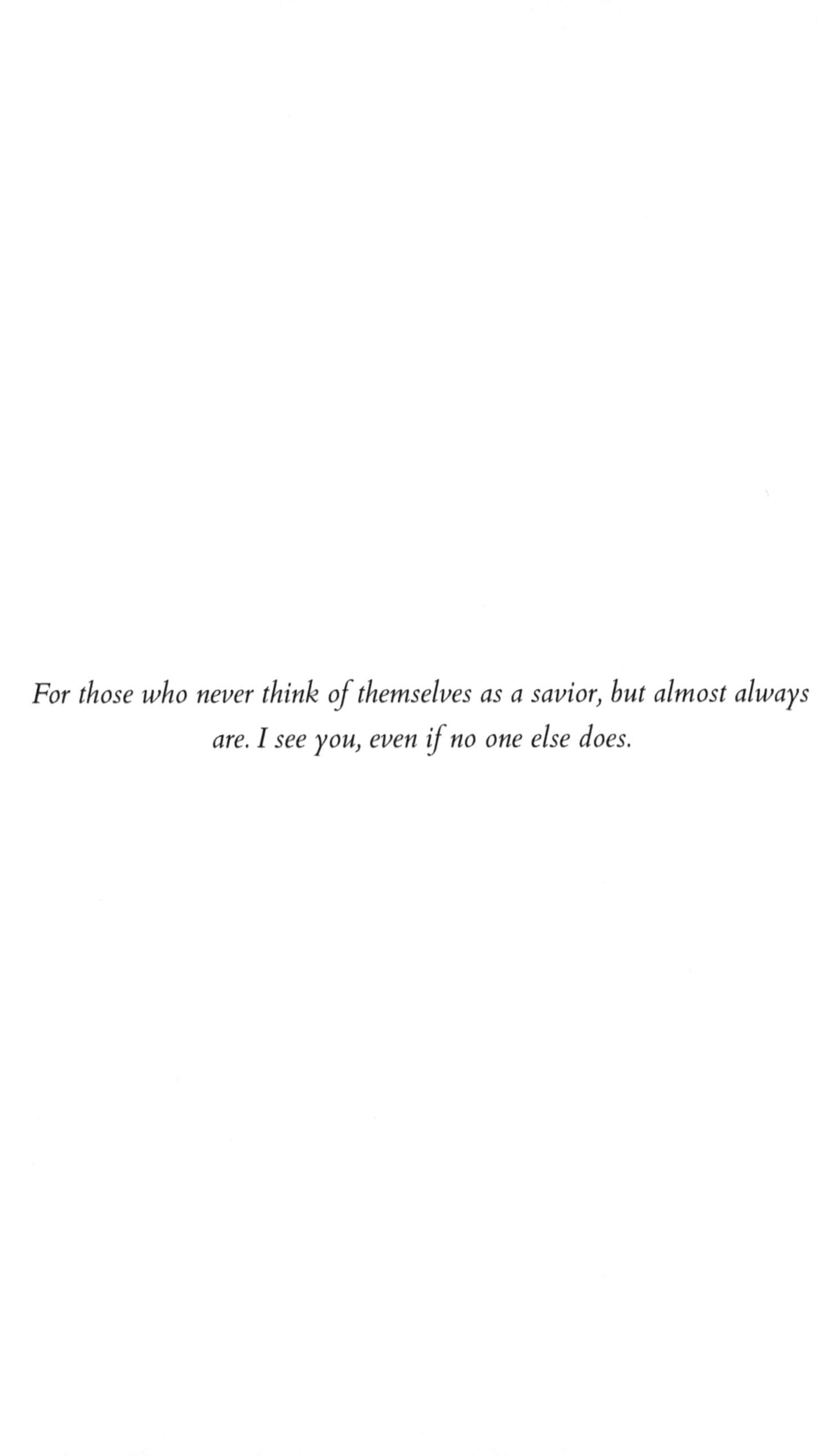

*For those who never think of themselves as a savior, but almost always
are. I see you, even if no one else does.*

Part One

Azalea Jinx and the Summer of Misery

CHAPTER 1

"Retrieve a child of jinx, but be warned.
Retrieve a child of jinx, and the world will mourn."
—Continued prophecy found inside Seer Arabella Cane's prophetic
journals, 106 B.G.

I had convinced myself I was a villain, a wicked person who did selfish things no matter the consequences, but…but now I know what a real villain is and what it's like to fall in love with one. And the villain I fell in love with…well, what was there not to love about him? From an objective standpoint, there may have been a few red flags—things others would see as unsavory or warnings about future behavior—but I couldn't be objective, or even logical, when it came to this particular villain. I couldn't think with my head instead of my heart because I didn't have a heart to use before him. Logic doesn't rule me anymore, my emotions do. And damn them for making me miss a man I desperately want to hate.

What does being a villain lover make me? A Grim fucker? Villain-adjacent? A villain-by-association? I don't know, and I don't care to find out.

For weeks now, a sinking feeling has lived underneath my skin and in my gut. It's an empty pit that only knows how to devour, and devour it does. When it eats, it leaves behind this mind-shattering numbness to envelop me, yet, somehow, I still manage to feel too little and too much all at once. I've never felt such hopelessness while still holding on to hope in my life; I've never felt like the world is ending while simultaneously believing it can be saved. That *he* can still be saved. It's a wish I shouldn't bother the stars with.

I glance down at the small SG tattooed in Shayde's handwriting on my wrist, a grim reminder of the man who turned out to be a literal Grim. It was a spontaneous decision made after our first real date, and the first tattoo I got because I wanted it. The other images marked on my skin I dreamed about first, which my love-addled mind didn't consider before jumping into the small tattoo at Shayde's first suggestion. I flinch at the sight of it now, commanding my heart to slow its desperate, rapid beats. Of course, it doesn't listen. The fist-sized organ in my chest is a fickle thing, something living and beating, designed specifically to torture me. Even now, it picks up its pace as Shayde Glover commandeers my thoughts—or is it Shayde Grim? Either way, I shouldn't be entertaining the palpitations that stutter to life at the mere thought of his presence. Shayde broke my fucking heart, and how dare it love him as much as it still seems to?

In more than one way, it's his fault my chest aches in the first place. If he hadn't swooped in to fix my heart in the first place, then none of this would be happening. I wish I could go back and warn myself that a life full of love and happiness isn't something that happens in reality—or in mirror worlds you so happen to find yourself in. Happy endings are what people sell you to entrap you into things like marriage and motherhood. It's a desperate ploy to make you do anything for love, including giving every piece of yourself up to feed that fantasy. But I won't do it.

I won't allow myself to be swallowed by this desperation to get Shayde back. I won't allow myself to hope for that future full of happiness and love, or risk everything to get a glimpse of it back. I wish I could return to feeling nothing but anger and rage; at least then I could be useful. At least then I would be capable of killing the son of a Grim.

Even now, I can't picture him as the evil overlord everyone believes him to be. Shayde was dark and mysterious, sure. He was a perfectly morally gray man who matched my darkest energies. But a cold-blooded villain? Someone willing to destroy the entire human world for me, because of me? Someone who thinks conquering a whole world is an equal exchange for my life, no matter the reason? Yeah, that's a very different side of Shayde. A side I wasn't privy to for our entire relationship. And I'm fucking *pissed* I didn't see it sooner. That I let these pesky emotions I'm suddenly full of block every ounce of logic living inside my body.

How the fuck does someone fall in love with a Grim? I may not have been born into this world, and I may not have come here with any pretense of doing things just because they were the right things to do, but seriously? The Grim is the Charmed version of the devil, a being I had been warned about within the first hour I crossed the threshold into this world. A being who has been killing for thousands of years, who creates hideous creatures known as Reapers, of which Shayde helped me kill. The same creatures who ripped apart my parents in the human world as they hid from the

Charmed, stealing their lives and my future as a not-orphaned kid in one brutal night.

Turns out it wasn't one guy, after all. It's been a dozen of them, generation after generation of Grims coming into the world, destroying hundreds of thousands of lives, and evading Conjurers all the while. Conjurers who, might I add, wouldn't even need to be trained in intense schools like Draxmere without the Grim's existence.

Isn't it ironic that I fell in love with one of the fuckers who could cause all that chaos and destruction? I, the savior, was brought to Draxmere to save the Charmed from the man I love…loved.

I truly never thought I would be capable of falling in love. Or loving in general. I was practically emotionless when I lived in the human world, full of a bitter horridness that drove me to do some incomprehensible things. Anger, jealousy, boredom—that's what controlled me for practically my entire life. Until Shayde came into my life, anyway. Shayde managed to make me feel *more*. He brought out things in me I had only hoped still existed somewhere deep inside, emotions I only ever dreamed of feeling again one day. Emotions the human world drained from me starting the day I was born.

That's what the human world does, apparently. It drains the Charmed race dry, and I lived there my entire life. I was cursed living there, killing anyone who got too close to me. Family members, friends, my ex-husband—they all died because of a death curse I was confident I had. Turns out my hidden powers were lashing out and stealing their Charm Levels to replenish my own. Fucked up, right? But if *my* Charm Levels had depleted, I would have been the one to die. I can't bring myself to regret it, even now.

I suppose that's why Shayde and I are—were—so drawn to one another. We both are capable of this…this darkness that not many understand. An unpleasantness no one else wants to admit they have. I was warned so many times about Shayde, most often by Demi. My best friend Demi, who Shayde's father turned into a Reaper right in front of me.

Anger surges through me, bright and new. Demi, the beautiful vampire who forced me into a friendship I couldn't help but accept. Demi, the first person I've ever truly loved. And that anger? It's all that's keeping me together now. Yes, I had been warned about Shayde over and over again, but Shayde was never warned about me.

I stare up at the ceiling of my dorm room, watching the fan hanging above my bed move in lazy circles. I hate this. I hate feeling sad, lonely, and weak. I hate knowing what I'm capable of; what I am going to be forced to do to the man I loved. I'm supposed to be a savior according to the prophecies Seers keep pumping out, but how can I save anyone when I can't even look at myself in the mirror? When, if I do look at myself, all I can think about is how much I hate myself for falling into Shayde's web of lies and how angry I am that I allowed this to happen. And then that hatred for myself turns into hatred for Shayde, and the whole self-pitying cycle starts all over again.

I think the worst part of it all is that I knew. I knew he wasn't a good person; he told me over and over and over. He told me he was a monster, and I believed him. The problem is, though, that I'm a monster, too. At least, I was. Maybe I still am.

I'm in no state to save anyone.

My hand drifts up to clutch the ring around my neck, gripping it so tightly it cuts into the skin of my palm. I should take it off, should fling it out the window, down a portal, into the woods. But I can't. I can't make myself get rid of the one thing that belonged to Shayde. I can't stop myself from greedily keeping it around my neck to remind me of all the things that made him *good*. To remind me of the mother he loved and mourned, of the pretty words that had me wrapped around his finger like a ring he molded for himself.

I'm a fucking mess.

I tried to keep talking to my other friends; I really did. But Ginny isn't Demi, and I can't stand watching her and the Thatcher triplets interact without the glue that held us all together. I can't stand to be around them without Demi happily chiming in, laughing, and making snarky replies. They've given me the space I requested shortly after the last faction meeting. Thank the Grim.

I probably shouldn't be saying that shit.

A bubbling laugh rises up and out of my throat, released into the cool air. Isn't that ironic? Me, the Grim fucker, telling myself not to use the Grim's name in vain. My mind reels back to the past as soon as the thought of him pops into it, images of interrogations flashing through my head. Yeah, that motherfucker landed me in *interrogations*.

In those first few days following Shayde's reveal, they practically locked me in a cell. I didn't know they had anything like that here, but oh boy, do they. The room had been a dungeon somewhere below the campus, dark and damp from lack of use. Spiders had crawled around every corner, and the constant *drip-drip* of a leak in the ceiling had annoyed me to no end. I sat locked inside that dark room, with my hands chained to a table. I tried to blast my way out of them, to no avail. Light-proof, I guess. They didn't even give me a chair to sit in, and I was forced to stand with an awkward tilt of my spine or sit with my arms reached up. I suppose that was part of the interrogation process, part of the torture to force me into giving up all my dirty secrets. The torture also involved a few punches that resulted in a broken nose and three broken ribs.

I understand why they did it. That's the saddest part of it all, I think. I wasn't even angry at them. I'm still not. I'm the Grim fucker, after all. I would have tortured and chained myself, too, if it meant there was a possibility to save hundreds of thousands of lives. In the end, I was found not guilty of treason against the Charmed race. What a relief, right?

I relived every moment with Shayde in those rooms, recounted every sexual encounter we ever had in hopes of finding something they could use. I admitted to knowing about his Grim form and then proceeded to admit how naive I was for believing it was some weird power I hadn't heard about before. Honestly, I never gave it much thought. For all I knew, it could have been some Shifter form Dean Delarosa never went over with me. Not that I can ask her anymore—Shayde's dad turned her, too, and I was forced to kill her in front of the entire student body. So, yeah. I didn't think too hard about it. I just told myself he was cursed, like me. But my curse was one of death, and now, I think his may be, too.

Death has been looking over my shoulder for years, smiting those closest to me so often that I distanced myself from people altogether. Everyone except Neil, whom I used in a misguided attempt to get my emotions back. When I was done with him, and my death curse hadn't taken him out yet, I got the job done instead. Me, my actions, the curse—all misguided factors influenced by my powers. Shayde's curse isn't some misguided attempt he can't control, though. His death curse is much, much worse. His curse twists Death's victims, keeps them alive through a process so horrible that Death refuses to take them back until they've been cleansed by the Light.

Watching Demi fall victim to that curse was the most painful moment of my life. It took three very large men to hold me back, to keep me from reaching her and possibly killing myself in the process, and even then, I almost managed to slip from their grasp. A sudden tear slides down my cheek as those last moments flash through my memories for what seems to be the thousandth time, remembering her last words to me before she became a Reaper.

"I don't think you were my doom, Azalea. I think you can still be my savior."

I fucking hate crying.

I was never able to cry when I thought I was human—I was physically incapable of it. There were times when I wanted to, needed to, but it was never possible. Not until Shayde and I got into an argument that involved him leaving me drunk, on the brink of an orgasm, in the woods. When he left me that night, I fell to my knees and wept like a baby for the first time in over a decade. I haven't had a day in over two weeks where I haven't cried similarly.

My heart hurts so bad, and my chest is in a constant state of ache in this never-ending grief that I just can't move away from. Shayde fixed me just to fucking break me all over again. I still don't understand why. Why would he tell me he didn't want to follow in his shady father's footsteps, why tell me he didn't want to bear any children, why promise he was different when he *wasn't*? Why would he tell me all these things when he planned on returning to his father all along? *What changed?* Or had anything changed at all?

My heart tells me it isn't true, it can't be. Of course he never planned on betraying me. But my mind…my mind yells at me to consider every angle. A year ago, I wouldn't have second-guessed myself at all. I would have followed the logical route—the Grim's son got the savior to fall in love with him so she wouldn't kill him. I can't accept that, not yet. Because if it is true…if it is true, Grim help him when I finally decide to get off my ass and do the job I was brought here to do.

I flinch when I hear a knock on the door. My mouth opens and closes as my slow, buzzing mind tries to decide whether to speak aloud. I know it's Jaymes—he's the only one I can tolerate anymore, and we agreed to meet at this time days ago. I hear the door creak open, hear the resounding sigh as he takes in the sight of me, limp on the bed. It floods me with shame, but I can't find it in me to care.

"You look like shit."

"Good morning to you, too," I slur, waving at him clumsily. I move to sit up but roll over instead, falling off the bed with a loud *oomph*. I blink away the dizziness in my vision, watching the overhead fan from the floor now.

"What are you on this time?" It comes out as a low growl, a warning I don't heed.

"Oh, I don't know," I murmur with a frown, holding up my hand and ticking down fingers as I count the things it *isn't*. It isn't weed, or meth, or cocaine—that much I know. I've done those before, and they don't feel like this.

"You took something without even asking what it was?" Exasperation now. I can see Jaymes absentmindedly rubbing away the wrinkles on his forehead when I tilt my eyes up, watching him approach.

"The guy next door gave me a whole bag of something in exchange for—"

"I do not want to know what you did for those drugs, Azalea," Jaymes hisses, suddenly vehemently angry.

"It wasn't anything bad. Nothing sexual." I roll my eyes. The guy wanted something of Shayde's, something that belonged to a bona fide Grim. I gave him one of Shayde's favorite shirts; that's what he gets for leaving it in my room to remind me what an idiot I am. The smell from that shirt had been so overwhelmingly *him* that I came back here and snorted as much of the black powder as I dared.

"Azalea, you can't just accept random drugs from people. Drugs here are different than they are in the human world, more dangerous. It was probably some version of Charmed opioids—it's a favorite on the market right now. Was it black? That's usually the signature for magical opioids."

"Oh, yeah. It was. Black as the Grim's heart." I giggle, rolling over onto my stomach with a sigh before placing my cheek on the soft carpet.

"Azalea, get up. We have to leave. We don't need to stick around campus any longer, okay? I've given you time, like you asked, but even the security teams are leaving. We won't be safe here if—"

"I won't be safe anywhere, Jaymes. If Shayde decides to come back for me, then he will leave a path of bodies to get to me," I grumble, pushing myself up into a sitting position and almost crashing over in the sudden wave of dizziness that follows.

"So you say."

"So I know."

"How come every time I stress the importance of your safety, you disregard it as though your life is insignificant?"

"Because it is."

Jaymes huffs, crossing the room and squatting in front of me. He grabs my chin harshly, pulling my dark brown eyes to meet his deep green ones. "Your life is not insignificant. And I'm not saying that because you're supposed to be our savior or because I feel like it's the right thing to say. I'm saying it because it's true. You are a good person, Azalea, and a strong warrior. Your presence here matters."

"Am I? A good person, I mean?" I don't feel like a good person. A good person wouldn't want Shayde back. A good person wouldn't have fallen in love with him in the first place. A good person wouldn't question why it matters if they are a good person or not.

"You are. Even if you are trying really hard not to be. Now, come on. My place is pretty far, so I'm going to have to portal us there." Jaymes takes my hand gently, warm calluses pulling me to my feet. I stumble into him, hands landing on a hard chest that moves with a sudden intake of breath. Then I'm leaning my hand onto his shoulder, weeping again.

I'm so fucking pitiful and *weak*. I thought the drugs would help, but all they've done so far is make my mind sharp and my lips loose. Well, that and make me feel like my body doesn't belong to me anymore.

"I think I hate him," I say, desperate for the feeling to go away. Everything fucking hurts, and no amount of drugs is capable of taking that feeling away.

"Some days, I think I do, too." I feel Jaymes swallow, the truth of his statement causing my ears to ring.

"Did you know? Did you know what he was?" I whisper, voicing the thought that has haunted me since the reveal. Shayde told me once there were things Jaymes couldn't accept about him, and that's why their romantic relationship ended. I suspect this is why.

"I did." He swallows again, his fingers tightening into my back. "I've known for years what he is, who he is. I just never cared."

"How? How did you get past it? How did you—" I pause, straining for the right words. "I didn't care when I knew that he was different, when I thought he was cursed like me. But when he told me in front of the entire Draxmere population and then some that he was a Grim, preceded by allowing my best friend to be turned into one of those mindless zombies, I realized that it had been entirely wrong of me not to care."

"I didn't care because, at the time, I was confident he wasn't a bad guy. I'm still not entirely convinced he's evil. Shayde never wanted to follow in his dad's footsteps, never wanted to be a Grim. Not until he met you."

"Oh, so it's my fault?" I don't allow my voice to wobble, my disbelief and anger biting through the cold air.

"No, I'm not saying that. I'm saying that his circumstances changed, and there may be more that's going on. We don't know—"

"You're defending him," I say, truly in disbelief now. I scoff as I back away, and I don't stop until my back hits something hard. I fall directly into the large mirror leaned up against my wall. The soft moss coating its edges brushes against my skin. It's another fucking thing in this room that reminds me of Shayde in this Grim-damned place.

"I'm not defending him," he says, all too defensively, white-blond brows furrowed together. "I'm just saying that the Shayde on the stage that day, and the one I know, aren't the same people. Shayde wouldn't do something like this unless he had a good reason. I'm not saying that he's a good person or that what he is doing is right. I'm just saying that he may be a little misguided in his attempts at heroism and—"

"Fucking stop, Jaymes!" I cover my ears and shake my head vehemently. I don't want to hear about Jaymes's belief in Shayde's morals. I, too, thought him to be incapable of something like this at one time. We were both wrong, it seems.

"Sorry." He deflates, taking a step toward me. "I'm sorry. I know you are still trying to cope with—"

I interrupt him again, fist slamming back into the mirror involuntarily. I ignore the shatter, my stinging skin and the broken mirror of little consequence right now. "I don't want to talk about Shayde right now. Or about all of the fucked up things he did. Or about all of the fucked up things he wanted *me* to do. I just—I'm over it all. I'm over him."

"I used to be in love with him, too, you know? Sometimes I wonder if I still am." His admission is a quiet and guilty one, and I let out a foreign, pitiful noise from the back of my throat as I let my head roll back into the mirror.

"Is that supposed to make me feel better? You telling me we are in love with the same person?"

"No. Yes. I mean—I just said it because I want you to know that I understand. Better than anyone else in the world, I'd wager."

"Yeah. Yeah, I suppose that's true." I kick off the mirror, taking a few steps before turning to look at it over my shoulder. Even through the cracks, I can feel Shayde's presence there, can see his eyes watching me as Jaymes's did once before bringing me into this new world. I can picture him behind me, gaze heated and heavy from a memory I shouldn't miss. With a war cry, I lift my already bleeding hand and hit the mirror again. Again. Again.

Jaymes shouts angrily, dragging me back and whispering hissed threats into my ear. I hardly feel the pain; the trickle of warm blood a faint sensation. Even through my angry sobs, even through the shards of missing glass, I still feel his presence here.

My bottom lip shakes as I hiss out to his ghostly presence, "You will not be my phantom, Shayde Glover, and I will not allow you to haunt me."

CHAPTER 2

"When Draxmere was first created, its architects were praised for their gorgeous work. The dark, gloomy castle may have been intimidating, but it was beautiful; no one could deny that. Those architects were set to build a similar school within the next year, but the location had not yet been determined at the time the contract was signed. That school was never created, however, because every single architect disappeared before the year was up."
—*Draxmere: A Tale as Old as the Grim*, written by Enhancer Kelvin Delaney in 1977 A.G.

Jaymes isn't careful or gentle as he drags me into a portal he created in the wall next to the mirror. I emerge ready with a string of curses, but pause as I take in the sage green house in front of us. Its exterior is fading and cracking, green bushes lined along the front of the house and trailing off around the corner out of sight. The greenery is covered with a blanket of snow, just like everything else in this freezing tundra. My gaze jumps to the bench swinging gently in the breeze on the front porch. A group of chairs and a tiny table sit neatly nearby.

I swivel my head around and take in the small countryside Jaymes's house sits in, the nearest house around half a mile away. Woods surround us on three separate sides, offering a sense of seclusion I've never experienced having always lived in large cities. As I turn back to the house, I try to take in the simplicity of the home and the feeling of being around something so *normal* for the first time since I was dragged out of the human world.

I hiss in pain as Jaymes drags me forward again, pulling me inside his home and slamming the door behind us. We emerge in a small foyer, a cozy living area directly in our path. Of the three walls I can see, all are lined with floor-to-ceiling bookshelves. Almost all of them are full. Two large reading chairs wait inside, plump and inviting. I think there is a couch, too, but Jaymes is blocking my view.

I catch a glimpse of a stunningly large kitchen to our right before being dragged even farther into the house, down a hallway that cuts between the two rooms. I glance at photos on the walls as I pass. Happy pictures of the Gravediggers hang everywhere I look. I ignore the pictures that have Shayde smiling down at me, just like I ignore the feeling seeing him brings to the surface.

The hall veers left, and Jaymes takes me to the door at the very end: a bathroom, I soon discover, as he slams me down onto the lid of a toilet. He crouches and swings the doors underneath the sink open, rifling through things and cursing my name all the while. When he pulls his hand back out, he's holding a first aid kit that he promptly proceeds to throw, along with a rag, onto the counter with a loud huff. He doesn't bother to be nice as he wets the rag and wipes every speck of blood from my skin, cleaning it roughly and efficiently before slathering on some kind of healing ointment.

Then he wraps it nice and tight, ignoring every sign of protest and every cry of pain.

With a sudden leap, I fall to my knees on the floor in front of the shiny white tub, ruining its pristine condition with my stomach's contents.

"Azalea?" Jaymes sighs, anger dissipating in mere seconds. "Are you okay?" He walks on his knees toward me, holding my hair away from my face and rubbing my back gently.

"No," I manage to say before vomiting again, my stomach pulling tightly as it tries to force out the little contents it has left.

"Hmm." I can hear the cockiness in that one syllable, and it aggravates me to no end.

"Don't say shit, Jaymes. I don't want to hear it. I don't want to hear—"

"I told you so?" He chuckles lightly, reaching for another rag underneath the sink. He runs it under warm water before handing it to me. It's dripping, but I wipe my mouth and face anyway.

I mutter a quick "Thanks." Then, with all the dignity I can muster, I turn to look at him. Silently, he releases my hair, watching me with a look in his eyes that gives me chills.

"No problem." His voice is husky, and I can't stand the heat in his gaze as he watches me unravel before him.

To avoid it, I quickly blurt out, "How do you afford this?"

"All Conjurers get a stipend for their work, Azalea, even those in training. Didn't anyone tell you that? If you make it into Draxmere, you are compensated for your time there. Then, once you graduate, your stipend is doubled. Before Draxmere, I was paid half what I am being paid now because I was attending the qualifier school."

I don't know what a qualifier school is, but I'm glad I didn't have to attend. I feel like a cheat jumping into things at Draxmere, but oh well. According to the Seers, rules don't apply to me, and I might as well take advantage of that.

"We…we get paid?"

Jaymes watches me carefully, surprise lighting up his features briefly. "No one told you?"

"Well, when I first arrived at Draxmere, you got all pissy with me. Then, Delarosa had to go through this elaborate explanation about what Conjurers were, why we fight Reapers, and what Draxmere trains us to do. I was a little overwhelmed with everything else, okay? I was just glad they weren't making *me* pay to attend the school."

"Azalea, no offense, but that's ridiculous. Why would we make you pay to train?"

"That's what humans do," I say stiffly, clutching tightly onto the wet rag. A puddle has begun to form below my fist next to the tub, but neither of us looks down toward it or makes a move to clean it up.

"Oh. Well, that's not how we do things."

"So, how much money are we talking about here?" My mouth is dry and clammy, my lips parched. Despite how painful it is to talk, I keep going. I don't want to be alone right now, coming off the high just to dip into the lowest of lows.

"Mmm. First-years start with two hundred fifty a year, and it goes up about fifty for each year you complete. When you graduate, you'll get five hundred for every year you live."

"Two hundred and fifty dollars? A year? Does money work differently here or something? Because that seems like…not a lot for fucking risking my life."

Jaymes bursts into laughter, reaching out to squeeze my arm comfortingly. "No, Azalea. Two hundred and fifty *thousand*."

My jaw drops, as does my stomach. That's how much I earned this year? Honestly, though, I fucking deserve it. I almost died how many times? I killed how many Reapers? Not to mention the whole savior thing everyone keeps throwing in my face. "No one told me about that," I manage to say, feeling nauseous as I take a deep breath and curse my heart for beating so readily. "How do they pay all of us so much? Is that not a lot of money here?"

"Oh, no. It is. We use the same money system as humans, though different parts of the world use different currencies. Around here, we use what is equivalent to…American dollars, I think? We tend to be sent into that region most often, so it made sense for us to just adapt to their ways. That's why English is the main language spoken in this area; we need to speak to locals quite often when on the hunt. As to how they pay us so much, well, the same way humans pay their government workers, I suppose: taxes."

"But why so much? Not that I'm complaining, but…" I think I'm going to be sick again. I've never *dreamed* of having that much money, much less actually possessing it.

"We die fast. For people to be willing to jump into a job of this nature, you have to pay them well. They want to be able to leave something behind for their families and want them to be taken care of. There are only five schools in the entire world that train Conjurers at the same level Draxmere does, and not all of those who train to go will actually make it that far. Most don't. On top of that, you have to graduate from one of those five to be considered a proper Conjurer. Otherwise, no job and no salary."

"That's…well, that's fucking amazing. How do I access this money, exactly?"

"Online, in your bank account. Didn't they show you this stuff? Seriously?"

"Well…no. I didn't know you guys had internet access. The fuck?"

"We don't have access on campus because they want our full attention on training. But, yes, we have the internet. The humans got the technology from somewhere, you know."

"And…and I can just order anything I want using that money? Have things sent here, just like back home?" I question, blinking rapidly as my pounding mind tries to process what this will mean for me. Having that amount of money sitting in a bank account is *unfathomable*. Back home, I was slinging fists in dirty venues to make a little cash for tattoos and basic necessities, but here I can take those skills and use them to do something good *while* getting paid. Maybe this whole Reaper-killing business isn't so bad after all. If you forget that it's my ex-boyfriend creating them, I mean.

"Of course you can." He chuckles, pushing himself into a standing position before holding a hand out to me. I sigh, taking it and allowing him to pull me up. He gestures toward the sink where a toothbrush waits, and I sigh happily.

"This isn't yours, right? I—" I pause when I see Jaymes holding a hairbrush next to my head, an elastic around his wrist. He moves to brush my hair, but I jerk my head to the side quickly with wide eyes. "You don't have to do that. I can—"

"Shut your pretty mouth and let me take care of you," Jaymes says with a bitter bite, and my heart plummets.

I consider Jaymes a friend, especially now that the two of us have bonded over a common pain. I mean, he's letting me stay at his house for summer break, for Grim's sake! But I also know it's all-too-possible he still wants more than friendship, despite his feelings for Shayde, because it's only been a few months since he told me he wanted me for himself. This, of course, was preceded by a passionate kiss, despite him knowing I was romantically tied up with his best friend. Unfortunately, a relationship is just something I won't be able to give him. Not now; probably not ever.

He reminds me too much of Shayde.

"Jaymes, I—"

"It's fine, Azalea. I don't want to talk about it."

"What if I do?"

"Are you that eager to reject me again?"

"You know it's not like that. You know—"

"I know, Azalea. Fuck, I know, okay? Brush your teeth with the new, unused toothbrush I left out for you, and let me talk."

I can only nod, shivering when his fingers touch my scalp. I feel the gentle pull of the hair brush as I ready the toothbrush. Our gazes meet in the square mirror above the marble sink. He's just as handsome as the first time I saw him, with his sharp features and crooked smile.

"If I had touched you first that day, would it have been me you took into your bed?" Jaymes clenches the hairbrush hard, his words barely above a whisper. I pause with the toothbrush only an inch from my mouth, my body tight and uncomfortable with the strange question.

"I d-don't know," I admit, squeezing my eyes shut. I jam the toothbrush into my mouth, brushing harshly to distract myself.

The first time I took Shayde into my bed was after an intense fight with a group of three Reapers, a fight that released some of my pent-up emotions and allowed me to feel a handful of new things for the first time in over a decade. Shayde had been the first to reach me after a close call with a Reaper, and his touch lit me up in a way I never knew was possible. I felt like a dead woman walking among the living before him, and our night together revived me, however briefly.

I don't know if things would have been different if Jaymes had been there first. I don't want to think it was a first-come, first-serve ordeal. I want to believe it was just Shayde and our undeniable chemistry that bonded me to him, like two elements coming together to form a molecule: inevitable.

"I convinced myself that you would have for months. That if I had just stayed by your side, you would have been mine. I was so sure about it, so sure that what I felt for you was real…until Shayde switched sides, and it muddled everything. Up until that point, I was sure I was falling in love with you, too. Shayde and I…" He pauses, running a hand over the stubble on his chin and clenching his jaw. "We've always been too similar. We make the same jokes, have the same taste in partners, and love the same people. When he joined the Grim…well, that changed everything. Because how can I be similar to a man like that? How can I want the same things he wants?"

"You mean, how could you want me? *A Grim fucker.*" My eyes shoot open as I hiss out the words, spitting out toothpaste aggressively. Jaymes pauses in his lazy brushing of my hair, eyes wide.

"Shit. No, Azalea. No, that's not what I meant. You know that I'm in the same boat as you when it comes to that. I think people are holding you to a higher standard because you are the prophesied savior, the person who can save or destroy our world. I don't hold you to that standard. I don't think less of you for being with Shayde or for wanting to be with him. I guess what I'm trying to say is, well, I've always wanted the things Shayde has. And vice versa. I've struggled my entire life to have an identity outside of him, even when we were no longer together romantically, and maybe I got caught up in that."

"So…you aren't attracted to me?" I raise an eyebrow, my still-muddled mind lost.

"Azalea, you're a fucking goddess." Jaymes finally meets my eyes in the mirror again, a soft smile tilting up the corner of his lips. He slowly begins to pull all of my hair to the back of my head, gathering wavy locks in his nimble hands. The once-vibrant amethyst purple has faded to a dull, almost gray color now that Demi is not here to refresh it. Even my bangs have grown unruly without her, their length so great that I can no longer wear them across my forehead. Demi last did my hair over two months ago, and I can't bring myself to refresh it without her here to help me. We had planned to have a night together after graduation, a final refresh before the break, but…

Jaymes continues, not noticing my inner struggle as I think of my Reaper best friend. "It's not that I'm not attracted to you. It's just…I guess this is the only way to convince myself to get over it. I have to tell myself that I only wanted you because Shayde did. Even if it isn't true. And if that's how I get past this, then please, just let me do it. I don't want you to be nervous around me or constantly questioning my motives. I don't want you to worry that I'm going to hit on you or that you shouldn't be staying in my house because I have impure motives. I care about you a lot, and I know Shayde would want me to take care of you since he can't. I just…I want you to understand that you are safe with me, and I am moving on."

I inhale softly, nodding as I reach up to squeeze one of his hands. "Okay. I can accept that."

Gently, he says, "Maybe the problem isn't that I'm in love with you, but that I'm still in love with him."

He said something similar earlier, and I still can't decide how to feel about it. In the end, I decided to distract us both with a new topic. "You just need to find someone who will reciprocate your feelings, Jaymes. You've been searching in all the wrong places."

"Hmph. I think I just need a break from all of this love bullshit entirely." Jaymes smiles, a visible tension releasing from his shoulders. He loops the elastic around my hair as I drop my hand, a move so obviously practiced it hurts. Did he do this with Shayde, too? It's a dangerous line of thought, one I quickly move on from.

"What, did Sellar wear you down?" I cackle as I purposely mispronounce her name. The stone lying on my chest lifts as the familiar banter takes form.

"I don't ever want to discuss Stella Stargrove with you." He scowls playfully before backing away from my form, jerking his head toward a door on the right I hadn't noticed before and gesturing for me to follow. I obediently do so, taking a few steps into a dark bedroom before violently stumbling back into the bathroom. What the fuck is that *smell*? Why does it—

"I'm sorry, Azalea. I paid someone to clean the house and very explicitly instructed them to remove anything of Shayde's, but…"

Jaymes refuses to look at me, choosing instead to pick at the corner of the deeply black duvet that is now visible.

"This was Shayde's room? He lived here with you?" My breath catches as I think about the two staying here, in this house. Is that how their relationship began? Did their nights apart slowly drift into nights spent together? No, no, I can't think about that. With a shake of my head, I cover my nose and mouth with my hand, refusing to breathe in any more of the intoxicating scent: Smoke, leather, and that elusive darkness that belongs only to him.

"He did. Technically, he also owns this place. We bought it together."

"Was this before or after the breakup?" I mutter bitterly, immediately regretting the words when he flinches.

"Does it matter?"

I step back into the room, approaching with caution. I feel more lucid, less drugged, but my damn mouth won't—can't—stop moving. "Jaymes, I—"

"It's fine, Azalea." But it's not, and neither of us can hide that from each other.

Chapter 3

"From a Grim, we cannot hide
our secrets, our strengths, our waning pride.
From a Grim we will seek
his secrets, his strength, and our souls to keep."
—Prophecy recorded inside student Seer Noor Owens's Prophetic
Journal, 2024 A.G.

I approach Jaymes, who sits on the edge of the bed, cautiously. A bed that was chosen by Shayde, in a dark room decorated by Shayde, all while being surrounded by his scent.

Abruptly, he says, "Shayde isn't what you think he is. He doesn't like to create Reapers, and he doesn't want to be a Grim."

"He…doesn't create Reapers?" As if Shayde watching as it happens makes it better or right.

"Not unless he has to."

"I don't understand. Why would he have to?" Did Shayde not choose to be the monster he proved himself to be?

"He didn't explain any of it to you? He didn't tell you how it works?" Jaymes's eyes crinkle together, his hand running across his face. "Fucking asshat."

"No. No, after I found out that he didn't just have some weird ass powers and that he was, in fact, a Grim, we didn't have much of a chance to talk. No, he disappeared the day after he showed me his Grim form and only came back again to kill his classmates. The last time I saw him was when he showed up at my door, begging for me to go with him." His Grim form was…terrifying.

He becomes nearly twelve feet tall, over double his usual height, and large antlers grow out of the sides of his head. His face is made of some kind of bone, animal-like in shape, and his eyes disappear. In their place are deep, empty holes that expose nothing but darkness. I see that form in my dreams, not because I'm scared of it, but because for me, the Grim is still just Shayde. I ran from him the first time I saw him like that, but only because he turned it into a fun game that ended with some of the best sex of my life. Other Conjurers can shift into things like werewolves, vampires, sirens, but the Grim? He becomes a monster no one else would dare look in the eyes. No one but me.

"Hmph." Jaymes glances me over, eyes softening. "How did he take the refusal?"

"I had to force him to leave," I admit quietly, wincing at the memory, the shame, of what I had done. I wish I could move past loving Shayde, wish I could not hate myself for hurting him, all while equally hating him for hurting me.

I wish I didn't have these emotions I clawed through hell to get back.

"You *forced* him? How?"

"I stabbed him."

Jaymes jerks away from me as though I am going to stab him, too. "You…you stabbed him?"

"Yeah. That a big deal or something?" I question dryly, placing my elbows on my knees and resting my head on my hands.

Jaymes throws his arms in the air, tilting his head back and groaning out, "You two are fucking meant for each other. Fucking psychopaths, the both of you."

"What else was I supposed to do, Jaymes? He wouldn't leave. He was on his knees, begging for me to go with him, to help him go fix Demi. *But I couldn't.* I couldn't forgive him. I still haven't. Maybe, if he had pulled this shit in the first semester, I could have. But it's too late now. He wanted me to feel. He made me this way. And this is all his fault. Everything that happened, the way I reacted…it's on him, and I hope he knows it."

"How did he take that betrayal?" Jaymes asks the question, but I'm certain he already knows the answer.

"Not well. He told me he wouldn't take me back unless I came to him on my knees and begged," I whisper, attempting to shut out that last, horrible memory.

"Okay, little flower." He chuckles humorlessly, eyes lit up with a coldness that doesn't belong there. "You want to betray me now? That's it? Fine. So be it. But I am going to make sure you feel every ounce of hurt with me. Your petals are going to fall off and decay, your leaves are going to die of thirst, your stem will never grow, and your roots will burn before they ever latch into the dirt. You will crawl to me and beg for water, beg for the sunshine you crave. And only then will you get it, not a moment before."

"Shayde, don't do this. Please, don't leave like this." I can barely see through my tears, can barely hear over the sound of my heart cracking into a million tiny pieces.

"Find me when you're ready to get on your knees and beg, *Azalea Jinx."*

Jaymes interrupts my thoughts, letting out another *hmph*. After a moment of silence, he adds, "Sounds like something he would say. Azalea…Grim's grow their antlers through the creation of Reapers. Once they hit the age a Conjurer does when coming into their full powers, they have to create Reapers once a year to live. So, that's what he's done every year since turning twelve, but only for survival. He claimed to only turn people who wanted it."

"His antlers…" I absentmindedly touch the spot on my back where those very antlers are tattooed, an idea I got from a dream before ever knowing about this world or the Grims.

"That's as much as I know about the subject, though. I think he just told me what I needed to hear for me to stick around."

"Him being a Grim…is that the thing you couldn't accept? The reason you couldn't be with him anymore?" I ask the question I've been dying to know, despite knowing it's the last thing I should be doing. It's none of my business why Jaymes is pining over a man he broke up with. Especially considering I'm in the same situation.

"You have to understand, Azalea. Growing up in this world, we are told from a very young age how evil and despicable the Grim is. Once I found out, I couldn't get the image of him out of my head every time the Grim was mentioned. In the end, I couldn't do it. I couldn't be with him when every time I looked at him, all I could see was evil. Even knowing he wasn't. And now…now I'm not sure I will ever be able to look at him the same again."

"I just…I don't understand how he could let Demi be turned. She was always so scared of the Gravediggers, the two of you in particular. She was terrified of what you would do to me. She told me over and over again that you guys would kill me, that I needed to play nice and listen to what you said. And the more often I disregarded her warnings, the more worried she got. It's all my fault this happened to her, and I'll never be able to apologize." I drop my head low, a single tear slipping from the corner of my eye.

Why can't I fucking stop crying?

Jaymes flinches as he watches me. He shifts his weight methodically between his feet before whispering nervously, "She had a right to be concerned. I guess it doesn't really matter now, so I'll tell you a secret Shayde and I have been holding for years. The very first time he showed me his true form at our old school, Demi saw him transform. Shayde and I hunted her down and threatened her within an inch of her life. We told her that if she didn't keep the secret, we would kill her. That if she didn't follow our orders, we would make sure she never made it into Draxmere." To his credit, Jaymes looks ashamed. Demi never mentioned going to school with them before Draxmere, only that…only that they ruled over every school the same way they did Draxmere. I guess she had first-hand experience with that.

"You…what?" Bile rises in my throat again, my heart clenching painfully. This is why she was so sure they would kill me. Why she was so worried about all the time I spent in their presence.

"I'm not proud of it, but Shayde had just finished explaining things to me when she came running through the woods, and we didn't know what else to do. We were only nineteen, Azalea. We did what we knew how to do."

I stumble off the bed, shaking my head furiously. "I think I need some fresh air. I'm going to go take a walk."

I need to get away so I can break down in peace. Fucking Demi and Shayde are still finding ways to break down my weakly enforced walls, and I don't know how to keep them from crawling past them. I need to be alone so I can—

"Azalea, wait! You don't know where you're going." He grabs me by the wrist, pleading with his eyes for me to stay.

"I'll figure it out." I dare him, with my own ferocious gaze, to hold me back. We stare at each other, and I clench my jaw tightly as Shadow and Light begin to dance in the air.

With a loud gulp, he says quickly, "Before you go, I need to tell you something else."

"What now, Jaymes? Would you like to tell me that you've been fucking Shayde behind my back? Ooh! Even better, you've been in contact with him and haven't told me?"

"No, Azalea." He scowls, releasing me from his tight grip. "I'm sorry I've upset you for the sake of being honest. Truly. But this is completely irrelevant to this conversation."

"Oh? Well, enlighten me, then."

"I am hosting a meeting here at ten in the morning. It's extremely important, and I need you to stay out of sight in your room. I'm serious about this, Azalea. These poor people can't know you are here or that you are involved."

"You don't want the Grim fucker around, do you?" I hiss, turning sharply on my heel.

"Azalea, that's not what—"

"Go to hell, Jaymes Bloodgood, and take your friends down with you," I call out the familiar phrase behind me, slinging up a finger he is all too familiar with.

I make sure to slam the door shut behind me, sparing a glance into the burgundy-painted bedroom across the hall before stumbling down the short hallway, past the kitchen, and to the front door. I grip the knob lightly, pulling sharply and forcing myself out into the freezing air. I don't bother to use a Balmy Charm to heat my skin; I like the cold that seeps into my pores. It's a reminder that I'm real, that the freeze I feel invading my body is real, and that this isn't some nightmarish world I've invented for myself.

I sit on the swinging bench on the front porch as I try to control my emotions, tears falling freely down my cheeks *again*. I want to be over this, want to move past whatever it is that Shayde has done to me. I don't know who I am without him, and I don't know how to live with his betrayal. I don't—

Light blazes to my fingertips as the hairs on the back of my neck stand. I spin my head in every direction, looking over houses and trees and yards in the far distance as I try to figure out what's caused the unease. A breeze shifts, and I feel it then: eyes on my back.

I twist my entire body around, blasting a ball of Light into thin air off the side of the porch and toward a section of the woods. No one and nothing awaits me, only the scent of a man I wish I could forget and a looming shadow that looks eerily similar to antlers in the distance. I scoff at myself, rubbing my eyes with the back of my hand to mop up the liquid blurring my vision. When I open them again, I see the branches forming the familiar shape, their twisting peaks making a mockery of my imagination. My mind is latched onto this man who doesn't care about me, who maybe never did, and it's high time I replace the heartbreak with something much more potent: *anger*.

CHAPTER 4

"The fox who loves
seeks the Seer who hounds.
Two parts of the puzzle
that keeps our savior above ground."
—Prophecy found inside Seer Cressida Payton's prophetic journals,
453 A.G.

The dreams always start with the ghost of a man, but they all end the same: I'm falling, falling, falling. This time, I'm sure I can see the body that waits in the shadows, can almost glimpse dark hair and a tall form. But I'm too scared to know who may be hiding in my dreams, and it's the unfamiliar threat of fear that has me stumbling back and tumbling over the cliff I never realize I'm standing on. I open my mouth to scream, but nothing comes out. The popping in my ears fills the empty air as I descend. The pit of my stomach drops as the light above me dims, and that masculine form comes into view. The first thing I catch a glimpse of, the first clear image I get, looms above me and sends my stomach rolling.

Antlers.

The fear turns into anger, the anger turns into defeat, and still I fall. I'm weightless, a sinking pit catapulting in my stomach as panic rises higher than the cliff above me. I fall, and I fall, and I fall, and I—

—jerk awake with a lurch, voices filtering into my ear. I'm curled up in a ball underneath a window outside of Jaymes's house, my ear tilted up toward it. I raised it last night without Jaymes's permission, allowing just enough space for the chilly breeze to gain access into his house without him noticing. I let out a trembling breath, watching the cloud form in the freezing air as I try to recover from the sickening feeling of plummeting to my death that I have experienced every time I close my eyes for the past two weeks. It's the reason bags have begun to form under my eyes; the reason, after sitting outside for only half an hour, I had drifted away into slumber without realizing. Last night I slept fitfully, the smell of Shayde comforting and achingly painful all at once. I woke too often to feel rested and have a sinking feeling that the rest of my nights here will be the same. At least that fitful sleep encouraged me to be on time for this meeting.

I curse at myself and focus on the fluttering voices inside, an attempt at distracting myself from trying to interpret the dream for the millionth time, and pick out two distinctly new ones floating in the air. One is clearly a man's, if its deep baritones are any indicator, but the other falls into a neutral territory I can't quite identify. Light and airy, with a hint of roughness hiding just underneath. Is it a woman's? Should I be upset if it is? No, probably not. There's no reason for me to be angry about another woman being in Jaymes's house when he said this was strictly business. Besides, there's a male in there, too. Jaymes could want either, or both, and I have no right to say a word to him if he did want to hang out with maybe, possibly, potential partners.

I may be lonely, but I'm not a monster: I won't make Jaymes be lonely with me. I won't tear away his friendships or force him to hole up in his house with me all summer—if you can even call this slightly above freezing temperature summer.

"—I understand that you may be holding some reservations when it comes to donations, especially under the current circumstances," Jaymes says, his voice calm and professional.

"Well, yes. I think that's quite obvious. Business is business, dear, and what you are trying to propose doesn't seem entirely beneficial. In fact, I would argue that you are getting the better end of the bargain." The lighter voice speaks with a quiet, disconcerting cackle that leaves a chill rushing down my spine.

I'm straining to hear more when the bushes shake, a black cat poking its head out. I open my mouth to greet it, but it's already approaching. It's small and young, but its purr is loud and ominous in the quiet morning. It crawls into my lap without fear, curling into a ball without pausing in its deep reverberations. It tilts its head back, exposing a large white dot underneath its chin.

"You could have rabies," I tell myself without conviction, running a hand over its sleek fur despite my words. The cat purrs louder in response, its small body practically shaking as it begins rolling around. I glance down to determine its sex, scoffing when I see it is a male. "Must I be plagued by men? Will I ever know peace?"

The cat digs its nails into me in response, proving my point entirely. I shake my head, trying to hone back in on the conversation I am missing and ignoring the swelling in my heart as the cat chooses to stay with me. Is it a coincidence that I mentioned feeling lonely just moments before he showed up?

"The Shadow Faction believes the best solution to the Grim problem is to offer extra compensation to Conjurers who wish to fight, no matter which faction they have pledged themselves to. Otherwise, a large majority of our people may be tempted to allow the human world to fall, a consequence I believe we all agree is not a welcome scenario." Jaymes again, now.

The strange man sighs impatiently, calmly stating, "What you are asking for is more than I am willing to give. I understand the situation, and I am taking note of the seriousness of this issue, but I cannot just *give* you such a large amount of money."

I know Jaymes very specifically asked me not to listen, but well, I couldn't stop myself. I don't want to be left out of anything important, especially not something that involves Shayde. Jaymes isn't allowed to be secretive here, and I don't give a fuck if he believes otherwise. I'm supposed to be the savior or whatever, right? So, shouldn't I know what's going on in the world I'm supposed to be saving?

Jaymes replies in a calm, professional tone, "Which is why we are asking for more than just money. We would like to offer a partnership, one in which—"

"What are you doing?"

I screech and blast Light in the direction of the voice. The familiar light cackle from before follows as a thin body bends to the left and allows my deadly blast to pass. I tilt my head back, meeting a man's pale eyes with a glare. I squint at him, hardly noticing the blue pigments in the depths of the eerie white surrounding it. The short man doesn't seem to mind me observing him, only reaching out a pale hand and offering me help. I decide not to take it, instead pushing myself into a standing position.

"You fucking scared me, asshat." I hate admitting I can feel this way: scared. I don't like being on edge all of the time or knowing that I have the capability of caring about shit like people startling me.

The man pulls his hand back and pushes it through his orange-tinted hair, black tips brushing back against his ears. My eyes are drawn to the singular braid dangling over his right ear, little gold rings dancing strategically down it. And, despite his short stature, I still have to look up at him when he speaks.

"What are you doing?" he repeats in that soft tone of his, seemingly bored.

"Just sitting with my cat. Grimsly." I quickly give it a name, gesturing vaguely at the cat who had leaped off me and tiptoed several feet away upon my abrupt position change. It's certainly...*an* alibi. Definitely not a good one.

"Who are you?"

"Fuck off, Fox," I scoff, running my eyes over his lithe body to assess the threat properly.

"Original." Those pale eyes watch me with disdain now, a disdain that quickly turns into amusement. "My name is Dagan Breather. *Who. Are. You?*"

I tilt my lips up into a dangerous smile, bowing slightly and waving my hand dramatically before saying, "Azalea Jinx, at your service."

"Ah. The savior. Yes, I know who you are. You and Jaymes are together, then? That's surprising, considering the rumors I've heard." Anger bubbles up into redness on my neck and cheeks, my gaze flickering to the scars on his arms as he takes a step forward. Their symmetry is what catches my eye. Each arm dotes a perfect band wrapped around each wrist and elbow. Pink skin puckers into white, the scars clean and long-since healed. *Just like Shayde's facial scar.*

The thought jars the anger right out of me, and I suck in a deep breath at the painful clenching in my heart that follows. I swear I can feel eyes on me again, as though the very thought of Shayde could summon his gaze. Absentmindedly, I rub my fingers over the ring around my neck, forcing myself back into the moment.

"Not exactly." I refuse to acknowledge the last statement and refuse to step away from his intruding form. I choose to glare at his round cheekbones instead, willing myself not to back down.

"Why are you spying on us, Azalea Jinx? Worried little Jaymsie was going to leave you out of the loop?"

That's exactly what I was fucking worried about.

"This is my house, too, you know? Temporarily, at least. I don't need permission from you, or Jaymes, or anyone else, to sit on my back porch and enjoy the cold air." Even now, our breaths form clouds around us, my body only warmed by the Balmy Charm I chose to perform this morning. It's laughable to think I was sitting outside because I enjoy this.

"Oh. Is that so? Is that why you were all curled up and hidden from sight?"

"I wasn't hiding—" I attempt to argue as Grimsly begins to purr in the distance.

"It doesn't matter, anyway. Why don't you join us?"

I flip my too-long bangs out of my face, scoffing at the strange man. "I don't think Jaymes would like that." I attempt to tuck a faded purple strand behind my ear now before saying, "Why are you out here bothering me, anyway? Shouldn't you be in that *very* important meeting?"

"No. That meeting has everything to do with my dad and nothing to do with me."

"Uh-huh. That so? Because I don't think people who have nothing to do with very important meetings are allowed to participate in said meetings, much less interrogate innocent bystanders outside of them."

"I like you, Azalea Jinx. Want a drink?" He ignores my snark and gives me a wicked grin, taking a few steps back. As he does so, I notice the limp in his right leg, one he is hiding very well. My short time as a Conjurer has proved that life is in the details. Maybe, if I had followed that motto with Shayde, I would have noticed the red flags and accepted them more readily.

"I don't hear that very often. And…what kind of drink?"

I probably shouldn't accept offers from strangers, but what do I have to lose? What does it matter if I'm poisoned on Jaymes's back porch? Shayde will still be gone, Demi will still be practically dead, and I will be lying six feet under.

"No, I'm sure you don't."

I frown, opening my mouth to argue, when he brandishes a bottle from out of seemingly mid-air. It's one of those drinks I had at the New Year's party at the end of my first semester, the delicious one that had me drunk in a mere ten minutes. Dragon's Breath, I believe it was called.

"Fuck, yes. Give me that shit!" I grab the bottle from his hand before he can object, relief flooding my features. Jaymes took my bag of drugs the day I came here and banned all alcohol from his cabinets, and I *need* this release. Now that I'm not numb, drugs and alcohol do the exact thing they are supposed to: provide relief.

"I got plenty more where that came from. My dad owns the company." Dagan slides down the wall, patting the ground next to him as he offers a place to sit. I do so begrudgingly, cold snow seeping into my pants once more when he adds, "I'm attending Draxmere with you this year."

I untwist the lid, taking a long sip before deciding to say, "You're a first-year, then?"

"I am."

"What do you do?" I glance over at him again, squinting. With his plain gray shirt and dark jeans, nothing screams *powerful*. Nothing other than the fact that his dad owns a huge alcohol company, apparently. I'm going to try not to linger on that fact, though.

"I speak to the dead."

"Oh, isn't that just lovely?" I wrinkle my nose in distaste before quickly trying to hide it: I keep forgetting I'm supposed to care about other people's feelings. "So, you're a Necromancer? I've never met one before."

"I am." He tilts his head again, reaching out to twirl a lock of my dull hair. I jerk at the small touch, but he doesn't seem to notice I'm uncomfortable with it. Or maybe he just doesn't care. "And you're an Elementalist. Quite a good one, I hear. Light and Shadows? I thought you would be mad, or close to it. You must be at war with yourself all the time."

"That's not the first time someone has assumed that. The truth is, I've never known inner peace to begin with, so I don't know if I would be able to tell if I was feeling an internal war caused solely by my powers." I take another long sip before smacking his hand down. "You shouldn't touch people without their permission. Next time, you'll lose the hand you touch me with."

"Oh, I've lost a hand before." He cackles, wiggling his fingers. I frown, pointedly glancing between the two hands he clearly still possesses.

"I don't think you have."

"Are you calling me a liar, Azalea Jinx?" That light tone turns abruptly devious; his small smile widens wickedly.

"What else should I call you?"

"Ha! I knew you wouldn't back down." He claps his hands gleefully, tilting his head back with a happy sigh. "I can be quite scary, sometimes."

"I only *get* scared sometimes," I retort just as his fingers reach out to trace the ring dangling between my breasts.

His finger grazes my chest, and before I can make good on my threat to take his hand, Grimsly bounds around the corner. He leaps directly at me, and a thin, translucent shield forms around the three of us, blocking the blow from the figure that drops before us. A Reaper has found me.

Dagan cackles at the sight of the ghastly figure, his laughter growing terrifyingly hysterical. My heart pounds as I stare at the creature, hesitation clouding my mind as it stares back. It doesn't move, only watches with an appallingly calm expression. *That could have easily been Demi.* With only a little regret, I thrust my hand up. Light pierces through the shield and into the Reaper that isn't actually Demi. Its ashes mix into the snow, a black-and-gray tinted spot left where its body once stood that forms itself into soft shapes. It's a muddled mess of beauty and darkness, like a painting only an artist who's experienced true pain could create.

Who had formed that shield? It isn't something an Elementalist or a Necromancer can do. I think. Was it…was it the cat? Is that another thing about this world I don't know? Another little tidbit of information no one bothered to explain? Because magic cats aren't important, obviously. And, I suppose, if bats having a bi-monthly shedding of their wings is normal, why can't shield-wielding cats be normal, too?

"I think we should go—" I start, but a flicker of movement on our right catches my attention. Three more Reapers have appeared.

Fucking Shayde.

This has his name written all over it, but why now? Has he finally deemed me worthy enough to kill? Has he decided my life isn't worth his, that he shouldn't risk any of those vague prophecies coming true just because he wants to keep me for himself? But I've been here for a full day already, and he had to know I was here the entire time. This is the only place I could've gone, the only person who would have helped me.

I feel the tingle of awareness that someone is watching again, and I whip my head around the open yard, desperate to find *something*. Something to confirm my suspicions, something to confirm that this is his doing. Because if this is him, if he's really attacking me right now, then there is no reason for me to hold on to this heart-wrecking hope. No reason for me not to hate him as much as the logical side of me knows I need to.

Shayde isn't waiting for me, but two more Reapers approaching from the woods on our left are.

Dagan stands beside me, placing a hand on my shoulder with a slow whisper, "Death is nearby."

"No shit," I hiss, blasting Light at the nearest Reaper. It dissolves into ashes, leaving four. But my surprise attacks are no longer surprises, and one of the Reapers leaps at me while I'm distracted.

It's Dagan who saves me.

A dagger is plunged into the neck of the Reaper. The Light infused into the blade blasts a hole through its throat and almost rips its head off entirely. I quickly spin and finish the job, gagging as the putrid smell of black goo leaking from its wounds hits my nose just before it explodes into ashes that rain down onto me. Leftover goo, mixed with ashes, lands on clothes, on skin, and burns whatever parts of me it touches. Red splotches form all over my body, the pain a side thought compared to the scene around me. I can feel the effects of the Dragon's Breath seeping into my bloodstream, my movements already slower than I need them to be.

"Can you do anything useful to distract them?" I question, eyes spinning between the three Reapers who are only feet away. They snarl at the Light blazing in my hands, unnaturally wide smiles spread across their cheeks and up to their ears. It's a painful reminder to see these creatures who look so similar to us, the small differences only prominent upon closer inspection: gray and mottled skin, sunken black eyes with dark bags underneath, pieces of flesh falling off and scabbed over, black veins, bloated bellies, and rows of sharp, discolored teeth. My heart sinks as I think about Demi looking like these…these *things*.

"Death is nearby," Dagan repeats, a hand coming up to clasp my shoulder. The ground rumbles underneath us in a way I can only imagine earthquakes could manage. Grimsly yelps and hisses at my feet as he leaps onto my pants. I ignore the biting sting of his claws as he climbs up my body, then take him into my arms protectively.

"Okay, great. Good to know, Dagan. But I need—" A bony hand reaches up to clasp around my ankle, and I scream in an embarrassingly high-pitched tone.

"Wrong one," Dagan hisses at the hand, which releases me abruptly. I watch in horror as a skeleton claws its way out from beneath the hard ground, snow caving in and falling onto its head. Dagan releases me, using both hands to direct the skeleton's movements.

Upon seeing us distracted again, a Reaper leaps at me. Before I can react, another shield sizzles up around us. The Reaper screams in utter agony, clawing at its chest and arms where the shield has burned its disgusting body. Black goo oozes from its wounds, already dripping down onto the grass below. I blast it with a beam of Light, turning my attention to the last two.

"Azalea!" I hear banging on the window behind me, and I risk glancing over my shoulder to see Jaymes pressed against the glass. "Azalea, I can't get out!"

"What do you mean you can't get out? Just use the fucking door, Jaymes. I'm not sure if you realized, but you are trying to escape out a window right now," I call back menacingly toward the useless man, tensing as a roar rises into the sky.

I turn as fast as I can back to the Reapers, the adrenaline helping me sober up. The skeleton has finally freed itself entirely, and it isn't a Reaper I hear but an achingly scary sound that comes from Dagan himself, who shakes from the force of tearing bones up and out of the ground. I watch in fascination and horror as the skeleton leaps toward the Reaper. It cries out in anger as the skeleton lands on it, flinging the pile of bones off to the side swiftly. The bones scatter, a disarray of what once was a person. I continue to watch, still intrigued despite the macabre sense of it all. Warning bells ring in my head as the pieces fly back together, the skeleton reforming. I hear Dagan's heavy breaths beside me, his hand reaching down to clasp my shoulder again for support as he focuses.

Jaymes is still screaming inside, saying, "The doors won't open, and I can't transport out! I can't even form a damn portal! Azalea, it's Shayde! Don't let him—"

I don't hear the rest of Jaymes's shouts over Shayde's voice emitting from the Reaper directly in front of me. "Azalea Jinx."

I almost fall to my knees, my body suddenly heavy and sharp. "What are you doing, Shayde?"

I try to keep my tone even and annoyed, but even I can hear the breathlessness in the simple sentence. Dagan directs the skeleton to attack the Reaper who isn't speaking with a flick of his hands that I barely notice, allowing me the time to blast it with Light before I can become too enamored by Shayde. Too distracted, too useless, too *weak*.

"I needed to see you. To speak to you." His voice is so clear it's as though it is him in front of me and not a Reaper. If I'm being truthful, I'm grateful it isn't Shayde standing here.

Seeing Shayde could only be devastating.

"I said all I needed to at our last meeting." The words are clipped and formal, as though this is a hindrance to my day and not world-shattering to my heart.

"Dagan, no! Don't do it, Dagan!" Jaymes calls from behind me, his pounding on the glass getting harder and faster. I hear something hit the glass, as though he's throwing things at the window to break it. I don't turn to look, focusing instead on the two daggers

Dagan has pierced into Shayde's chest. No, no, that isn't Shayde. It's only his voice, not him, inside this body.

I reach forward with Light blazing at my fingertips, screaming for Dagan to move as the Reaper tilts its head to look at him with an ear-splitting smile, but Reapers are so, so fast. Dagan's body is flung into the air, soaring high above us. I race toward the Reaper, but it is dragged to the side by some invisible force. I shout for Dagan, spinning and tilting my head up just in time to see him hit the roof with a loud groan. He rolls down the side of the house, and I take off running, terrified I won't reach him in time. I reach out my arms in desperation as he crashes down, leaping like a track runner over hurdles. Dagan miraculously tumbles into me, and we both fall to the ground with the force of the impact. I cushion his fall, but nothing cushions mine. I hear the crack of my ribs, feel the pain that accompanies it. Dagan sits on top of me, heavy and unmoving.

"Azalea!" Jaymes is frantic, and I can see him slamming a table chair into his window with no luck. The look in his eyes is one of pure terror, and I have to turn away to keep myself from crying. I will not let these stupid fucking emotions I begged to have control me, will not let them stop me from becoming the savior over some pesky little relationship they tried to convince me was *love*.

"Azalea!" Another voice cries my name now, this one belonging to the man who I'm certain visits my dreams.

"Shayde." I can't help myself, can't stop from calling out to him in my slightly intoxicated, pained state.

Dagan's body rolls off me, pushed away by the Reaper. That same Reaper crouches down before me, gingerly touching my cheek in a show of affection unlike anything I've ever seen before. Its face isn't cracked into that unnerving smile I've become accustomed to, its body shaking as it is forced into being gentle with its prey. It looks…remarkably human.

I blink through the pain in my right side, whispering, "How are you doing this?"

"What can be created can also be controlled." I try not to gag underneath the touch of the Reaper, closing my eyes so I can picture Shayde instead.

"I should kill this Reaper," I say, though even I am unconvinced by the statement. Fuck, why do I *miss* him?

"You should," he agrees before echoing my thoughts. "But you miss me."

I swallow. "What do you want?"

"I told you that I wanted to speak to you. I had to. You know that I love you, Azalea, and if you would just listen to me—"

"You came here to try and convince me to go with you? How well did that work out for you last time? Tell me, did I leave a scar?" I scoff, reaching up to grasp the Reaper's wrist and pulling it off my cheek. Light ignites in my hand, causing the Reaper to cry out and stumble a few feet away. It hurts to move, hurts to breathe, but I have to hold it in. I've had a broken rib recently, and I managed through the pain. I'll manage through it again if I can make Shayde retreat.

"I have Demi," he blurts. The Reaper steps forward and goes as still as a statue above me. "I can bring you to her."

"I don't want to see her." How dare he bring her into this? Dangle her as some sort of prize for complying with his demands? Demi is a fucking Reaper, and nothing can change that now. She will never be *Demi* again.

"You have to come with me!" The anger that I now know he possesses takes over, his shouts enough to have Jaymes flinging his body against the glass in desperation.

Shayde doesn't scare me, though. So, as defiantly as I can, I hiss, "No, Shayde. I don't."

"You and I are meant to be together, Azalea. *I love you.*"

"Why can't you understand and accept that what you did was *wrong*? I can't love someone who is okay with turning a blind eye to their own faults. I can't love you if you can't fucking own up to this shit and at least try to fix it!"

"Azalea, my father—"

"You are *not* your father!" I shout, pushing myself up to my elbows. I groan in pain as I do so, tears springing to my eyes.

"I have to do what he says, Azalea. You don't understand."

"No. I don't."

I don't understand how he could kill an entire planet full of people, how he could offer up fucking living, breathing beings just for his father to be pleased. I don't understand how he can go back on everything he told me, how he can be this horrifically evil person when I *know* he isn't, how he can make the wrong choice over and over again and still feel justified in doing so.

I have been wallowing in misery for two weeks, grieving and desperate for things to be different. But now that I see nothing has changed, and nothing will change, I'm not going to let myself be sad anymore. No; now I'm fucking pissed.

"I love you enough to come back and try to fix this, but you don't love me enough to hear me out?"

"I told you I cannot love you and if…" I pause, jaw ticking as I clench my teeth together angrily.

"If what?" He seems almost desperate for an answer, his tone pleading. I force myself to stand up and, despite the pain that radiates throughout me, I reach out and place a hand over the Reaper's heart.

Before blasting the Reaper with Light, I say, "If I cannot love you, then I will hate you instead."

CHAPTER 5

"Scythe Partners are a rare and incredibly powerful phenomenon. These animals are named from a human myth, after a weapon used by a character known as the Grim Reaper when he collects the souls of the dead. Similarly, Scythe Partners help Conjurers collect the twisted souls trapped inside Reapers. The chance of you having a Scythe Partner is two point three percent, a very low probability. If a Scythe Partner finds you, usually in the form of a cat but sometimes in other animals, it is a sign of your great power. Conjurers with Scythe Partners are historically the most powerful of their generations."

—*You and Your Scythe*, written by Shifter Marcellus Stone in 1998 A.G.

The ward around the house disappears when the last Reaper does, and with it comes an explosion of motion. Every window shatters and every door slams open, some flying off their hinges completely. I can vividly hear the cracking of wood, the splintering of glass, and the shouts of surprise and discord from inside.

I turn my head to see Jaymes running so hard that I'm certain he's going to trip and fall, but he reaches my side with no such incident. I've fallen onto my back now, but his arm wraps underneath and around my waist. His free hand cups my cheek with such gentleness, such care, that I don't have it in me to resist. I don't have the energy to push him away and bark about not being fragile.

"Are you okay?" His dark green eyes roam my body, examining every inch of me with such depth that I shiver.

"Physically? Sure," I manage out, wincing as the words vibrate my aching ribs. Jaymes helps me to my feet, hands moving silently as he casts some sort of healing Charm that warms my entire body. My ribs still ache, but at least they don't feel snapped in half anymore. Mostly bruised, I think.

"Azalea…" He trails, swallowing hard. "Did he…was he…?"

"He wanted to talk." I shut my eyes, wishing I didn't have to recall the conversation I'm sure will be echoing inside my mind for weeks to come.

"He wasn't trying to kill you? You're sure?" He pants out the words, but I don't think it's from the exertion of his run.

"Very. I'm not sure I'll be able to repeat the sentiments if we meet again, though." *If I cannot love you, then I will hate you instead.*

"What did you say to him, Azalea?"

"The truth." I shrug from his hold, taking a shuddering breath.

"So he's going to come after you now? We need to put together a plan, get security, and move you to a secure location—"

"No, we don't."

"Azalea, you don't understand the ramifications—"

"Shayde can attack me if he has the balls to do it. Isn't that what the prophecies are about? Me kicking his ass and bringing about world peace or whatever?"

"I don't think they go exactly like that, but—"

"Great, then we agree. I will stay here with my new pet cat and Shayde can go fuck himself."

"Your new cat?"

Dagan answers this time, his light laugh leaving a shiver down my spine. "She has a Scythe Partner."

"What the fuck does that mean?" I frown, searching for the black cat who saved my life and probably Dagan's.

"A Scythe Partner is an animal that chooses to bind itself to you for the remainder of its life, or yours. Your souls are tied together, providing the animal with a small amount of protective magic. It's an incredibly rare phenomenon, Azalea Jinx. Consider yourself lucky." This is the first time Dagan's father has spoken to me directly, and I stiffen as my eyes roam over the wide man. His balding gray hair is what catches my attention first, but I am quick to move my gaze to his more prominent features: sparkling hazel eyes and lips that are practically nonexistent. He holds the straps of his suspenders with meaty hands, rounded belly shifting from the force of a light chuckle. His legs are small compared to the rest of him, and there, at his feet, lays my new pet.

"It's small." I frown again, ignoring the businessman as I bend to pick Grimsly up.

"Looks around a year old," Dagan's father comments, body jiggling as he chuckles heartily.

"He was born on the day you entered this world." Jaymes's eyes harden as he stares at the dark ball of fur in my arms. The cat's eyes are a striking blue, and they peer at Jaymes as though he is prey Grimsly is preparing to eat for his next meal.

"How would you even *know*—" I start, flabbergasted.

"Prophecies."

"You Charmed and your Seers," I grumble, annoyed. I lift the cat briefly, displaying him proudly. "A boy!" I announce, as though everyone were waiting for a gender reveal. "Grimsly."

"Azalea." Jaymes runs a hand over his face, shaking his head and looking up at the sky. "You can't name your cat after the Grim."

"After *a* Grim. And it's my cat, I'll name it what I want. It's a good name, one he earned after saving my life from a Grim."

"A hero," Dagan remarks, nodding solemnly. He seems to be mostly unharmed, with only a few tears in his clothes from the hard impacts he made. He's bound to be sore and aching by this time tomorrow, though.

As though sensing where my mind went, Jaymes turns to the man. "I have medicine in the house and know a few basic healing Charms. Why don't we all go back in, and I'll take care of your wounds?"

"A pretty nurse to tend to my wounds? I've never dreamed of something so enticing." Dagan's eyes glitter in amusement, his tone flirty despite the seriousness of the moment.

I swear I can see a blush tinting Jaymes's cheeks, the sight making me blink in surprise. "Alright, come on, then. Let's finish this meeting while we're at it, hmm?"

And they do. Only this time, I'm allowed to partake. I listen with rapt attention as Jaymes discusses the future of the Shadow Faction, his fierce passion striking me in the heart with a brutal blow. It seems he takes after his mother in more than physical traits.

Mr. Breather declares, "Okay, Bloodgood. You know what? You have a deal."

Jaymes doesn't let on his surprise, but I do. Mr. Breather seemed to have been adamantly against giving either faction money, based on the way he's repeated those sentiments multiple times in the past two hours. Even his son seems a little surprised, head tilting curiously.

"Great, why don't we write—"

"I will provide donations and help you raise money through my products if your team implements them in their businesses and the businesses of their faction members, but only if you meet another request."

"Oh?" Jaymes's brows crinkle, concern barely concealed across his features.

"I want my child to be a part of your little group, the Gravediggers. I want assurance of his survival in this war. If I uphold our end of the bargain, which I fully plan on doing, then you will abide by these terms."

To Jaymes's credit, he doesn't let the outrage I'm sure he feels show. "I can't do that."

"You have an opening, don't you?"

"I will not replace Shayde." Jaymes's voice is hard, his body stiffening. The room is coated with a sudden awkwardness that Dagan's father tries to shove away with harsh truths.

"You mean you won't replace a Grim? Come, now, child. Surely you can see the issue in that statement? Surely you can see the issue with still calling him by his name and not acknowledging his deceit?"

"I acknowledge his deceit. I acknowledge his inheritance. But I also acknowledge that the man I knew and loved is not the same one we see now. So, no, I will not dishonor his memory or his person by replacing him so easily. Shayde is not someone you can *replace*."

"I don't want to replace him. I want to live." Dagan smiles in that way that leaves fear racing through my heart. There's something so…off about him. Something inherently *wrong*.

Jaymes takes a deep, steadying breath before saying, "I can do that. I won't call you a Gravedigger. I won't acknowledge you as a member of the group. But I will allow you to stay by our side and teach you what we know. Does that sound agreeable?"

"Sure." Dagan leans back in his chair, crossing one leg over another and tilting back. His head dips over the back of the chair, arms crossing across his chest. "When do I start?"

Jaymes stares at his elongated neck for a good while, contemplating or just plain distracted, I can't be entirely sure. "Two weeks. Come back in two weeks, and I will have the others here."

"Ugh. That's just lovely," I groan under my breath as Jaymes spins to Mr. Breather.

"Leader Fellows will be in touch with you to discuss the exact numbers of this deal. Our main point of contact going forward will be your son, but Leader Fellows is always available in times of utmost importance. I have these papers to sign if…"

Jaymes's voice fades away as I turn to look out the window, a prickly sensation running down the back of my neck. I see movement in the distance, near the woods that run down the other side of the street. I squint, heart already racing, as I search for someone who should not be there. Someone I shouldn't *want* to be here.

I stop breathing when a pair of antlers emerges and let out a shaky sigh when a stag steps through the trees. I run my fingers over the ring dangling from my neck, the rough edges a comfort despite who and what it represents. With one last lingering look, I turn away from the windows.

That prickly sensation doesn't leave until I'm tucked away in my room, Shayde's room, and buried underneath a comforter whose smell won't leave.

"You've lost weight." The words are calm and quiet, attached to a mouth I cannot look away from. I've known it was him hiding in my dreams, known the shadowy figure couldn't have been anyone else. I'm too fixated on him in my waking moments not to dream about him, too. And now, as I stare at him, I can't look away. I can't even take those precarious steps back and fall like usual.

"Yes," I admit, eyes roaming over Shayde's body. He's wearing a dark suit, tailored perfectly to his sculpted body. I swallow hard, my mouth watering. I've never seen him wear a suit before. Of course this would be the image my mind constructs. Of course it would bring me a version of him I wouldn't want to resist.

"Because of me?"

"Yes." Can I say anything else? Can I form more than one syllable in his overpowering presence?

"I'm sorry."

"It's too late for 'sorry'." There. I did it.

His light green eyes bore into me, lips pursed tightly as he takes a step closer and forces me to take a step back toward the ledge. "You hate me." It's not a question.

"I told you I did." I hold a hand out to stop him from coming any closer; I won't be able to control myself if he touches me.

"You tell me lots of things." He pushes close enough now to touch my outstretched palm, pressing against it with a hushed whisper escaping chapped lips. "Things you would never tell anyone else."

"I can't deny what happened in our past, but I can forge a new future. One without you in it." It's a little cathartic to speak so freely, to get my twisted, warped thoughts out and say them directly to him. Even if the real him will never know a word of them.

"Is that what you want, little flower?" He reaches out and twists a strand of my hair, much calmer than he should be.

I ignore his question, saying, "You shouldn't be here. How are you here?"

"I'm here because you want me to be."

I can't deny that. My subconscious has clearly missed him.

"This isn't real, though."

"Hmm. You've had some other, very real, dreams before, haven't you, darling?"

"Those were different. I saw images, words, symbols. I didn't—I never saw *you.*"

"Then maybe I'm not here." He shrugs, pushing harder into my palm. My elbow relaxes of its own accord, and suddenly his body is pushed flush against mine. His arm wraps around my waist, hand moving from my hair to my cheek.

I close my eyes tightly, shaking underneath his touch. "I don't know who you are anymore."

"You know exactly who I am, little flower. You know my secrets, my weaknesses, my strengths. *You know me.*"

"I know nothing about you. I don't know your mother's name, your favorite color, your middle name, your deepest fears. *I don't know you.*"

"Her name was Sakura. She was named after a flower, just like you. She came from a different region of our world but made the hard decision to journey here to join Draxmere. That's where my father found her." Shayde opens his mouth, then closes it, closing his eyes and pressing his forehead to mine. Good Grim, it feels so *real.* "My favorite color is brown. Specifically, the shade of your eyes. My middle name is Ren, after my mother's father. My deepest fear is losing you."

"No, Shayde. You can't…you can't say—"

He interrupts me, his body stiffening. "The truth? I can't say the truth? I can't tell you the things you want to know?"

"It doesn't matter, anyway. None of this is real. It's all made up shit my brain formed to cope with the loss of you."

"Keep telling yourself that." He huffs, pressing his nose against mine. "You like to tell yourself a lot of things that aren't true."

"Like what?" I can barely breathe with him so close to me, can barely feel anything past the points where our skin makes contact.

"Like your decision to hate me. The decision to make me your enemy."

"You are my enemy, Shayde. You didn't have to be, but…you decided for us both."

"I love you." His lips brush against mine, light and brief. "I love you, and I want to be with you."

"I don't want to be with you. Not anymore." I swallow the lump in my throat, cursing my dream-addled brain for forcing me into this situation.

"You are determined to hate me?" His voice is harsh and viscous, a stark change to the gentle demeanor he's been using the entire conversation.

"I cannot love you," I tell myself, despite my lack of conviction.

"Then I will give you a real reason to hate me, Azalea Jinx."

Shayde pulls me even tighter into his body, lips meeting mine in a harsh and bruising motion. I can't help but wrap my arms around his neck, hands tangling into his long, dark hair and pulling. Our kiss is fast and fleeting, harsh and regrettable. When Shayde steps back, his eyes are pooled with anger, a wide smirk flashing at me just before I am pushed over the ledge. I fall, fall, fall, until the eyes staring down at me from so high above become nothing more than little green specks.

CHAPTER 6

"With the help of a jinx, a curse, an ill-fitted match,
the world shall fall by a trusted savior's hands.
In the Shadows, in the mind, a plan will hatch,
and in the Light, in the open, the evil shall stand."
—Prophecy recorded inside student Seer Allia Jordan's Prophetic
Journal, 2024 A.G.

My feet pad lightly on the cold wooden floors, my anger radiating around me in the form of a cloud of shadows. I can hear Jaymes's stern voice in the kitchen, his tone harsh and brutal. Then I hear Arlo's charming laugh, his unserious attitude only angering Jaymes further.

"Give the kid a break, Arlo. He doesn't know that you're pulling his tail," I say dryly upon entering the room, stealing Jaymes's coffee mug from his hands and taking a long sip.

"I don't have a tail," he grinds out, glaring down at his mug but not moving to steal it back.

"You don't?" I raise an eyebrow, dramatically peering around his body.

"Okay, Azalea, that's enough. I—"

"Is it? Enough, I mean? Because I think I am just starting, and I'm quite sure you aren't going to like what else I have to say."

Jaymes rubs the bridge of his nose in aggravation, waving at me dismissively. "I never like the things you have to say, Azalea Jinx."

"Great, then you are going to *love* this." I put down the cup, my smile misleadingly bright. "You have no control over my actions. You do not get to tell me when or where I go, and you most certainly don't have the right to lock me inside your house. I am no prisoner, Jaymes Bloodgood, and I will not be treated as one."

"That's not what I'm trying to do." He stares down at the mug, his words quiet and pleading.

"Oh, I know. I know all of the protective bullshit you've been telling yourself because you're a macho man and have this innate need to protect me, the helpless woman. Except, I'm not helpless, and I do not follow orders from *you.*"

"Oh shit." Arlo grins as his eyes flicker between us, lifting himself onto the kitchen counter and propping his chin on his hands. "Nox, got any popcorn?"

"Shut up," Jaymes seethes at his two friends, turning his attention back to me. "Quit being such a whiny baby, Azalea. I know Shayde, and—"

"So do I. Remember? I know him just as intimately as *you.*" I don't allow myself to linger on that thought, on the many intimate moments my mind conjures to remind me exactly how well Shayde and I know one another's bodies. Clenching my teeth, I push past the memories and snarl, "I will not sit back and let you guys go have fun at a club and leave me here. I'm bored, Jaymes. It's been a month, okay? I'm as okay as I will ever be. I stopped doing drugs and only drink occasionally now. I deserve a night of drinking and dancing. I deserve a distraction. Shayde hasn't shown his face here once. *Not. A. Single. Time.* What makes you think he will show up now?" That statement isn't necessarily true, but Jaymes doesn't have to know that. He doesn't have to know Shayde *might* be stalking me. Between the constant prickling on my neck and Grimsly's hisses at the window in my room…Yeah, I think it's a strong possibility. I should probably be concerned about that, honestly.

"Let her come, Jaymes," Nox rumbles, blue eyes falling to me.

I nod my thanks, throwing my hands up as though to say, "See?"

"I don't know, Azalea. Going out…" Jaymes gnaws on his bottom lip, contemplating.

Hand on my hip, I cluck my tongue and say, "Wouldn't it be worse if I were here alone? What if he found out I was on my own and decided to come snatch me up?" I don't have any legitimate worries about that, but I'm desperate to get away from this house and Jaymes's overprotective energy.

"The house is warded against him now." Jaymes waves his hand dismissively, watching me wearily. "I—" Jaymes is interrupted by a knock on the door; a breathy sigh leaves his lips.

"Ooh, is that Dagan?" I bounce from toe to toe, grinning. I've teased Jaymes for the past few weeks about Dagan and the blush I know I saw on his cheeks.

"I'm sure." Jaymes strides toward the door, ignoring the three of us snickering at his retreating form. Jaymes throws open the door, his mouth opening to say something, but his entire body freezes instead.

"Hi, Dagan," I call as I approach, jaw popping open when I see the person at the door. It isn't Dagan…but it is. The woman standing there has the same foxy hair, the same face, the same body, but…

"Hello, Azalea," she calls, smiling. Her silver dress is skintight, hugging every curve and emphasizing her long legs. She flips her long hair over her shoulder, moving to push past Jaymes. The limp I noticed our first meeting confirms this *is* Dagan, and I worry briefly over how the tall stilettos she wears will affect her stability.

"Nox. Arlo." Her tone is professional, her smile still bright. She points at each boy when she says their names, somehow knowing who is who. She strides past us to shake their hands, and Jaymes and I turn simultaneously to watch her walk away. Even *I* stare at her ass.

"I thought you said Dagan was a dude," Arlo manages out, shaking her hand firmly. He turns to us with wide eyes when she moves on to Nox, shaking his hand as though it hurts.

"I am sometimes," she says brightly, shaking Nox's hand just as harshly. "Today, I am not."

"Got it," Arlo mutters, cradling his hand. "But…"

"Just ask," she says bluntly, sensing the hesitation. "I won't be offended."

"Well, how do you choose?" Arlo blinks at her innocently, genuinely curious.

"It's not about choosing, it's about feeling." With that, she dismisses him, turning back to me and frowning.

"Why aren't you dressed, Azalea?"

"Yeah, Jaymes, why am I not dressed?" I tilt my head and narrow my eyes in challenge, the corners of my lip tilting upward in a smirk as I dare him to deny me again.

"Oh, fuck off, Azalea. Go put on a dress already. You have twenty minutes." I can't stop the laugh that escapes me, followed by a wink and a blown kiss to piss him off further. Then, slyly, I shoot him the middle finger as I turn to leave.

"I'll help you, Azalea."

Dagan follows dutifully, an extra swing in her step as she struts after me. "Please tell me you have something hot to wear. It would be a shame for you to hide that body behind ugly clothes."

"I have something." I swallow, remembering Demi's red, glittering dress sitting in the back of my closet.

"Great. Do you want me to help you with your hair and makeup? Twenty minutes is—" I hold up a hand to stop her, shaking my head vehemently.

"I-I appreciate the offer, but I can't. It reminds me too much of…" I shudder, clenching my eyes shut.

"Oh. Right. Your Reaper friend. I'm sorry; I should have realized."

"It's fine. Really. Demi is just a sensitive topic."

Dagan only nods, her voice quiet and sure as she says, "I know Death. Your friend, Demi? She reeks of life."

I spin, shoving her against Jaymes's bedroom door and pinning her by the wrists in a move so fast she doesn't have time to scream. "What did you just say?"

She stares at me with interest, starting by saying, "I said—"

"Yes, yes. I know. But how do *you* know that?"

"Because she's been here." Dagan frowns before laughing maniacally. "I felt her presence the last time I was here. I always feel the presence of a Reaper. They are so close to Death, so near extinction, that their scent is always hovering in the air. And Demi? I only recognized her because her presence was so similar to *yours*. The two of you...you smell like him. Like the Grim." Panic seizes my body so tightly I can't breathe, can't think, for a few precious seconds. I...I *smell* like him? Demi smells like him? Have we been marked by a Grim somehow? No...no. I can't let myself dive into that bottomless waterhole. With a full body shudder, I pull myself out of those particular thoughts and delve into an alcove full of other, just as dangerous ones.

"How? How can you do that? If she were here, why didn't she attack me too? Why didn't she...?" I trail off, slowly backing away. She didn't attack me because Shayde had been here, too, just like I suspected. And he didn't want me to kill her.

"It's a Necromancer thing. A powerful Necromancer knows when Reapers are near: We can feel it in our bones. It's like...someone whispering into my ear. Like a strong smell wafting into my nose. I can recognize a Reaper with my eyes closed."

"And you can tell who they used to be?"

"Not always. If I knew them in life, sure."

"You didn't know Demi in..." I don't want to say in life because I don't want to think of her as *dead*.

"No, I didn't. But like I said: She smells like you." The smile that follows is the creepy one Dagan often uses, the kind that leaves you unsettled and desperate to get away from them, and I shudder at its presence.

"Okay. Okay, great, thanks for the information," I say numbly, leading her into my room.

Demi had been here. Demi had been here. *Demi had been here.*

The Gravediggers take us to a club bursting with life despite its contradictory name, Deathly Deviances, illuminated in pink neon letters on the back wall. The number of bodies in this place is astronomical for its size; people press against each other so tightly that I'm not sure how there is room to move. Our every step is constricted, and Jaymes holds tightly onto my hand to keep me nearby as we navigate through the crowd. I hold onto Dagan's bony hand, dragging her after me as we push toward a bar in the back corner. The flashing multi-colored lights in the otherwise dark room are the only thing aiding our journey, that and the growling Nox, who is convincing people to jump out of our way.

"It's so…loud!" I shout, which is answered by a cackling Dagan.

"You've never been clubbing?" she questions, stumbling over a wayward foot.

"Not really, no!"

"Ooh, you are in for a treat, Azalea Jinx!"

Jaymes shakes his head at us, white-blond hair flopping over his face with the movement.

"I hope so!" I need this. I need to be distracted, to have something other than *Shayde* to think about.

When we reach the bar, Arlo orders a round of shots for everyone. The bartender hands us a neon green liquid in small, clear glasses, and I wrinkle my nose in distaste. "What the fuck is this?"

"Just drink it, Azalea!" Dagan throws hers back without so much as a wince, which could be expected from the heir of a large alcohol company, I suppose. With a shrug, I toss the drink back. It tastes almost like an apple, sweet but with a hint of bitterness. It burns, but I don't mind it.

"Got any Dragon's Breath?" Dagan shouts over the music, gesturing at the five of us. The guy nods, ducking down below him.

"I love this stuff," I sigh as the man pops back up, placing all five bottles down on the table. Dagan passes him a handful of cash, not looking to see the total, and waves him away. She grabs two, handing one to me, and pops the lid off hers. I follow suit, clinking our drinks together with a genuine grin.

"Don't drink that too fast," Jaymes says into my ear, chuckling as I pause.

"Don't listen to him! Drinking it fast makes it work quicker." Dagan cackles, draining hers in one go. I laugh, sending Jaymes a mischievous grin before mimicking her actions.

"I think *I* should be warning *you* not to drink too much," I shout, enjoying the flush that spreads across his cheeks as he remembers the night I'm referencing. A night that resulted in us kissing, Shayde beating the hell out of him, and me crying in the woods.

"That won't happen again."

"I know it won't." I glance over toward Nox and Arlo, who are already knee-deep in conversations with two very pretty girls. "Do you think he misses Demi?" Demi, a tiny little vamp, was obsessed with Arlo, a large wolf, and had warned me multiple times that he was off limits because she was claiming him for herself. Nothing ever happened between them, as far as I'm aware, but in the end, I know he wanted it just as badly as she did.

"Of course he does. But she's a Reaper now, Azalea. He has no choice; he has to move on."

"Right. Of course." I swallow, hating the burning in my throat that has nothing to do with alcohol.

"Let's dance!" Dagan practically drags me away from Jaymes and toward the dance floor. She is quick to find us a pair of dance partners, two men who eye us hungrily. I don't notice their features, don't find out their names. I only melt into their bodies, switching partners with Dagan on occasion. That is, until Jaymes and Arlo come to sweep us away.

"Boo," I pout, head swimming.

"Dance with me, Azalea." Arlo doesn't ask, he *demands*. When Arlo takes me into his arms and begins to dance, he doesn't do it in a possessive "I want to go home with you" way. He is gentle and kind, endearing and slow despite his earlier attitude. He holds me closely, my back against his chest, but it isn't the same way a lover might dance with me. It's more protective, as though to keep me away from the crowd.

"I don't know anything about you," I shout, tilting my head back against his chest to look into his hazel eyes.

"What do you want to know?" His dark eyes sparkle in the lights, a wolfish smile on his lips.

"How did you meet Jaymes?" *And Shayde,* I think, but don't say.

He leans closer to speak into my ear so I can hear him properly. "Through our parents. We've known each other since we were really young. Jaymes, Nox, and I were together before we were out of diapers."

"Shayde came later?"

"Shayde came later," he agrees, lips pursed.

"Jaymes isn't taking it as hard as I thought he would," I say, watching him dance with Dagan. He looks so uncomfortable that it's funny, and he seems not to know where to place his hands. Dagan is unfazed by his charming shyness, grinding on him like he's a lover and not a man she is doing business dealings with.

"Jaymes is too optimistic sometimes," comes Arlo's reply, his sigh reverberating down my spine.

"You don't think—"

"No. I don't think any of us should be considering giving Shayde the benefit of the doubt. Especially not Jaymes. Especially not *you*."

"I'm not going to."

"I know. That's not the type of person you are."

"What's that supposed to mean?"

"It means you're a hard ass." Arlo grins, his pointed canines flashing.

"Bah, humbug," I mutter, turning to face him and shoving him lightly. "Why don't you find a girl who actually wants to dance with you? I'm fine on my own."

"Jaymes said—"

"Jaymes isn't my master. He doesn't own me." I glower, shoving him harder. "Go on. He isn't going to notice." I jab my finger in his direction.

"He definitely won't," Arlo agrees.

Jaymes has melted into Dagan's body, a blush still spread across his cheeks, but his eyes are alight with lust. His hands have moved to her hips, his lips pressed against her ear. He had been so confident with me on the dance floor all those months ago that seeing him like *this* is comical.

I waltz away from Arlo before he can object any further, bumping into another redheaded individual instead. Her strawberry blond curls flip over her shoulder as she spins around to see me, gray eyes flashing as she takes me in. "Sorry!" I shout with what I hope is a sincere smile.

"It's fine. Want to dance?"

Just like that, I am whisked into a stranger's arms, her tall form grinding into me song after song. Just when I am starting to sober up, she pulls me from the dance floor, but not toward the bar like I had suspected. Instead, she brings me to a small side door in a hidden alcove, pushing me out into the cold night air. I do us both a favor and place a Balmy Charm over our forms, protecting us from the cold despite this being the warmest weather I've felt in this world by far. I glance around the dark alley we have found ourselves in, raising an eyebrow.

"Pretty and powerful," she says shyly, a cloud forming around us as her words hit the light, snow-filled breeze.

"Yes," I say simply, gaze roaming over her body. She isn't my usual type, with her boyish frame and small breasts, but that's good. I don't want my *usual*. I don't want anything that reminds me of Shayde, or Demi, for that matter. And this girl? She is nothing like either of them, the total opposite of everyone who has been involved in my life for the past year. And, fuck, do I hope that means something good for me.

I shove the woman into the wall with a lustful gleam in my eyes, blocking her in with my body as I reach up on my tip-toes and grab her cheeks into my hands. Our lips meet in a frantic, desperate moment and I try *so hard* to feel butterflies, or at least a little damn lust. But my mind screams at me *not Shayde, not Shayde, not Shayde,* and damn him for making me feel like this. For ruining sex and attraction and fucking *lust.*

I shove my tongue into the girl's mouth just as her hands come down to my waist, small moans leaving her warm mouth. I move to cup her breasts with one hand, the other skimming down her tight black dress and stopping at her thighs where it ends. I push the ends of that dress up with confidence, whispering, "Is this okay?"

The woman nods frantically, pulling me closer into her body. My fingers inch up her bare thigh, tracing over her lacy underwear. She moans again, back arching and hips raising as I begin to trail kisses down her neck and fall back flatly on my feet. I rub small circles over the outside of that lacy underwear, teasing, testing, taking.

"Fucking Grim," I murmur, wishing I felt more than annoyance at performing this task. I used to *like* this. Well, at least I used to *want* to do this. Like is a strong word for someone who couldn't feel lust or attraction. But, really, is anything different now? Because I still feel nothing for this woman. No heat in the pit of my stomach, no flutters, no pulsing between my thighs. Nothing other than the hope that I can get there, other than the wish to find someone else just as worthy as Shayde for my body to cling to. It makes me so annoyed, so hopeless, so *angry* that Shayde has ruined me for anyone else. That I can't even properly use this woman, or anyone else, to get him out of my head.

"You would know about fucking a Grim, wouldn't you, Azalea Jinx?" The body pressed against mine is ripped away on a phantom wind, torn from my body in one fluid motion. Her screams echo in the night air, her long hair whipping me on the way out. And that *voice*.

"What are you doing here?" I shake as I spin toward the direction of it, pure, cold *hatred* filling my bones.

"Hello, little flower." His shadows have pulled her to him, her back flush against his chest and his hand against her throat. Tears leak from her eyes, panic on display in those blown-out pupils.

"Cut the bullshit, Shayde. Give me my plaything back," I scowl, forcing my racing heart to calm. *No,* I tell it. *We do not want him anymore.*

"I can't check on you, darling?"

"No. You can't." How can I get her away from him? How can I convince him to let her go? Maybe, if I—

"Well, it's a good thing I did, because it seems you weren't following my rules."

My alcohol-addled mind searches for an explanation but comes up with none. "What rules?"

"Rule number three: If anyone ever puts their hands on what's mine, I kill them."

"Shayde, that's ridi—" Before I can finish my sentence, Shayde grabs the woman by the head and snaps her neck. No noise leaves my lips, no fleeting sounds of panic. My eyes don't even widen. Behavior like this from Shayde can no longer surprise or scare me.

"Asshole," I hiss out on an exhale of breath, my Light blaring to life. From one second to the next, I am blasting him, Light burning a hole in his arm. Shayde jerks away in surprise, dropping the body unceremoniously to the ground.

"You hit me," he breathes, glaring down at the wound as though he can will it away. It's bloody and raw, a painful reminder of what we are to one another now: enemies.

"Yes, and I'm about to do it again." I throw another blast his way, stumbling forward as I try to force my mind to focus. I may have sobered up some from having the drinks I consumed a couple of hours ago upon arrival, but that doesn't make me *sober*. I still feel light-headed, still feel obnoxiously calm, still feel inebriated past the point of what a situation like this calls for. And Grimsly…Grimsly isn't here. I left my protector, my Scythe Partner, at home, and I'm so unbelievably *stupid* for thinking Shayde wouldn't show up here.

"You hurt me," he whispers, throwing out a blast of Shadow to block my attack.

"I will do more than hurt you, Shayde Glover. Or is it Shayde Grim now?" I tilt my outstretched hand out of sight so I don't have to see the small SG printed there.

"Are you going to kill me? Is that it, Azalea? Do you think this will all go away if I die?" My attacks become frenzied, but I know better than anyone how powerful Shayde truly is. I've trained with him and fought by his side. Logically, I *know* that I can't kill him. But, as I am so often reminded by myself, I am no longer ruled by logic.

I don't answer Shayde, refusing to acknowledge his pain or mine. Instead, I keep attacking. With each one, I inch closer, unsure of what I will do once I get close enough to strike a truly lethal blow. Will I be able to do it? I suppose I'll have to because I know how easily he could kill me.

"I killed her."

"I know, I fucking watched it happen." A gurgling, hysterical laugh leaves my lips. I watched him kill an innocent girl, one I called my plaything right before she died. I watched and I couldn't do *anything*.

"Not your plaything, as you so lovingly called her. *Demi*."

"What?" My emotions rule me now, and my body comes to a grinding halt on their behalf. In those few seconds, Shayde has me trapped in his shadows, tendrils wrapping around me tightly like ropes. I struggle against the bindings, hands pinned to my sides. Fuck, fuck, *fuck*.

"I brought her to see you one last time. It was on the night we had a lovely chat at Jaymes's house. I let her know that you loved her, allowing you to be her last sight. Then I killed her."

"*No*." I didn't realize how hopeful I had been that I could save her, how desperate I was for her to be alive and well. But she isn't. A heartbroken noise escapes my lips, something demented and torn coming straight from my soul.

"Isn't that what you wanted?" He tilts his head curiously, watching me with a confused expression. "Didn't you say she was practically dead already?"

"I-I-" I can't form words, or thoughts, or noises. *Dead, dead, dead.*

"What should I do with you now, Azalea Jinx?" Those are the words that have me slamming back into myself, my expression hardening and my eyes turning deadly. He killed Demi, and I will make sure her death *meant something.*

"You should kill me while you can," I warn, voice hard and detached.

Shayde chuckles as though I told a joke. "Why would I do that?"

"Because I have no reason to let you live." My Light blasts from my entire body, burning each of those shadowy tendrils entrapping me right off. Shayde jumps away with a hiss, the muscles in his jaw clenching. Before he can decide what to do next, I am holding my hands out, chanting a prayer in my mind and begging myself to do what has to be done. I form a multicolored ball, which I only managed to do once before, the effort making my intoxicated body shake. But I continue to form the ball, flinging it at Shayde in one mighty move as soon as I deem it large enough.

The Light and Shadow mixture hits him square in the chest, his body flying up and out of sight. And, like a coward, I flee. I flee back into the club, slamming the door to the alley, and search the crowd for a familiar face. The first one I find is Nox, his bulky form only mere feet from me.

"He's here," I call as I shove past sweaty bodies, panting. "Nox, he's here!" Nox knows immediately who I am talking about, his face solemn with pursed lips as I approach, and he is much more efficient at making people move. He sweeps me under one of his beefy arms, pulling me toward the D.J. booth. "What are you—"

Nox grabs the microphone from the man, his stern and serious voice filling the room instead of music. "There has been a Grim sighting nearby. All of you need to get the fuck out *now*."

There was no hesitation in the crowd. Even the bartender flees the scene, the thundering footsteps and fearful cries vanishing into the night as over two hundred people disappear in mere minutes. Only Jaymes, Dagan, and Arlo stay in the building with us, all looking at each other wearily. That is, until Jaymes looks at me. A look that says *Are you okay?*, to which I respond verbally:

"No. I'm not."

CHAPTER 7

"There will be no end to the Grim
until a Grim can make amends.
There will be no jinx to save the world
until a jinx no longer forgives."
—Continued prophecy recovered in the prophetic journals of
Abraham Delowosky, 377 A.G.

DEMI

"I told her I killed you."

I flick my eyes over to the emotional boy, wishing I could get out of this cage and suck all of that delicious Charm right out of his body. But my master told me to obey the boy, so I will. Even if I disagree with his decision. Even if I desperately wish to please my master in any other way. Even if I desperately wish to be free to do the things I was created for.

"She didn't take it very well," he sighs, slowly inching down the wall until he falls into a seated position. Then he continues, despite my lack of response. "I thought it would make her feel better, but it only made her angry. And it's not like I can take it back. She hates me, Demi."

Annoyance surges through me; I close my eyes so I don't have to watch the weak offspring of my master wallow. I'm so tired of listening to him *pine* over this woman. I would have killed her already if I were him. From the sounds of things, she is destined to be his downfall. Why take the risk? Survival is more important than something fickle like *love*.

"And it's getting worse. The memory loss, the loss of self, the inconsistencies in my mind. I don't know why I keep doing these bad things. I don't want to do them," he wails, banging the back of his head against the wall.

This, too, is another thing he cannot stop talking about. The master's offspring has inherited gifts that he should be thankful for, but he only complains about them. He says he doesn't like to kill, that he doesn't want to be a Grim. He says that I didn't want to be a Reaper, either. But I don't care what I wanted before because now I want more than I ever did before. I want to devour, to eat, to grow. I want to be powerful and important. I want to be my master's favorite. But the sad boy won't allow me to devour. He won't allow me to fulfill my full potential.

It's annoying.

"My father is an awful person, but now that I've begun to experience this…this *confusion*…I wonder, was he always evil? Did he always want to be the Grim? Or did the Grim take over, despite his wants and his wishes? Every time I change, I can feel it taking over my mind, can hear these insidious thoughts. All it wants is chaos and power and destruction, and *I don't want those things*."

I make a small noise, my best impression of a sigh. The boy never wants any of the things I want. He doesn't understand why chaos and power and destruction are *good* things. These things balance out the carefully placed goodness in the world—we need to be bad to make things even. If we aren't bad, then who will be? If we don't choose chaos, then who will? Besides, being good isn't fun. Being good wouldn't make me strong *or* sated.

"She told me she hates me," he moans, head now in his hands. "She told me that to my face, Demi. You know her—she doesn't half-ass anything. She's truthful and brave, and she most certainly hates me."

Good. Maybe he will stop pining and move on. Maybe heartbreak will be the thing that finally corrupts that selfless soul.

"I don't know how to stop myself from changing. I don't know how to help you. I'm lost, Demi, and I'm not sure how I'm supposed to find the pieces of me that have been scattered in the wind.

"Did you know I attacked her? I just couldn't stop myself. I saw her pressing that woman up against the wall, and I got so *angry*. Honestly, that wasn't even the Grim inside me. It was just me. *I told her.* I told her she wasn't allowed to touch anyone else, and she doesn't get to break the rules just because she doesn't think she's mine anymore. Because she *is* mine. That's why you have to help me, Demi. You know her. You love her. How do I fix myself so I can fix this mess? How can I tell her that I don't want to work with my dad? That I'm doing all of this for *her*?" He's still seated against the wall, but his hands move around in distress and his head shakes so violently that I wonder if it will fall off entirely.

I stay silent, but not because I have nothing to say. No, it's because I do not have the ability to speak. So, instead, I flash him one of my grins that seem to creep normal people out. It only spurs the offspring on.

"Ugh, I know. I know. You're right. I need to keep looking for the Grimoire. It will tell me how to stop this, and then I can bring the book to her, and she can fix me."

The Grimoire: some ancient tome that the master's offspring says details everything about their creation. I think it's stupid to dig up something so ancient and all-knowing. It's been hidden for a reason. My master knows this, and so does his son. This book could be the end of his life, which could mean the end of mine. I want him to forget the book ever existed, if only so I never have to *worry* about never existing.

"I think the book would tell me how to fix you. Surely the first Grim made mistakes, changed people he didn't mean to. Surely there's a Charm or something I can perform. Maybe there's a ritual? I don't know, I don't want to speculate." The offspring continues to ramble, pulling at his long hair.

I watch in annoyance as he stands, beginning to pace outside my cell. I'm so tired of watching him unravel, of seeing his wrinkled clothes and baggy eyes. He is *weak* and undeserving of the great power he wields. All because of a *woman.*

"Fuck, here it comes again." His head jerks to one side, twitching as his jaw ticks. "When my mind shuts off, don't let me do anything Azalea wouldn't approve of, okay?" Then he's collapsing, a dull heap on the floor. I make another noise, leaning against the bars as I wait for his head to lift.

A cackle escapes from his lips before that dark mop of hair moves, his body spasming with his laughs. "Oh, I fucking love her. I love her audacity, her strength, her boldness. Everything about her compliments everything about me. I can't wait to destroy her mind, body, and soul. I can't wait to *own* her."

Here we go again. This version of the offspring likes to talk about possessing the girl and too often goes into detail about all of the unusual things he wants to do with her body. I don't understand sexual attraction, but it is fascinating to listen to him speak of those things.

"She thinks I'm going to try and kill her now, and I'm certainly going to make it seem that way. I'm going to be vicious in my endeavors, but all with one goal in mind: To capture her. I'll put her right next to you, and eventually, she won't be able to resist falling back in love. And once she falls back in love with me, I will use her to take over both worlds. With a power like hers, we'd be unstoppable." He cackles again, jerking up like a vampire rising from a coffin.

I watch as he jumps to his feet, waving away the lock on my cell. The door swings open, and I step out, following him as he strides down the room. I like this version of the offspring most of the time; *he* knows how important chaos is. Even if that chaos always has to surround *her*.

"How about we go pay her a visit, hmm? I *so* enjoy having my eyes on her."

Chapter 8

"Reapers were my first and only creation, and they are *everything*. They are exactly what the Charmed can never be: chaotic, hungry, power-driven creatures. They are the balance between good and evil, and they are the only things that can keep a Grim alive. Creating these creatures and causing chaos in the world is our only purpose. We are not good. We are not heroes. *We are here to balance the universe.* It is your sacred duty as a Grim to continue on our legacy, to sacrifice your body and mind until, eventually, it is just you and your creations left to rule the world. Don't let the Charmed fool you; the world would be better with a Grim at its helm."

—*The Grimoire*, written by the first, unnamed Grim, 1 A.G.

This dream is different. It starts with the same shadowy man in the distance I now know to be Shayde, but this time, the scene has changed. I'm not standing on the edge of a cliff, I'm standing in a kitchen. It's unfamiliar, its small size leaving me hardly any room to explore. Aging wood cabinets stare down at me, brassy knobs gleaming under a flickering light. I glance up and snicker at the boob-like fixture. When I tilt my head back down, Shayde is emerging from the shadowy distance I won't dare explore. His lips are tilted up into a smile he's trying to hide, his eyes roaming my body freely. This time he's in a gray t-shirt and dark jeans, casual wear I'd seen him in many times before.

"Why did you come back?" I don't know why I bother asking, he's just a figment of my imagination. Obviously, I wanted him here despite all the best reasons not to.

"I don't want to fight in your dreams. Your dreams are the one place we are allowed to *exist*."

"We exist in the real world," I say, confused.

"But we are not allowed to exist *together*." The words are a solemn admission.

"You know I don't give a damn about what is allowed. I care about who you are, who you were supposed to be. About what a disappointment you turned out to be." Hurt flashes across his features, eyes wide in disbelief for brief seconds before that carefully neutral mask returns. He shrugs, as though he doesn't care what I think of him.

"Dreams are the only time I can be what you need me to be. The only time I can defend myself against your beliefs."

"Last time I had a dream about you, you told me you would give me a real reason to hate you."

"Oh, I will. *I have*. But I'm also going to give you reasons to love me, too."

"I don't want that."

"You want to hate me?"

No. Yes. I don't know. Absolutely. Never. "I want you to be the man I thought you were. But I guess we don't always get what we want, do we?"

He smiles sadly, saying only, "Do you want to make cookies?"

"I don't know how to cook, much less bake." I furrow my brows, turning my attention to the ingredients on the yellowing counters. In the human world, I wasn't given the opportunity while growing up to learn basic skills like cooking. Once I turned eighteen and was on my own, I usually only bought things that could go in the microwave or oven with little interference. I also ordered takeout when I had the funds.

"But I do." My eyes fall on the cake mix, the eggs, the vegetable oil, and the powdered sugar. That's it. That's all that is there.

"Are you sure? Because that looks like things to bake a cake. Not cookies."

Shayde laughs, and my spine tingles at the joyful sound. How often have I heard him laugh like that? Truly laugh with no care? Not very. Shayde is a serious man, and I've never seen him not on edge. Even on our one date in the city of Maladara, he was tense and aware of our every surrounding. I was the one who had let my guard fall, I was the one who let myself fall prey to his advances. Is this the way my mind is going to torture me? By showing me images of him relaxing in a home that could have easily been ours? By picturing us as a normal couple with a normal life that would never have been written in our futures?

"Cake mix cookies, I think they call them. My mom used to make them with me. We'd roll the dough into fun little shapes and cut little stars or hearts out before rolling them in the powdered sugar. Delicious and fun. An easy way to entertain a child."

I don't like how my mind is forming such a convoluted backstory for such a simple man. He is the son of a Grim, which in turn makes him a Grim. Not a devil by association, but a devil truly. I'm not allowed to turn him into…into a *human*. I'm not allowed to give him feelings and make him seem reasonable.

"I don't want to cook with you."

"Yes, you do." He approaches so quickly that I have no choice but to face him head-on, my arms crossing across my chest as he presses into me.

Angrily, I hiss up at him, "You think you know me so well? You think you know my feelings, my thoughts?" I'm arguing with myself, and I'm going to lose because, *yes*. Yes, this Shayde I created does know everything about me.

"I want to know you more. I want to hear every thought, every feeling. I want to know you the way you know yourself." It isn't what I expected him to say, and my arms drop in defeat as I take in his solemn expression.

"Fine. I don't care. Invade my dreams and show me the life we could have had. Show me what it means to miss you, what it would be like to love you still. But this is the only place I will allow you to control my feelings, Shayde Glover. This is the only place *we* exist."

"I will take whatever I can from you, Azalea. Good or bad. Give whatever scraps of yourself you can to me, and I will devour them with the passion of a dying man." I shiver underneath his heated gaze, wincing as his arms move to wrap around me. I dodge that touch, jerking into an aging counter and shaking my head furiously.

"I can't do this, Shayde. I can't…we can't be together like that. Not even here. I can pretend that we are a normal couple, that we live normal lives and do normal things. But I can't pretend to be fucking you. That's crossing a line."

"It was just a touch, Azalea." The slightest hint of a smirk graces his lips, and he takes a step back as he shoves his hands deeply into the pockets of his dark jeans. "But glad to know your mind went straight to the gutter."

I scowl, sputtering with blazing cheeks, "I know where your innocent touches lead, Shayde Grim."

The flinch he releases has his head jerking back as though I slapped him. "Don't call me that. Please, just don't."

"Was Glover your mother's last name?" It's a quiet question, one that lingers as I turn back toward our meager ingredients.

"It was." I feel his presence behind me, long arms reaching up to grab a bowl out of a cabinet.

"How did you know that was there?"

"This home used to be my grandfather's. That's why it looks so outdated. My mother would bring me here whenever my father was feeling particularly nasty." He puts the bowl down before reaching into a drawer and pulling out a spatula and a flower cookie cutter.

"I really need to stop giving you such detailed backstories," I murmur to myself, shaking my head. Clearly, this recipe, this house—it's all hidden somewhere deep inside my damaged mind.

"Hmph," he huffs, fingers gently brushing against mine on the counter. "Did you ever consider that I'm not a figment of your imagination?"

I jerk my hand away, wide brown eyes looking up to meet his light green ones. "What did you say?"

"You heard me." He seems amused. Relief floods me, my fluttering heart calming its rapid pace.

"Fuck, I thought you were being serious."

"Well, I *am* a serious man." The exact thought I had not moments ago. Definitely a figment, then.

"Alright, alright. How do we make these cake cookies, Shayde?" I've never made cake mix cookies before. Or any cookie. I doubt this recipe could be remade outside of a dreamscape, honestly. But Shayde is certain in his movements, and he shows me how to mix everything to create a thick batter. He shows me how to flatten it out and use the cookie cutter, and we cover each one in the messy powdered sugar with glee. By the time we are sticking them in the oven, both of us have relaxed significantly.

I rub at my nose with the back of my hand when I feel an itch, smiling softly, sadly. "I've never seen you like this."

"Like what?" He watches every move I make with rapt attention, gaze heated.

"Like…like you have no cares, no regrets, no worries. You just are. You're calm and fun, not just frantic and frenzied."

"I thought you liked it when I was frantic and frenzied," he murmurs with a smirk, leaning his right hip against the counter with an unwavering gaze as his arms cross over his chest.

"Well, yeah. Especially at first when I didn't know…" *When I didn't know how long I would have to enjoy you,* I think, but don't say. As it turns out, I had less time than I would have ever imagined.

"Do you prefer it when I'm slow? Do you prefer it when I am deliberate and patient?" His words definitely have a sexual undertone, and my stomach flips at the thought of having him above me, despite my earlier words advocating against it. I'm so *fucked.*

"I don't know. Maybe I do, if I'm dreaming about it."

"The cookies still have another ten minutes. Until then…" he drifts off, suddenly nervous.

"Until then?" I raise an eyebrow, my breath hitching when he gets closer.

"Until then…" This time, when his lips meet mine in a gentle caress, I know what he means. Shayde has never kissed me like this: slow, easy, searching. His tongue creeps out and licks a path along my bottom lip, slipping inside my mouth and exploring me in a way I've never experienced before. And it all feels so *real*. His taste, his smell, his touch. I've never hoped to dream up something so *good* from a man who is anything but.

Shayde's hand moves to cup my face, the other placed firmly on my hip. I press myself into him, unable to stop myself, groaning when I feel how hard he is. But he doesn't take things any further like I expect him to. He only kisses me, despite my hips shamelessly grinding against his. Despite my hands wandering up his shirt and across his hard muscles. He only groans and curses into my mouth, keeping that deliberate, patient pace he promised. I'm so distracted that when the timer goes off, I jump, jerking out of his arms in a hurry. He chuckles, moving to grab an oven mitt and pulling the cookies out.

"Fuck. I can't…we can't…"

"Make out like horny teenagers?" he finishes for me, grinning deviously.

"Yes. That. We can't do that." I touch my lips absentmindedly, the absence of him leaving a fiery burn across my swollen skin.

"Can we at least eat the cookies we made?" He raises an eyebrow, gesturing at the red velvet-flavored flowers.

"Sure. Yeah. We can definitely do that." I swallow down the part of me screaming this is wrong, even though it feels so right. I approach him with caution, reaching up on my tiptoes to peek over his shoulder at the hot cookies. They *do* look good…

Later, when we've had four cookies each and our stomachs are full and warm, I begin to wash the dishes. It's such a mundane task, but it's one I haven't done in a while. Shayde inches up behind me, leaning down to whisper in my ear, "I wanted this kind of life with you."

His words are innocent, but they leave an earth-shattering *need* in their wake. My body trembles, my heart races, and it takes everything in me to control the urge to take him here and now. *I will not have a wet dream about Shayde,* I tell myself, *I will not have a wet dream about Shayde. I will not…*

"I've never wanted this kind of life," I admit, refusing to allow this to happen. None of it is even *real.*

"You didn't?" He seems surprised, as though he pictured me as the type of girl to settle down with kids in a suburban home full of love and content.

"No. I wanted adventure. I wanted extremes. I wanted to *live.*"

His arms wrap around me, pulling me into his chest as he questions lightly, "Do you still want those things?"

"Yes." I shake as I turn the water off, refusing to turn and press myself against that hard body even farther.

A finger curls through my hair as he murmurs into my ear, "Do you think you'll ever have enough of adventures? Enough of fighting and longing and wishing?"

I release a shaky sigh, shivers running down my spine. "I don't know. Have you tired of it yet?" The question isn't bitter or sarcastic, only curious.

He lets out a bitter laugh. "No. I'm not sure I ever will."

"Well, if it ever does become tiring, let me know. I'd like to long for normal things."

"What do you long for that isn't normal?"

"*You.*" I can't help myself, can't stop the whimper that follows.

"Azalea," he breathes into my ear, hands encapsulating my wrists as he pins me against the sink. "Don't be ashamed of wanting things no one else does. Don't be ashamed of your desires, of *me.*"

"But I am. I'm so ashamed that I can't even allow myself to want you in my dreams, Shayde. I'm so ashamed that I'm creating this fake version of you just to justify this insatiable *want.*"

The heat of his body is suddenly gone, and I whirl around to see him stalking toward the shadows. "Where are you going?" I call, eyes wide.

"Back to the darkness you created me from." Then he's gone, and I'm stumbling backward in shock and despair. I stumble and fall, tumbling off a cliff I never knew was there.

I fall, and I fall, and I fall.

CHAPTER 9

"Maybe once, on a hollow, lifeless night, creating Draxmere seemed like a good idea. Maybe a great one, even. But there is no good in a place born of evil, and there is no greatness in a place created with ill intent. Draxmere is not, and will never be, a satisfactory home for our children. And if, somehow, it becomes one…we should be ashamed."
—*Draxmere: A Tale as Old as the Grim*, written by Enhancer Kelvin Delaney in 1977 A.G.

Another month passes, and I refuse to tell Jaymes about the dreams. I don't want him to think I still possess the insane hope of Shayde being more than the double-crossing Grim that he is. I don't want him to push me to forgiveness, because I'm not ready to forgive. My mind is desperate to give Shayde an escape, desperate to make it seem like my life isn't so hopeless. He's only visited me once since the cookie dream, but he had been silent and watchful the entire time. It was strange to see him so quiet and reserved, and I wrote it off as my subconscious wanting him to be nearby even if we didn't say a word to one another.

In just three weeks, we have to return to Draxmere, and I'm not sure if I should be grateful or fearful. I don't want to face my peers, don't want the sad eyes and suspicious gazes. However, I do want to return to the place I have called home over the past year. I want to go back to the place my parents met, the place they became legends, the place I became a savior.

Jaymes and I are lounging in his large sitting room, snuggled together in one of his large loveseats. My head rests in his lap, my legs stretched across the arm of the loveseat as I lie on my side. It's become a normal occurrence this month, me seeking comfort from him and him allowing it. We've spent all day, every day together, bonding in a way I've bonded with few people before. Jaymes runs a hand through my hair absentmindedly, deeply interested in a book floating in front of his face, whose pages he turns every few minutes. "What do you know about my parents?"

"Not much," he admits reluctantly, gaze tearing away from the book and down to me. His eyes roam my form, pupils dilating as he takes me in. It's the same look of longing and want I find myself sending him some days.

I probably shouldn't have crawled into this mini sofa with him the first time he asked a few weeks ago, but I did it anyway. Jaymes is warm, familiar, my *friend*.

"I never asked anyone about them because I didn't want to know. I was so focused on myself, so selfish about my needs and my wants, I just…I never looked into them, or my history, or even the history of Draxmere."

"Well, I can help with the Draxmere history dump, but I can't say I know much about your parents. They were a legendary couple, and your dad was set to inherit a seat on the council. But then, one day…*poof*. They disappeared. Their names were written in the papers, and the situation was investigated, but…they left willingly. No one could make them come back. And if anyone knew why they left, they never came out and revealed it. The whole situation was pretty weird, in my opinion. Of course, this was well before my time. I'm just repeating speculation and rumor. The only reason anyone ever talks about it is because of you. Most people think a Seer must have told them something that got them spooked, so they left. Some think it was to protect you, but I can't see why that would be the case. I don't think anyone would have killed you; they want a savior."

"You don't think Mr. G would have hunted me down?" I trace patterns on his thigh absentmindedly, not acknowledging the goosebumps that form on his bare arm.

"Maybe. Maybe not. Who knows? Maybe if you had never left, you would have never become the savior."

"I'm still not certain I *am* the savior."

"Well, maybe you aren't yet, but you will be."

"And what if I don't make the right choices? What if I fuck everything up?"

"You won't."

"But the prophecies say I can be the difference between saving the world and ending it, right? So what if—"

"You won't." He tugs on my hair until I look at him, passion blazing in those dark green eyes.

"Tell me about Draxmere," I murmur, gaze drifting to his lips. Fuck. I can't do this. *I can't.*

"It was formed fifteen years after the Grim was created. The Reapers had become such a problem that the leaders knew interference was necessary, and Draxmere was the very first school built to help create that interference. At first, anyone who wanted to fight was allowed to attend. Some only attended for a few years before they were ready, others for much longer. Within the first twenty years, it became abundantly clear things needed to change. And, with such a large number of Conjurers wanting to fight, they knew they would need to develop a better system. Hence, the creation of the other top four schools. They, too, took anyone who wanted to fight for a while. But after a hundred years had passed, things were in disarray. The schools overflowed with students they couldn't house, there weren't enough professors, and there was no way to properly instruct students who had no idea what they were doing.

"At first, no one knew what to do. Eventually, someone recommended training Conjurers from a young age to fight, and everyone thought it was brilliant. Thus, an army was born. School after school was built, and eventually, it all became a competition. Draxmere wouldn't let you in unless you were strong enough to finish the other schools, wouldn't let you become a fighter unless you proved yourself to be tough enough to last. But they never wavered in their inclusiveness. They don't care who you are, as long as you prove yourself worthy. Shifter, Elementalist, Seer. None of that matters as long as you put in the work."

"I don't think I did. Put in the work, I mean. I just…showed up and they let me in."

"The Seers—"

"I know what the Seers said, Jaymes, but even *you* were upset I was allowed in."

"I was," he admits in a low tone, suddenly very serious. I push myself up into a seated position similar to his, holding my breath.

"But then I saw what you could do. I saw the power you hold in that gorgeous body of yours, and I knew I was wrong. I knew you deserved a place here, even if you hadn't worked as hard for it. But you *did* put in the work, it was just a different kind. You fought to keep yourself alive in the human world, even when you didn't know it. And you still sought out training, some part of you recognizing the need for that strength and knowledge to survive.

"You put in the work, Azalea, and I'm proud of you. I'm proud of you for trying, even though I know you didn't always want to do it for pure reasons. I'm proud of you for the way you've handled this new life, for the way you have shown such resilience in the face of danger. I am proud of you for never letting the world affect who you *are*."

I can't stop myself from leaning forward and pressing my treacherous lips against those dangerously sweet ones, can't stop myself from pressing my body against his even as I tell myself this is a *horrible* idea. I miss Shayde, I miss the intimacy, and I'm a downright bitch for using his best friend this way; for attaching myself to the one person who is as close to Shayde as I will ever get without having the real thing. For trying to replace, to replicate, what I had with the man who's trying to distance himself from the monster I crave. It's just…I'm too selfish to stop.

Jaymes's eyes widen briefly, but I squeeze mine shut before I can interpret that look as anything more than surprise. I arch into him as his hands grip onto my hips, his lips moving at a fervent pace. The kiss is fast and hard, and my hands end up tangling in that fluffy blond hair I've always admired as my knees move to either side of his lap. I don't let myself think any further about what I'm doing, don't let the voice inside my head screaming, *not Shayde, not*

Shayde, not Shayde, take over. I grind against Jaymes, willing the friction to distract me from the torturous voice trying to punish me for taking what I want.

"Azalea," he groans into my mouth, hips jerking up involuntarily. A shiver runs down my spine at the pure *need* that drips from that one word, and I press myself closer, closer, closer.

"Are you sure?" Nimble fingers work their way underneath my shirt, brushing against my bra as he asks for permission. I nod, unable to form words as heat trails to my core. Heat that I haven't felt since Shayde, heat that I was missing, heat that I—

"Fuck," I moan as his large hand slides underneath my bra, squeezing my breast with just enough pressure.

"Azalea," he says again, breathless, before standing and bringing me with him. I cling to him like my life depends on it, eyes and mouth popping open as I start to question him. But then I'm being dropped onto the soft, cushioned loveseat, and Jaymes is falling to his knees before me, and all my questions dissolve into the air. Shit, this is actually happening. Can I let it go any further? Can I do this to myself? To Shayde? Wait. No. Fuck Shayde. I'll seek my pleasure wherever I want to seek it. He lost any right to my body the night he let my best friend become a creature of nightmares.

"Jaymes." His whole body tenses when his name leaves my lips, the hand inching up my leg pausing briefly.

"Say it again." His eyes meet mine with the demand, hand moving up to the waistband of my dark leggings.

I lift my hips as he tugs on them, giving in to the command and letting out another breathless, "Jaymes."

"Fuck." He gulps down air as though he had been drowning, ripping the leggings cleanly off my body. My skin breaks out in goosebumps at the sudden cold, but he doesn't seem to notice or care. Instead, he begins pressing a kiss against my ankle, mirroring the motion as he moves up my calf, to my thigh. I'm practically shaking when he presses a kiss to my inner thigh, my head dropped back against the chair as I wait for him to reach the spot where I so desperately need him. His fingers move to pull at my plain underwear, readying to bare myself to him, when he pauses and lifts his head.

"Jaymes, please—" I start, lifting my head back up with pleading eyes.

"Those are *my* eyes." He isn't looking at me when he says it, but at the thigh I have bared to him, staring directly into the full-color rendering of his eyes on my skin.

"Yes, they are." I swallow, wincing as I wait for the anger, the hurt, *something*.

"Wh-why? When did you get this? Why not…?"

"Why not Shayde's, you mean?" I go to pull my leg away, but he stops me, hand firmly placed on my thigh as he stares at the beautiful piece of art on my skin.

"Yes." Now those matching eyes meet mine, and they aren't angry or hurt or upset. They're conflicted, confused, caught in a moment of vulnerability.

"I got them tattooed when I was in the human world. Before I ever knew you. Before…" *Before Shayde.*

"I don't understand." He still doesn't move from his knelt position before me, gaze falling back to the detailed image. "How would you know…?"

"I dreamed of them. And I thought they were so beautiful, so…so worthy of praise. I couldn't get them out of my head, and I just…went to the nearest shop and had it done. It's the only way I ever get the dreams out of my head."

"You have more dreams like this?" His head snaps back up, the heat and vulnerability replaced with suspicion.

"Um, yeah. Sure. Lots of them. At least, I did when I was in the human world. I haven't had another one until recently."

"What kind of dreams were they? Did you only see images, or were there messages, too? Was it like a scene playing out, or was it just sounds?"

"Is this really important right now? Because this seems like a bad time to be discussing—"

"Answer the questions, Azalea." He nips my thigh, and I jump, mind spinning dizzily.

"No, they weren't sounds or scenes playing out. Just images. Sometimes images of words or phrases, but usually an image of some sort. And every time I had one, I couldn't forget about it, I couldn't stop the pictures or the words from running through my mind obsessively all day. So I just decided to get them tattooed. It was the only way I could move on, the only way things got better. But in the end, it just paved the way for new dreams. They used to be so simple, so boring." I pause as his fingers begin tracing patterns on my leg, tracing images and words with a gentleness I don't deserve. His fingers dip in convoluted spirals and loops, tracing waves and mythical creatures and poems. He admires each tattoo, admires my skin, admires *me*.

"You had a dream about every single one of these?" he questions, his touch leaving a gentle heat over my skin.

"All but one." I finger the delicate *SG* on my wrist, wishing we didn't have to talk about this right now. Not when I was so close to getting over *him*.

"All but one," he repeats, glancing up to meet my gaze again before murmuring, "You said that's how the dreams used to be. How are they now?" Then he dips back down and begins peppering kisses over every tattoo and tiny bites on the few patches of blank skin.

"I'm not sure if they are the same," I admit, my voice high-pitched. "I started having this dream where I am on the edge of a foggy cliff, and there is a figure in the distance. But as they approach, I take a step back, and then I'm falling over the edge."

"And that's it? That's all that happens?" His kisses now make their way over clothed skin, right over the wet patch in my underwear. I shiver, arching up into him as his hands grip my thighs tightly, and he shudders.

"Well…" I shouldn't tell him about Dream Shayde, because then he won't want to do this anymore. He will get up and leave and I'll never be able to get over the fucking Grim because no one else has come close to making me feel lust like this. No one else is similar enough to give me the same thrill.

"Well?" Fingers inch just underneath the fabric, brushing against me in a teasing move. And I *know*. I know he is using seduction tactics to make me tell the truth, but I'm so full of…guilt, and remorse, and *lust* that I tell him anyway.

"Well, a few times, Shayde has come out of the shadows. He told me once he'd give me a real reason to hate him. I think it's just my subconscious trying to make sense of it all." I wave my hand frantically, the other coming to rest in the hair at the back of his neck.

"And you always fall?" He frowns when he asks, fingers slipping tantalizing close to my clit.

"Always," I lie, refusing to admit that the cliff isn't the only place I've seen Dream Shayde.

"Hmm," he hums, slowly pulling the fabric down, down, down until it hits my ankles. He stares at my core with a ravenous gaze, licking his lips before meeting my eyes again. "You're sure this is okay?"

"Fuck, Jaymes, yes. I already told you—"

Jaymes bends forward with a sudden urgency, tongue dancing across me in the most delicious way. I buck against him, grateful for the hands on my thighs keeping me pressed into the sofa. Jaymes is slow and deliberate with each lick, each suck, each tiny little bite he pleasures me with. It's exactly what I expected from him, and it's just enough to keep me mindless.

"Jaymes," I pant, both hands in his hair now as I press him closer, closer, closer.

"You taste so…*sweet*, Azalea Jinx," he whispers as he lifts his head, a wicked smile on his lips. Then one of those strong hands is lifting off my thigh, fingers pressing against my entrance as his mouth falls back down to my clit. Each thrust has me closer to ecstasy, my release coming closer and closer as he turns me into a panting mess.

"Please," I beg, but I don't know why. Jaymes wouldn't stop. Jaymes wouldn't leave me on the edge of release, not even as a punishment I deserved. Jaymes is the type of man who would give me everything I wanted and more, and he'd never ask for anything in return.

Jaymes doesn't change his pace or his rhythm, and I explode in a quick and brutal moment. My orgasm crashes through me like a wrecking ball, and Jaymes has to hold me down again to keep me from melting off the sofa entirely. Shadows I hadn't noticed before slip down my arms, dripping into a pile on either side of the chair. When was the last time I lost control like this?

Jaymes leans back on his heels after licking up every last drop of my release, green eyes luminous as he watches me try to recover. "I think you may be a Seer."

"What the fuck?" I hiss, enraged. "This is really not the conversation I want to have right now."

"What would you rather talk about?" he asks, amused.

"I'd rather not do any talking!" I'm sitting here, half-naked, my orgasm dripping from *his* lips, and this is what he wants to discuss?

Jaymes laughs, moving to a crouch as he leans over my body. I stop breathing as his lips hover over mine, his hard length pressing into me from behind too many layers and giving me just enough friction to cause another wave of pleasure to zap through me.

"I think you may be a Seer," he repeats, staring at me intently. "And I think your dreams have been pointing you here, to this world, for a very long time."

"I'm not a Seer. I'm already a Dual-Wielder. I can't be a…a triple Wielder!"

"Why not?"

"Because I can't," I seethe, outraged. "Because those don't exist."

"Sure they do," he shrugs, watching me all too eagerly. "And you're one of them."

"Jaymes, can't we just put this conversation on the back burner? I really want to finish what we started, so maybe we could—"

"I think your dreams are leading you back to Shayde," he interrupts, running a hand through his light hair.

"Seriously, Jaymes, what the *fuck*—"

"I'm going to tell the new dean that you need to be put in Seer classes as well," he interrupts again, regret dancing in his eyes.

"You can't just decide these things for me, Jaymes Bloodgood. You can't distract me with oral just to butter me up for shit like this. I'm not a Seer, I will not attend Seer classes, I most certainly won't be led back to fucking Shayde, and I would really like to get back to the whole sex thing we were in the middle of!" I pant at the end of the tangent, pushing hair out of my face and glaring.

"I wasn't trying to distract you," he whispers, sorrowful. "And I don't want to lead you back to Shayde. And I *really* want to go back to the sex thing we were in the middle of, but I can't."

"Why the fuck not?" I cross my arms over my chest, wishing I could pull my legs closed. But Jaymes is still between them, still leaning over me as though he's about to kiss me senseless.

"Because if you are a Seer and these dreams you're having are real, then I know what they mean. I won't get in the middle of a cosmic event, even if I'm desperate to keep you for myself."

"How do you know what they mean?" I throw my hands up, flabbergasted.

"I know because I've been around Seers my whole life, Azalea. The fog and the shadowy figures? It means your future is uncertain around this particular person. The edge of a cliff means you have a decision to make: a leap of faith or a fall to your doom. You clearly have unresolved business with Shayde, and I am not going to be involved with you if it means I'm the one getting hurt in the end."

"Seers speak in riddles," I try again, deflating. "They don't have funny dreams and crazy tattoos."

"You got these all in the human world, correct?" I nod, unsure of where he's going with this. A finger jabs somewhere on my thigh, his words suddenly harsh and all too serious. "This is a Charm for healing cuts and bruises." Another jab. "This one is a prophecy recorded hundreds of years ago and is known as one of the most popular prophecies of our time."

"So what?" I whisper, shaking.

Another jab. "This one is a Charm to create wards, a very complex and difficult Charm. This one is the Shifter symbol, half completed. This one is a small version of Draxmere. This one is—"

"So what?" I hiss again, interrupting him. "What does it matter? Maybe my parents told me some of these things, and I just remembered them. Maybe they brought me here and I don't remember that."

A hand slides under my shirt, to my back. "This one is an exact replica of the youngest Grim's antlers."

"Please, Jaymes, don't. *Please.*"

"Should I tell you what each and every one of these means? Do you want me to explore your entire body so I can tell you how intimately entwined you were with this world before you ever knew about it?"

"How about we start with the body exploring and then…" I start in an attempt to deflect, but I hastily stop when I see the murderous look in his gaze.

"You were chosen to be the savior for a reason, Azalea. And if you are having dreams about Shayde, then you are more powerful than any of us ever realized. Seers can't *see* other Seers."

"I've had other dreams," I say after a brief pause, mind reeling as I think about the repercussions of what this could mean.

"With Shayde in them?"

"Yes. I've had three now that felt so, so *real*. Like I was having an actual conversation with him."

"Maybe you were."

"Stop, Jaymes. No. I'll never sleep again if I think those were real. It was just my mind trying to soften the blow of his betrayal. Nothing more."

"If you say so," he whispers, blinking down at me sadly.

"Why dreams?" I question, still confused. "I don't...I haven't spoken in riddles."

"No, but your tattoos have." Fingers trail from one phrase to another, his mind connecting phrases I had never put together before. I refuse to look at them, refuse to connect the pieces of each separate piece myself.

In her darkest hours, she'll crave a sinner, a monster, a digger's grave.

If all else fails, a savior will rise, but only through ashes will we survive.

Light and dark will combine in the girl who has no time.

A heart split in two has one desire: The girl with split powers and a burning ire.

"I'll be killed," I say eventually, sighing when he finally backs away from me. When the Conjurers at Draxmere found out I was a Dual Wielder, they almost attacked me then and there. They were angry, defiant, hysterical. Dean Delarosa pulled me out of the room before anyone could attack, but this is different. I've never heard of someone having three powers. How angry will the Conjurers be now? How likely are they to attack me just so I can't climb to the top? I've already been deemed a Grim fucker; will this be the final block that topples my tower?

"I won't let you be." Jaymes gently starts helping me pull my pants back on, gaze heated as he stares unflinchingly at my core again.

"Why did you…why did you do this if you suspected that it wouldn't work between us?" I gesture down at my half-naked body, lifting my hips as he slides my leggings back up to cover me. It's an intimate move, being dressed by someone. It's much more sensual than being *undressed*.

"Because I'm a selfish man, Azalea Jinx, and I just wanted to taste you one time." His voice is rough and mournful, and it almost has me sliding the leggings right back off.

"And now that you have?"

He smiles lightly, holding up my underwear before shoving it into the back pocket of his jeans. "Now that I have, I'll take this souvenir and my memory and cherish it for as long as I live."

"Jaymes," I groan, covering my face to hide the infuriating blush. "What happened to the whole 'I only liked you because Shayde did' thing?"

"I lied," he says simply before striding away. And as he leaves, my neck tingles with awareness. My gaze snaps toward the window by the front door. It's there that I see a shadow, a movement, and then all is calm once more.

Grimsly jumps into my lap almost protectively, curling up and staring rigidly at the door. I stare with him, too lost in thought to care about what could be out there. I stroke the sleek black fur of my cat absentmindedly, dread wrapping itself around my entire body.

I'm not a Dual-Wielder.

I'm a fucking mutated Wielding freak who shouldn't exist.

Chapter 10

"Look for one with light and dark within,
the one with a burden, a poison, a sin.
She'll sneak and she'll creep,
and she'll become everything you wish you didn't need."
—Prophecy tattooed on Azalea Jinx, first found inside Seer Reed
Henderson's prophetic journals, 217 A.G. (often used in poetry and
song lyrics from other years)

"What did you do?"

Shayde knows something is wrong, can sense it in the foggy air around us as we stand on that fucking cliff again. My foot is only inches away from causing me to plummet to my death, or to whatever hell awaits me at the bottom.

"I don't know what you're talking about," I lie, eyebrow raised as he steps into view. I don't take a step back, overly aware of what outcome *that* would bring.

Shayde inches closer, closer, closer. I shift from one foot to the other, panicking and jumping into his chest when the rocks beneath my left foot begin to crumble. He pulls me to him, pressing his nose into the crook of my neck and inhaling deeply.

"His scent is all over you."

"Oh, that's bullshit. You can't *smell* him on me."

"I fucking knew it," he scowls, glaring down at me as he clenches his jaw.

"You only know because I know." I sniff indigently, glancing back at the ground wearily. I can't step away, but Shayde's grip has become punishing as his fingers dig into my skin.

"*I know because I saw you.* I told you I would kill anyone who put their hands on what's mine, proved it to you, and you still let him taste something that belongs to me?" *Shit.* I didn't even think about that. I was being so overtly selfish, so needy…

"I don't belong to anyone but myself," I hiss, daring a shove to his chest. Shayde doesn't budge, his annoyingly handsome face not even slightly amused.

"It was *Jaymes*," he says quietly, almost…sad. Betrayed. Confused.

"Well…I…we aren't together, Shayde. And Jaymes is the closest thing to you I can get, the closest feeling I've experienced that even compares to what you gave me," I admit into the foggy air, wincing. I used Jaymes, wish I could still use him, just so I don't have to experience *this*. I'm such a bitch.

"Yeah? And did you get what you wanted from him? Did you get what you needed?"

"I came." I shrug, refusing to meet his gaze; refusing to make this mean more than it does.

"I don't just make you come, though, do I, darling?" He places a hand under my chin and tilts my head up, smirking. "I make you feel. I make you come alive. I give you an experience no one will ever be able to replicate. I revive you, Azalea Jinx. But look at you. This is not revival because no part of you wants to *live*."

"I'm not…I want to live, Shayde."

"But you don't want to live as *you*."

"No." I twitch in his hold, my treacherous heart picking up its pace as his unwavering gaze holds me steady. Then, with a gurgle, I say, "Are you real?"

"Is anything inside your mind ever real, Azalea?" He tilts his head, hand still on my chin.

"Sometimes. Sometimes I have dreams that are real. Ones that represent life, or parts of a life I never recognized. Sometimes I have dreams that make me think I'm crazy, or delusional, or a witch. I guess one of those things turned out to be true."

The corner of his mouth twitches up, a light chuckle escaping. "You're a Conjurer, not a witch. That's just offensive to every Conjurer in the world."

I glance toward the edge of the cliff, wondering if I should make a break for it just so I can avoid *this*. Seeing him, speaking to him. "Ah, right. The magical beings from this world don't want to be confused with the magical beings of another," I say with a roll of my eyes, annoyed by my own dream apparition of Shayde.

"So you aren't real?" I question again, wanting a straightforward answer. "Jaymes thinks you could be. But Jaymes also thinks I could be a Seer."

"You're a Seer?" This news hits him hard, and he drags me away from the edge of that cliff with a ferocity he shouldn't have. He watches that cliff with a new edge, scowling over at it.

"I might be."

"Your tattoos," he whispers, pieces clicking together. "You…you said you dreamed them, but I didn't realize…"

"No, you didn't. But Jaymes did." I pull out of his grip now that I am closer to safety, wishing I could disappear in the fog like he does.

"When he was between your legs, you mean?" His voice is harsh, tone dripping with disdain.

"You've been between my legs plenty of times, and *you* never noticed. You hardly paid attention to my tattoos, much less their meanings."

"You know I paid very close attention to your body, little flower. I know exactly where you have tattoos. Don't you remember the little heart on your breast? The tiny one, hidden like a freckle? Did you dream of that one, too? What about the crescent moon on your ass? What dream did *that* one derive from?" He looks at me with so much want, so much *need*, as he says it that I have to look away.

I smile cruelly, turning to meet his eyes again as I say, "I dreamed of them when I was lying next to my husband. And when I dreamed about them it wasn't *my* tits I was seeing, or my ass." Unbridled fury races across his features, nose scrunching as he scowls.

"I paid attention to your body, Azalea. I paid attention to the way your legs shake when you come, I paid attention to the way you like me to suck on those delicious tits, I paid attention to the way your lips feel sliding over my cock. I pay attention to every part of you, inside and out."

"Paying attention to the parts of my body you *like* isn't the same as paying attention to *me.*" I stand my ground, suddenly angry. *Good.* Maybe this anger will finally drive him from my mind and banish him from my dreams. "Maybe I don't want you to memorize how I like sex. Maybe instead, I want you to memorize the number of tattoos I have, or the number of freckles on my shoulders. Maybe I want you to know if my belly button is an innie or an outie, or if my left boob is bigger than my right. Maybe I want you to know me so intimately that you would have known immediately what I was. It took Jaymes one look, Shayde. *One look and he knew.*" My voice cracks by the end, my entire speech shaky and more emotional than I intended.

"One hundred thirteen, if you haven't gotten any new ones. Thirty-seven on the left, thirty-nine on the right. It's an innie. The right boob is larger, but only barely." His answers are short and clipped, eyes boring into me as I blink at him in surprise. We dance around each other for a few precious seconds, my mind reeling as I try to figure out his next move. Then he leaps, pulling me to him in a gentle but firm move. I cry out, struggling to escape his grip, but he holds just tight enough to keep me in his arms.

"You think I don't know you more intimately than anyone else? Do you know those things about my body? Have you counted my tattoos? Memorized all my scars? Measured the length of my dick? No? I didn't think so." He flings me away, scoffing. I stumble back, surprised.

"You're right," I whisper, suddenly ashamed. "You're right. I was using you for so long to get what I wanted, and then suddenly it wasn't about me, but about *us*. And maybe I jumped into that too quickly. Fell too hard. Because I wasn't ready for this. I wasn't ready to give someone the kind of love I wanted."

"Are you ready now?" He watches me like my answer will make or break him, like the whole world would come crashing down if I say *no*.

"*I don't know.*" And even if I did, it couldn't be with him. It couldn't be with the man who sided with the Grim, who *is* a Grim.

"Then I won't come back until you do."

The ground beneath me rocks and sizzles, a giant crack forming inches from my feet. Shayde doesn't bother to glance back as he strides away into the fog, doesn't listen to my screams for him to come back. I weep as the earthquake shakes the ground beneath me again, and I tumble, falling into the deep abyss that had formed beneath us. My hair whips around me as I fall, tears drying in the frigid air as I reach for something, anything to stop me from repeating history.

I fall, and I fall, and I fall.

CHAPTER 11

"With the help of a jinx, a curse, an ill-fated match,
the world shall fall into a trusted savior's hands.
In the Shadows, in the mind, a plan will hatch,
and in the Light, in the open, the evil still stands."
—Prophecy found inside Seer Jodi Maldonado's prophetic journals,
2011 A.G.

"**H**appy birthday!" the chorus of voices shouts, their cheeriness way too much for me to process this early in the morning.

"What the fuckkkk," I groan, covering myself with the comforter that *still* smells like Shayde. I won't comment on the fact that I've slept better here than I've slept anywhere else in my entire life.

"Get up, Azalea Jinx. We have a full day planned. This is the last chance we all have to hang out before we go to Draxmere, and I plan on taking advantage of every second of it, starting with the hair appointment we have to be at in thirty minutes." Dagan is next to me now, light, wispy voice purring in my ear.

I pop open one eye and push the comforter back down, taking her in before saying, "I don't want to spend the day with you."

"Well, that's great, because it isn't just me." Dagan beams, gesturing toward the shadows in the doorway. Jaymes is at the front of the group, Nox and Arlo flanking him on either side with large smiles.

"What the fuckkkk," I groan again, screeching when the warm comforter is ripped from my body.

"Up we go!" Dagan cackles, dropping the fabric unceremoniously onto the floor.

"Jaymes." I roll onto my side and turn pleading eyes to him, but he only sends me a soft smile and takes me in slowly before shaking his head no.

"Maybe you should put some clothes on, Azalea," Arlo coughs from behind him, pointedly looking away as I throw my legs over the side of the bed and stand.

I glance down, frowning with a shrug. "First of all, you were the one who walked in here uninvited. This is my space. Second of all, I have underwear on, Arlo. Don't be a prude."

"But it's a fucking thong, Azalea. Good Grim, and put a bra on!"

"Prude," I say with a wave of my hand, heading for the adjoined bathroom. Dagan follows behind me, chatting brightly. I interrupt, questioning, "How did you know it was my birthday?"

"Jaymes told us."

"And how did he know?" I scowl as she flips her long hair over her shoulder, rolling her eyes.

"I don't know. He texted me two weeks ago, said, 'July twenty-fifth. My house. Azalea's birthday.' So I told him I would come and not to worry because I would make you feel special. But he said he already made some appointments for us to go do things and that—"

"He made the hair appointment?" My eyebrows draw in, confusion and unease settling in my stomach.

"Yes, and the nail appointment, and the spa appointment. We are really busy today, so really, Azalea, you need to stop asking so many questions and hurry along."

"I don't…why would he do that?"

"Probably because he looks at you like you're his own personal snack," she cackles, clearly amused by that fact.

"You should have seen the way Shayde looked at me, then, if you think Jaymes likes me," I murmur, taking a brush to my knotted hair.

"Ooh, was it worse? How did he look at you?"

"Like he was going to devour me," I say, wincing. "Body, mind, and soul."

"How did you manage to get two hot guys to fall in love with you? I swear, if Jaymes looked at me the way he looks at you, I would be caving so fast. I don't know how you've been holding off on him."

"Jaymes is…he's nice. He's sweet and caring; unyielding and full of love. But Shayde…Shayde is fire and brimstone, he's demanding and formidable. He's overpowering. Shayde became me, and I became him, and now I don't know how to untangle myself from the person I became with his guidance. Jaymes and I…"

"It's complicated?" she surmises, smiling softly. "I get it. But I'd still tap that."

"I tried," I sigh, which results in her demanding I explain the full story. So, I do, and I forget Shayde more and more as I recount the way Jaymes touched me; as I get more and more excited for the day to come; as I realize that Jaymes is so thoughtful and amazing and…I don't deserve any of it.

"You look beautiful, Azalea."

Dagan is right: I do look beautiful. The salon Jaymes sent us to is high-end, with its gorgeous models on the walls and prices nearly in the thousands. When she told me the total, I vomited a little in my mouth, but Dagan pulled out a silver card with Jaymes's name on it and said little more on the subject.

I stare at myself in the mirror now, tossing my hair around and watching it bounce. It falls just past my ears in a wavy bob that feels so good. The curtain bangs hang perfectly across my face, framing it in a way that is so flattering, I couldn't help but gasp at the first glance. And my highlights…those are new. No longer the amethyst purple I have worn for over a year, but a vibrant red to burn alongside my anger. I feel like a new person, a new version of Azalea I have yet to meet. I feel like a gorgeous badass who could destroy the world…or save it.

"Alright, quit gawking at yourself. Nails are next." Dagan drags me away from the mirror and out of the door, pulling me a few blocks down from the salon. This isn't the city of Maladara, so I'm unfamiliar with its terrain. It's not as pretty as Maladara either, the environment is much more plain and human than I would have expected from the Charmed. It's more…normal. No flying fabrics or dancing hats, no crazy colors and floating people. Just…normal buildings with normal products. I tried to ask Dagan about where we are, to learn more about the world of the Charmed, but she only told me it's named Grokburgh and didn't explain more until we were in the middle of our manicures.

Dagan forces me to get red nails to match my hair, gushing about how pretty I look and how exciting it is to do all this with someone. She rattles on about this city, its people, and how her father sells alcohol to almost every vendor in the area. It's mundane, average talk that feels so good. No talk of Reapers, or Grims, or fucking Shayde to ruin it all.

I almost melt when we go to get massages; the hour-long back rub eases sore muscles I didn't even know I had. By the time I'm walking away, I'm feeling gooey and slightly sore, my tired eyes barely staying open through the process. Dagan is having none of it, though. She tells me there is no time for naps, that we have to finish our shopping before the party tonight.

"What party?" I question, agitated.

"Oh. Um. Not a party. A get-together."

"Uh-huh. And who's going to be at this get-together?"

"Me, and you, and Jaymes, Nox, Arlo…um, you…" She ticks names off on her fingers, eyes fluttering over to me nervously.

"He sent you to distract me all day so he could set up a surprise party, didn't he?" I rub the space between my eyebrows as tension begins to build, an unfamiliar feeling grating at my chest: A warmth, a tinge of friendship rising.

"Well…maybe…"

"Well." I drop my hand, straightening. "I suppose it's a good thing I'm having fun, then, isn't it?"

Dagan squeals and throws her arms around me, causing us to stumble back into a bench and tumble over. "What the fuckkkk," I groan, repeating a phrase that's come out of my mouth far too many times today.

"Ooh, come on. I want to take you to my favorite place. It's so good. The lingerie is to die for, and the clothes are so soft you'll never want to take them off."

"I don't need lingerie," I hiss while allowing her to pull me up and drag me to the other side of the street.

"Oh, yes, you do. If you want Jaymes to fuck you, or Shayde to devour you, or yourself to feel good, then you need new lingerie."

"I don't want…I don't—"

"Ah, I don't care for the lies you tell yourself, Azalea. Trust me, the taste of them gets old fast." Dagan goes on as though she hasn't shattered my mind, as though she didn't just crush my stoic thoughts between her French-tipped fingers.

I let her drag me to that store, let her convince me to buy a new wardrobe and new lingerie. All the while, I try to convince myself I'm not trying to impress anybody for any reason, convince myself that my impending future and what might come of it have no relation to this trip. Anything to not feel like *me*. And by the time she's done with me and we are loaded up with bags, the sun is setting in the sky. Snow drifts down softly, the lightest of touches compared to the blizzards I have experienced at the top of the mountain while attending Draxmere.

Some of the things Dagan forced me to buy were winter clothes. She said that my wardrobe is heavily lacking, and to be fair, it is. Florida isn't the place for someone to need heavy winter clothes, much less experience fucking blizzards. I've mostly been relying on Balmy Charms to survive here, and that has been enough.

I was so conscious about prices at first, too, but Dagan scowled and belittled me for it. She said Jaymes has no bills, no girlfriend, not even a best friend to spend money on. He wanted to do this. Dagan, herself, even buys me some things, stating I shouldn't spend my own money on my birthday. It made me a little emotional because I barely know Dagan, but she still treats me as though we have known each other our entire lives. Kind of like Demi.

My heart twists a little, especially knowing how much Demi would enjoy this. She would have loved Dagan, and she would have loved helping me pick out lingerie. Not because she would want me to look good for Shayde, or Jaymes, or anyone else I may decide to take to bed. No, she would have wanted to help me feel confident and sexy, and she would have had some damn good taste.

By the time we meet Jaymes at the meet-up spot where he first left us near the salon, my stomach is gurgling and making some pretty loud whale noises. He almost seems to hear it when we approach, a gentle smile on his face as he looks me over and says, "You girls hungry?"

Dagan nods enthusiastically, and I shrug, chewing on my bottom lip as I wait for his reaction to the giant haul we are bringing back with us. But the only thing he does is grab my wrist and pull me to him, whispering roughly, "You look beautiful, Azalea," before grabbing Dagan by the shoulder. We are all transported away, reappearing on the cozy front porch of Jaymes's house.

Loud music blasts from inside, and I groan, turning to Jaymes with a plea in my eyes. "Why?"

"Because I knew you'd hate it," he snickers jokingly, taking mine and Dagan's bags.

"I don't hate it. I just…I don't want to be the Grim Fucker, you know? I don't want to walk into the room and watch everyone fall silent as they whisper about my past. I don't want to hear Shayde's name or read it on every pair of lips I see." That's what happened when I came back the very first day after Shayde had announced himself as the son of a Grim, and I hated every second of it. Things didn't change in those two weeks I stayed on campus, and it's the main reason I'd holed myself up in my room. That, and I wanted to get high, or drunk, or both, just to try and get back that numbness I had before.

"No one here is going to judge you, Azalea. The people here are my friends, and they are all aware of how much you mean to me. They won't say anything about Shayde, or the Grim, or call you names. It's your birthday, Azalea. No one should be alone on their birthday."

I smile sadly, looking up at him as I whisper, "I've been alone most of my life, Jaymes Bloodgood. Birthdays were never an exception."

"Well, this one is."

With that, he leads me inside, Dagan having abandoned us at some point without me noticing. When we walk in, the music seems to get impossibly louder, and Jaymes pops out of existence with my things before reappearing by my side, bags gone.

People shout and cheer as Jaymes brings me into the crowd, the small house almost full of strangers I've never met. Jaymes whispers about them being classmates, friends and admirers of theirs. Second-years—wait, no—third, now. These people are third-year Conjurers on the verge of graduation. These strangers clap Jaymes on the back, holding up plastic black cups and sloshing liquid around haphazardly.

"Dagan sponsored your party," Jaymes shouts over the music, grinning.

"Fucking Grim, Jaymes, why haven't you already gotten me a drink?" He laughs, dragging me by the hand into the kitchen to do just that. I sip on my drink the second it's pressed into my hands, smiling as Nox and Arlo approach, and I slap two slices of pizza onto a plate.

"Happy birthday, Azalea!" Arlo cries, leaping forward to pull me into his arms. "This is such a great party. You know, I'm pretty sure I saw your friends. The triplets and the redhead? They were so excited to be here. You should definitely find them," he rambles, clearly intoxicated as he sways us around. I lift my eyes to meet Nox's, grunting as I try to push Arlo off with my elbow so I don't drop my things. With a grin, Nox puts his arms around Arlo's waist, dragging him away.

"Happy birthday," Nox grunts, blue eyes boring into mine. I only nod, blinking at the intensity of the stare. I don't have much time to decipher it, though, because the very friends Arlo had mentioned come leaping out of the crowd like foxes on the hunt.

"Azzie!" Ginny cries, and I flinch at the nickname, trying to plaster on a smile despite the absolute gut-wrenching pull happening in my stomach. I don't snap at her, though, like I want. Like I almost let myself do. Instead, I let Willow, Wren, and Reese circle me, the four girls crowding around and chattering away as I begin to devour my food.

"You'll never guess what we've been doing—" Wren starts.

"The whole summer has been—" Willow interrupts.

"No, you guys, ask about her first—" Reese says.

"Wow, okay, you three." Ginny scowls, shoving at them. "Give her some space. You're overwhelming the woman."

"No, no. That's okay. I'd love to hear about your summers. Actually, let me introduce you to someone. This is Dagan, Jaymes's friend."

"Your friend," Dagan corrects as I pull her into the fray, foxy hair swaying as she raises her glass in greeting.

The five of us strike up a conversation about our summers, the impending school semester, and the new dean that no one seems to know the name of. It's all so mundane and normal and *fun*. And the more we hang out, the more I think about Shayde, the more I miss him, and I *can't* let that happen.

When I get three drinks in, and the thoughts of Shayde become too much, I leave the girls, on the hunt for Jaymes and determined to make him kiss me again. Surely he owes it to me to try, or maybe I owe him? Or maybe neither of us owes each other. Maybe the world owes us a chance. Wouldn't that be funny and downright diabolical of the world? To put the two Grim Fuckers in a relationship when neither are over said Grim? Do I even want a relationship with Jaymes? I don't think so, but I don't know. If it means getting over Shayde, I'll do anything, even hook up with his best friend.

I stumble out of the house and into the frigid air, wrapping my arms around myself after casting a quick and clumsy Balmy Charm.

Almost immediately, the hair on the back of my neck stands up, but I can't seem to recall why that should bother me. Dagan said she saw Jaymes out here ten minutes ago, but I don't see him now. I stumble down the few steps on the front porch, taking several strides into the yard so I can look around for him. I see a trail of footprints in the snow and make the foolish decision to follow them, despite the prickly warning that now has goosebumps rising on my flesh.

"Grimsly!" I call as the dark cat comes bounding up to me, rubbing against my legs and purring. "Why are you out here in the cold? Shouldn't you be asleep on my bed? Did you miss me? Is that it?" I bend down to pet the cat, losing my balance and falling on my ass. I laugh, tossing my head back as he crawls into my lap. My ass is quickly getting wet, but I ignore the sensation as I tilt my spinning head up.

"Jaymes!" I call, glancing around. I somehow made it across the road, the footprints veering off into the trees. With a sigh, I pick up Grimsly and manage to get up on my feet. I stomp off into the woods, huffing and watching the cloud form in the air.

"You are such a pain, Jaymes," I try again, stumbling over fallen branches. "Why are you out here anyway? I hope I'm not interrupting something." I cackle at my own joke, not expecting the answer that comes my way.

"Oh, no, darling. You aren't interrupting; you are the guest of honor."

Grimsly hisses, back arching as he clings to me. Slowly, I spin around, blinking in the darkness as I stare at the giant figure in the woods. Giant antlers, skull-like head, empty eye sockets. Yeah, that's definitely a Grim.

My heart begins to thud, my head suddenly clear, and I know what I have to do. Before, I would have told myself to ask questions first, to start a conversation, to distract so I didn't have to attack. But I don't care anymore. I don't care about Shayde or his motives. I don't care that he won't leave me the fuck alone. I'm not the type of girl you get to fuck around with. I'm the type to destroy you before I, in turn, get destroyed.

Shayde Glover is not allowed to be my downfall. He isn't allowed to ruin everything I've worked for all year long. I'm the fucking savior, and it's about time I start doing the job I was brought here to do.

I raise my arm, and I blast.

CHAPTER 12

"Reapers are unique creatures. They are not like Conjurers—they're better. They aren't held back by emotions or relationships. They'll kill each other over a meal if you let them get too close to one another. You never need to worry about their loyalty or their priorities because it is *you* they are indebted to. I have designed them to be loyal, self-sustaining creatures with only one motive: Hunger. And once my creatures begin to thrive…they'll eat the entire world and any others we stumble upon. All you have to do is create them. "
—*The Grimoire*, written by the first, unnamed Grim, 1 A.G.

DEMI

I can see the master's offspring shrinking back down into his Charmed form as I peek around the tree I'm hiding behind a few feet away, his face pinched. I know him well enough now to see that he is attempting to hide his shock over the fact that she didn't bother to greet him. He had such romantic notions about this meeting, had sworn up and down that she couldn't resist the present he got her for her birthday. Except, it seems he wasn't able to make it that far into the plan. It seems the strongly scented Conjurer doesn't care for presents.

"I'm getting tired of this same greeting every time I come to visit, darling," he hisses, pushing his glasses up on his nose. He very rarely wears them, but tonight he wanted to look good for her. He tied his hair half up, wore a black silk button-down, and even shaved the stubble he'd been sporting for two weeks now.

The girl still doesn't speak, only blasts another burning beam of Light at the master's offspring. He throws up a dark cloud of Shadow, cursing under his breath. I snort, or something akin to it, as she takes a step forward, wobbling. The offspring hesitates, clearly battling with his next steps. But the short woman doesn't give him time for hesitation, a full battle bursting into fruition before me.

Light and dark come together in a beautiful combination, her powers deadly and brilliant. The multicolored balls she throws his way are hard to evade, and the offspring doesn't manage to get away from all of them. The master stumbles and groans when one smacks him in the thigh, another following to his chest. They burn through his clothes and onto his skin, red blisters and bubbles form-ing instantaneously. The beast in her hands forms a few shields, blocking the offspring's advancing attacks quite effectively. And, oh, the air smells so *delicious*.

"You fucking came to ruin my night, didn't you?" the small one hisses, anger propelling her moves as she clutches the beast tightly to her chest. I ache to jump into the fray, to devour her Charm Levels, but my instructions were clear: No matter how hungry I get, no matter how badly I want to take a bite, I am not to move from this spot until the offspring comes to get me. How utterly *boring*.

"Not quite, but it seems you're hell bent on ruining mine," the offspring bites back, panting. I watch in anticipation as he seems to deteriorate, the mixed orbs the small one keeps throwing taking a toll on his limited strength. I glance over his body and notice the giant hole that has been scorched on his side, the skin underneath red and irritated.

"Why can't I get away from you?" she whispers to herself, and I almost release a laughing noise but refrain. My laugh would only scare her. The offspring said not to do that.

The offspring clutches his side, taking a shaky step forward as his shadows curl into the air like tentacles. "I see you found my gift." He jerks his head toward the small beast in her hands, the dark creature hissing and scowling at the offspring.

"Your gift?" She falters in her brutal attack, and it's enough for the offspring's dark tentacles to snap out and grab her. Her wrists are the first thing to be captured, the shadows pulling on them and causing her to drop the creature, the gift, in her hands. It tries to form another shield, but it seems the fight has depleted it. So, instead, it stays by her feet and lashes out with claws and fangs at the shadows. It grows to be three times its size as it attacks, viscous and unyielding. I admire the ugly thing—strength and determination are such good qualities to possess in one so small.

"Yes, quite useful, isn't it?" The offspring grins as shadows encircle the small one's ankles, pulling her legs apart as she lifts into the air. Another latches around her neck like a collar, tight but not restricting.

"Grimsly!" The small one fights against her restraints, thrashing around like the wild creature she is. It would be cute if it weren't so irritating. I wish the offspring would get over this useless plight and let me eat her.

"You named it after me?" The offspring blinks, staring up at the girl just before the enlarged beast strikes. It leaps onto him, foam dripping from its snarling mouth. He screams as it bites down on his arm, his neck, his chest, sharp teeth doing anything to get inside his skin.

"Grimsly, no! Stop, Grimsly! He'll kill you!" the short one weeps, Light escaping from various places as she tries to melt her restraints away. She only succeeds in freeing one wrist, but it's enough. She blasts at the offspring again, hitting him in the cheek. The offspring howls, enraged, and stumbles back into a thick trunk before landing on his knees. *Finally,* I think. *Finally, he is going to do something about this.*

The creature is flung off my master's offspring with a blast of darkness. It flies into a nearby tree and collapses after a thunderous *snap* resonates through the air. It still breathes, but barely. The man rises, wobbling on his legs, but still manages to snap another shadow restraint around the ferocious one's free wrist.

"I'm tiring of this game, Azalea Jinx." His voice is devoid of all emotion, the excited leer long gone. This hasn't been the fun night he was expecting, not the welcome greeting he was sure he would receive.

"Can't take the heat?" she hisses, downright furious as she continues her struggle.

The offspring sighs, pushing his now-crooked reading glasses back up his nose. "I can take heat, and I can give it, but being uninterested in it is an entirely different thing altogether."

Kill her, kill her, kill her, I beg him silently.

"What is the point of all this? Why are you here? Why not just kill me?" She deflates, as though she's given up. Maybe she isn't the ferocious one, after all.

"It's your birthday," he replies, as though that answers everything.

"I didn't know you knew my birthday." She seems weary now, maybe even a little annoyed.

"Of course I do. Do you know mine?" She doesn't answer verbally, but it's the only answer he needs. "It's October twenty-fifth. Isn't that a fun coincidence?"

"You mean that we both happened to be born on the same number? Yeah, what a hoot." She's bitter now, staring anywhere but at him as the shadows encircle her lovingly. They dance across her skin like rolling smoke, caressing her with gentleness and devotion.

"I think it is, yeah."

"Well, bless your heart." The words are bitter and sound funny coming from her lips, more…

"There's that southern accent you try so hard to hide." The off-spring is grinning as though she offered him a little treat, beaming as though she used this…*accent* just for him.

"It happens sometimes when I'm insulting people. I'm sure you'll be hearing more of it in the future."

"That didn't sound like an insult."

"Yeah, that's the point." She winces, finally ceasing her escape efforts. "You're here because it's my birthday, right? You got a gift for me or something? One you won't try to kill in front of me?" Her glare is gloriously deadly, and I can feel the power building inside of her. Should I warn the offspring? Should I come out? But, no, he told me not to. He said she couldn't know I was here or alive.

"Yes, I got you a gift." He grabs the strands of Shadow trailing off his body, pulling them harshly and forcing her to fly to him at a harrowing speed. The ferocious one doesn't even scream; she mostly still seems annoyed. I understand because the offspring annoys me, too.

"Fuck you *and* your gift. I don't want anything you have to give me, *Grim*." She spits at him, a wad of saliva landing on his cheek. The insult! I should eat her. I *will* eat her.

"Oh, Azalea, darling," he sighs, letting her spit drip down his face as though it's insignificant. "When will you stop being mad at me?"

"I'm not fucking mad, Shayde. I'm furious. What you did to Demi…" My name from her lips is a sad sound, and for some reason, I want to…comfort her? Is that what this weird feeling that wants me to come out and prove I'm fine is?

"That's why I'm here, Azalea. This is as much an apology gift as it is a birthday gift." The offspring is gentle now, a switch flipped once again. That is what infuriates me the most: he's all these different people in the same body, and it can be *so* confusing. I don't have the patience to deal with all these sides, nor the desire. I just want to eat, and he never lets me.

"Really? Because it seems like another excuse to come see me."

"Don't pretend like you don't want to see me, too. Like you don't miss me," he snaps, eyes searching for something in her that even I know he won't find. He talks about her so lovingly, so obsessively, but watching her these weeks has shown me the truth he can't face: She's stubborn and unwilling to give him what he wants. Or herself.

She's not going to come back to him.

"I miss the you I thought I knew. But that guy doesn't exist, so what's left to miss?"

The shadows waver in their conviction to hold her up, her body rocking around in the air only briefly before they solidify around her once more. "I like having you spread open like this," the offspring says casually, devouring her with his gaze. I know he won't eat her, though. He won't let me, either.

"Fuck off, Grim. Give me whatever it is you have and leave. I have a party I'm missing."

"Yes, the one Jaymes is throwing for you. How is my room, by the way? Cozy? I hope you didn't change too much; I quite liked how things were." The offspring reaches a hand down into his pocket, trying to prolong this moment. I wish he wouldn't. I'm tired of being out here when I could be eating.

"Good Grim, you're relentless." She throws her head back and growls low, clearly raging again.

"It's another piece of my mother's jewelry. A bracelet." I watch as he slips it over her right wrist, gentle and hesitant. Oh, she's about to flay him alive. How delightful! Go on, ferocious one. Convince him to kill you with your unforgiving tongue.

"Quit giving me sentimental shit, Grim. As a matter of fact, take this fucking ring back while you're at it." He flinches at her calling him "Grim" again. She's so devoid of emotion, so utterly over the whole situation. It's quite comical.

"I won't." He lets his fingers linger over the small sliver of bare skin, eyes ravenous as he stares down at that bracelet. "These pieces of her, they're the only things untouched by the poison of my bloodline. She wasn't untouched by it, though, and neither are you. This—me, the Grim—I didn't want any of it to affect you. To…to ruin you. But it has. You may not forgive me now, but you will. And when you do, you'll be a lot more grateful for my gifts."

She scoffs, tilting her head back down in a terrifyingly slow moment. "Doubtful."

"Of which part?" He raises a brow, amused.

"Which part should I start with? The forgiveness? The gratefulness? This—us—isn't happening ever again. I shouldn't have to constantly remind you that I am the savior, and you are the thing I'm supposed to be saving the world from. *We are enemies, not lovers.*"

"But I love you." He tries so hard to make her understand through those meaningless words, but she doesn't.

"And I hate you." There is no bitterness in her tone, no sense of regret. Only honesty, and I admire it. I hate the offspring, too.

The offspring doesn't speak again. He only grabs those thick strands of shadows and flings her into the nearest tree. He breathes harshly through his nose at the action, eyes wide as if he can't believe he did it. Then he cackles, his personality flip-flopping inside of him like a fish out of water. The ferocious one is immediately out cold, her eyes closing and her breathing slowing. All that power she had been building up releases in a giant burst of light. The offspring cries out as he is burned by her outrageous amount of power. He, too, collapses.

I let out a muffled noise, irritated. I crawl out of my hiding spot from behind the trees, approaching him with little caution. I pick the offspring up, carrying him in my arms like a baby. Then I walk away, leaving the ferocious one injured in the cold.

Maybe, after she's dead, the offspring will release me and I can finally be free to eat whoever I want. Maybe I'll start with the party I can scent even here, miles away from the unconscious savior.

Chapter 13

"Scythe Partners are known for their fierce protection of their partners. Each Scythe has different methods of protection, but the most common method is Shielding. Similar to the Wielding the Charmed perform, Scythe's Shields come from the Charmed Levels they have been graced with. No one knows how or why these animals are chosen, as normal animals do not have even an ounce of Charm Levels inside them. Powers beyond Shielding are rare, but not impossible. It is as common as a Conjurer being a Dual-Wielder, to put it in layman's terms. If your Scythe Partner is a Dual-Wielder, be grateful and be wary: Your future is certain to be full of danger."

—*You and Your Scythe*, written by Shifter Marcellus Stone in 1998 A.G.

The terrified screams that echo in the dark, chilly night are what wakes me.

The next sensation that hits me is pain. Pain in my throbbing head, in my sore back, in my aching body. It takes a lot of effort to sit up, and the moment I do, the many alcoholic drinks I've consumed end up on the forest floor. I groan, shivering as I wipe my mouth before the vomit can freeze to my lips. That's a disgusting thought—one that quickly has me performing a Balmy Charm. My body is cold, despite the patch of warmth my head lies upon. Oh, wait; that's blood.

"Fuck," I groan aloud, scanning my surroundings. Shayde is gone, but the memories of what he did aren't. He...he threw me into a tree and left me here to die. I know I told him to just kill me already, but damn, I didn't think he would *actually* do it. And that thought hurts more than any physical pain he caused.

And Grimsly...Grimsly was hurt, too. Where is he? He turned into that...that giant beast and tried to protect me. I need to find him. I need to—

The screaming that woke me grabs my attention again, and I hastily pull myself to my feet and take off at a sprint in the direction of the noise. I shove at branches, my movements sluggish and uncoordinated. I reach up and touch the back of my head as I run, hissing when my fingers prod the gash there. So that's where the blood came from. It doesn't seem deep, but head wounds always bleed more. The back of my shirt is stained with it, a fact I'm only aware of because of the fabric sticking to my back. But I can't think about it right now. I have to figure out where the screaming is coming from.

I emerge from the trees after receiving more than a few cuts. Jaymes's house is still too far away. I can see it in the distance, and I know immediately that his house is where the screaming is coming from. I sprint as fast as my intoxicated body will take me, as fast as my injuries will allow. Did he decide to go attack Jaymes? Did Shayde decide that none of us matter, that he can just find other people to befriend? Is he really that far gone?

I'm not paying attention to what is in front of or below me, and I trip unexpectedly. I let out a noise of surprise as I fall, hitting my side and rolling. A groan sounds from the thing I just tripped over, and I quickly pull myself up to my knees to see what it is that I've hit.

"Shayde?" I whisper, eyes wide. There he is, passed out, with Grimsly lying over his chest and purring. "Grimsly? What the fuck are you doing? Get off of him! You just attacked this man. He *hurt* you, you dumb fuck. Come here, kitty kitty." I crawl over, reaching to pluck him off of Shayde's body. Grimsly snarls and bites at me, glaring.

"Azalea?" Shayde whispers, quiet and confused. "Am I dreaming?"

"Grimsly, what the fuck? You're *my* Scythe Partner, not the fucking Grim's. *Come on.*" I try to reach for him again, but this time he actually *does* bite me, and it takes everything in me not just to leave him.

"Azalea, I'm sorry," Shayde says abruptly, breathless and stumbling over his words. "I'm so sorry."

"See? He's out of his mind right now, Grimsly, so you need to leave him be." How do I get Grimsly away from Shayde? I am definitely not going to pick up the little creature who can turn into something that resembles an extra-large dog when he doesn't want to be picked up. Would he come for treats? Shit, I don't have treats. But I can't leave him. He's my Scythe Partner: He protects me. At least, he's supposed to. The least I can do is protect him in return, either way.

"My mind is split," Shayde continues, shivering now. And, damn it, I feel bad for him. These stupid emotions have my hands waving, warming him, and hating myself for it all the while.

"Your mind is split," I parrot to distract him, reaching to pet Grimsly. He allows it since I'm not actively trying to grab him. "Got it."

"Sometimes I'm me, and sometimes I'm not. I don't always know what I'm doing until it's too late, and I'm sorry. I'm so sorry," he continues, lifting an arm to cover his eyes.

"Right. Makes total sense," I say, not really digesting his words as I put a second hand on Grimsly.

"It's the Grim in me. It takes over, and I…I become *him*."

"Wait, what?" I pause, squinting my eyes down at him. Is he trying to say that…that the Grim inside him is forcing him to do all these horrible things? That's…that's a load of bullshit.

"You are the one thing I can rely on, Azalea. The only thing that keeps me coming back. And I'm so sorry. I'm so sorry. *I'm so sorry.*" He begins to sob, and I realize I've never seen him so vulnerable. Does he still think he's dreaming? He must. Should I…should I kill him while he's like this? Do my job as the savior and take care of the only heir to the Grim? My fingers leave Grimsly's fur and dance into my boot, where a dagger lies in wait.

I slip the Light-infused dagger out, not allowing myself to think about what I am doing and who I am doing it to. Shayde asked me once if I would kill one person to save many.

"Would you kill someone to save another life?" It's as if he reads my mind, jumping straight into talk of murder. "Would you use an innocent person to find and kill the monster you are hunting? Could you use your

bare hands to take a life? Could you look them in their eyes as you murder them? Those are the questions you need to answer, Azalea."

"Why? What does murdering people have to do with those beast things we hunt?"

"You'll be surprised, Azalea, at the lengths those beasts will go to to seem human. Answer me. Will you kill?"

My answer was quick: Yes, I would. It's time to prove to the man who helped train me that I'm capable of doing all of the horrible things he knew I would need to do.

I raise the dagger above my head, preparing to do the unthinkable, just as Shayde says, "You have always haunted my dreams, too."

"You have haunted my dreams since the day I met you, Shayde Glover. As long as you're there, what does it matter which kind of dream you're in?"

I freeze, swallowing hard as I gather the courage to ignore my aching heart. I don't let out a noise as I swing down, aiming for the sensitive organs in his gut to avoid hitting Grimsly. Except…except, the dagger flings out of my hands and I'm thrown ten feet away. Grimsly snarls and hisses at me, a shield wavering in and out of existence around him and the Grim.

"Why?" I whisper, wincing as I push myself back up into a sitting position. I land on my back; the pain radiates down my spine as my vision becomes even more fuzzy than before. How does he even have the energy *left* to form a shield?

Grimsly, of course, doesn't answer me. He only begins to knead his paws on Shayde, watching me with cold orange eyes. The screams from before come into focus so vividly that I jump, clambering to my feet and running back toward the house and forgetting the injured Grim in the middle of the road.

"Jaymes!" I scream, pushing my feet faster. I'm still off balance, the drinks from the night weighing heavily on my limbs as well as the blood loss that contributes to my weakness. I almost lean to the side and vomit from the exertion, but I stop myself just in time. I'm already covered in blood, I don't need to add vomit to the list of bodily fluids on me; I narrowly avoided that fate once already tonight.

"Azalea!" I hear a call from inside the house just as a dark figure takes off at an awkward run through the backyard, far enough away that I can't tell if it's a Reaper or a Conjurer. Charmed are fleeing from the small house, transporting away as soon as they are a safe distance from others. I shove through the crowd as I make my way inside, the vomit from before trying to make another appearance when the smell of blood and gore hits my nostrils.

"What…what happened?" I fling myself into the kitchen, finding the Gravediggers speaking in hushed whispers to one another.

"Reapers," Arlo says, relief in his hazel eyes when I come into view.

"Where the *fuck* were you?" Jaymes demands, stomping over to me and grabbing me by the shoulders. "I thought…I thought—"

"I went out looking for you." I shove at his chest harshly, forcing him to release me. "I went looking for you and found our ex-lover instead."

"Shayde was here?" Nox questions, stepping forward and dabbing at his bloody lip with a rag.

"Yeah. He's passed out in the middle of the road, actually. Grimsly is fucking out there protecting him." I jerk my head in the direction I left Shayde, and Jaymes snaps at Arlo and Nox twice before pointing. The two leave with no questions on their tongues, transporting away to investigate.

Jaymes turns back to me, lips pursed as he asks, "Why is Grimsly protecting him?" He reaches forward to touch the back of my head, exhaling roughly when he feels the gash there. His hands wave briefly, and I can *feel* the cut stitching itself back together slowly.

"Beats me. I tried to stab the Grim, but he—"

"You tried to stab him? Azalea Jinx what would ever possess you to stab a fucking Grim?"

"I've done it once, I didn't think it would be very hard to do it again." I shrug, pretending it's not as big of a deal as it is, as his eyes inspect me for more injuries.

"Azalea, a Grim can't die like normal people can. No one knows what kills a Grim, besides old age, apparently." Jaymes rubs at his forehead, clearly annoyed with me.

"Glad the savior was informed about that important information," I deadpan, glancing around. Two bodies lay on the ground in the living room, a blood trail following them down into the hallway. Two males, it seems—not my friends. "Ginny and the Thatcher sisters? And Dagan? Are they…?"

"I sent them home as soon as the first Reaper showed up. Everyone's safe," he whispers, reaching out as though to console me before dropping his arm.

"The first…?"

"Shayde sent about five of them," he confirms, sighing. "The house was so crowded that it was hard to fight them. Everyone was running over each other, transporting, trying to escape. It was chaos. One got away, but we took care of the other four."

"Shayde didn't send them," I say, confused. "He couldn't have. We argued, and he…he knocked me out. But when I came to, it couldn't have been very long. I hardly had any snow on me, and I was still just as drunk as I had been before. I heard screaming and made my way out of the woods just to find him on the ground, as unconscious as I had been. He was mumbling about me, and it seemed as if he thought he was dreaming. He…sounded normal. Like himself. Not like…"

"Like a Grim?" Jaymes winces, shaking his head. "Maybe he did it before you woke up. There's a small window there, surely he could have–"

"But who knocked him out? And if he did do it, then why is Grimsly protecting him?"

"I don't know." Jaymes stares out of the window above his sink, watching the spot I had left Shayde, where Nox and Arlo now stand intently. "I don't know."

Part Two

Azalea Jinx and the Fall of Enemies

CHAPTER 14

"In darkness and evil,
a savior awaits.
In light and good,
a hero can not escape."
—Prophecy found inside Seer Rosalyn Wheeler's prophetic journals, 303 B.G.

Jaymes won't stop insisting Shayde attacked his party, despite the lack of evidence. I'm all for criminalizing Shayde. Truly, I am. But this? This couldn't have been him, so who was it? Had Grim Senior ordered the hit? But that doesn't make sense, either. Shayde has him convinced I'm their little bitch to breed, and he didn't seem willing to kill me with the possibility of producing the most powerful Grim in existence dangling inside his malicious head.

I don't want to make Shayde seem like a good guy—he isn't. He's so far away from good that I shouldn't even be considering his innocence. Except…my mind is *screaming* at me that something is off. Grimsly wouldn't have protected him from me if Shayde were a danger to me or Jaymes. He wouldn't…right? I searched "Scythe

Partner" on the laptop Jaymes provided me, and all the articles I read say that a Scythe Partner is bound to their chosen one. *Me.* So why? *Why, why, why?*

Jaymes's insistence is putting me on edge. The constant frown on his face, the refusal to speak about it after I'd pestered him throughout our final days alone. It was strange and unlike him. I thought he would be ready to defend Shayde; he's done it plenty of times before, but he seems to be latching on to this event, this attack, and using it to turn Shayde into the villain. Not that he *isn't* the villain, but…well, I'm not sure he's the mastermind who orchestrated this.

Jaymes won't even talk about Shayde now. I was the one refusing to bring him up before, the one who demanded Jaymes let me hate him in peace. I don't know what's wrong with me. I feel hot all over, and the thought that he might still be Shayde douses me with the iciest of waters. When I think about what he said, about his mind being split…I don't want it to make sense. I don't want to reconcile the old Shayde with the new one. I don't want there to be two different versions of Shayde to consider at all. Fuck, I just need to ignore this whole situation. That's what people who feel things do, right? They shove all the bad things down until there's nothing left to feel bad about.

Staring at the school now, I know that coming back to Draxmere is the highlight of my week, my month, my *year;* it's exactly what I need to move past this entire confusing summer. Now that I'm not being dragged through a portal by a hot kidnapper, I'm able to enjoy the fresh start of the school year. Last year, I came into the semester late, but now I get to see the fresh chaos of move-in day for myself. It's exhilarating, and I finally feel like I've come back home. I'm not sure I've ever felt like I had a home until I came here.

I don't think I would have chosen Draxmere if I hadn't been forced to. I would have never done anything for anyone else, much less put myself through the shitload of work attending this school requires. But I'm glad I did. Do I feel like a cheat sometimes because I didn't have to go through all the rigorous testing everyone else did? Sure, sometimes. Then I remember the Seers are the ones to blame for that, not me, so there's nothing to worry about. It's not my fault my talent is raw. I'm working on it, okay?

Seeing Draxmere again fills me with crude emotions: ecstasy, relief, dread. When I left a couple months ago I was the Grim fucker, and they will all still see me that way. But I'm over that. Yeah, I fucked a Grim. Yeah, it was the best sex I've ever had. But I'm never falling back into Shayde's bed, so what's the point of lingering on that? If other people want to, then, well, I'll let them. That's not on my conscience, it's on theirs.

I stare up at the beautiful school, at the dragon fountain out front and the hundreds of students piling around it trying to get into the door. None of us have books, or bags, or personal items of any sort. Everything awaits us inside our new rooms. Will this room look like before? Will it be another sad imitation of my life in the human world? I hope not. I can do without the reminder of my life there and how pathetic it truly was.

"Azalea!" For a brief moment, I think it's Demi squealing in delight, but it's only Ginny. She races toward me, throwing her arms around me tightly. Her bouncy auburn curls swarm my shoulders, invading my space and flooding my senses with her evergreen scent.

"Hi," I say on a choked swallow, forcing myself to forget about Demi. She is another reason I have feelings of dread about returning: this whole place reminds me of her, is full of memories of her.

"I was so worried about you the other day! Jaymes forced us to leave before we could find you. He insisted you were okay but none of us knew where you were so how could we be sure? But obviously you are!" Her words come out so fast I can barely digest their meaning.

"Ah, yeah, sorry about that. I drank way too much and wandered off, passed out briefly, and came to when I heard screaming. I came as fast as I could, but he had already sent everyone home by the time I made it back. I missed out on all the action." I shrug, unwilling to admit what I had actually been doing, that I had tried to kill a Grim and failed. *I won't be the Grim fucker.*

"I forgive you." She releases me from her tight hold, grabbing my hand and dragging me to the entryway. We shove past students who are roaming around on the grounds, their shouts and outcries falling on deaf ears.

"We are on the second floor this year, right?" I question as we enter the gloomy castle, instantly feeling the weight on my chest lighten.

"Yes! Isn't that so exciting?" She acts as though it's a huge upgrade, but I don't think a single flight of stairs is that big of a deal.

"Sure, sure," I remark dryly, crinkling my brows in confusion when we start heading toward the training gym. "Where are we going?"

"Ah, they have a mandatory student meeting at the beginning of the school year. We still have fifteen minutes, but I want to get good seats. Besides, we might get a glimpse of the new dean before everyone else!"

I flinch at her excitement. "Right. I forgot about that." I didn't, but I don't want to admit that I think about killing Delarosa.

Ginny leads me to a spot directly in the middle of the front row of bleachers. Three grinning brunettes watch us with brilliant smiles. I smile back hesitantly, twitching my fingers at them in a wave as we approach. No mole, left mole, right mole: Reese, Wren, Willow. It's the way I've learned to tell the triplets apart, even though it makes me feel like an asshole. They're plain girls with soft, round faces; sirens who don't stand apart much in a crowd. I know I should be able to tell the differences in the cadence of their voices, in the movements of their bodies, in the tiny differences in expressions, but…I've never bothered to try.

"Azalea! I'm so glad you're okay. I called Nox probably thirty times after that whole fiasco at Jaymes's house to make sure you were okay." Reese beams, clearly happy to see me.

"You…called?" I frown, realizing I've never seen a Conjurer with a phone. "You guys have phones?"

"What's a phone?" Willow frowns, confused.

"What you call people on?" I say blandly, probably more confused than they are.

"Well, whatever that is, we don't use it. We have Charms to call each other. It's like…little live bubbles where we can see and hear each other," Reese explains, a small frown on her lips. "You've never seen anyone do that? It's Charmling level stuff."

"First of all, that's a video chat. We do that on phones in the human world. Second of all, what the fuck is a Charmling?"

"Toddlers," Wren grins, amused. "Reese is saying you don't have Charm intelligence past the point of toddlerhood."

"Ouch." I rub my chest as though my heart hurts from the insult, but I can't stop my lips from rising in amusement.

"Oh, hush, Wren. Azalea, that's not what I meant. I just—"

"It is what you meant," I interrupt, shrugging. "And that's okay. Will you show me how to do it?" Reese's cheeks tint red, but she nods anyway and begins to move her hands into position to show me. She uses both hands to make the shape of a rectangle, leaving one flat on the bottom and using the other to shoot straight up.

"Just think about who you want to see, and if it doesn't work, try saying their name. Be careful, though. Sometimes you catch people in situations that…are unsightly, to say the least." Reese shudders, shaking her head as though disgusted.

"Remember that time you called Nox when he was jer—" Reese slaps a hand over Willow's mouth and blushes so furiously that her entire face turns red.

"I don't want to remember that," she says adamantly, though her eyes trail over to the man in question. He and the remaining Gravediggers stand by the entrance, clearly keeping guard. But why do we not have the team of guards from last year? The ones who were supposed to be helping us when one of the Grims inevitably attacks?

"Why are you calling Nox so often, anyway?" Ginny raises a brow, clearly amused.

"We are friends. That's all. Tentative friends, anyway."

"Where are the guards?" I question, interrupting the girls before they can go off on a tangent about Reese and her possible relationship with Nox.

"Oh." Ginny glances around, a frown tilting her lips downward. "I don't know. That's weird. Shouldn't they be at a meeting like this? I mean, this is the meeting where *everyone* has to attend. Why wouldn't they keep this place under lock and key? Yes, we can all defend ourselves rather well, but with the chaos that's been happening in this school the past year? Yeah, I think it wouldn't hurt to have some extra help."

"Who do you think the new dean will be?" Willow whispers, watching the doors wearily. "Do you think they are the ones who called off the guards?"

"Who else would have had the power to do that?" I murmur, watching Jaymes absentmindedly. His whole body is tense, his blond hair gleaming underneath the bright lights.

"I think it's going to be—" Ginny is interrupted as a series of gasps echo across the room.

I jerk my eyes back to the door, away from Jaymes, only to find another head coated with the same white-blond hair. No…no, no, no. *She* can't be here. She must just be announcing the new dean. *She must be.*

"Good morning, Draxmere Academy of Conjuring," the woman bellows, her crisp white suit harsh against the sea of black.

"Good morning, Leader Bloodgood," the chorus of replies sounds back.

She smiles wickedly. "For today, and the foreseeable future, I will not be Leader Bloodgood to you. To you, my students, I am Dean Bloodgood."

I grind my teeth as the gasps sound again, my eyes flashing toward Jaymes. I expect to see him fuming, or upset at the very least, but…he only seems resigned. Did he know before we came? Had he suspected and not told me?

"No way," Ginny whispers, eyes wide. "How is that even allowed?"

"I am excited to lead this prestigious school and to get to know the new Conjurers preparing to fight in our war. Dean Delarosa was a great friend of mine, and it was a major loss for our people. I can only hope that I succeed her in the way she would have wanted me to." She pauses for dramatic effect, wiping away a stray tear. A tear that probably doesn't exist. "Now, I know you were all expecting a great speech. I had one prepared, truly. But now that I'm here, I'm seeing a lot of disturbing reactions. Some of you seem to be upset about my presence here. So, I'd like to open the floor to questions and comments. I want to reassure you that I am here as an ally, not an enemy. Please, stand up and raise a hand if you would like to voice your thoughts."

I know that the smile on her face seems pleasant and genuine, that she seems as though she's trying to make an effort to make things better, but I suspect this was all a ploy. She never planned on a big speech. She wanted to make herself seem relatable, and oh, has she.

A first-year student on the opposite side of the room from us stands, hand raised: Dagan. "How do you plan on leading an entire faction *and* a school?"

"Ah, great question." She beams at him, but Dagan doesn't return the sentiment. He only stuffs his hands down in his pockets, eyebrows raised.

"Then answer it," he challenges, cackling in that maniacal way of his.

"Of course." She watches him with interest now, as though he is some kind of experiment. "My role as the Light Faction Leader is now being split between me and my second in command. The two of us will make big decisions together, but for now, he will be handling the side of things I don't need to worry myself with as your dean."

"And will you get paid for doing both jobs?" Dagan questions, and Ginny slaps a hand over her mouth to keep from laughing.

"…yes," she admits, smiling through pursed lips. "Any more questions from the crowd?" Dagan sits, but others stand.

Question after question is asked, some as menial as "Will we still have the buffet?" and others just as valid as Dagan's, like, "Will you treat the Shadow Faction members differently just because we aren't in your faction? Will you show favoritism to your members?" That one was answered with a "definitely not" and quickly pushed to the side.

"Your job—isn't it a conflict of interest in this position?" Reese now, a defiant brow raised high.

"Maybe in normal circumstances," Haiden Bloodgood says slowly, debating her next words carefully. "But Draxmere has a board of councils, and it is the board that hired me. The factions ultimately have a say in curriculum, but not in hiring. As a sign of good faith, there will be representatives from both factions working inside the school, though. Don't worry about any conflicts of interest, there are plenty of checks and balances in place for a situation like this." This is the first question that truly rattles her, and unfortunately for her, the hard-hitting ones keep coming.

After forty-five minutes of questions, though, Dean Bloodgood tries to end things by saying, "Alright. I think that will have to be all the questions for today. If you have any more pressing concerns, you can always visit me in my office."

I stand, raising a hand and snapping my fingers in the air to capture her attention. "I have one final question for you, Dean Bloodgood."

"Azalea Jinx." She turns to me hesitantly, gritting her teeth. "As I said—"

I ignore her attempt to stop me. "Where are the guards?"

"The guards?"

"Yes, the guards. The teams that were placed around campus for a whole semester last year? The ones the school had follow me around and were all up in my business? *Those guards.*"

"They weren't necessary this year." She sniffs, making to turn away from me.

"Why? Is it easier for you if more of us die?"

She gasps, turning back to me with eyes too wide. "Why would you ever say such a thing?"

"Because you want us to give in to the Grim? Because if there are fewer of us to fight you on the issue, then it will be easier to get what you want? *Where are the guards?*" Simmering rage is exposed on my face now, the scowl on my lips intimidating and the glare in my eyes deadly.

"The Grims gave us a year to make a decision, Azalea. They won't attack us until after that time is up. We do not need guards because we do not suspect we will be under attack anytime soon. As for the first part of what you said, that's not what I want. I want our world to survive. My opinions may differ from yours, but that's okay. I'm not trying to get rid of Conjurers who disagree with me, unlike the Grims, who I've heard you are very *intimately* associated with."

"No, she didn't," Ginny gasps, moving to stand beside me. I shove her back down harshly, glaring at the new dean. Did she really just play the Grim fucker card?

"My sexual history is none of your concern, nor anyone else's," I say defiantly, my face heating. No, no, no. I can't be…blushing. I can't be *embarrassed*. Nothing embarrasses me, and I certainly won't let this bitch embarrass me over *sex*.

"Of course not, dear. It's just a security risk, you see. Your history, I mean."

"I was questioned already, *Bloodgood*. Those trained teams didn't seem to find my history to be a security risk to anyone but myself." I refuse to back down now, not in front of all these people.

"So they did." She purses her lips, opening her mouth and then closing it. "Do make sure that your next partner isn't a Grim bent on destroying the world, yeah?" Just like that, she has won, and by the small upturned corners of her lips, she knows it.

I'm pulled down harshly by several sets of hands, but I can barely feel myself sitting over the overpowering force of my rage. Ginny whispers something to me, reassurances, probably. I can't hear them over my pounding heart, over the pressure of my anger as it builds and builds and builds. Shadows lick around my feet, Light bursts from my hands. It starts—

Jaymes's arms wrap around me, his soothing voice in my ear the only one to break through. "You can't kill her right now, Azalea."

"Why not?" I hiss, turning to face him. I stare into those familiar green eyes, into that spot of brown, and the pressure in me begins to release at the steadiest of paces.

"Because if you kill her, we will have to find a new dean." He smirks, running a hand over my hair and tangling his fingers at the nape of my neck.

"Great, I don't like the one we have, anyway," I say, brows crinkling in as his face inches toward mine. "What are you doing?"

"I'm kissing you." And he does. He leans in and lets those soft lips press against mine, the tiniest of pecks but the boldest of statements.

"Why would you do that?" I hiss underneath his lips, low enough that the others can't hear.

"She's watching us," he says simply, tucking a strand of hair behind my ear. I tilt slightly to see Leader Bloodgood watching, her mouth pressed so tightly that the area around her lips is turning white.

"Oh." I grin, meeting his eyes again. I didn't lose, because now her son has declared his alliances publicly, and they aren't with her.

"You don't want to be the Grim fucker anymore, right?" I shake my head, despite my heart screaming *yes*. "Good. Then this is how you get past it, okay? You've moved on. I've moved on. We're together. You can't be the Grim fucker when you're in a relationship with the dean's son. A dean who also happens to be the leader of the Light Faction."

"I don't want to be in a relationship," I whisper, extremely confused. We fooled around, yeah, but that didn't mean I wanted to date him. I wanted fun, a distraction, not…not *this*. Whatever this is.

"I know. It doesn't have to be real, Azalea. Things don't have to change. I just…I just can't let everyone take turns destroying you. I can't watch my mother embarrass you as though you aren't the only hope we have left. I just…I want to protect you, okay? This is the only way I know how."

"Okay," I say, because how can I say no? I've never been protected before. No one's ever cared enough to try. And I think…I think I would like to be worthy enough to save.

CHAPTER 15

"In truth hides lies,
and in trust hides deceit.
In a villain hides an ally,
and in a hero hides defeat."
—Prophecy recorded inside student Seer Allia Jordan's Prophetic
Journal, 2024 A.G.

My room is in the dead middle of the second floor's left wing, and my heart *aches* when I swing the door open. This time, it isn't a mirrored replica of my room in the human world; it's somehow sensed that things have changed, that *I* have changed, and is now an exact copy of my room at Jaymes's house.

Shayde's room.

The whole place still smells like him, that smoke and leather mixed with darkness so invasive that I don't want to breathe. I got used to it over the summer, my nostrils eventually leaving it behind, but here…it's like it's being pumped through the fucking vents.

I choke as I shut the door behind me, covering my mouth and my nose as I am enveloped in *him*. How did the room know the exact way to torture me? The exact way to put my body at ease while ensuring my mind panics? This isn't right, it isn't fair, it isn't—

I close my eyes, taking a few deep breaths before allowing myself to open them, and drop my hand. I take another startled inhale as I glance around, noticing that the things I had saved from Demi's room are sitting outside the bathroom door. And there, on the nightstand, is the bracelet Shayde gave me that I had torn off and shoved down into a drawer and conveniently forgotten to pack. A process I repeat now, burying the stupid thing under underwear and socks. I swallow hard, closing my eyes again and taking a deep breath.

This room is my worst nightmare. It makes me *feel*.

I force myself to lie in the bed—*his* bed—and stare up at the white ceiling as though it holds all the answers. I think of Shayde and how badly I miss him, even though I hate letting myself acknowledge that. I think of Demi and how much I want her to be here with me, fixing my hair and makeup in the morning and telling me all the juicy gossip she heard during the assembly. I want someone to tell me that it's going to be okay, that I'm going to be okay, and I want that person to mean it.

What I want means nothing in this world.

I thought things would be different here, and they were. They are. But some things don't change, and one of those things is how I view the world. Everything is white or black, there is no gray, and I have to be what I am told to be. I don't get to be the savior and also fall in love with the villain. I don't get to have a best friend or a dean who gives a damn about me. Those things are distractions, and I can't afford distractions in a world as deadly as this one. I have to focus on my future, the future of this world, *and* the humans', if I ever want to have those things again.

A world where a Grim exists is one I can't enjoy.

A schedule is attached to my door with a Charm, and I grab it on my way to breakfast after doing my own makeup and hair.

I hated every second of it, cried when I saw the first curl, and puked by the time it was all over from how hollow my gut felt. But I did it. It's the first step to healing, to moving on, and I have to force myself to continue forward.

My new schedule isn't very different.

I glance down at the neat piece of paper with the school's emblem, signed by Dean Bloodgood.

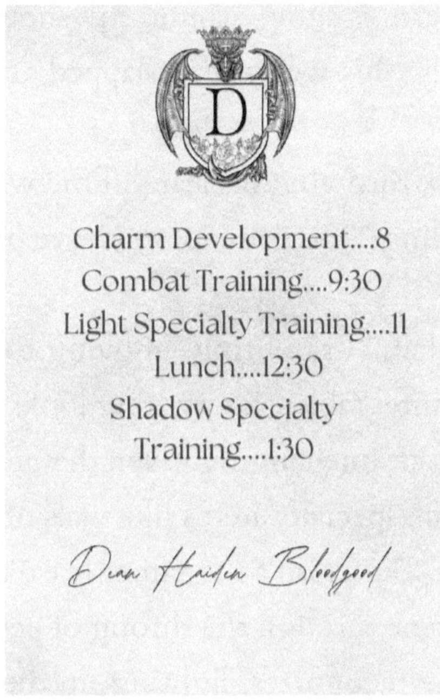

I scowl at that signature, crumpling the paper and throwing it into the mostly empty hallway to leave behind. I already have the schedule memorized: Charm Development at eight, Combat Training at nine thirty, Light Specialty Training at eleven, lunch at twelve thirty, and Shadow Specialty Training at one thirty. The only things that have changed are the times of Charm Development and Combat Training, which have just been switched. Easy enough to memorize, right? At least now I can eat a decent breakfast without worrying about throwing it all back up during Combat.

The short trip to the cafeteria is uneventful, and I manage to avoid every single interaction possible. People stare, some move to stop me, but I ignore everyone. I don't want to talk to people I don't know, and I certainly don't want them to think *I* want to talk to *them*.

"Azalea!" Arlo's arm is slung around my shoulder before I even enter the room fully, his wolfy grin slapped across his handsome face.

"Hi, pup," I snarl, throwing his arm off me with a huff.

"I'm no pup, darling." His grin doesn't leave his face, and I flinch at the nickname.

"Don't call me that," I say firmly, moving to grab a plate from one of the many buffet tables. Everything looks the same, the dark decor and table layout unchanging. Even the order of the bar setup is the same, with the specialty items like vials of blood and piles of raw meat up front. But it isn't the same. It isn't the same because Demi isn't leading me through the throng of people, calling out to every Conjurer she recognizes, lighting up the room. It isn't the same because—

"My bad." He holds up his hands placatingly, throwing the biggest steak I've ever seen onto an all too small plate.

I don't say anything, placing a bagel and a cup of fruit onto my plate before spinning around to walk away. "See you, pup."

"Wait, Azalea!" Arlo stops me with a hand on my elbow, watching me meaningfully. "Come sit with me and the boys. Jaymes is waiting for you."

"Why should I care what Jaymes wants? I want to sit with my friends." I don't, really, but I don't want to be alone, either. Demi wouldn't want that.

Arlo groans, rubbing his face with his hand like I'm some annoying task he's trying to complete. "Come on, Azalea. Don't be like that."

"Tell Jaymes that you were a good dog and listened to your master," I say, brushing by him to go toward the booth on the other side of the room where I see auburn hair waiting for me.

"Azalea," Arlo grabs my elbow again, harsher now. "Go sit with Jaymes."

"Excuse you? Are you seriously demanding I do things now? You think you can just tell me to do something and I'll listen? You think you can bully *me*?" I rip myself away, stomping away before he has a chance to lay hands on me again. I move toward the other side of the room, but suddenly an arm is wrapped around my waist, and I am being dragged to the long table at the center of the room.

"Do you ever just fucking listen?" Jaymes grumbles, pulling me along as though I weigh nothing.

"Jaymes Bloodgood, if you don't let me go this instant…" I snarl, Light flashing at my fingertips. It draws the attention of nearby students, but I don't care.

"Azalea, *stop*. Stop fighting me, stop resisting this, stop being so ignorant. It's going to be expected that you sit with me."

"Did you just call me fucking ignorant?" I hiss, spinning to face him fully. "And since when do I care about what is expected of me?"

"I call things as I see them. And since *now*. I told you yesterday that I'm trying to protect you, Azalea, and sitting with me will provide protection. When you're by my side no one will mess with you, or call you names, or any bullshit like that. If you don't sit with me, or interact with me, or act like you fucking like me, then this whole ordeal is going to fall apart before it even starts. Go along with this, *please*. For once, just…don't fight me."

My movements falter, my feet stumbling lightly as I begin willingly following behind him. "You're serious about this whole relationship thing?"

"Fake relationship, right?" He reminds me with a grim smile but nods all the same. "Yeah, I am. I'm worried about you, *for* you, Azalea. At least when you're next to me…"

"Right," I whisper, swallowing hard. "You think I need protection."

"I know you do."

"You don't think I'm capable of taking care of myself?" I snarl, forgetting momentarily what he asked of me.

"I know you can take care of yourself, Azalea. That's not why I'm worried."

"Then why…" I stop, realization setting in. "You think people are going to actually attack me? Not just verbally, but like…kill me?"

"Yes, I do," he says softly, glancing down at me with those deep green eyes.

"Shit." I allow him to guide me into a seat, allow him to curl into my side and hold my free hand.

I don't like this. I don't like this pretend relationship or these fake romantic notions. I liked how we were before. I liked getting surprise head in his house, I liked getting to know him as a person, I liked the tension and the ease of our friendship.

"I'll take care of you, Azalea," he says, knowing the exact thing I need to hear.

"I know you will," I murmur, nibbling on a strawberry with a sigh.

I shouldn't allow this. I shouldn't let him treat me like I'm his little bitch, like I'm under his thumb and will do whatever he asks. I don't want people to think I'm under his spell, or that I moved on from Shayde to him. I just…I don't want any of this.

But I still want him to take care of me. Even if it means giving up parts of myself to make that happen.

CHAPTER 16

"Draxmere was haunted by its past in its first few decades of being built. Students were hesitant to come, and even more hesitant to stay. Some say that the building is cold and uninviting because the energy of a Grim lives inside. Others theorize that the Grim can see what happens inside the walls, that he knows exactly what happens on the land where he was born. I've been told by multiple sources that the library is the worst room to be in, that it leaves you feeling helpless and fearful. Maybe that's where the Grim's energy lives. Maybe not. Maybe it's all a figment of the imagination, a conjured idea from the minds of the fearful. For the students' sake, I hope it is."

—*Draxmere: A Tale as Old as the Grim*, written by Enhancer Kelvin Delaney in 1977 A.G.

The mile-long trek uphill to reach the small building on the outskirts of campus that Charm Development is held in is a little easier now that I've built up some muscle and tolerance. Professor Canmore greets me with the sinister smile I'm accustomed to, her crow-like features just as creepy and off-putting as ever. Her gray hair hits her shoulders now, the thin strands brittle and dry.

Her black eyes track my every movement, despite the hundred or so students in the room she could be watching instead. That sharp and crooked nose is tilted up, her face even more wrinkly than usual as she looks down it at me.

"Good morning, class," she says, maneuvering her way through the room toward me. I chose to sit in the very back, near Ginny, but she doesn't seem to mind. She looks like she has lost weight, but her larger body still manages to bump into a few desks in her determination to reach me.

"Good morning," my peers chime back, but my mouth does not move. I watch her approach with a sigh, pushing my back into the chair and crossing my arms across my chest.

"Azalea Jinx," she says when she reaches me, tapping my desk with long, pointed nails that are painted the deepest of blacks.

"Professor Canmore." I nod my acknowledgment, waiting.

"I'm surprised to see you back here."

"Why?" I raise an eyebrow, perplexed. "Did you think I ran off with the Grim?"

"I thought you'd give up," she says simply, as though it made sense.

"Give up?" I scoff, shaking my head sharply. Brown curls fall across my face, the blood-red highlights vibrant and distracting. "I'm not a quitter."

"Oh, no. No, I see that now." Her smile is sinister as she watches me with a quiet fixation, adding on, "It will take more than a little heartbreak to break you, won't it? How…endearing."

"Great, glad you approve," I drawl, earning quiet laughs from those close enough to hear.

"You were a good student," she muses, tapping those nails again. One, two, three, four. One, two, three, four.

"I still am," I snap back, annoyed.

"Well, we will see about that, won't we?" She spins suddenly, striding back down the row as though she wasn't acting strange at all.

"That was so weird," Ginny whispers from my side, leaning across the space between us. "Do you think she was hoping you had quit?"

"That old loon?" I question, rolling my eyes. "I'm sure of it."

Professor Canmore had been nice enough last year, but something about her always set me on edge. She was squirrely at best, utterly terrifying at worst. The looks she would send me during class…they made me feel like a sinner in church. They were scorching, to say the least, and I never understood why. I was a good student, like she said. This was my highest-ranking class. I scored better than the majority of people here, despite my general lack of knowledge on Charms. Charms come naturally to me, hence my interest in performing well. The knowledge I gain from this class is used every day, and I like that. Even if this fucking professor doesn't like *me*.

"This year, we have a lot of ground to cover. The dean is requiring a new curriculum, which equates to almost double the amount of work we had before." Professor Canmore starts, earning groans of protest among her students. "Now, now. No complaining. You are supposed to be the best, are you not? If you cannot learn some simple Charms, then why should we include you in that category? Why should we allow you to fight against a Reaper if you can't even perform simple tasks?" The groans fall silent, and the room becomes still. I'm so frustrated already that I wish I had Grimsly here to distract me. I left him on my bed this morning, but I saw the little shit racing out into the woods on my trek here.

"Bloodgood doesn't think it might be a little difficult for us to double our curriculum when our training is also doubling?" I ask, not bothering to raise my hand. It was a whispered rumor this morning, one I'm certain is true.

"*Dean* Bloodgood wants what is best for her students, and she feels the curriculum at Draxmere can be improved upon. So, that's what we are doing. It's not my job, or yours, to question her intelligence."

I don't respond to that, silently fuming as Professor Canmore begins to explain that we are going to be using the same textbook from last year, *Advanced Charming*. I hardly pay attention as she assigns chapters to us for homework, as well as an essay on said chapters. I zone out entirely until she begins calling on random students to perform her Charm of choice, testing our memory and skill.

"Azalea," she calls toward the end of class, fingers snapping dramatically. "Do you want to show us the Enchantment Charm?"

I watch her wearily, saying, "I've never heard of that."

"Oh, no, sweetie. That's just not right. You did read your textbook last year, didn't you?"

"I read the assigned chapters," I say slowly, meaningfully. "They didn't include the Enchantment Charm."

"Well, I'm afraid that you must show me the Charm. If you don't, you'll receive a penalty."

"A…A penalty?" I question, face scrunching up wearily. "Is that another new rule our lovely dean has instilled?"

"It is." That sinister smile makes a reappearance, and even Ginny gasps at the sight of it. "If you cannot perform tasks in class, misbehave, or simply don't follow rules, you are now subject to receiving penalties. At the end of the week, the amount of penalties you receive will be tallied up and your punishment will be doled out accordingly."

"Punishment? Like detention or something?" Are they fucking for real right now? This isn't high school!

"Or something," she says, tapping those fingers again. One, two, three, four. One, two, three, four. "You won't perform the task I asked you to perform?"

I grit my teeth, grinding out, "I can't."

"Then congratulations, Azalea Jinx. You are my first student to receive a penalty."

"That's not fair," Ginny tries to defend me, pushing out of her chair.

"Only a professor can decide what is and isn't fair," Canmore sighs, looking at Ginny as though she's a pest. "Are you a professor, dear? No? Sit down, then." Ginny glances over at me, gnawing on her bottom lip, but I nod to let her know it's okay.

"You can give me as many penalties as you want," I tell Canmore, smiling just as cruelly. "And Bloodgood can give me as many punishments as she wants. *I'm not quitting.*"

"Not yet, you aren't, dear. But the kinds of punishments she mentioned to me…you may be reconsidering in a few weeks." She watches me with a sudden seriousness, beady eyes narrowed. Then she smiles brightly, waving at everyone. "Find chapter thirty-four and write a thousand-word essay on the subject. Tomorrow we will perform the Charm that it discusses. Complete the assignment, turn it in, and you're dismissed."

"What was that? And how can she just change the curriculum? Both factions are supposed to agree on curriculum changes! And the amount of work Canmore's assigned us already? It's an outrage!" Ginny fumes an hour later as we walk back toward campus, our pace heightened so we can make it to the gym in time for Combat Training.

"That was dear Dean Bloodgood showing me that her influence reaches far greater places than mine. And I don't know about the curriculum stuff. Maybe the dean has more power over the curriculum than the factions?" Light snaps at my fingertips, anger rising. A brief flash of that Light explodes from my eyes and blinds Ginny, her screech alarming me and everyone in the nearby vicinity.

"What the Grim, Azalea?" she cries, holding her face and moaning.

"I'm so sorry! I don't know what that was. That's never happened before. Stress-induced, maybe?" I reach out a hand, stopping just short of touching her before dropping it. No, I don't need to get any closer to Ginny than I already am. I don't need to do casual touches and warm embraces. Been there, done that, and I don't want any more of it. Friendships only hurt in the end.

"You flashed me." She rubs her eyes before blinking them open, glaring at me. They are rimmed in red and watery, her eyeliner slightly smudged.

"Why are you flashing Ginny, Azalea?" Willow appears at her side, a maniacal grin on her face.

"Sorry, should I include you three, too?" I murmur, eyebrows raised as I move to pull at the hem of my shirt.

"For Grim's sake, Azalea, no!" Wren shouts, covering her eyes.

"Are you sure? Because the cold really makes my nip—"

"No, no, no!" Ginny slaps at my arm now, despite the grin on her face. "That is not the kind of flashing I was discussing here!"

"I mean, I know they're big, but come on, no need to be harsh about it. Pepperonis are perfectly normal on someone of my size, you know?" I laugh at her horrified expression and the blush creeping up her face.

"Azalea, please don't traumatize the innocent girl," Reese chastises as we enter one of the side doors of the main building, the darkness waiting for us inside comforting. Not that it is bright outside or anything. The Charmed world is just lit like a cheesy teen two-thousand's movie—dim and gloomy.

"I'm not innocent," she hisses, face as red as her hair. She glances over at Willow, swallowing hard. "Where have you three been, anyway? You missed class this morning."

"Ah, yeah. We got pulled into a meeting for the sirens," Reese grumbles, clearly annoyed by it.

"You guys have meetings?" I've never had any meetings outside of my specialty classes. Is it just a…species thing?

"Yeah, apparently there's been an influx of sirens quitting," Willow says conspiratorially, her voice a hushed whisper. "They practically begged those of us left to stay."

"Dean Bloodgood did?" I question, shocked.

"Of course not," Wren scoffs, shaking her head. "It was just our specialty professor, Alec Larkman. He was really sad that our numbers shrank so much over the break."

"Why are so many quitting?" I ask, though I think I may know why. It isn't like sirens are land fighters. Their voices are great, yeah, but everyone knows they are more comfortable in water.

"They don't feel valuable," Reese shrugs, tossing her murky brown hair over her shoulder. "They think that no matter what, the Grim is going to win, and there is no point in them wasting their lives on protecting something that is going to die anyway."

"You mean the human world?" My words are bitter, my mouth scrunching up sourly.

"Azalea…" Ginny starts, hand on my shoulder. I shrug it off as we approach the doors of the gym, glancing over them all nonchalantly.

"I'm not offended. I understand why people think humans aren't worth saving. *I'm* not sure they're worth saving; I don't have a single person there I would miss if they died. But it isn't about people proving their worth or even proving that they *aren't* worthy. It's about real, living people who are just like us. They shouldn't have to prove they are worthy for us to save them. We should just *do it* because that's what we *do*." I sling the doors open, tossing over my shoulder, "I don't give a shit about what other people do or think. Their opinions won't change the truth. Killing off an entire species is wrong. No debate will convince me otherwise."

The five of us are quiet as we make it into the locker rooms to change, as are most of the girls around us. A few send quiet looks my way, which doesn't surprise me after what happened in my last class. I ignore them all, striding out the second I'm done and not bothering to wait for my friends.

"Azalea Jinx." I pause my strides, glancing to my left at the blond figure stretching at the sidelines.

"Sarah Sourgarden," I respond, trying to hide the twitch of my lips when Stella Stargrove's fists clench at her sides.

"You know my name."

"Yeah, I know. I just said it, didn't I?"

"Listen, Azalea—" she starts, fuming, but is interrupted by Professor Grey Donovan.

"No time for catching up, girls. Get in formation," he barks, pointing toward the center of the room. I nod, striding off to stand in line with the others who are already waiting. By the time everyone is out, we stand in five rows of twenty-five, just like we were taught. I'm sure there are a few more stragglers, but our numbers were only at one hundred twenty-five at the end of the year. Though with the amount of deaths and people quitting, I can't say for sure what our class size stands at now. Some of these rows *do* look a little short. Demi told me once that no more than five hundred students attend Draxmere at a time, which allows for some wiggle room, but I've never bothered to count and probably never will.

Professor Donovan's body is just as large and threatening as ever, those ghastly scars on his dark skin prominent. His muscles bulge with every movement, his deep brown eyes stuck on me. I choose to focus on his gleaming bald head because it's much easier than staring into that sharp gaze of his.

He strokes his full beard for a few long moments before saying, "Congratulations on making it to your second year at Draxmere. Not everyone did, so you should be proud of yourselves." My heart thumps, my eyes shutting on their own accord. *Demi didn't make it.* "This year is going to be harder. I'm going to push you as far as you can go and then some. Got it?"

I nod my head, murmuring, "Yes, sir," along with the others. Professor Donovan still watches me, as though trying to convey a message through his gaze.

He taps his Necromancer pin, grinning. "Don't worry, if I push you too far, I'll revive you so you can cuss me out appropriately." A few laughs follow, but I'm not one of them. I've seen what a Necromancer can do, and if he's half as powerful as Dagan…that's not a gift to laugh at. "A few announcements before we begin. The first one will likely be a disappointment to many of you: There will be no second-year Conjuring trips. Yes, that means that you will not be going in the field this year, as is tradition."

Groans sound in the room, complaints reaching my ears. "That's bullshit," Reese growls under her breath nearby. "How are we supposed to get any real experience now?"

"Some of us don't need to worry about getting any real experience," I murmur, glaring over at her. "Not sure why you want more Reaper attacks to play hero in."

"That isn't what I meant, Azalea." Reese deflates, eyes wide as she stares at me. "I know we fought in an actual battle last semester, but I don't think that is qualifying enough—"

Professor Donovan cuts off Reese and the others chattering around us, calling out, "Alright, quiet down, class. Now, the next announcement is—"

"Are you ready to introduce me yet, Grey?" a high-pitched voice interrupts from nearby. All I can see from here is the small height, long brown hair, and the hint of muscle in the limbs of the person posted by the door.

"This is Catrina Gordo. They are my assistant this year and will be helping me evaluate your progress." His eyes are back on me, insistent. Fuck, is this a plant from Bloodgood?

"Nice to meet you all," they say, thin lips smiling at us politely. I take in blue eyes, a wide nose, and tan skin. They can't be any older than twenty-five, so…they must be a recent graduate. The pin on their white training gear shows them to be an Enhancer. "I'm a Light Faction representative here to evaluate Draxmere's weaknesses and strengths. My Shadow Faction counterpart is on campus as well, whom I'm sure you will meet soon. I'm here only to interfere when necessary, not to teach. Ignore my presence and behave as usual."

"Right. Now that that's over…" Donovan drawls, stroking his beard again. "Who's up for some sparring? I think we need to evaluate skill levels again to see which of your group kept up with their training over the break." I swallow hard, breathing harshly through my nose. I was *not* one of those people who kept up with training. I was hoping today would consist of one of the brutal workouts I was used to…not straight-up sparring matches. *Fuck.*

"Genevieve Brady," Catrina calls, smiling so cruelly that I almost take a step back. "You'll be paired with Azalea Jinx today."

"Oh, shit," Reese gasps from beside me, eyes wide.

I shrug, moving onto the large mat as directed. I'm not going to let Bloodgood's little minion affect me.

"Azalea," Ginny whispers as she approaches, brown eyes pleading with my own.

"Don't," I say, messily pulling up my red-streaked hair. "They want us to react, but we aren't going to. Just fight me, Ginny. Pretend we aren't friends."

"That's easier said than done." She plants her long legs apart firmly, fists rising in front of her. I watch the freckles on her pale face to avoid her sad eyes, mimicking her.

"Did you mention the new rule this year, Professor Donovan?" Catrina asks, watching us with a predatory gaze.

"No." He sighs, rubbing his beard again. "Listen up, second-years! Catrina is here to help me evaluate how much effort you guys are putting into your training. You show up every day and put in your all, or you don't show up at all. If you aren't putting in your all, you get a penalty. Catrina or I will decide if you deserve one or not by the end of class, or in cases like today, the end of your matches."

"They want us to take it easy on each other so you'll be punished," Ginny whispers frantically, her words barely reaching my ears. "You can't let them punish you."

I feel Donovan's eyes on me again as I give her a grim smile. "I can."

Professor Donovan blows his whistle, announcing the start of our match. Ginny bounces around for a second, letting out a noise of unease as she swings. I block the swing easily, jabbing at her lamely. We both follow this routine a few times, but neither of us put any pack into the punches. Unfortunately, it's rather obvious.

"I've seen enough," Catrina calls, snapping at us to end the fight. "You're both receiving a penalty."

"What? No way," Willow cries out, trying to defend us. "You didn't give them a chance—"

"They are both stronger than this, even I know that. Next match is Stella Stargrove and Beau Turner." They don't bother to look at either of us before announcing the next match, not giving us the chance to argue our case.

"I'm sorry, Ginny," I say for the second time in under an hour.

"It's fine, Azalea. The punishment isn't about me, anyway. It's all about you." She gives me a sad smile, taking my hand and patting it gently.

Dean Bloodgood is sending me a clear message: *If you don't go down gently, I'll take your friends down, too.*

CHAPTER 17

"A Scythe uses their Charm Levels to form their shields, but those powers are easily deflated. Most Scythes get in a good three shields before they are weakened, unless their Charm Levels are higher than the average Scythe. This usually only happens if the Scythe has more than one ability, at which point we have concluded that their Charm Levels are equal to those of a Charmed child. Watch for signs of depletion in your partner: small shields, stumbling, and noises of distress are the most common. Like with Conjurers, Charm Levels will replete eventually."

—*You and Your Scythe*, written by Shifter Marcellus Stone in 1998 A.G.

I skipped lunch, deciding instead to smoke some weird Charmed concoction with a few first-years in the front courtyard. I have a pleasant buzz by the time I approach my Light Specialty Training professor, her brown hair covered in a lot more gray streaks than before. It's still pulled up in her signature tight bun, leaving her eyebrow piercing visible for all. I can still see that wrinkly floral tattoo peeking out above her chest, and I almost laugh at the sight of it. Why is seeing an older person with tattoos and piercings so jarring? It's entirely normal, but I'm also entirely high.

"Professor Battle wants me to help you again this year," Jaymes says in a way of greeting, his arm wrapping around my middle and pulling me to him.

"You going to penalize me too?" I ask, stumbling into his embrace.

"Grim, Azalea, you smell like…" He groans, pushing me away. "You're high, aren't you?"

"So what if I am?" I cross my arms, watching Professor Battle chat vehemently with a first-year student across the way. We're outside, practicing in the back corner of the courtyard. It's snowing hard today, but at least the snow on the ground isn't ankle deep like usual.

"Azalea, you can't use substances to hide from your emotions. You can't dive down into a bottle, or anything else, just to drown your sorrows. You can't use drugs or alcohol as a coping method. It isn't *healthy*."

"I don't care about my health," I say truthfully, smiling lightly. "I just care about the hiding part."

"Yes, you've made that much clear." He frowns, fingers splaying across my hip.

"What are we doing today?" I question, allowing Light to dance between us in a small ball.

"She's focused on the first-years today. She just wants everyone to practice a little while she gets them settled in. The first few weeks are usually like that. We kind of just make sure to—"

"Azalea Jinx," Stella Stargrove purrs as she strides up to me, nose wrinkling as her head tilts back.

"What do you want, Sora?" I murmur, detesting the grin on her face.

"You were ratted out. You're getting another penalty for smoking contraband."

"Oh, please, Stella." Jaymes scoffs, pushing me behind him harshly. Protecting *me* from fucking *Stella*. "No one has ever cared before about contraband."

"Your mother cares," she purrs, blinking up at him seductively. "I'm just doing what she asked me to. You understand that, don't you?" She reaches out to touch him, stroking his arm gently.

"All too well," he says, flicking her hand away with a scowl. "Message delivered. You can leave now." She looks up at him sadly but nods, turning and strutting away without another word.

"Bitch," I call after her, laughing at the middle finger she throws up behind her.

"How many penalties is that now, Azalea?" he asks carefully, brows creased in worry.

"Three," I say cheerfully, collapsing onto the ground. "One per class. How many do you think I can get in one day? I want to set the record."

"Azalea, this isn't funny."

"Sure it is. I can take her punishment." I smile sweetly, blinking up at him lazily. "I've been a bad girl my entire life, Jaymes. I'm used to getting spanked."

"Azalea." His voice is low and husky, his expression pained. "I'm not doing this with you."

"Doing what?" I ask innocently, collapsing onto my back and sighing contentedly.

"I told you I won't be with you like that if you're still hung up on Shayde."

"Why? Because you respect him?" I scoff, closing my eyes. Before I can stop myself, I add something meaner. Something more truthful to my situation than his. "Or maybe you're so in love with him that fucking around with me is the next best thing."

Jaymes stares at me in shock for a few precious seconds, face contorting into something ugly as he hisses, "No, Azalea, it's because I respect *you*. I won't fuck with your emotions like that. Or his."

"That didn't stop you from going down on me in your house," I murmur, not entirely sure how we got here.

"I told you I'm selfish, Azalea, but I'm also not immune to my own feelings. Just like you aren't. I don't want to be hurt. If we…if we go past kissing and jump straight into the physical…you can't give me what I want."

"Shayde would have fucked me without hesitation if I asked," I say, because it's true. The first time we had sex, it wasn't because he wanted emotion. He just wanted *me*.

"I'm not Shayde," he says darkly, backing away.

"I've noticed." I don't mean it to sound as bitter and regretful as it does, but I can't stop myself. I don't know how to handle the things inside me right now, how to stop the hurt from pouring out into others.

"I know I'm not the one you want, Azalea." He lunges forward suddenly, crouching down and leaning over me. "I know you'll never love me. *I know that.* You don't have to shove it in my face. You don't have to be fucking cruel."

I stare, wide-eyed, at his enraged face. "I'm not trying—"

"See, that's the problem, isn't it? You aren't trying. You aren't trying to get over him, you're just trying to shove what you feel so far down that it won't resurface. But that won't work, Azalea. You can't just ignore the things you feel. I wish that's how it worked. I wish I could ignore the things I feel for you. But I can't. *I won't.* I'll fucking stay by your side and pretend to date you so the whole world can believe you've moved on when you haven't. So Shayde will think we both betrayed him. So that you'll have a minuscule amount of protection in a world I can't protect you from. I'm going to let my heart break a little every single day just to help *you.* I'm going to break, and fall, and then I'm going to get back up and let you do it to me again just so I can stay in your orbit."

"I didn't ask you to do that," I say quietly, just as furious. "I didn't ask you to fall in love with me. I didn't ask you to protect me. I certainly didn't ask you to fake date me."

"You didn't have to," he hisses, deep green eyes blazing. "That's what love is, Azalea. It's all give and it's no take. You may not love me romantically, but we are friends, aren't we? You can at least pretend to care about me."

"I do care. I care more than I fucking should!" I shout, Light snapping between us. We are far enough away from others that my shouts are inconsequential, my Light only an indication of following instructions. "*That's* my problem. I care about people, and they get hurt because of me." Tears spring to my eyes, my damn emotions controlling me *again.*

"What happened to Demi was tragic, Azalea, but it wasn't because of you. You can't close yourself up because of that. Because of Shayde."

"I think my reaction has been entirely normal, Jaymes, but what about you? You don't seem to care at all. First, you were saying we could save him, and recently you've been treating him like a villain. I don't—"

"He *is* a villain," he shouts, shaking me harshly. My head wobbles and my vision blurs briefly, the anger making everything hazy. "What don't you fucking understand about that? He killed Demi. *He hurt you.*"

"I know exactly what he did." My eyes harden as I blast Jaymes with the strongest ball of Shadow and Light I can form, sending him flying ten feet away. I force myself to my feet and strut over to him. Then I crouch down over *his* body, crossing my arms across my knees casually as he groans in pain.

"If I cannot love him, then I will hate him instead," I say quietly, calmly. "That's what I have been telling myself every day. And every day it gets a little easier. But I can't just forget what I had with him. Not when he's showing up in my dreams, not when you tell me my story with him is unfinished, not when everyone is constantly reminding me of all the reasons I was with him in the first place. What do you want me to do, Jaymes? You want me to be the husk I was when I first got here? The emotionless little girl who would have done anything to get what she wanted? Because sometimes I wish I were still her, too, but I'm not. I can't be. If I become her again, I would damn this world and every other world I pleased if it meant I got to be with Shayde again. But like I said, I'm not her. I never will be again. I'm not some damsel in distress, Jaymes. I know what I'm doing. What Shayde did. And fuck you for throwing that in my face all over again."

I stand, not bothering to stick around for his reply, and stride off. I don't have time for his overprotective alpha bullshit today. Or any other day. If he wants to fake a relationship, fine. If he wants to pretend that Shayde's the only villain in this story, fine. But I'm not delusional. I know that the Grim is a figurehead and that there is more going on behind the scenes. I know that I can't be with Shayde, and I don't want to be. I'll let Jaymes swallow me up in his protective arms, I'll let him hold me close and keep me shielded from my peers. I'll gladly do it just so I can keep myself out of the black hole of thoughts that revolve around Demi and Shayde.

But I won't be gladly ignorant.

Professor Slateman was so preoccupied with the first-years in Shadow Specialty Training that he didn't even notice me. And, this time, I don't have Shayde to show me the ropes. I don't have anyone here I trust, and I don't know how I am going to succeed without help. He didn't bother to send an older student my way like he had last year, much less to tell me what I should be working on. So, instead, I sit with a tree behind my back and toss a black ball of Shadow around, watching the first-years preen at the balding brown-haired man with disgust. Professor Slateman is bulky and his ears are too large, but his kind blue eyes make up for all of that. You can take one look at the man and know that he *cares*.

So, when a student approaches me later, a brown-haired beefy girl with a permanent snarl set into her lips, I know it isn't him who sent her. "Let me guess," I say before she can speak. "I'm getting another penalty?"

Those lips tilt up, her eyes hard and devious. "You haven't done anything all class."

"What was I supposed to do?" I scoff, flinging the harmless ball I'd been tossing around at her. "Professor Slateman was too busy with the first-years to bother with me."

"That's not my problem," she says with a nonchalant shrug, that smirk stuck on her face. "You were reported for disobedience."

"Hence the penalty," I say in a sigh, rolling my eyes. "What's up with all the messengers? You one of Bloodgood's little minions?"

"We are part of a special team. The Black Cloaks," she hisses, spine straightening as she points to the pin on her chest bearing a hooded figure wearing a dark cloak. "Dean Bloodgood is applying a lot of new rules around here; she needs people she trusts to dole out the consequences and make sure those rules are being followed."

"Minions," I repeat, pushing to my feet. "Spy on me all you want, little birds, I'm not going to break." I strut away from her, abandoning the last ten minutes of class entirely. What's the point in staying, anyway? I've already received the penalty and will take whatever punishments the combination of those leads to.

My heart thuds heavily in my chest, the traitorous bitch; Dean Bloodgood holds a lot of power in this situation, and I'm scared.

I'm fucking scared that I'm going to get kicked out. That the one place I've felt at home will be taken away from me.

I'm scared she is going to break me.

CHAPTER 18

"A heart split in two has one desire:
The girl with split powers and a burning ire.
Evil lingers inside that wicked heart,
but goodness spreads even as the world falls apart."
—Prophecy found inside Seer Tamra Liu's prophetic journals, 303
B.G.

"You told me you weren't coming back."

My heart races as I stare, taking in his rugged appearance. He's got on those fucking glasses, the ones that make him look so nerdy and attractive all at once.

"I hate what they're doing to you," he whispers, not answering. I'm standing on the edge of a familiar cliff, rocks crumbling into the abyss as I shift from one foot to the other. I know what I should say, what I should do. But here, I'm dreaming. Here, it doesn't matter if I cave because only I will know how easily I fell into temptation.

Shayde's hair is pulled halfway back, the bags under his eyes dark and heavy. His red sleeves are rolled up to his elbows, his hands shoved down into the pockets of his dark jeans. He watches me with a sadness I can't comprehend, with an adoration I can't accept.

"You told me you weren't coming back," I repeat, swallowing hard. He looks so…irresistible. It isn't fair that he's here, it isn't fair that I can conjure an image so fucking *realistic.*

"I know what I told you." There's no bite to his tone, no fight. "But I can't stop myself, Azalea. Not when it comes to you. I know what they are doing to you, and I…"

"You what?" I question when he stops, taking a step forward just to get away from that deathly fall.

"I blame myself."

"Good, because it's your fault," I hiss, jabbing a finger in his direction and stumbling forward as a chunk of the ground beneath me crumbles and falls just after I step off it.

"I know it is." Still no bite. No anger.

"This isn't you," I say, gaze softening. "Where did you go?"

"Has it really been me this whole time?" He misdirects the question, smiling sadly.

"Considering none of this is real…no." I laugh shakily, running a hand through my hair.

"You're so beautiful," he whispers, watching me with reverence. "Shayde…"

"I hate what they're doing to you," he says again, softer this time.

"I hate that I have to let them do it," I reply truthfully, taking a few more cautious steps forward. I gravitate toward him, my body heating and my heart thumping.

"You don't have to. You know that." He tilts his head, an invitation in his words.

"What else would you have me do?"

"Come with me."

"You know I can't do that, Shayde," I whisper, shaking my head furiously. "You know better than to ask that of me." And, even though I would never admit it out loud, there has to be some part of me that wants to go. There must be, if my mind is so hung up on the idea.

He lifts his shirt to finger a pink scar with a grim smile. "Going to give me another one?"

"If I have to."

"I know." He drops his shirt and smiles sadly again. "And you know what the worst part of this whole thing is? I would let you. I would let you take all your anger out on me, kill me, if that's what it took to make you heal. To make you…*you* again."

I finally approach him, running a hand down his cheek. "My mind only conjured you because I had a bad day."

"You'll keep having bad days as long as you are there."

"Yes," I say, nodding. "I will."

"Then why won't you come with me?" He sounds so sad, so desperate, so lonely. He sounds as empty as I feel.

"I can't, Shayde."

"Why?" he repeats, still not even an ounce of anger in his words.

"Because you're a Grim!" I cry, dropping my hand. "Because you betrayed me. Because you *hurt* me. Because you killed Demi." *That.* That last bit is the most important thing of all, the one misdeed I can never forgive him for.

"It's not my fault I was born to be a monster; I didn't get to choose who my father was."

"No, but you did get to choose what direction you would follow. *You chose wrong.*"

He flinches at the harsh truth, lips pursed as he pauses to think over his next words.

"There are things you don't understand," he tries again, moaning as he puts his face in his hands.

"Like what? Explain them to me."

"Like I'm not *me*," he whispers into his palms, holding them there to block me from his expression.

I scoff, rolling my eyes. "Obviously. You're a figment of my imagination." This is the best excuse my mind can come up with for his behavior?

"Am I?" He drops his hands, suddenly looking at me with an intensity that *hurts*.

He…he is a figment of imagination, isn't he? This is just a dream, isn't it? Dream walking isn't a thing. Right? "I…I don't understand."

"I'm not me," he repeats, watching me carefully. "Not all the time."

"Do you expect me to believe that?" I whisper, shaking my head. "Do you expect me to believe this is you? That these dreams are you? Because I don't. This? Us? These dreams? This is what I want. What my mind is too afraid to admit in the light so it brings it out in the dark. This isn't really *you*. Even if I desperately want it to be."

"Can I convince you otherwise?"

"No." I outright laugh now, taking a step away.

"Can I try?" He looks so fucking *broken*. So, I waver.

"Knock yourself out." I wave my hand dismissively, turning away so I don't have to see what I've done to him.

"I need your help. I need…I need to not feel like this anymore. Like I'm a bunch of fragmented pieces that no longer fit together." His voice is dry now, rough and honest.

"I don't know what that means."

"I don't expect you to. I just…being a Grim is a curse, Azalea. It's a curse that was placed on my family long before I ever deserved it."

"You don't deserve it now," I say truthfully, turning so my gaze finds his once more. "Doing bad things doesn't make you a bad person. I would know."

"Even killing your best friend? That doesn't make me bad?" He smiles weakly, tilting his head back to look up into the darkness.

"I…" I don't know how to respond to that because the answer is *yes*. Yes, killing Demi makes him bad. So bad that I can't see past it. If he had been honest with me, if he had just told me *what* and *who* he was the second he showed me his Grim form, I may have been able to forgive him; the betrayal wouldn't have cut so deeply, the truth wouldn't have burned so harshly. If he gave me a good reason right now, I would forgive him for sacrificing the world. I've done horrific, viscous, vile things for piss poor reasons and I have forgiven myself for them. There isn't a lot I *can't* forgive. But Demi? Demi is one of those things, and we both know it.

"Exactly." He swallows hard, watching me carefully again before saying, "But I'm still going to ask for your help. I've been trying on my own, and I'm slipping away faster than I expected. Here, in your dreams, is the only place I feel like me. The only place my sanity lingers. You're the only person in the entire world I trust with this knowledge. The only person in the entire world who can save me."

"Because I'm the savior?" I whisper bitterly, scoffing.

"Yes. And because you love me, even if you don't want to. And I love you despite it. Because all the prophecies say you will be the savior, but they don't say *who* you will save."

"I was supposed to save Demi," I say, swallowing. "That prophecy said I would be her savior or her doom. Guess what my success rate is so far at being the savior?"

He flinches, taking a deep breath. "You can still be her savior."

"You killed her, remember?" The words are like poison leaving my mouth.

"Did I?" He tilts his head, watching me closely.

"Yes, you…Fuck you, Shayde. You don't get to toy with my mind like I'm your little puppet!" I scream, shoving at his chest.

"I thought I wasn't real? I'm just a figment of that imagination of yours, aren't I?"

"Oh, fuck off," I seethe, holding my head in my hands. "What do you want from me?"

"I want you to save me. I told you already."

"How? How does one save a Grim?" I throw my hands in the air, laughing at myself. I can't believe I'm even *entertaining* this.

"I—shit. I have to go, Azalea. Listen to me, please."

"What do you mean you have to go? I'll wake up when I damn please."

"No, you'll wake up when dear Dean Bloodgood bursts through your door and drags you out of bed in a few minutes. Just fucking listen to me for once, Azalea Jinx!" He's frantic now, holding my shoulders and digging his fingers in so tightly that it hurts.

"I'm listening! Good Grim, man, let me go!"

Shayde does no such thing. "I need the Grimoire. Please, Azalea. I've been searching everywhere I know to look, but I can't find it, and I need your help. The Grimoire could save Demi, could save other Reapers, too. It could save me. I don't know how to find it, but I need it. I need it if I want to not be fractured anymore, Azalea."

"What's a Grimoire? That sounds like a spell book or something." Could my mind make up something like this? Could I dream something so complicated?

"Or something." He glances behind me, words picking up their pace. They fly from his mouth, a jumble of murmurs I can hardly understand. "I need to find it. I have to. It'll look like a giant book. It'll feel evil. It'll want to devour you. Just don't let it. Just…find it. Bring it to me. You're my only chance, Azalea. You're the Reapers' only chance."

"I don't understand. What does this book do? What does it look like?"

Shayde shoves at me hard, pointing toward the edge of the cliff. "Do you want me to come back here?"

"I don't know." *Yes. No. Of course. Definitely not.*

"You still aren't sure if you can give me the kind of love you want," he says sadly, closing his eyes and taking a deep breath before racing forward and shoving me again.

"Quit that, Shayde." I make to shove back angrily, but he points again, back at the edge of the cliff.

"Run and jump, Azalea."

"You want me to jump off a cliff?" I raise an eyebrow, shaking my head in disgust. I can't believe him. After all that—

"No. I want you to wake yourself up before they get in your room. They aren't warded anymore, and I need you to prepare yourself. Get dressed. Arm yourself. They're coming."

"Who? Who's coming?"

"Wake up, Azalea!" he shouts, desperate and panicked. The look in his eyes is pleading, his entire body shaking as he points again at the edge of the cliff. I only hesitate for a brief second, swallowing and nodding before turning away.

My heart beats dangerously as I race forward. Despite the fear that threatens to overtake me, I jump.

CHAPTER 19

"A savior cannot bear the weight of her fate,
nor the weight of her sorrow.
And now the resurrection of a hero starts too late,
reliant on the time we borrow."
—Prophecy tattooed on Azalea Jinx, first found inside Seer Titus
Grant's prophetic journals, 2001 A.G.

I gasp when I wake, fingers sliding across the Light-imbued dagger underneath my pillow. I jump to my feet, glancing out the dark window next to my bed. It's before sunrise, well before anyone should be awake. Despite the panic racing through me, I dress, sliding on black leather pants with deep pockets. I've barely gotten on my tank top when the door bursts open. Two men stand at the entrance with stony expressions.

"Azalea Jinx," the blond one says, eyeing me up. I swallow hard, taking a single step back and crouching low.

"We have orders to retrieve you," the black-haired one says, scowling. I grab the matching leather jacket hidden just underneath my bed, standing and slipping it on. They watch me wearily, glancing at each other before fully stepping into my room. Fuck,

Dream Shayde was right. I had a total of five minutes before these bozos strutted in like they owned the place.

"Orders from who?" I shove my hand inside my jacket, patting the hidden pocket inside that holds two more daggers to reassure myself that they are still there.

"Your dean. It's time to cash in your penalties." That's what this is fucking about? It's Saturday for Grim's sake! This is supposed to be a *rest* day.

"And if I don't want to?" I flip the dagger lazily, letting shadows coat the floor around my feet in warning.

"Then we will drag you out by your hair," the blond says with a shrug, annoyingly calm.

"Think you can manage it?" I ask sweetly, letting Light crackle at my fingertips. They glance at each other again, taking a synchronized step forward. I laugh, tucking my dagger away. "Relax, boys. I was only joking."

I prance forward, sliding out into the hallway after a few quick strides and turning back to watch the two with a raised eyebrow. The blond says, "Follow us," and shoves me into the wall harshly on his way by.

I scowl, gripping my shoulder that now throbs. "You two sure know how to treat a lady."

My escorts say nothing. They stride down the long hall, assuming I'm following. And I do. I follow because what else am I supposed to do? Stay in my room and freak out about Dream Shayde predicting the future? About the possibility that he could be real? No. No, I can't do that. I can't sit around and fucking mope. I also can't just kill Dean Bloodgood's little helpers; she'll only send more. Whatever punishment I'm about to endure...they think I deserve it. Maybe I do. Maybe I don't. Either way, I'm going to let them do it. I won't let them scare or intimidate me.

I'm not escorted to Bloodgood's office like I expect. I'm taken out to the front courtyard where a small group of people wait for us. I can only see two other guards, one male and one female. When they part, my heart stops entirely, and all I see is *red*.

"Why is she here? This is *my* punishment," I hiss, jabbing my finger at Ginny. She's sitting on the edge of the fountain, staring at the dragon inside numbly.

Dean Bloodgood smiles brightly from beside her, patting Ginny's shoulder roughly before rising. "Ginny here has almost accumulated as many penalties as you this week, Azalea."

"Has she now?" I murmur, glaring. "The only reason she has any penalties is because—"

"Because of you?" Bloodgood shoves her hands down into her pockets, that familiar blond hair whipping back in the wind. "Yes. That's exactly right. I've heard all about your refusal to fight each other in Combat Training. It's disappointing, really."

"We are training to fight Reapers, not each other," I say blandly, glancing over at Ginny. She still hasn't moved, her shoulders hunched, her normally perfect hair erratic and poofy. My eyes trail over her body, noticing the fluffy pajama pants and the thin tank top. She didn't have a Dream Shayde to warn her to get up and get dressed.

"Reapers are us." She shrugs as we come to stand before her. "Your little friend…Demi, right? She was your friend, and now she's a member of our greatest enemy's army. If you ever find her, you'll have to kill her. I'm preparing you for that reality."

"She's already dead." That has Ginny's head snapping up, her vacant eyes watching me carefully. Her lip is split, blood staining her chin.

"Then you understand," she says, not unkindly, and glances down at Ginny. "Ginny *doesn't* understand. The two of you are disobedient, and I won't tolerate that at my school. Your penalties are…unfortunate. Punishments aren't usually kind."

I've received nearly twenty penalties in five days, most of which have been in Combat Training because I've refused to fight Ginny every single day. Ginny, in turn, has refused to fight me. I knew she was getting penalties for it, but she insisted she didn't care. But this Ginny? Her punishment has already begun, and it's clear that she *does* care.

"Ginny," I whisper, swallowing hard. I only know of ten penalties; when did she get the other ones? How many did she get? Surely she didn't get as many as me?

Ginny doesn't answer, so Bloodgood continues. "You're being sent to the human world today, girls."

"The human world? Why would we—" I pause, noticing Ginny wrap her arms around herself in a shiver. Not because she's cold; she's *scared*. "You're sending us into combat."

"In a way," she smiles cruelly, snapping her fingers. "I'm sending you to be bait."

Ginny screams as arms wrap around her and her body is lifted into the air. She kicks her legs, rearing down and biting the arm around her. I wish I could cheer her on to bite harder, but arms wrap around me, too, wrenching me from the ground. I'm slung around to face a portal only feet away, guarded by the two men who came to get me earlier.

"It's okay, Ginny!" I scream, letting them carry me to the portal. "It's okay!"

"How can you say that?" She sobs from nearby, and I hear her captor shout out in pain. I smile, proud of the fiery redhead.

"I have Light, remember? I can kill whatever Reaper they are using us as bait for."

"Can you?" Dean Bloodgood smiles, snapping her fingers a second time. The blond man comes barreling forward, malice gleaming in his eyes as he raises a vial in front of his face.

"Shit. I take back what I said. It's not okay!" I kick and scream, throwing my head back into the person holding me, but they don't let go. The blond man grabs my chin with his hand, prying my mouth open. A finger slips into my mouth, and I bite. *Hard*. He screams, and his hand falls, blood dripping from the broken skin.

"Fuck you, bitch," he hisses, hand closing around my throat. I fight even harder than before, trying to make contact with *anything*, but my vision quickly begins fading, my brain focused on one thing only: oxygen. The moment he releases me, my mouth opens of its own accord to gasp for air. As soon as it does, the liquid is poured down my throat. A hand covers my mouth and plugs my nose to force me to swallow.

"Swallow," the woman behind me hisses, squeezing me tighter. I do as I'm told, coughing and sputtering when they finally let me breathe again.

"I'm not a spitter," I say bitterly, blinking to bring my vision back into focus. I see Ginny on the ground beside me, a man on top of her pouring the strange liquid down her throat, too. Fear, strong and true, invades my body like a foreign virus. It infects everything it touches, leaving me shaky and unwell. "What did you do to us?" The question is aimed at Bloodgood, and it's she who answers.

"It'll numb your powers for a little while. The Reapers will be able to smell your Charm Levels, of course, but you won't have access to your power yourself."

"You…you took our powers away?" I whisper, wide-eyed. I immediately reach for my Light, my Shadow, *anything*. Only the whisper of what I had before remains.

"This is a punishment, Azalea. It's not meant to be pretty."

"Our punishment is death?" I laugh manically, heart racing in the face of horrific fear.

"Of course not. A team is waiting nearby to take care of any Reapers who may show." She says it so calmly, her hand waving as though my concern is dismissive.

"Let me guess: It's a team you chose?"

"Of course. I wanted professionals, after all." She wanted people who were willing to let me die.

"And what happens if a Grim finds out where I am?" I question breathlessly, not sure if I *want* Shayde to show up. I definitely don't want Grim Senior popping in for a surprise visit.

"Then we will kill it," she says on a shrug.

"You don't know how to kill a Grim," I say, laughing humor-ously again.

"No, but you know how to charm one." She smiles again, snap-ping her fingers. "Talk your way out of it, Azalea. From what I understand, you're good with your mouth." My cheeks blaze in embarrassment and anger, but it doesn't matter. I don't have a chance to mouth off, to show her *exactly* what good comes from my wicked mouth.

Ginny screams and cries as they throw me into the portal. The noises silence once I tumble into gooey darkness.

If a fucking Grim does show up, Dean Bloodgood better pray to whatever entity she thinks will help her the most that I don't decide to side with the evil beasts after this.

CHAPTER 20

"Our line has been blessed as Dual-Wielders. As Dimineers, we excel, but as Seers? As Seers, we *thrive*. We can live off the secrets our abilities provide us, off the hints we are blessed to be given. My prophecies have led me to many a poor soul: It's the easiest way to find someone to willingly turn, after all. Use your abilities to blend in, but also use them wisely. We are strong, we are glorious, and we are Grims.

Don't fuck it up."

—*The Grimoire*, written by the first, unnamed Grim, 1 A.G.

"**G**et it off, get it off, get it off!" Ginny screeches as she tumbles to the ground in front of me, fighting with a black ball on her chest.

"Grimsly!" I practically sigh in relief at the sight of the fickle creature, feeling safer already. "Where the fuck have you been all week?" For a cat whose sole purpose is supposed to be protecting me, he isn't very good at it.

"You're familiar with this…creature?" Ginny pants out, finally dislodging Grimsly from her chest. She manages to pull herself to her feet, dusting snow and dirt off her clothes with a scowl.

"That's my Scythe Partner." I sigh, crouching down and opening my arms. He leaps onto my chest with a howl, staring up at me with those insanely observant orange eyes.

"You have a Scythe Partner and didn't tell me?" Ginny cries, pointing at me accusingly.

"I didn't?" I scratch him behind the ears, daring a glance around. "Well, it doesn't matter right now, either way. We need to figure out where we are and what we are going to do when one of those fucking Reapers show up."

"Just one?" Ginny asks quietly.

"If we're lucky," I say, sighing heavily. "I can't tell where we are." We are surrounded by trees, but a walking trail leads toward a cabin in the distance, which I can barely make out. It's pretty warm and definitely not snowing here. My ears popped, I think, so that could mean we are in the mountains somewhere.

"Well, don't expect me to be any help on that front." She snorts, kicking at the ground. "I wasn't prepared for an excursion."

"Neither was I," I murmur, taking a step toward the walking trail.

Ginny scowls, hissing, "Are you joking? I'm in fuzzy pajamas and you're in full-on Conjurer gear. I think one of us was a little more prepared than the other."

"Yeah, well, I couldn't sleep," I lie, gesturing for her to follow me.

"You couldn't sleep, so you decided to get dressed for battle?"

"I couldn't sleep, so I decided to get dressed, period. I can wear what I want, you know? It doesn't always have to be those ugly uniforms." The short black skirts and matching vests, the white blouse whose buttons are pushed to their limits across my chest—yeah, we both know it's a decent excuse to wear something, *anything*, else.

"No, but it doesn't have to be battle gear, either. Who told you, and why didn't you tell *me*?"

"I had a bad dream," I say, refusing to turn around and look at her. "It freaked me out, so I got up and got dressed."

"Oh. I see." She doesn't. She can't. But it doesn't matter because she's here anyway.

"I'm sorry that I dragged you into this mess."

"Don't be. You aren't in this alone, Azalea. We all know what a bitch Bloodgood is. It's in everyone's best interest to not do things that are in *her* best interest." Ginny stomps loudly behind me, cracking sticks left and right. "Where are we going anyway?"

"That cabin," I say, pointing. It's closer now, probably a thirty-minute walk. "I figure it'll be easier to defend ourselves in an enclosed space where we can keep an eye on all the exits."

"Yeah, you're probably right." She falls silent for another five minutes before saying, "Why are they doing this?"

"Because I'm a Grim fucker." I turn back and flash her a self-deprecating smile. "Because I stood up to them and they didn't like that."

"You're the savior. It's your whole shtick. What did they expect you to do, lie down and take it?"

"Yeah, I'm more of an active participant."

Ginny laughs, saying, "Yeah, you've made that pretty clear."

"I don't know if they want me dead," I say quietly, turning back to glance at her again. "But if they do, then sending me to the middle of nowhere surrounded by Reapers without my powers would be the way to do it."

"I can't believe they took our powers." Ginny shakes her head, jogging to come by my side.

"Yeah, since when do Conjurers have potions? What the fuck was that?"

"We *don't* do potions. I've never heard of anything like that."

"Isn't that fantastic?" I say bitterly, glancing around when I hear the snap of a twig that wasn't caused by Ginny. "Could you be any louder? Aren't you highly trained for combat? Isn't being quiet on your to-do list for training?"

"Oh, hush." Ginny scowls at me, purposely taking another loud step. "I didn't—What is that?" Ginny points in the distance at a large black creature standing on its hind legs, giant paws swiping up at something in the trees.

"A bear," I say, raising an eyebrow. "You've never seen a bear?"

"We don't have bears." She scrunches her nose, watching it wearily.

"Just be quiet, okay? Don't draw its attention. Ignore it. If it comes near, we get out of its way. And if it decides we are a tasty meal, then I'll stab it." I pull out one of my daggers before handing it to her. "Or you will."

"You brought daggers? Azalea, how did you know—"

"I already told you, Ginny. Don't make me lie to you again, okay?"

"Right." She huffs, sending me a withering glare. "You're good at secrets, aren't you?"

"Let's not argue, okay? We are in some serious shit right now. And if this is how they decide to punish us every time we get penalties? Well, then, we'd better prepare to be dead before the end of our second year."

"I just don't get it," she says softly, glancing at me out of the corner of her eyes. "Aren't they worried Shayde will show up?"

"I think they're banking on it." I tilt my head back to look at the rising sun, swallowing hard.

"Will he kill you if he shows up?"

"I don't know." I don't know what's real anymore. I don't know who Shayde is or who I want him to be.

Slowly, softly, she says, "You've fought him a couple of times now. Has he ever gone for a death blow?"

"Not once," I whisper, refusing to look at her.

"He's still in love with you."

"Of course he is." I try to laugh, gesturing at my body. "Who wouldn't love this?"

"Azalea, please tell me you aren't still in love with him. I swear to the Grim, if you guys are still in a relationship and you're pulling me by the tail—"

"We aren't together, Ginny, don't worry. I'm with Jaymes now, remember?" I try not to sound bitter, but it comes out that way anyway.

"You *are* still in love with him." She groans, slapping her forehead and sliding her palm down her face. "That makes things awkward, doesn't it? Considering the mortal enemies aspect to this whole dynamic?"

"Ginny, I've had emotions like love for less than a year, okay? Give me a break. Have you ever tried to fall out of love before? It fucking sucks. *I'm trying.*"

"I know you are," she says softly, smiling gently. "I know you wouldn't let Demi's killer back into your life."

"Right." I clear my throat, continuing down the path. "I wouldn't dream of it." Except I *do*.

When we reach the cabin, the sun has fully risen. Reapers don't usually come out during the day, but from what I understand, they don't usually travel in packs either. I rush Ginny into the unlocked cabin, locking the door behind us and shoving a leather recliner in front of it.

"Now what?" she questions, glancing around. The cabin seems clean, though I have to admit the bear decor littering the kitchen and living room is overkill. Black bears fill paintings on the walls, images on the dish towels, and even the blankets sitting atop a softly lined gray couch. Accompanying them are black and red checkered towels and pillows. "This place is…" She trails off, wincing.

"Tacky?" I suggest with a scoff. I pick up a note from the wooden table as Grimsly jumps out of my arms, glancing down at the bold words in soft lettering accompanied by a heart drawn at the bottom of the page.

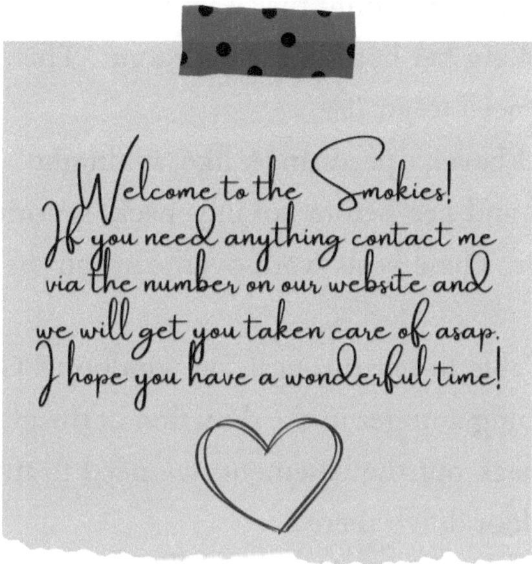

"Welcome to the Smokies. If you need anything, contact me via the number on our website and we will get you taken care of asap. I hope you have a wonderful time," I read aloud, groaning.

"The Smokies?" Ginny murmurs, walking deeper into the cabin to assess the situation. I watch Grimsly curl up on the couch, his soft purrs loud in the quiet of the cabin.

"It's in Tennessee. Apparently, I'm only allowed to visit Southern states," I say, tossing the note back down. "This must be one of those places families rent on vacation down here."

"People willingly come here? With their families?" She shudders, glancing at the horrifying decor again.

"Yeah, Reapers, bears, and all." I follow her into the living room. There's a wall of windows against the farthest wall, showing off a gorgeous view of the tops of trees. Great; we're close to the edge of a cliff. There's a set of stairs leading up and a set leading down, and a single bedroom off to the side.

"To be fair, it's really only the bears they know about," Ginny points out, poking her head in the bedroom. "There's a bathroom in here if you need to go."

"Ah, good. I haven't peed since, like, midnight." I wander into the bathroom and pee before coming back, ignoring the creepy bear comforter. These hosts went overboard on the theme, to say the least.

"They'll be able to get through the windows," Ginny says as I approach, jabbing a finger in the direction of the glass.

"Let's go check out the basement; we need to make sure there isn't another door down there."

We follow the staircase down into the basement, the chilly air hitting us quickly. There isn't a door as far as I can see, but there is a small swimming pool.

"Do you think it's heated?" Ginny murmurs, strutting forward and dipping her toe inside the clear water. "The answer to that is a resounding *no*."

"I wish we had a door to shut," I murmur, glancing around. There are a couple of chairs, but not enough to bar the doorway.

"Well, if we don't feel like being ambushed, down here's probably our best bet. One way in, one way out," she says confidently.

"Yep," I agree, plopping into one of the chairs. "The good news is we will hear one of those things long before they ever make it down here, and we have our own alarm system in the form of a hissing feline."

"The bad news?" She sits in the chair opposite me, leaning back with a sigh.

"If there isn't a team ready to dispatch, I can't kill it."

"Yeah, well, let's hope I was right about Shayde being in love with you still."

We fall silent, our bodies tense and our breaths light. We wait for hours, listening for any sign of an intruder. We never hear one. I go up to the kitchen after our stomach aches become too painful, but there isn't much in the cabinets. I find some stale crackers, a half-empty gallon of milk, and a jar of peanut butter. We split the jar, taking turns with a mostly clean spoon left in the dishwasher. The milk hadn't spoiled yet, so we sip on that, too. It's better than nothing, I guess.

"Why haven't they come yet?" Ginny asks when it hits nightfall, the sunlight streaming down the stairs now gone.

"I don't know," I say honestly, just as confused as her.

"Do you think they've been killing them outside as they show up?"

"No, I think Bloodgood would have wanted at least one to come in here and scare us."

"True." She falls silent for another moment before whispering, "Do you think Shayde knows you're here?"

"It's possible." I shift uncomfortably in my chair, eyes on the doorway. Dream Shayde had warned me about what was coming, knew what was about to happen. I finger the ring around my neck, contemplating. Is Dream Shayde a manifestation of my Seer abilities? Is it my mind's new way of relaying messages?

"Why did he attack the party that night?" Her voice is barely above a whisper as she fidgets uncomfortably in her seat.

"Ah, I don't know. Who am I to guess at a Grim's motivations?" *It wasn't him, it wasn't him, it wasn't him,* I scream in my mind.

"You don't think it was him, do you?"

I glance over at her, meeting her soft brown eyes. The rest of her is sharp, but her eyes? They are the softest feature she owns. "And if I don't?"

"Then I think you really *are* still in love with him," Ginny says with a sneer. I scoff, glancing at the doorway again. Grimsly still hasn't come down here, which is probably a good sign. He must not detect any threats if he isn't worried about my safety.

"I just—" I stop, shaking my head. "What I think doesn't matter. I don't think Shayde or his father want me dead. Shayde still thinks he has a chance and his dad…well, he thinks I'm going to be the mother of the next Grim."

"That's so…disturbing to think about." Ginny scrunches her nose, making a disgusted face. "Do you think they come out with the antlers?"

I laugh, shaking my head. "Of course not. Their bodies are as normal as ours. From what I've gathered, they don't get their Grim power until they are like twelve or something."

"Ah. Like Conjurers," she says with a nod, watching me too closely. "Do you want to have his kids?"

"What I want doesn't matter, I'll never have kids."

"Why not?"

"I can't." I shrug, pointing at my stomach. "I don't have my tubes anymore." Neil and I were trying to have kids early on in our marriage, and one of my failed pregnancies ended up being ectopic. I ruptured one tube, and the other was infected. So… bye-bye tubes, I suppose. It ruined my marriage, but I think it may have saved my life. If I were to have a kid right now with two Grims on the hunt…

"Oh. Oh, Azalea, I'm—"

"Don't say you're sorry. It isn't a big deal, really." Except for Conjurers, it *is*.

"You aren't sad about it?"

"No, I don't think so," I say, glancing her way again. "I've never had motherly instincts."

"But the Grim—Shayde's dad, I mean—he thinks you can have kids still?"

"Shayde lied to him."

"To keep you alive," Ginny whispers, eyes wide. "So he wouldn't kill you for being the savior. He thinks it will be worth keeping you around."

"The two of us having a kid? That would more than likely produce an astronomical amount of power in one person."

"Oh, Azalea, he's obsessed with you, isn't he? What are you going to do?"

"The only thing I know *to* do: Kill him." I try not to flinch when I say it, but I think it only results in my face being pinched.

"Azalea…"

I sigh, plucking up my courage as I grind out, "Listen, Ginny, this is the last time I want to talk about this, okay? I'm the savior according to all these prophecies everyone's been jabbering on about. You know what that means? That means I have to save people. My destiny has already been written in the stars. I'm supposed to kill the Grims to save everyone else. What happened between Shayde and me…" I stop, wiping at my mouth to hide the whimper that escapes. "It's a damn travesty. But I have a job to do. A world to save. I fell head over heels in love with a Grim because he was the first person to show me any affection, the first person to make me *feel*. So, yeah, I fell for him, and yes, I'm still brokenhearted. But I'm not going to allow myself to love him. Because if I allow myself to love him, to want him, then I'll go running back into his arms and damn the entire world when I do."

The two of us fall quiet, and Ginny never responds. We don't speak again until Grimsly comes bounding down the stairs, leaping into my arms with a loud *meow* that makes me wince. Following him are two Conjurers, both scowling at us. They weren't at Draxmere this morning, but it's clear whose side they are on in this situation.

They lead us to a portal in the floor above us, silent and brooding. We are shoved through with little mercy, and I almost swallow a lung full of goo at the suddenness. But then we emerge at Draxmere, Dean Bloodgood waiting for us at the dragon fountain in the front courtyard where we left her.

"It seems the Reapers weren't interested in the bait we offered today," she says through clenched teeth, clearly trying to keep her composure. "Do you know anything about that, Azalea?"

"Why would I?" I stare her down unabashedly, waiting for her to question me. To accuse me of what I know she's thinking.

"If we find out you've been in contact with the Grim…" She pauses, watching me carefully. "Well, we won't need Reapers to dish out our punishment."

"Read my mail," I say blandly, grabbing Ginny by the hand and tugging her along. "I'm sure you'll find the love letters you're looking for there."

Ginny struggles to hide her laugh, shaking her head lightly. Dean Bloodgood is enraged simply by the fact that we don't *get* mail. And even if we did, Shayde wouldn't be stupid enough to communicate through a way that could be tracked.

He'd find a way to communicate secretly.

CHAPTER 21

"And if a savior cannot learn,
if a friend cannot forgive,
our world won't just burn:
She'll reap it until it ends.
—Continued prophecy found inside Seer Abraham Delowosky's
prophetic journals, 377 A.G."

Within a month of the new school year, I have been sent to the human world six times: once alone, once with each Thatcher sister, and twice with Ginny. As far as I'm aware, no one else has been sent out into combat. And all six times…not a single Reaper has shown its ugly face. Each time I'm sent somewhere new, always secluded and always in a Southern state. My best guess? They don't want me anywhere that would make me smile.

Poor Willow was terrified when we were sent out into the field, but I did my best to reassure her there was nothing to worry about since that was the one trip they left us with our powers. I'm a Dimineer *and* an Illuminoor; I can set a trap and kill a Reaper before it has a chance to hurt her. Plus, with her ear-piercing screams, she can easily distract the thing while I blast it. Of course, having a plan is one thing; executing it is another. Reapers are, as a whole, terrifying for the average person. Yes, it's what we are being trained for. Yes, they don't scare me the way they do others. And yes, that all means jack shit when you are being overwhelmed and people around you are dropping like flies. After fighting our way out of that graduation battle a few months ago, everyone is a little scared of how many Reapers may appear at any given time and whether or not a Grim will be accompanying them.

I'm not cut out for comforting people, though. After the third time Willow sought reassurance, I kind of snapped and said some pretty mean things. She's still a little angry about that, I think. Ginny is, too, if her constant glares are any indication. I don't know what they expected out of me, though. I'm not the snugly, tell you everything will be alright kind of gal. I'm honest and mean, which is no fault of mine.

On top of the field punishments, Dean Bloodgood has also assigned me to cleaning duty. So far I've had to dive into the Olympic sized pool to clean a million little pieces of confetti out after a party by *hand*, scrub the necromancers horrid-smelling, nightmare-inducing white room with a toothbrush two separate times after training sessions, prepare the vampire blood vials (which resulted in my being covered in fucking blood for *hours* after spilling it several times), and clean up the dining hall three nights a week (a disgusting task to do without using Charms because these students leave blood and raw meat and trash *everywhere*).

All of the small tasks I've done distract me from schoolwork, and I've fallen behind considering every class has doubled the coursework. I get punished every day in Combat Training, even after Ginny and I decided just to hit each other on the mat and get it out of the way on the days we spar. They still pair us up some days, but after we gave up being nice, they didn't care anymore. I didn't train over the summer break, and my muscles hate me for it. I've lost a small amount of weight since coming to this school, but mostly gained muscle, and this amount of training is not for the weak. I've been left heaving off to the side of the mat several times, my body too new at this level of physicality to keep up. I get a penalty every time I dry heave, and two every time it's more than dry.

During all of these punishments, Bloodgood hasn't made an appearance. It seems her work balance isn't going as well as she hoped because most days she disappears entirely. Today is the first day I've seen her since she first sent me out into the human world, and her pure white suit mocks me from the gym floor for this assembly. That woman is anything *but* pure.

"How's Grimsly?" I glance over at the sound of the light voice, taking in fox hair briefly before glancing away.

"He likes to stay in my room and sulk because I'm not there. That is when he's not disappearing entirely," I say, and Dagan chuckles under his breath. "What are you doing over here? Shouldn't you be sitting with the first years?"

"I missed you," he says plainly, patting my thigh. "I've hardly seen you this entire month."

"I thought you were avoiding me," I murmur, watching as the rest of the Light Faction council enters the gym.

"Why would I avoid you?" He runs a hand through his orange, black, and cream hair, following my line of sight.

"Because of Jaymes." When he still looks confused, I add, "You have a thing for him."

"Ah, sure, but who doesn't? I can't blame anyone for climbing that tree if they were presented with the opportunity to do so." He cackles, the familiar noise bringing my lips into a lopsided smile.

"I've also been busy being punished." I lean back into the empty seat behind me. I got here early to observe the faction members' interactions, but most students are still trickling in.

"Yeah, I heard. I've gotten my fair share of penalties, but the things they're making you do? It's just plain nasty." He shakes his head, strands of hair falling into his face.

"Yeah, well, I wouldn't expect anything less than nasty from that particular Bloodgood. You may not want to be seen talking to me. She'll take things out on you next."

"Let her." He scoffs in the dean's direction, blowing his hair out of the way. "I'm not easily spooked."

"Mmm, yeah, I guess all the dead people will do that to you, won't they?"

"Something like that." He cackles again, and this time the subtle hint of maliciousness sends a chill running down my spine.

"Dagan," Jaymes greets, eyes roaming his body before flicking over to me. "What are you doing over here?"

"Visiting Azalea." He dismisses Jaymes with a glance, eyes now locked onto the Shadow Faction council members walking through the door.

"I told you not to—"

"I know what you told me," he says blandly, turning to raise an eyebrow at Jaymes. "I think you'll find that I don't listen to rules very often."

"What did he tell you not to do?" I question, squinting my eyes at Dagan.

"Don't—" Jaymes starts, but Dagan doesn't give a shit what Jaymes has to say about this.

"He told me not to hang out with you because his mom will punish me, but I don't give a rat's ass about that. I usually don't see you, anyway, but I'm not going to purposely ignore you just because Jaymes has a hero complex."

"Dagan—"

"You think you have the right?" I hiss at Jaymes, interrupting whatever he was about to say.

"You are *mine* to protect now," he snarls, leaning down to get in my face. Then he glances over at Dagan as though to say, "So is he." It seems as though Jaymes hasn't forgotten the deal he struck with Dagan's father.

I stand, glaring up into his beautifully bright green eyes. "I am no one's property."

"You agreed—"

"I agreed that you can try to protect me," I say, jabbing a finger into his chest. "I agreed that you can take care of me. I agreed because I felt fucking vulnerable, and I still do, but being vulnerable doesn't equate to being owned. I am not *yours*."

"Then whose are you, hmm? *Shayde's*? Do I need to remind you how *that* turned out?"

"That's uncalled for," Dagan defends me, standing up to his full height. He's still shorter than Jaymes, but he's very much taller than me.

Jaymes's eyes flick over to Dagan, and his bravado falters briefly, his mouth opening and closing before he breathes harshly out of his nose and meets my gaze again. "I want what's best for you."

"I know," I say, because I do. "But that doesn't mean you get to dictate my actions, or the actions of my friends. It doesn't mean you get to control my life. It doesn't mean you get to be an asshole just because you aren't getting your way."

Jaymes wraps an arm around my waist and pulls me into him, leaning down and pressing his forehead to mine. "I'm sorry."

"You should be." I press my hands to his chest and allow him to hold me, to touch me, because I want this so bad. A year ago, I wouldn't have been craving human touch, comfort, or friendship. I wouldn't crave normalcy the way I do now. But Jaymes is what I have left of Shayde, as horrible as that sounds. Jaymes is familiar, warm, and *here*.

His lips brush against mine, the touch light and soft. I wish my stomach would flip at least once or that desire would race through me the way it always did with Shayde. I wish that I could use Jaymes to move on, to fuck, to forget. But his touch won't erase Shayde's, and his lips won't, either.

"Hello, Draxmere Academy," Dean Bloodgood calls, pointedly clearing her throat. Jaymes holds me for a second longer, fingers gripped on my chin as he presses another chaste kiss to my lips. The two of us sit down, his hand twisting in mine. I sigh softly, eyes widening when Dagan takes my hand, too.

"I can be here for you, too, Azalea. You don't have to be alone," he whispers in my ear, squeezing gently. "I won't even make you pretend to date me."

"I'm not…"

"You are. I barely know you, Azalea, but I can see the ghosts in your eyes. You're trying to make yourself feel things you aren't ready to feel. That isn't how emotions work, sweetie. You don't get to choose how quickly you develop feelings, and you certainly don't get to choose how quickly you rid yourself of them."

I don't reply to *that* analysis, my back tensing. Instead, I say, "Thanks for the offer."

I watch Bloodgood's eyes flick over to us, narrowing as she continues, saying, "We are gathered here to discuss your options in the coming months when it comes to choosing a faction. December first is your deadline, which means you have just three months to make a decision. Some of you may have already decided, particularly those of you who were supposed to choose at the end of your first year and didn't get the chance to. Today, the factions and their leaders have gathered to present themselves to you. This will be more of a Q and A type of meeting, but we will hold two more meetings that will get into the nitty gritty details of it all. As most of you know, I am the Light Faction leader, Leader Bloodgood, AKA your dean." A few chuckles sound, but most students are alarmingly silent.

"My name is Leader Fellows." The familiar man steps forward, dark skin with even darker tattoos bulging underneath his casual t-shirt depicting a bloody dagger and the large bold words "we fight or we die" across the front. His bald head gleams underneath the blaring lights, and I quickly drag my attention down to the glasses falling off his crooked nose to avoid the glare. "I am the Shadow Faction leader." Four people flank him, two of whom I know to be Nox's parents. I'm not sure which ones, though, because Demi never pointed them out specifically.

I flinch at the thought of Demi, turning my eyes instead to Arlo's parents next to Bloodgood. His dad is her second, if I remember correctly. The one who's supposed to be ruling things in her place while she's here. "Today's discussion is going to be a deep one: The Grims. The Light and Shadow Factions are working together to make a united decision, but we are still split on the subject. So, let's discuss it with you, the very people who will be affected by this decision. The Grims gave us an ultimatum last year during graduation: Let them take over the human world to save our world, or fight, and we all die."

"Fighting doesn't mean death," Fellows interrupts, glaring at her and pushing his glasses back up to sit on his nose. His brown eyes are hard, his lips pursed.

"No, I suppose not," she corrects herself, giving him a placating smile. "But with two Grims, it isn't bold of me to make assumptions."

"One Grim was here for years living right underneath y'alls noses and it didn't change a *thing*," I mutter under my breath, pulling my hands into my lap.

"Are you seriously defending him right now?" Jaymes hisses under his breath, and I can feel the glare hitting my cheek.

"No, just stating facts."

"It is just facts," Dagan agrees, not taking his eyes off our leaders.

"The Light Faction's stance on this is well known: We say give up the humans."

"The Shadow Faction says we should fight." Fellows steps forward, waving his large arms around to gesture at us all. "We as a whole know what we signed up for when we chose our career paths. We knew the danger that becoming a Conjurer would expose us to. We knew, and yet we still chose to be here."

"How often have you asked yourself what the point of all of this is?" Bloodgood shouts, holding her hands out placatingly.

"How often have we thought, 'Will this fight ever end?' Well, we don't have to do that anymore! War means sacrifice! War means compromise! We don't get to save everyone. I don't live in a fairy tale world where that happens, and neither should you. And, from what I've heard, sacrificing the humans wouldn't be that great of a loss in the end."

Leader Fellows cuts in now, booming out, "We have someone here, in this room, who knows exactly what goes on in the human world. Who was raised there, has lived there, and knows exactly what kind of loss it would be. Who knows that there are more innocents than there are guilty, that there are children we would be condemning to death. Who chose to leave them and join us so they could fight in the war and hopefully change the tide. They chose this life to save the very people you say don't deserve to live!" I sink as far as I can without being inconspicuous, groaning quietly. He makes it sound like my choice was a choice at all. Like I wasn't a selfish bitch who was looking for my next fix. He makes me sound like...*like a savior*. I guess that's the point.

"Yes, and that same person almost condemned us all with their relationship with our greatest, oldest enemy." Bloodgood watches me intently, and I raise both my middle fingers silently to piss her off. Beside me, Dagan does the same.

"You're so getting punished," I snicker, watching the leader's cheeks flare red.

"We aren't here to condemn our own," Fellows fires back. "Especially not when that person could be our only hope to finally end this war."

"This is a conversation for a private meeting among the factions," she replies steadily, taking a deep breath before a bright smile animates her face. "But, now that we have presented our stand on the matter, it's time we take questions. We want you to think critically, to ask questions so you know exactly what kind of decision you will be making when you choose a side."

"Exactly right, Leader Bloodgood. We know how important this is, and we know what a critical time this is to be making the decision. So, please, raise your hands and ask anything." Fellows waits patiently for a few silent seconds, but no one raises their hands. So I do. "Azalea Jinx." He smirks, probably because he knows anything that comes out of my mouth is going to be a challenge to Bloodgood.

"What happens when they get tired of the humans? What happens when that world is overrun with Reapers who can't feed anymore because, quite simply, there are no humans left?"

Dagan coughs beside me, eyes wide. "That's a damn good question," he says, clapping me on the back enthusiastically.

"Great question, Azalea. Leader Bloodgood, would you care to elaborate?" Fellows is grinning like a lunatic, clearly pleased.

"It is a great question, Azalea. And, to put it quite simply, it would take a very long time for that to happen. It's a problem to discuss in a century or so when that seems more probable." Bloodgood's jaw ticks, and she moves to tuck a stray strand of white-blond hair behind her ear.

"So your solution is that it's a problem for our grandchildren, or great-grandchildren?" Dagan shouts, eliciting cries of outrage among the crowd.

"That's no solution at all!" someone calls, and many shouts follow.

"We must think about ourselves right now, and we must consider whether or not we will be able to create a future with that possibility at all. If we choose to ignore the Grims' demands, then we may never have the chance to have great-grandchildren. It's a risk our faction is willing to take at this point in time."

Rapid-fire questions come after that, most poking holes in the plans the Light Faction is trying to create. I zone out after a while, then stand to slip out silently after thirty minutes go by. Jaymes tries to stop me with a tug of his hand, but I jerk away without looking and stride out confidently, hands shoved down into my skirt pockets.

"We are not done here, Azalea Jinx," Bloodgood calls behind me.

"I'm done," I say, pausing at the door. "I'd rather spend my time somewhere doing something more productive."

"If you leave, I will forgo penalties and dive straight into punishments."

"Go ahead." I tilt my head back over my shoulder, giving her a secretive smile. "We both know you were going to do that anyway." I flip her off a second time, shoving the door open and striding out. I walk only a few doors down, opening a familiar one on my right and slipping inside. Then, I sit in the comfortable chair behind the chaotic desk and I wait.

"Azalea Jinx."

I sigh, spinning around as the door slams open an hour later. "My name coming from your mouth doesn't give me the rush I usually prefer."

"Get out of my chair."

"I kind of like it, though." I do another spin, smirking cockily. "Besides, who's going to make me move? You?"

"I'm a lot stronger than you are, Azalea," Bloodgood seethes, nostrils flaring.

"But are you more powerful?" I spin a name plate in my hand, turning my back to her again to prove a point. The truth is, I'm untrained. Undisciplined. She could probably wipe the floor with me if she wanted. But I have raw power, and a lot of it. I'm not sure who would win this battle, but we both know I'd have a damn good shot at it.

"Did you need something or are you here to bother me?" She crosses her arms across her chest, glaring.

"I had more questions that couldn't be answered in front of a crowd," I say with a shrug, facing her fully.

"By all means." She waves her hand and scoffs, waiting.

"Why do you hate me?"

"I don't hate you." She strides over and sits in one of the chairs across from me, raising a perfectly arched brow. "I hate what you represent."

"Hope?" I laugh, shaking my head. "Since I've come to this damn school everyone has acted as though my presence means better times. Why is that so bad?"

"Because it isn't true."

"The prophecies claim—"

"Azalea, I'm not going to groom you for delusion like Delarosa did. I'm not going to lie to you and tell you that you are our only saving grace. You're not. Sure, there are a lot of prophecies that say you will save us. There are also just as many that say you'll kill us all."

"What?" I drop the nameplate, heart racing. *She's lying.* She has to be.

"See, no one's mentioned that little fact, have they? Everyone tries to tell you that you are destined for greatness, but the truth is that no one knows what you're destined for. The prophecies are vague, as though they can't really see your future. Do you know why that is?" I swallow, shaking my head and shrugging. Her eyes narrow, and my heart leaps. *She knows.*

"Why would no one tell me?"

"Ignorance means plausible deniability. If you only see yourself as a kind, heroic savior, then how could you ever go dark? If you truly believe yourself to be our only hope, then why would you make a decision that would risk the entire world?"

"I'm not ignorant anymore," I say bitterly, clenching my fists in my lap. "Why would you tell me?"

"Because I don't believe in that bullshit." She leans forward, whispering over the desk, "I don't believe that hiding the truth will make you a good person. In fact, I'm not sure there's any good inside you. I mean, what kind of savior sleeps with the very person they are supposed to kill?"

"I didn't know," I say defensively, clenching my teeth.

She smiles gently, chuckling softly under her breath. "But you do now. Tell me, how tempted are you to go running back into the Grim's arms?"

"Temptation has no hold over me." I stand, moving to leave, but her next words make me pause.

"Deny, deny, deny. It's your only defense in all of this, isn't it? *I didn't know, I don't want him, I don't communicate with him.* Is *any* of it true?"

"What is truth but a careful balance of lies?" I look at her innocently under my lashes, feeling triumphant when Light crackles at her fingertips. I continue my path toward the door, freezing with my hand on the knob. "Does Jaymes know?"

"Of course he does. Didn't you ever wonder why he hated you so much when you first met?"

"How did you know—"

"I know a lot of things about a lot of things. Go talk to my son, Azalea Jinx, and let me know how bitter the taste of betrayal is."

I swallow hard, forcing my tone into one of boredom and nonchalance. "I've already tasted it, actually; it's just as horrible as I'd expected it to be."

CHAPTER 22

"Is it worth saving, is it worth the time?
Is it worth her living, is it worth her lies?
She questions and seeks answers,
she fights and receives truth.
In the wake of clarity with her romancer,
she'll find a reason to save *you*."
—Prophecy found inside Seer Margery Frazier's prophetic journals,
2013 A.G.

I didn't want to ask Jaymes about the prophecies, so I left well enough alone. Jaymes doesn't share the same sentiments, though.

"You talked to my mother?" He blasts a sphere of Light at me, and I form a shield with my own, the ball bouncing back toward him at record speed. He dodges, and the ball hits the tree behind him, rattling the trunk so hard I hear a crack.

"Wonderful job, Azalea!" Professor Battle calls in the distance, but I'm too annoyed with Jaymes to care.

"So what if I did?" I scowl, blasting a half-hearted beam in his direction. "How do you know about that, anyway?"

"Nox saw you leaving." He throws back his own beam, the two slamming into each other with a force so strong that I stumble back. I grit my teeth, shoving as hard as I can, but it still isn't enough to defeat someone like Jaymes. "Want to tell me what you talked about?"

"If I did, I would have told you already."

"I tried to give you some space, Azalea, but you're going to have to talk to me."

"No, I'm not."

"That's always your first move, isn't it? You're so fucking predictable." He laughs humorlessly, pushing so hard that my Light tapers off and I fall to the ground. The beam streams over my head, tumbling into the distance to find another victim. "You can never just open up; you always have to force us to figure out what's going on inside your head. You always fucking hide things!"

"So do you, apparently," I snarl, rubbing my throbbing hip from the fall.

"She told you about the prophecies, didn't she?" He goes from angry to resigned so fast that I hardly see it.

"Hmm, what gave it away? Is the evil inside me extra present today?"

"You aren't evil, Azalea." He's slowly pushing forward, leaving me no choice but to retreat lest I be hit head-on.

"I didn't think Shayde was, either, but here we are."

"This is different. *You* are different." Another step forward, followed by my step back. A dance that the two of us know well by now.

"Am I? Shayde and I are two kids living in our parents' shadows, doing our best to be just like them. We are powerful Dual-Wielders who have been ostracized by the people around us. We are sad, lonely creatures who just want *help*. When you put it on paper, Jaymes, we aren't very different at all." I don't say I'm a triple-Wielder because I haven't had a single prediction dream since coming to Draxmere, other than the weird Shayde dreams, and I'm not entirely sure it counts anymore.

"You never said you wanted help. That you were lonely or sad," he whispers, so close that he now reaches for me. I let him hold my cheek, glaring into his magnetizing eyes.

"I was *screaming* for help, Jaymes. I was doing drugs and drinking, I was taking pills to put myself to sleep, I was dreaming about Shayde because my mind was desperate to cling to the person I thought I knew. And I thought you understood when you brought me to your home, when you took care of me, when you offered to protect me. But I don't think you understand at all."

"Make me understand," he begs, his face open and vulnerable in a way I never see in anyone else. "Tell me what to do to help you. To make this better. To make you see that you aren't evil."

Shayde would have already known, I think, but don't say.

"I can't tell you because there is *nothing* in this world that will make this feeling go away. Nothing that will make things better. Can you bring Demi back? Can you go back in time and convince Shayde not to fucking stab me in the heart? Can you convince me that Seers are ever wrong?"

"I don't know what to say. What to do," he whispers, pressing his forehead against mine.

"Just be my friend, Jaymes. Not my boyfriend or my protector. I just...I just want you. I don't want all that egotistical protective bullshit you've been doing since we got to Draxmere. I tried to let it happen, to be okay with it, because I just wanted to be taken care of. But being here, being punished every week, being forced to study ten times more than everyone else…I've realized that the only person who can take care of me is myself." I can't keep pretending to be okay with his behavior, but I can't pretend I don't need him, either. I have no one else to lean on, despite what Dagan and the others say. They don't understand like Jaymes does. They don't get the absolute madness that Shayde will drive you to. The madness that still consumes me.

"Okay," he whispers before joking, "Does that mean no more kissing?"

"When I want a kiss, I'll ask for one." I smile, the tension that has been sitting inside me for the past four days finally releasing.

"I can live with that," he says, smiling back. "Do you want me to tell people we broke up?"

"I don't give a shit what people think," I say truthfully, shrugging out of his grip. "Tell them or don't. I don't care. We know the truth, and that's all that matters."

"Then I won't. I know that it doesn't offer you much protection, but what little it does…" He trails off, shrugging. "I think it's worth not letting people know the truth."

"I can live with that," I repeat his sentiments from earlier, pausing before saying, "I'm sorry I can't let it be real."

"I know I told you before I wasn't going to interfere until you'd figured out what's going on between you and Shayde, but…sometimes it's really hard not to give in. Hard to not pursue you the way I want, to give you all of me like I want you to give me all of you."

"I can't go back to Shayde," I whisper, truthful once again. "Despite what my dreams say. I won't. Maybe one day, when this isn't all so…so *fresh*, we can try for real."

"If we don't die?" he asks, smiling sadly.

"We won't die. I'm the savior, remember?" I smile, too, lips dropping as I realize something. "You never told her that I might be a Seer. You never got me into classes."

"When I realized who the dean was…" He doesn't say anything else, mostly because he doesn't need to.

"A bitch?" I fill in, grinning when he chokes on a laugh.

"Exactly that," he agrees, reaching out to squeeze my hand. "I'm glad you came into my life, Azalea Jinx."

I beam up at him, smirking as I say, "I'm glad you pulled me into it."

The next day, I don't wake up in my bed.

"What the—" I murmur, my vision blurry and my mind racing. My hands are tied above my head, my body dangling just low enough for my toes to graze the ground. Pain wracks through my shoulders, wave after wave rolling by. I'm fairly certain my shoulders are dislocated, and I breathe deeply as I try not to let my thoughts linger on it.

"Look who's finally awake," a cold voice calls from somewhere behind me, an unrecognizable entity that jars me into full consciousness.

"Where am I?" I try to use my powers, but I can't feel them there. Fucking Grim. *They drugged me.*

"An undisclosed location."

"Real helpful," I hiss, glancing around. The walls and floor are concrete, the light gray below me stained dark in large splotches that look horrifyingly like the color of blood. And Grimsly…my Grimsly isn't here. He doesn't know where here is, doesn't know how to find me. Or…or have they locked him up somewhere, too, in anticipation of this? If they hurt my Grimsly…

"I'm not here to be helpful." The man moves to stand in front of me, his cold gray eyes watching me with a hateful glare. His pointy nose jabs forward as he leans into my face, thin lips curling up menacingly. I can see every wrinkle in his forehead, every crinkle around his eyes, every gray hair on his balding head. "I'm here to get information."

"Ah." I lean away. The chains dangle me barely above the ground, and my toes drag backward. Pain jerks through my shoulders again, and I have to bite down on my lip to keep from crying out. "Good luck."

He chuckles, pressing down his sleek black suit as though worried about wrinkles. "I don't need luck, Azalea Jinx. I just need *you.*"

"I don't know what you mean." The dim lighting makes his light skin even lighter, and for a moment, I imagine him as a ghost in my dreams, another figment of my imagination.

"Where is the Grim located?" His face has turned alarmingly delighted, a hand twitching over a dagger fastened to a sheath on his side.

He's about to torture me, isn't he? Oh fuck, he definitely is. "Which one?" I smirk, heart pounding.

"Let me make this quite clear." He surges forward and grabs me by the throat, dragging me near until he's so close that his breath slaps against my face. "We can do this the easy way or the hard way. The hard way involves *your* blood forming new stains on *this* floor. The easy way involves you walking out unharmed."

"These are the only choices you people ever offer, aren't they? Always easy or hard. Never a nice medium-paced way." I'm rewarded for the sarcasm with the hardest punch I've ever received to my gut. I cough and sputter, struggling to breathe.

"I'm so glad you chose the hard way," he says with a malicious smile, letting go of my throat. I swing back unceremoniously, still struggling with unproductive, gasping breaths. My arms are becoming numb, a slow tingling rising in the limbs. But that pain in my shoulders...*that* still remains. "I was told you were known for disobedience. *I can't wait to break you.*"

"I'm already broken." He doesn't like that answer, so he punches me in the jaw this time instead. Pain blossoms in my face, the sensation only briefly drowning out the pain in my shoulders and gut. My body can't decide which one to focus on, and each area aches in flashes.

"Where is the Grim?" he repeats, snarling at me. Blood trickles out of my mouth and down my chin, but I stay silent. I receive another punch as recognition of that silence. "Where is the Grim?"

More blood fills my mouth, and I can't help but release a gurgling laugh. I laugh until I can no longer breathe, until the blood has dried and I don't see red. Until my vision is blurry and I think for one brief, blessed moment that I am going to pass out.

"Care to tune me in to the joke?"

"You wouldn't get it," I say, turning my own glare to him. "Ignorance isn't a good look, you know? Has anyone ever told you how unattractive stupidity really is?"

"You know where the Grim is." He ignores my jabs, grabbing me by the throat and squeezing hard. "Tell me."

"I wish I did know," I rasp, not letting my eyes leave his. "Because if I did, I would go kill the motherfucker myself."

"Liar!"

A punch to the gut, a kick to the back, and a hair pull later, he's gotten no further into his questioning. I vomit once onto the ground below me, just off to the side of where he stands. It's mostly liquid, but it was enough to splatter onto his shoes and give me brief satisfaction. "Do I need to move on to different methods?" he questions, smiling as he cracks his fingers ominously.

"Do what you want," I croak, my entire body screaming in pain. My arms are long past numb, my toes rubbed raw. I'm only wearing the thin camisole I went to bed in, and the draft in this place has me shivering. The pain could be helping with that, though.

"So glad to hear you say that."

I finally release a scream when he reaches up and snaps the first finger. I scream again when he does the second one just for fun.

"I don't know where he is," I snarl, grunting when I accept another punch to the gut. The consequential swing of my body leaves my shoulder screaming, leaves the darkness I crave just out of my reach. "I haven't seen him in months."

"But you have seen him?"

"Everyone knows he attacked me twice over the summer. It's common knowledge," I pant, wishing beyond anything that I could summon even an ounce of power to blast him with.

He grips my chin, forcing me to look into his cold gray eyes. "I'm not talking about the supposed *attacks*. I'm talking about visits outside of the little show you two have been putting on."

I stare back, just as cold, just as deadly. With a bloody smile, I say, "Besides in my dreams?" That earns me a whole handful of broken fingers.

"*The truth!*" Spittle flies from his lips, his anger palpable. "The truth will set you free."

"My powers would set me free," I say calmly, doing my best to ignore the fiery pain radiating from my hand down the entire length of my previously numb arm. "But you were too much of a coward to let me keep those, weren't you?"

"Such a smart mouth," he purrs, running a thumb down my lips. "Such pretty lips."

"Useful, too," I say before spitting the biggest blob of saliva I can, a good amount of my blood mixed in with it. "I hope I have some dormant disease that I just passed on to you."

"How thoughtful," he says, sighing and wiping his face lightly. "Alright. I guess I'll move on to a different method, then. We do have all day together, after all."

The man pulls the dagger I spotted earlier from the sheath at his side, and I eye it warily. "That thing got Light imbued in it? Because if it does—" I fall silent when the cold blade touches my neck, feeling a cut form as he presses into my skin with just enough pressure to cause blood to emerge.

"Speak again, and I will make sure this dagger does more than just cut you." He pulls it away slowly, grinning as he says, "Oh, and if you scream, I'll add on to your punishment."

I watch with wide eyes as he slowly crouches, dragging the dagger down with him. The light touch doesn't cut me, but it does unnerve me. Then, with a harsh grip, he grabs my left thigh and begins to slice. I grimace and whimper, tears eventually falling out of my eyes involuntarily, but I don't scream again. I won't give him the satisfaction of seeing me cave, of seeing me break. After he carves the first letter, I tilt my head back so I don't have to look. I stare at the ceiling, wishing that it would be over. Wishing I could find it in me to escape inside my mind and never emerge again.

"The first word is done, do you want to see?" he mocks from below, tapping me with the pointed tip of the blade. I don't respond at first and he continues, saying, "You can speak for now."

"No, thanks. I trust my artists," I whisper through the tears, keeping my head tilted back to stare at my broken and bruised fingers. This position makes my shoulders ache in a new way, but at this point, what on me doesn't ache? My vision faded in and out as he cut, but the darkness refused to consume me.

"*Look.*" The one word has me snapping my head back down in a moment of consciousness, his tone not one to question. I'm not in a situation to defy him—that's been made clear.

"Grim." The one word breaks as it crosses my lips, and I close my eyes tightly. He said the *first* word is done.

"You like that nickname, don't you? *Grim fucker?*"

"*Fuck you,*" I seethe, jerking against my restraints. "That Grim fucks better than you on his worst days."

"Want to put that to the test?" He drops the dagger abruptly, standing so quickly that I don't have time to see the slap coming. "I don't think you realize what kind of position you're in right now."

"I understand completely. It's you who doesn't understand the situation." I smile cruelly, leaning forward as best I can. "If Shayde finds out what you've done to me…" I pause to relish the fear that briefly flashes in his eyes before the coldness seeps back in. "And if he leaves you alive, then you can fucking *bet* I won't."

"You think you're that important to him? That he would care about you that much, even after you betrayed him?" The necklace around my neck feels so heavy now, the reminder of exactly what I mean to Shayde constricting my air flow.

"No, but you do," I whisper, wishing I could scratch the itch on my face. "Otherwise, I wouldn't be here."

He snarls, hand around his belt, "Do you think he will still want you after I'm through with you? Do you think he'll appreciate you once you're broken?" With a snap, the belt is out of his pants, the *crack* from his swift movement making me flinch.

I laugh, unable to help myself. "I'm already broken. Anything you can do to me is nothing compared to what I've done to myself."

I scream when the belt comes slapping down without restraint, both thighs now aching.

"What did I say about screaming?" He slaps me again, this time on the hip, and I have to bite my lip to keep from crying out. Blood instantly pools out of my bottom lip, but I don't release it in case a lingering whimper tries to escape. "Where is your Grim now, Azalea? Where is *your* savior?"

His words have a flash of Shayde filling my vision, and with a sudden agony, my entire body stiffens and convulses. My head pounds, my surroundings fade, and my body becomes weightless. In front of me is no longer a damp basement but an open field; a dozen or so Conjurers surround a door leading somewhere underground. From the shadows, I see a giant pair of antlers and a set of soulless eyes. When the Grim steps out into the open, the Conjurers begin to scream. They blast, they fight, they die. No one can touch Shayde, and not a single Reaper steps out of the woods to aid their master. It's like…he didn't bring any. Wherever this is.

With a gasp, I'm thrown out of the vision, my gaze homing in on the man in front of me. My body is more sore than before, indicating I've been hit a few more times. But as I look at him, realization hits me so hard I jerk. I laugh, the sound rough and hysterical. The man pauses, seething at the audacity.

"You got a dozen guards up there, don't you?" I question between breathless laughs, feeling the tingle of power awakening inside my system.

"How did you—"

I don't let him finish his sentence, warming my entire body with Light instead. I don't have my hands to aim, don't have a conduit to get out the energy that's hit me so hard I convulse, but I force it to leave me anyway. My entire body is consumed in heat and white light, and I hear my captor scream and stumble back. The chains above me crack and snap with a force so strong I have no time to catch myself. I fall to my knees, unable to move any of my limbs properly. And as the light fades, I see the man holding his eyes and blood coating his face. He crawls toward me unknowingly, searching for something.

"I told you," I whisper, spotting the dagger only inches away. I force my hand to reach for it, trying to teach myself the basic use of my limbs despite being unable to feel them. This hand still has three usable fingers, the others not even bothering to twitch around the handle. "If Shayde didn't kill you, I would. It seems he isn't going to make it in time to claim the death blow."

I force myself to raise the dagger as high as I can manage, biting back screams of pain with each move I make. My hands and arms shake, my entire body sore and tingling. He can't see me coming, I realize, because his eyes are *gone*. The majority of his body is burnt and bloody, skin peeling off in layers. This is a mercy killing, honestly.

I manage to raise the blade above his head, my shoulders and hands crying out in agony, and I whisper, "I don't need a savior; *I am one*."

I stab him once, twice, three times just to make sure I get the job done. I don't hesitate. I only scream. Partly because of the pain, partly because of the anger inside me that I can't escape. Anger has always kept me company, and today, this moment is no different than any other.

"Drop the dagger, Little Flower." I spin on my knees as fast as I can, my body finding relief in the shadows that surround me despite my mind screaming at me to run.

"Why? You worried I'll stab you, too?"

"I know you will." He chuckles, striding forward with hands shoved down into his pockets. "I still have the scar to prove it."

I smile lightly, swaying as I try to force myself to stand. Shayde rushes over, gripping my arms lightly to keep me still. "No, Azalea. Don't move. You've already done enough damage while finishing the deed. You're in no condition to stand." A pause as he looks me over before adding, "Do you want me to pop them back into place?"

I shudder but nod anyway, bracing myself for the pain. But no amount of bracing could prepare me for when his hands shove strategically on my shoulder, the sound as it pops back in reverberating through my skull. My scream rattles inside the room, breaking and forming when he does the second one just as quickly as the first. Tears stream down my face, but I'm thankful for the trained soldier before me who knows exactly what to do in a situation like this.

"Did you kill them?" I whisper, allowing him to scoop me into his arms without a fight. He was right: I'm in no condition to stand, or do much of anything else, actually.

"They sat outside and listened to you scream." He grits his teeth, his hold around me gentle and avoiding any bloody or bruised areas as best as possible. "They allowed this to happen to you."

"I'm glad you killed them," I say, tucking my head into his chest. Maybe that does make me evil, despite all the things Jaymes believes me to be. Maybe it's okay that I'm not a good person.

"I'll kill anyone who hurts you. Anyone who gets in my way when I'm trying to find you."

"How did you know where I was?" I whisper, groaning as he begins to walk.

"Shh, it's okay. I've got a portal waiting outside," he murmurs, brushing stiff hair out of my face. "And I always know where you are, Azalea. I keep close tabs on the girl who's supposedly destined to kill me." His fingers brush against the necklace on my neck, against the ring he gave me that I haven't brought myself to take off.

"No one ever said I had to kill you," I say, the thought I've had for a month now finally escaping. "Just that I will save the world. Saving doesn't equate to killing."

"You thought it did."

"I was pissed off."

"And you aren't anymore?"

"No, I'm still very much pissed off."

Shayde laughs lightly as he walks up a flight of stairs. I grunt and groan the whole way up, tears still streaming from my eyes. My vision is foggy, and I still feel as though I'm dangling, the pain that vibrates throughout my entire body strong and agonizing.

"But not enough to tell me to fuck off," he notes, shadows stretching up to push the door open. I groan at the sudden sunlight, tucking my head even further into his chest with my eyes closed.

"I have someone else to prioritize on the pissed off list now," I say into his hard chest, listening to the comforting, steady beat of his heart.

"So do I."

"You don't get to kill her, Shayde," I hiss, heat flaring inside me as my powers try to rise again. "Her death is mine to claim."

He chuckles, striding off into a nearby building with little care. "What a violent little flower you've become."

"It's what they've turned me into," I say quietly. "It's what they wanted."

"Do you always give people what they want?"

"Never."

"Good girl."

I smile at his words, heart fluttering treacherously. "Where are you going to take me?"

"I'm taking you home." He says it so matter-of-factly, so sure of himself.

"You have to take me back to *my* home," I say, hating the words as they leave me.

"No, I don't. *They* did this to you. They—"

"Will do it again if you take me. You'll confirm everything they thought. You'll—"

"I'll what? I'll save your fucking life? I'll keep you safe? I'll make sure they never do this shit again?" He's angry, and rightfully so. Despite how badly I want to hate him right now, I would be in the same boat if they were torturing him in a shady basement.

"You'll make them suspect me."

"You want to go with me," he accuses, practically growling as he speaks.

"Of course I do," I whisper, crying for an entirely different reason now. "I want to go with you and get away from all of this. I want to forget about being the savior and forget what you are. But I can't. I can't go with you because I know I'll just regret it in the morning."

"You can't keep doing this. You can't let me near you, let me inside of that beautiful brain of yours, and throw me back out."

"I'm weak," I say, swallowing hard. "You make me weak. You make me forget, until I don't."

"I wish I could take it all back, but I can't. I won't."

"Hmm." I pause before saying, "You sound…"

"Sane?" he suggests, chuckling at me again. "Yeah, realizing you were in danger will do that to me." Shayde glances down at me again, not pausing in his long strides. He doesn't falter once, as though he knows the path we are taking intimately.

"I never know what version of you I'm talking to lately." Good Grim, why am I talking to him right now? *I've gone insane.* It must be the head wound, or the pain, or the trauma of the entire situation.

"I never know, either." He swallows hard, pausing before a long mirror in the hall at the end of the first floor. "Let me heal you a little, please. I don't know a lot of healing Charms, but I can—"

"No." I snap my head up, staring into those light green eyes. "I want you to leave me like this. I want you to bring me to the front steps of the school and drop me off so they all know exactly what happened to me."

"Azalea," he moans, gaze roaming over my body. "*Please.* It kills me to see you like this." His perusal stops at my thigh, where the bloody word is now visible, the skin raw and puckering. The word slices right through my beautiful tattoos.

"I'm officially marked as yours," I say gently, moaning in pain when his fingers graze against it.

"I'm so sorry, Azalea. I never meant…"

"I know you didn't. We both made decisions we shouldn't have. But I don't blame myself, or you, for this. I blame the Bloodgood bitch."

"Then it seems we are on the same page." His wicked voice rumbles deep inside my chest, lighting my body up in a way I don't think anyone else ever will. Ah, definitely the head wound making me feel this way. "Are you sure you can't come with me?"

"I'm sure."

"Give me a second." He sighs, shifting to place me on the ground gently. "I made this portal to go to *my* home, not yours."

"*My home*," I say quietly, closing my eyes so I don't have to see his expression as a truth slips out unwittingly, "is nothing without you."

CHAPTER 23

"The only thing in the entire world that could bring a Scythe Partner to abandon their chosen one is love. Love for their chosen one is love for the people in that person's life, including significant others. In very rare cases, we have seen Scythes abandon their partners to protect their significant other in times of distress. However, they will only do this if they sense that this is what their partner *wants* them to do."
—*You and Your Scythe*, written by Shifter Marcellus Stone in 1998 A.G.

Going through the goo of a portal is even more miserable when you're already struggling to breathe.

I force myself not to gasp or inhale, the cool gel soothing against my raw and sore skin. When we emerge, Shayde steps into the water fountain, exiting straight out of the dragon in the front courtyard of Draxmere. Students are lingering around in the yard and on the steps, but they don't notice us right away. Not until Shayde transforms into his Grim form, my body lifted by his shadows as he grows. Then he gently cups me in those giant hands, empty eyes watching our surroundings diligently as Conjurers scream.

"Bring out your dean!" he shouts, the deep, terrifying voice as commanding as it is broken.

"You said you wouldn't kill her," I murmur, feeling dizzy and overwhelmingly weak. Weak enough to wish this moment wouldn't end, weak enough not to care that a Grim is cradling me with a tenderness no monster should possess.

"And I won't," he hisses back under his breath, dismissing me.

"What is the meaning of this?" Dean Bloodgood is out faster than I expect, considering she's hardly on campus anymore, much less in her office or nearby. Professors have come out, too, along with most of the third years. They watch wearily, either scared to attack a Grim or afraid to hurt me.

"You tell me," he snaps, crouching down so everyone can see my bruised and broken body. "You are the one who did this to her."

Students murmur among themselves, staring at Bloodgood warily as her face pales and she says, "I did no such thing."

"Well, not with your own hands, no. It just happened on your orders, didn't it?"

Bloodgood pauses before saying, "She knew what would happen if she continued to disobey. She knew what would happen if she posed a threat to our community."

"Posed a threat?" He roars so loudly that the trees shake, birds flying off in every direction.

"Yes." Bloodgood purses her lips, doubling down on her assessment of me. "Look at her; she's in the arms of a *Grim*. If that's not threatening, I don't know what is." I'm shifted into one of his giant hands, the other reaching out to grab Bloodgood. She doesn't scream, to her credit, but she does try to blast him with Light. It seems to deflect right off him, falling fruitlessly to the ground. But I know he isn't immune to Light because *I've* hurt him before.

Shayde leans in close so that Bloodgood can get a very good, very close-up look at his skull-like features and the giant antlers atop his head. "If I find out you've *punished* her again, I'll come back and rip your fucking head off. If I hear of you mistreating her in anyway, I'll come back and rip your fucking head off. If I have to save her from the people who are supposed to be protecting her, I'll come back and rip your fucking head off. Do you understand, or should I keep going?"

Bloodgood has gone so pale that she looks like a ghost, but she nods anyway. *You deserve to be scared shitless,* I think, taking satisfaction in the moment.

"Shayde!" I hear Jaymes call from below, frantic and confused. "Let her go!"

"Mind your business, Jay," Shayde calls back, dropping his best friend's mother unceremoniously. She has the sense to move before she hits the ground, managing to tuck and roll and come out unharmed. "Actually, no, don't listen to that advice. You minding your business is why she's been subject to punishments."

"Azalea." His eyes move from Shayde to me, his body moving down the first step so subtly I hardly notice. "What happened?"

"Ask your mother." Shayde points at him threateningly, glancing around. "And don't come any closer. Where's the redhead?"

"Ginny," I whisper, feeling so, so sleepy.

"Where's Ginny?" he corrects himself, eyes squinting at the crowd. Not a single one attacks, not after seeing Bloodgood be so easily overtaken. Not after watching her Light bounce off harmlessly.

"I'll find her," Arlo volunteers from somewhere behind Jaymes, and I hear footsteps retreating. The silence that follows is eerie, but it doesn't seem to bother Shayde.

"Azalea!" Ginny shouts, bounding from the front doors and racing down the steps without fear.

Shayde holds my body up with shadows again, transforming in front of everyone once more. Once back in his normal form, he drags me over to him again, but he doesn't take me into his arms. "If I touch you again, I might not let you go," he whispers, brushing crusty hair out of my face. "I don't want to leave you here, with these people."

"You have to," I say, tilting my head back and groaning softly as a rush of pain runs through me. My legs hang lifelessly, my arms limp and drooping at the sides of my body. And my *hand*…it throbs so badly that it manages to overtake everything else in brief flashes.

"No, I don't, but I'm doing it anyway because you asked me to." He turns to Ginny, who stops only a foot away, her glare so magnificent it could kill. Then, he begins to shout, "Your dean did this to your savior! She ordered her to be tortured, to be punished, all because Azalea is associated with *me*. What does that say about your people when a Grim has to be the one to bring back your savior safely? What does that say when she has to save herself from *you* and not the other way around?

"The next person who lays a hand on Azalea Jinx will no longer *have* a hand, and that's if I'm feeling generous. Treat your savior right, or I will." He grins, dark hair moving gently in the breeze. And damn, if I don't love the hint of insanity hiding in those green eyes. "I am only giving her back because she wants to be here. She made her choice twice now. Honor it. And if you don't…" He shrugs, shoving his hands down into his pockets. "I'm sure I could find a lot of ways to make use of a Draxmere-sized army."

"They won't stop," I say more to myself than him.

"Oh, I'm betting on it." He runs his hand down my cheek, and I wince at the flash of pain the small touch leaves in its wake. "Because I *want* to come here and massacre them all. Seeing you like this…it brings out the side of me I've been trying really hard to repress. The side I warned you about, the one that has nothing to do with being a Grim and everything to do with loving you."

"I'll heal," I whisper, going for the kill as I add on, "Physical wounds heal quicker than the emotional ones." He flinches, nodding understandingly.

Loud enough for everyone to hear, he demands, "Ginny. You're the only one I trust with her right now. You care for her, don't you?"

"She's my friend," Ginny says, fierce and loyal all the way through.

"Good." Shayde's gaze flicks to Jaymes, who stares in shock, confusion and hurt spread across his features. "I know what you've been up to, Jaymes Bloodgood, and I don't approve in the slightest."

"You been stalking me, Glover?" I murmur, smiling slightly. Am I crazy? I must be, to think that stalking is sweet.

"I am nothing without you," he says matter-of-factly, bending down to press a kiss to my lips. It's gentle but long, and he's careful to avoid putting too much pressure. I don't have the energy to fight back, much less care that I'm kissing a Grim in front of half the school. I feel myself floating over to Ginny, feel her arms wrap around me with such gentle determination.

In the distance, I see a figure hunched over, watching me longingly. I see the Reaper through a haze, but I *know* who that is. I would know her a mile away, a meter away, an inch away. I would know her just like I'm sure she knows me.

Demi is alive.

Shayde forms a portal in the dragon once more, quiet and unbothered by the attention on his form. I watch through a hazy gaze as he turns his head back over his shoulder, smiling gently as he says, "See you in your dreams, darling."

My eyes widen, my body jerking up suddenly as the Reaper turns and retreats at a run into the woods. Ginny shouts at me, forcing me back down into her arms and screaming for someone to help her get me to the infirmary. It hurts so bad, from the jerking to the push, but I can't focus on anything but Shayde and his words.

See you in your dreams, darling.

That *motherfucker*.

CHAPTER 24

"And in that grave, she'd watch the world fall.
In that grave, she'll know the Reaper's joy was worth it all."
—Continued prophecy recorded inside student Seer Allia Jordan's
Prophetic Journal, 2023 A.G.

DEMI

I growl at the weak offspring, sniffing the nearly dead prey he drops at my feet. I hate being fed such pitiful meals, and I especially hate when he delivers them to me already on Death's doorstep. What is the point in eating if I can't even hunt? And it leaves me so *hungry*. Always so hungry.

"Eat it, Demi. I'm in no mood to argue with you today." He's never in the mood to argue. Not that I *can* argue verbally. I mostly just snarl and hiss because it's the only thing I can do to defy him. That and sneak off to eat his friends. Though that *is* the reason I'm no longer allowed out of my cage when we are home.

I make the noise I usually make when I disagree with the off-spring's antics, bending over to eat my meal anyway. The blood is sour this close to death, too coagulated and cold to properly enjoy. I don't know where the offspring gets these meals, but he's not a very good hunter.

"We are going to have to get her, Demi. She asked me not to, but…" I glance up as he pulls on long strands of dark hair, green eyes opening and closing before he lets out a dark laugh. "I'm not sure I care what she asks for anymore."

Here we go again with the pining.

"She is mine, and she doesn't understand," he growls, pointedly glaring at me. "Just like you." He says I was friends with the girl once; this is probably why.

I can't remember what life was before I was his. Before my master gifted me to him. I hope it was better than this, better than the constant hunger and feeding off weak prey that doesn't keep me satiated. This is why I had to go off on my own, why I decided to invite others to join me. The offspring is too *weak* to understand my plight. He's too *good* to do anything more than allow me to exist for the sake of the girl.

"But she still hasn't found the Grimoire. I don't know if she's even been looking. It's been *months*." He is whispering now, an annoying trait that makes me angry. Everything about him makes me angry, actually. If my true master hadn't gifted me to his offspring, I would tear him into pieces and eat all of the magnificent power inside of him. He smells *so* good…

"I'm going to have to visit her again. I keep telling her I won't, but I do it anyway. She has this control over me I just can't shake." He bangs a fist against the wall, raging again. I make another annoyed noise, tossing my small meal to the side. Well, the pieces left of it, anyway. He's so hot and cold all the time; I'm sick of it.

"I'm going to have to get her back here, with me. I don't have a choice, do I? Those Conjurers have no idea what they've done. My little flower isn't going to take their bullshit." He cackles, throwing his head back and smiling maliciously. "She's going to make them pay. And when she does, I'll be waiting for her. Mark my words, Demi: Azalea Jinx will come back to me voluntarily. She'll come back to me on her knees and *beg*, just like I told her she would have to do."

I snarl again, retreating to the back of my cage and curling up in my nest. I've heard this all before, and I'm sure I'll hear it all again. My opinion on the matter?

Azalea Jinx isn't going to be the one on her knees begging.

Chapter 25

"The stones that Draxmere was constructed out of have been infused with protection Charms, but they can't keep evil out of its walls. Not when it's been hiding inside all along. No, these protections are purely structural. Draxmere will not fall. But those inside it? *They can fall harder than any stone ever could.*"
—*Draxmere: A Tale as Old as the Grim*, written by Enhancer Kelvin Delaney in 1977 A.G.

The third and final meeting for the Light and Shadow Factions happens in the two weeks before finals, which just so happens to also align with Reaping week. I don't go to the meeting, despite the mandatory attendance clause, because they are too scared to punish me for breaking the rules now. And they should be. Not because they should fear Shayde, though. They should fear *me*.

I've gone to classes, pushed myself to work harder and keep up with the work, and managed to improve in the few weeks I've had since being tortured. Vampire blood healed most of my injuries within the first few days, and I decided from the moment I returned that I wouldn't let myself be complacent in this school any longer. I've kept my head down, I've allowed them to punish me for the sake of being good, but where did that get me? What's the point of *being* good if they won't *treat* me as though I'm good?

Fuck that.

I want to learn and I want to stay at Draxmere, but I won't sacrifice myself for the sake of their power trip. I won't be treated as less than just because I'm new, because I'm different from the rest of them.

"Which side are you going to choose, Azalea?" Willow asks when we sit down for dinner, my plate mostly empty. I've had a hard time stomaching food since coming back, and the tiny bowl of mysteriously dark soup and the piece of bread beside it are the best I will be able to do.

"Is that even a question?" I scoff, moving my spoon around so it taps on the ceramic bowl.

"Did you hear what they announced?" Reese asks, sending a pointed look to her sister.

"No, I don't care much for their announcements and proclamations," I murmur, listening to the methodical *clink clink clink* as I talk.

"You'll care about this one," Wren says, sighing and shaking her head.

"What have they done this time? Is torture *allowed* now?" The factions had a huge fight about what Bloodgood did to me, from what I heard. The Shadow Faction was pissed, but the Light Faction argued I could be siding with their greatest enemy. If they hadn't tortured me, I wouldn't be considering doing just that.

"No." Ginny glances between the sisters with a hint of worry, but I ignore it. "They are giving people the chance to change sides."

"They're…what?" *That* I certainly wasn't expecting.

"I know, right?" Wren exclaims, banging her fists on the table. "They're trying to recruit more people to the Light Faction!"

"Some of the Light Faction might leave, too," Ginny argues weakly, rubbing her forehead as though it hurts.

"They won't," I say, watching the liquid stirring in my bowl and listening to the *clink clink clink.*

"How do you know that? They could—" Willow starts, trying to defend Ginny, but I stop her.

"There may be a few," I amend, watching a piece of chicken float to the surface. What I think is chicken, anyway. "But the Light Faction is full of cowards. They think giving the humans to the Grims is fine, that things for them will finally be better."

"And they're scared," Reese whispers, tapping long nails onto the table. "They don't want to die, and they certainly don't want their families to die."

"I'd understand that, I suppose, if I had a family." A curled noodle bobs up now, floating up and disappearing with another stir.

"You do have a family, Azalea." Ginny grabs my hand under the table, holding it steady as she stares at me.

I don't lift my head, too busy with the soup. "Sure," I say. I don't want to hurt her feelings, but these people don't understand me; they don't get it.

"Azalea," she whispers, squeezing gently. "The bags under your eyes have gotten so heavy, you don't eat anymore, you work yourself to death…"

"I have nightmares," I defend myself, snapping my head up to meet her worried gaze with a deathly glare. "And I work myself to death because I am not *immune* to death."

Ginny gapes at me, finally saying through a harsh intake of breath, "You think Shayde's going to kill you?"

"No, actually, I don't. I think he made that quite clear when he rescued me from the people who are supposed to *not* be killing me, remember?"

"You rescued yourself," Reese reminds me, hissing, "He just carried you home."

"Is this my home anymore?" I ask quietly, going back to clinking my spoon around. "Because I no longer feel safe here. Shouldn't a home be safe?"

"Are you…" Ginny can't finish her question, her mouth twisting in a way that makes her face pinch.

"Ask me, Ginny." I can't stand having people beat around the bush. Am I angry? Grim, yes. Am I tired? Grim, yes. Am I going to leave? *Grim, yes.*

"Are you going to take him back?" She finally gets out the question, her eyes wide as though surprised with herself for being so bold.

"I cannot love him." I try to make it sound convincing, try to remind myself to hate him. Try to remind myself that he isn't who I thought he was, who I want, who I crave. He's different now. He won't ever be the same. It should matter, but I don't think it does anymore, and that *terrifies* me.

"You're going to leave, aren't you?" Willow's voice cracks, realizing much sooner than everyone else the meaning behind my words.

I smile bitterly, closing my eyes. *Clink, clink, clink.* "I want to."

"Don't," Ginny begs, squeezing my hand so tightly it hurts. A hand that had been broken so badly that even vampire blood could not take away the pain for weeks. "Please, Azalea. You can't be out there on your own. I know they've done some horrible things. I know because I've been there with you. We all have. But you can't—"

"*You* weren't in that basement," I snarl, shoving my bowl to the side and standing. "*You* weren't hanging by your wrists. *You* weren't beaten bloody. *You weren't carved into like a pumpkin on Halloween!*" I scream the last sentence, panting as Light and Shadow swirl around me in a beautiful and deadly dance. I've been so out of control, so lost, so miserable.

I take a deep breath, inhaling through my nose before saying firmly, "I'm not leaving yet. I haven't made a final decision. I'm going to stay and I'm going to choose Shadow Faction to piss off Bloodgood. I'm going to do my best to acclimate, to try and be the person I was before. But I'm not. What they did to me…they showed me who they are. I don't want any part of saving that."

I turn and leave, my soup cold and untouched. My stomach churns at the thought of eating, my mind reeling. My fingers roam to smooth over my skirt, directly over the spot on my thigh that now reads "Grim". Tears spring to my eyes; tears that I cannot stop. This feels worse than Shayde betraying me, worse than losing Demi. It's worse because I expected them to be capable of something like this, but I didn't prepare myself for it. It's worse because I betrayed myself.

Six months ago, I would have never considered siding with a Grim. I would have told Shayde to kick rocks and never come back. *I would have, I would have, I would have.* But I'm not. I'm not going to fight for people who torture me. I'm not going to save a spot in my heart for those who don't trust me. I'm not going to be their savior.

But I will be Demi's.

Demi is the only person who was there for me, the only one who cared before I did. She stayed by my side through it all, warned me about the Gravediggers before I could understand what there was to be warned about. *She* tried to save *me*. It's only fair I do the same for her.

If Shayde really has been in my dreams, if that's even a possibility, then he already gave me the key to survival. He told me to find the Grimoire. He was convinced it was here. So I'm going to find that fucking book and I'm going to bring it to him so we can comb over every inch of it together.

Then I'm going to come back and kill anyone who dares tell me I can't save the others.

CHAPTER 26

"Weak Charmed are easy to sway. So many are born practically powerless, their desperation reeking in the air of our world. I've found that I don't need to go to them; they come to me. They come looking for a chance to be better, to do better. The easiest way to convince them to turn is to tell them that, after they consume enough Charm Levels, they will become like me. Then, I show them my son as 'proof'. They eat it up. And my wonderful, wicked son, never lets on that it's a passed-on trait. They see a strong, capable young man who became powerful through *me*. And they're so desperate, they don't understand they've been fooled until it's too late."

—*The Grimoire*, written by the first, unnamed Grim, 1 A.G.

The Reaping Ceremony doesn't involve parents like graduation. We do stand out in the back courtyard, the maze magically expanded in the same way. Except this time, the large line of students waiting to cross the stage is over double what it was all those months ago, due to both first and second-year students having to participate. Only third years stand in front of the stage, seated comfortably and chatting. I see the Gravediggers among them, their faces stoic and serious.

"Jaymes looks constipated," Dagan remarks, popping up beside me with a grin. Today, she's donning her natural short hair, but her eyes and outfit present the most Gothic aesthetic I've ever seen her wear. She's dressed like she's attending a funeral, her black dress covering almost every inch of skin. The collar rises high, flaring out at the top in the same dramatic way the sleeves do. I almost laugh at the sight of her because the atmosphere *is* similar to a funeral. I didn't wear anything so dramatic. I'm just in my uniform.

"Maybe he is."

Dagan lifts a dainty hand and wiggles her fingers at him, winking for added effect. Jaymes's neck turns red, his gaze bouncing from her to me in a flurry of movement. "No, I think he's just nervous for you."

"For me?" I scoff, kicking my feet. "He knows exactly what I'm choosing."

"That's the problem." She smiles softly, watching him with a longing I can't describe.

"I don't see how—"

"Welcome, Draxmere students!" Dean Bloodgood calls from her podium at the center of the stage, the other faction members flanking her on either side.

"Got to go," Dagan says, whisking away to find her place in the front of the line. They placed us in alphabetical order, so as a Breather, she's in the front of the line near Ginny, who's a Brady. I'm placed in the middle, far away from them, and the Thatcher triplets, and anyone else I might like. I don't mind too much, though. Lately, the insistent, meaningless chatter of friends has become too much for me to bear.

"Today is about you. Today is about the future. We are excited to place you among others who believe in the things you believe in, among people who understand exactly who you are. We have stood exactly where you are once, and we know how nerve-wracking this process can be. Despite your nerves, we ask you to make the right choice for you. Don't take into consideration anyone else, only yourself." She steps aside to let Leader Fellows speak, his eyes weary and the bags underneath prominent—just like mine.

"When you step onto this stage, you will be presented with two spheres." We all watch as those spheres appear, one full of darkness and the other filled with light. "To make your decision, choose the sphere that reflects your choice. Your body will absorb the sphere, but it won't hurt or affect you in any way. This is a symbolic process, one we pride ourselves on partaking in. Do not fear, and do not worry. Only you know what choice is right." His gaze flicks over us, landing on me for so long that I shift on my feet awkwardly.

"Well, without further ado, let's begin!" Dean Bloodgood cries, gesturing for the first student to approach. It's a girl with short blue hair; a first-year, I think. She only hesitates for half a second before choosing the ball of darkness, causing cheers to erupt around the yard.

"Excellent choice!" Fellows calls, shaking her hand firmly and clapping her on the back. "It seems as though we get to claim the first pick this year, Haiden." He taunts Bloodgood openly, a satisfied smirk on his lips.

I don't recognize the first ten people who walk onto that stage, but I do recognize that the majority of them choose the Light Faction. By the time Ginny steps up, the Light Faction is ahead by about four students, but both Ginny and Dagan help to lower that number. I assumed they would choose the Shadow Faction, and part of me is a little relieved. I'm not sure I could still be friends with people who choose to follow *her*.

The line slowly moves up and the numbers begin to blur. I lose count after thirty people choose the Light Faction and twenty choose the Shadow Faction. By the time I've made it to the stage, I know those numbers have changed drastically. At least a hundred students have come up here already, and there will be at least a hundred more after me.

Silence falls as I step onto the stage, but I don't mind it. My heart doesn't pound with nerves, my pulse unchanging. I keep my eyes on Dean Bloodgood as I approach, her cold gaze turning colder.

"Azalea," she starts, as though about to try and convince me to join her side.

"Don't bother," I snarl, grabbing the hem of my skirt and lifting it so she can see the prominent scarred word there. "I already know what happens to people under your leadership."

I grab the ball of darkness so fast that it almost slips from my hands, shoving it into my chest harshly without breaking eye contact. Shadows explode from my body so brilliantly that people gasp, eyes wide and confused. The ball hadn't *exploded* for anyone else. I turn my head to catch Jaymes's eye, to see if he is as proud of me as I am, but my vision is overtaken in a flash.

I see Shayde and Jaymes together, arguing, screaming. I can't tell what words are being said, can't hear what they are so angry about.

Jaymes is holding a ball of Light, his entire body shaking with anger and agony. Shayde doesn't threaten him back, his back rigid and his eyes hard. From behind Shayde, I see myself emerge, and Jaymes's Light crackles and fails. His shoulders droop, a tear slipping down his cheek as he turns and looks over in my direction.

"Forgive me, Azalea."

For what? I try to say, but a series of words are shouting over my own.

The voice is old and sincere, the embodiment of truth. "Be wary of the beast inside, be wary of a friend who lied. Don't query the Grim who hides, don't query the friend who chooses sides. Don't bury the secrets that died, don't bury the truth you find."

"What does that mean?" I shout, my head pounding as I reach up to cover my ears.

I release a scream when the voice starts again, louder than before, and fall to my knees. "Be wary of the beast inside, be wary of a friend who lied. Don't query the Grim who hides, don't query the friend who chooses sides. Don't bury the secrets that died, don't bury the truth you find."

"I don't know what it means," I cry, holding my head tighter as the pain increases. It feels like my head is about to split in *half.*

"Be wary of the beast inside, be wary of a friend who lied. Don't query the Grim who hides, don't query the friend who chooses sides. Don't bury the secrets that died, don't bury the truth you find," it says again, shouting so loudly now that it pierces through my screams.

So, I repeat the words back to it. I repeat the words over and over, tears streaming down my face as I beg it to stop. As I attempt to demonstrate that I've received the message and obtained the necessary knowledge. After the fifth time of repeating the phrase, I hear something new, something familiar.

Jaymes.

"Azalea? Azalea, please, wake up. Azalea!"

My eyes are suddenly open, taking in the sight of Jaymes leaning over me. When had I closed my eyes? Why was I lying down? And my *head…*

"Jaymes?" I whisper, turning my head slightly. Something wet sounds with the movement, and a stab of pain jolts through me. I groan, closing my eyes briefly before flickering them back open. I'm still on the stage, a crowd of students watching me with wide and panicked gazes.

"It's okay, Azalea. You're okay," he soothes, cupping my face gently.

"What happened?" I ask the question, but I don't need to. *I just had a vision.* But how? How had I seen Shayde in my vision? Seers can't see Seers, that's rule number one. At least, they can't see more than vague nonsense, hence the many prophecies about a savior and a jinx that everyone believes refer to me. Was the prophecy about me, Jaymes, and Shayde? Or was the vision that went along with it something else entirely?

"You just proved my theory about you to be right." He grins, blond hair tipping over his face as he moves to help me stand. I never told him about what happened the day I was taken and tortured. I never told anyone the full truth of what happened that day, actually.

"In front of everyone," I grumble, my head full of a stabbing pain that might not just be a result of the prophecy. I reach back and touch my head, feeling the slick blood immediately. At least it matches my hair.

"Yep," he pops the 'p', guiding me toward the steps to exit the stage. "Show off."

"Azalea Jinx," Dean Bloodgood calls, stomping over to us before we can escape. "You've been hiding a third ability," she accuses, jabbing her finger at me.

"No, she hasn't," Jaymes says calmly, looking at his mother in boredom. "She just manifested it. If she had known about it, she wouldn't have dropped like a sack of bricks and started screaming at the top of her lungs."

"I…" she starts, but stops, mouth opening and closing like she can't decide what to say.

"Congratulations, Azalea Jinx," Leader Fellows says, approaching to shake my hand. I do so hesitantly, feeling weak and dizzy. "On joining the Shadow Faction and on your new ability. You're going to do great things."

I chuckle, eyes flickering over to Dean Bloodgood. "Or horrible ones."

Dean Bloodgood ordered me to attend Seer Specialty Training at the beginning of next semester, a class starting at seven in the morning because, "Predictions are most accurate after a good rest." I don't argue or deny this order, not that I was given the chance to. A note with the instructions was slipped under my door the same night as the Reaping Ceremony.

Only three days later, the entire population of Draxmere is now leaving for winter break. The entire population minus me, anyway.

"Please, Azalea," Jaymes calls from outside my door, fist tapping against it for what seems to be the hundredth time. "I don't like the idea of leaving you here by yourself."

"I think being alone is exactly what I need right now." I need the chance to search the school uninterrupted, the chance to find the Grimoire so I can get the hell out.

"I don't want to leave you," he says softly, just loud enough for me to hear him.

"It's not about what *you* want." I curl up tighter under my dark comforter, the scent of Shayde so strong today that it's overwhelming. After all this time, it still hasn't faded. I can't spray it away, can't wash it away, can't will it away. Through it all, the scent lingers. For better or for worse.

He sighs, groaning loudly. "I know. You'll be okay, right?"

"I always am."

"Okay." He pauses as though searching for the right words. "I love you, you know?"

"I know you do," I say gently, frowning.

"I'm trying to be less controlling, but—"

"If you walk away now, you'll succeed in that."

"Azalea, just let me be concerned about you! Let me worry about your mental and physical health without ridiculing me for it for once!" He is screaming now, angry and hurt.

"I don't know how to do that," I admit, closing my eyes tightly.

"That's always the problem with us, isn't it? One of us always feels too much and the other just doesn't feel enough." The words are a slap to the face, a reminder of who I was and who, some days, I am desperate to still be.

"Jaymes…" I hear his footsteps retreating before I can finish, before I can convince myself to step out of bed and open the door. I sigh, throwing the comforter over my head and letting Shayde's scent truly swallow me whole.

At least I still have one piece of him left that didn't turn sour.

PART THREE

AZALEA JINX AND THE WINTER OF REDEMPTION

CHAPTER 27

"Before a dreary morning dawns,
the newly crowned queen will send her pawns.
The little flower will wilt and die,
her petals will fall and turn to ice.
The sweet nectar once found inside
converges and takes form in a bitter blight.
The winds of change bring wings to fly,
and in the freshly dug dirt, she'll plant her seeds of spite."
—Part of a recovered prophecy recorded inside Seer Shayde
Glover's prophetic journals, 2024 A.G.

I attempt to contact Shayde through my dreams the very first night I'm alone, despite the rational part of me screaming that it's a mistake. I don't know how this connection between us works, how we can see each other so vividly, but I want to control it, too. I want to be able to seek him out for answers and push him away when I don't. And now that I know it was all real…I want to know what's happening to him. If he told me the truth about his mind being split, then…well, that might change things for me.

I lay on my bed and try to manifest him as I fade into sleep—my brain hones in on his face, his body, his smell. I don't see him that night.

The second night, I try to force it, not just ask the emptiness inside of my mind. I demand Shayde appear; demand my power to connect me to his. I don't see him that night, either.

By the third night, I'm desperate enough to beg and plead and cry myself to sleep. Apparently, tears are the key to success.

Within moments of drifting off, I'm on the edge of my cliff and no longer lying in my comfortable bed at Draxmere. I can't see Shayde through the fog in the distance, but I stride forward anyway. I head straight into that fog despite not knowing what waits inside; despite the fear of it that's held me at bay all this time.

At first, it's just endless fog and rocky mountains that I barely manage to avoid. No signs of Shayde, past or present, linger. That is until I stumble into the small kitchen with aging wood cabinets and brassy knobs. The one with a flickering, dim boob light hanging from the ceiling. And…there, on the counter. *There* he is.

"I've been looking for you," I whisper, wrapping my arms around myself to keep myself from running right into his arms.

"Azalea." He jumps and lifts his head, eyes wide. He says my name like it's the answer to a prayer, looks at me as though I've granted his only wish. "How did you get here?"

"With a lot of bitter tears," I remark, looking him up and down. "You look…"

"Destroyed?" he suggests, closing his eyes before rubbing them harshly. With a broken voice, he whispers, "This is real, isn't it?"

"You tell me," I say plainly. He smiles softly, tilting his head back so it hits the cabinet behind him.

"I need answers." I lick my lips, dropping my hands and stepping up between his legs. "I need you to tell me the truth."

"I've always told you the truth, you just don't always like to hear it." His head drops back down until our faces are inches away, fingers twitching as though aching to move. I know because mine are doing the same thing, desperate to make contact. I hold them as steady as I can, gripping onto the counter on either side of him to keep myself from touching him.

"How did you know Bloodgood was about to send her goons to my door? You knew the day, the time, and you knew how to seek me out. How?"

"You never ask easy questions, do you?" He smiles bitterly, clearing his throat before saying, "I saw it. I told you I was a Seer, and I...I saw her coming to get you. I only knew the day and the time because I saw the sun rising outside your window, and the prophecy I was given mentioned dawn. It was long and a pain to memorize. And that prophecy..." He shivers, as though the thought of it scares him.

"How are we doing this? How are we seeing each other? Seers can't..."

"I don't know, Azalea. I just went to bed one day, pining over you, and woke up next to that cliff, hiding in the shadows. It was easy to come back after I knew how. At first, I returned because I wanted to see you, but then I physically couldn't stop myself from coming to you. My best guess? We're connected by an ancient kind of power that only existed when the Grim was first created." A power I'm sure he's hoping is detailed in the Grimoire.

"Is the Grimoire real?"

"Very." He sighs, folding his hands over each other and twisting them around, around, around. "I have it on good knowledge that it's kept somewhere inside the school. It's the one place I haven't checked, the one place I no longer have access to. They've warded the entire academy against me; I haven't been able to go farther than the front courtyard without getting blasted back. The dragon statue is as far as I can go."

"How am I supposed to find it? I don't even know what it looks like!"

"It's old and full of dark magic; you'll find it. You're drawn to the darkness like a moth is drawn to the light, Azalea. You'll know it the second you're in its presence."

"And you swear it can save Demi? You swear you can bring her back?" I clench the counter hard, staring into those beautiful green eyes and waiting.

"I can't swear that, Azalea, because I've never actually read the thing. I only suspect the knowledge it contains. I only hope." He looks sad, as though he truly wishes he could promise this to me.

"Suspect is not good enough," I snarl, slamming my hand onto the hard surface.

"It's all I can do until you find it."

"You told me she was dead," I accuse, unable to back away from him. I'm supposed to be the one caging him in right now, but I feel more like a dog on a leash than I should.

"I did." He swallows, his Adam's apple bobbing from the motion. "I wanted you to hate me."

"I did. I–I do."

"You don't, or you wouldn't be here."

"I hate you less than I love her," I whisper, unable to stop my hand from drifting to one of those muscular thighs. "I'll do whatever it takes, be whoever I need to be, to get her back."

"I never meant for her to get involved in this," he whispers, hand moving to cover mine. The other moves to cup my cheek, and he sighs in relief, as though he really hadn't been sure I was real until just now.

"You let it happen." A tear slips down my cheek, slow and full. "And I can't forget it."

"I wasn't myself," he whispers, using his thumb to wipe it away. "I spent those months away from you entirely in my Grim form. My dad forced me, and…and it changed me. I used what little energy I had left to warn you, to save you, and even then it wasn't enough. I'm sorry it happened, but I'm not sorry it wasn't you."

"I can't forget it," I repeat, his words washing over me. What's happening to him?

"I don't want you to forget what I did. I just want you to forgive it." He bends down to press our foreheads together, sucking in so hard that his entire body shakes.

With a steady, calm voice, I ask, "It's the Grim changing you?"

"Yes."

My eyes flicker shut, another tear escaping. "What is it doing to you?"

"It's taking over," he says simply, our lips so close they almost brush against each other now. "The Grim is a creature of evil, of chaos. The more you use its abilities, the longer you go with it living inside of you, the more of yourself is lost. It feels like I've been split in half, like there's this evil doppelganger who's pretending to be me and isn't. I'm trapped inside my own mind, watching myself do all of these horrible things I would have never *considered* doing before. I've made it longer than most of my ancestors, but I can't hold out forever. I've probably got a few months left, six at the max, before there's no longer a piece of me left outside of my dreams."

"And the Grimoire…it can help you, too?"

"I think so. I heard the stories from my father as a young child, and from my father's father. They both mentioned being able to return the power to the place it originated, but I don't know what that means or how to do it. I don't know if it will cure me."

"Do you want to be cured?"

"What else would I want?"

"Me to still love you." Does he care about being evil, or is he doing it because he thinks that's what I want him to do?

"Can't it be both?" His thumb runs along my cheek again, steady and gentle.

"You can't make decisions because of me. You have to make decisions because it's what you want, because—"

"This *is* what I want!" He has both hands on my cheeks now, pressing into me firmly with wild eyes. "*You* are what I want."

"You told me you didn't want to be like him," I whisper, a shiver running down my spine.

"I don't."

"Good." I swallow, nodding. "I…I'm not sure what's right or wrong anymore."

"Right and wrong are what we make them to be." He shrugs, pushing me gently as he slides off the counter. He towers over me in a comforting way, in a way I missed so fucking much. His hand trails down my body, knuckles brushing up under my skirt and to the scar on my thigh. "And this? This is wrong."

"I know. That's why I'm here," I admit softly. "Because you helped me after *they* hurt me."

"You want revenge?" His smile is malicious and seductive, as though the very thought turns him on.

"So very badly." His hand trails back up to my waist, the other following on the opposite side. "It comes second only to Demi."

His nose brushes against my ear as he promises, "I will make all of your dreams come true."

"I don't have dreams, only nightmares."

"And what wicked things speak to you at night?" He nibbles on my earlobe, and I gasp, involuntarily arching my back and pressing my chest into his.

"A creature with antlers on its head and inky words inside its mouth," I murmur, heart pounding and stomach pulsing.

"Inky words or a slippery tongue?" Another nibble now, just below my ear. It's followed by a slow, sensual lick and a trail of kisses to my shoulder.

"Can't it be both?" I repeat his sentiments from earlier, smiling as his hands drag me into his body harshly.

"Can I tell you something?"

"Anything." I am the last person Shayde should confide in, but I'm the only one I want him to do it with.

"Even when I'm not myself, I can't get you out of my mind. I've watched you, I've hunted you, I've sought you out in my dreams. Even if you can't forgive me, I will always forgive you. I am so blindly driven by this aching need for you that I do horrible things just to get to you. I will never be able to let you go. And if that means I have to work for the rest of my life to earn your forgiveness, then I will."

"Why do you need to forgive me?" I whisper, my breathing labored as his hands slip over my ass and squeeze.

"You hurt me, too, Azalea. If my words are slick like ink, then yours are deadly like *poison*."

"I didn't want to love you anymore," I whisper, heat flushing my cheeks.

"And you thought Jaymes was the best person to help you fall out of love?" he growls into my neck, squeezing me tighter. "You thought sleeping with my best friend would make this all go away?"

"I didn't sleep with him!"

I yelp when he slaps my ass, lips back at my ear. "No, but you tried damn hard to."

"If I can forgive you for all of the horrible things you did, then surely you can forgive me, too." I smile up at him, running my hand through his long hair and cupping the back of his neck.

"And do you? Forgive me, I mean?" He searches my eyes for the truth, pleading with his gaze.

"I wouldn't be here if I didn't." The admission is loud in the quiet kitchen.

"I told you what my conditions would be if you wanted to earn my forgiveness." He smirks, tugging on red strands of hair playfully.

I release him, sinking onto my knees before him. I look up at him with glossy eyes, the ache inside me so strong I can hardly breathe. "Please, Shayde," I whisper, hands inching up his legs toward his belt. "*Please* forgive me."

"Good Grim, Azalea," he groans, hands tangling into my hair. "Seeing you like this…"

"I can prove that I deserve it," I say, the sound of his belt buckle unclipping echoing behind my words. "Will you let me?"

"Only if you'll let me worship you in return. Only if you agree to be mine."

"I've always been yours; I just didn't always realize it."

"I should tell you to stop," he hisses as I unbutton his jeans, the zipper sliding down with a quick flick of my finger. "Because this isn't what I meant when I said I wanted you begging on your knees. But only a good man would tell you to stop, Azalea, and I am not good."

"You may not be the hero in my story, Shayde, but if you let me, I'll be the hero in yours."

He lets out a noise that almost seems like a whimper, fingers clenching in my hair as I reach in to grab him. Another noise now, a new one, and it has my stomach fluttering so hard I almost fall back to sit on my heels from the sensation. But I keep going, determined, pulling his dick out and licking my lips. It's been so long since we've been together, so long without him inside me, that I've forgotten how thick he is.

"Azalea," he whispers, groaning when I lick the tip. I smile, licking, teasing, exploring. I've never had the time to explore him like this, never felt the need to. Before, I was so focused on the newness of it all, on the emotions he awakened inside me. But now...now I can focus on everything else, too. I can be overwhelmed in an entirely new way.

With slow precision, I take him into my mouth, tongue swirling around his tip before I lower myself farther. He reaches back to steady himself with a hand on the counter, his eyes flickering shut as his head tilts back. I watch him as I retreat, then take all of him again, gagging slightly from the abruptness. That noise seems to put him on edge, the hand still in my hair pulling now. He isn't guiding me, only giving himself a way to touch me.

Watching Shayde come undone is something I've never paid attention to before. I've never watched as his body stiffened and twitched, never listened properly to the loud moans and exclamations as he came. And when he looks down to see me swallowing, he loses it all over again.

Slowly, I rise to my feet, pressing in to cage him against the counter. "Was that proof enough?"

"I don't know," he breathes, smirking as his chest heaves. "I may need to make sure you learned your lesson a few more times."

I laugh, the sound full of promise and seduction. "I'll take whatever punishment you deem necessary."

"I know this is just in our dreams, but I swear to the Grim, Azalea, the things I want to do to you…they are meant for the real world." He bends down to press a harsh kiss to my lips, so unwound that he can't control himself. He breathes against me, a reminder of his earlier sentiments, "Next time I see you, Azalea Jinx, I'm going to worship you."

"Next time I see you, Shayde Glover, I'm going to give you a reason to."

Chapter 28

"The Draxmere Academy of Conjuring was always set to be named as such. Though many arguments led to this. Both Light and Shadow Faction Leaders at the time wanted the school to be named after them, as they both considered themselves majorly responsible for its creation. Drax Love and Mira Villegas were stubborn, but good, leaders. In the end, it was Drax's second, Tommie Camacho, who suggested combining Drax's name with Mira's nickname 'Mere' to form the official name. It was the only suggestion that ever caught traction, so it stuck."

—*Draxmere: A Tale as Old as the Grim*, written by Enhancer Kelvin Delaney in 1977 A.G.

The first place I check for the Grimoire is the most obvious: the library. I don't come here often, if at all, and I'm not entirely familiar with my surroundings. Honestly, the entire place is overwhelming. Stepping in, the smell of paper and ink is imbued in every inch of the space, and the aisles of tall shelves loom in the mostly dark room. One light hangs above me, dim and not entirely useful. I glance to my right at the mostly empty desk—a large calendar is left on top, along with a few forms to sign if anyone happens to borrow books during the break. If I find what I'm looking for, I won't be signing a damn thing.

I take a hesitant step toward the first aisle directly ahead of me, sighing deeply. There are *thousands* of books in this place, and I know that the Grimoire is probably not going to be hanging out among the normies. But this is the most logical place to look, and even if I don't find the Grimoire, I might find books that hint at its whereabouts.

I don't know what I'm looking for, exactly, as I slowly pace down the aisle. Shayde said I would know when I found it; that its old and dark power would call to me. If that is true, then I doubt the book will be hidden here, where it can be found so easily. I'm sure I'm not the only one the darkness likes to call to.

I notice after a while that things are organized by genre and by alphabetical order after that. Most of the books are also numbered, but I've never cared about the Dewey Decimal System before, and I can't bring myself to learn it now. I do briefly stop at the 'G's' in nonfiction after ten different aisles, heart racing as my fingers dance across spines. Of course, the book isn't here. I find out after three hours that it isn't anywhere in this room, actually.

I huff when I finally finish the tedious task of checking every single shelf in the stupid library, my frustration growing. I knew it wouldn't be easy—Shayde can't find the damn thing, after all—but I had hoped I wouldn't have to spend my whole break searching the castle; that I wouldn't need to be constantly on the lookout for a strange feeling or secret passageways as I stride down Draxmere's halls.

I pause on my way back up the aisles, stopping when a large book in the D's catches my attention.

Its spine is a deep brown, the word *Draxmere* printed on the side in such a fancy script that I grab it impulsively. I flip it over, noting the title *Draxmere: A Tale as Old as the Grim* by Kelvin Delaney. I open the aging cover to the first page, eyes wide as I see a detailed map of Draxmere lining the first pages. The contents list many chapters with titles hinting at the history of Draxmere, the secrets it hides, and its dark past. I tuck the book under my arm, nodding to myself.

Maybe this wasn't a wasted trip, after all.

The Draxmere Academy of Conjuring was built on a land born of evil and depravity. Many of the Charmed gathered at the site in large groups from all around the world to protest its construction, and many more protested in their hometowns. In the end, none of the protests were enough. The factions decided that Draxmere needed to be created, and they were determined that the land it lay on would be one that held historical significance. I'm sure at this point you're asking yourself, what could be the reason the world was so divided about this issue? Don't worry, I'll break it to you gently.

Draxmere was built in the same place where the first Grim was created.

When the first Grim came into existence, the world of the Charmed changed in a horrible, despicable way. We began having to fight for our lives, began having to train our children and each other to kill monsters in the night. To this day, we do not yet have a solution to the problem that was created, and we do not know who, exactly, created this problem. Was it nature trying to balance out the good and the bad? Was it a Charm gone wrong? No one knows, and no one can find out.

Many Charmed believe that the school of Conjuring should not be built on this hated land because they are worried it is the land itself that is cursed. They worry over what kind of monsters this school can turn their children into, and they worry that another Grim will rise. These concerns were heard by the factions, but both sides unanimously agreed that they were to be dismissed. It was a highly controversial decision.

I pause in my reading, shaking my head and closing the book at the end of the first chapter. The land Draxmere was built on was the place where the first Grim was created…so is that why the Grimoire is here? Did the first Grim leave it here on purpose, or was it stolen and forgotten through time? If any Conjurers here know about the Grimoire, surely they would be looking for it, too?

Maybe no one *should* know about the Grimoire. The fewer people involved, the better for me. As soon as I can recover the book and leave this supposedly cursed place, the better.

Within a week, I've searched everywhere I can think of in the school. It's not hidden in any of the rooms used on the bottom floor, not in the Charms classroom on the edge of campus, and as far as I can tell, not in any of the dorm rooms. I feel no pull, no magnetism, no darkness calling. The Grimoire is not here.

I've settled down in my dark bed to mope, prepared to sit and stare at the ceiling with despairing thoughts for hours, when a knock sounds at the door. It startles me so greatly that Light blasts from the tips of my fingers, burning the wall in several spots. No one should return to campus for another week, and I haven't run into a single person since break began. Who could be at the door? My body stiffens and shakes as I consider the one possibility that's greater than any other: Dean Bloodgood.

I quickly form a Charm to see through the door, my entire body sagging in relief when I see Dagan standing outside with a hand on his hip.

I scowl at the door, calling out bitterly, "What do you want?"

"Let me in, Azalea Jinx, or face the wrath of the dead!" Despite the harsh tones and wicked cackle, Dagan's face is soft and non-threatening. I grumble but force myself up, padding over to the door, releasing my Charm, and swinging it open.

"Are you going to tell me why you're here?" I mumble as he strides in, that limp I notice occasionally now present and his hair longer than the last time I saw him. When was the last time I saw him, anyway? Was it that brief encounter at the Reaping? I think it was. And that had been the first time I had seen him in a month, since the last school-sanctioned assembly. Good Grim, I'm a shitty friend.

"Do I need a reason to come visit my friend?" He glances around the room, sniffing hard and wrinkling his nose. "It smells…ew, have you been having sex this whole time? I was worried about you, and you've been here getting busy with some guy?"

"How do you know it was a guy?" I say blandly, not wanting to admit that the man he's smelling is Shayde and that it has nothing to do with us having sex. His scent lingers like a bad stomach bug.

"Are you kidding? It smells like testosterone and a six pack in here." Dagan drops the bag he was holding onto my bed, flopping down on his back with a huff and spreading his arms and legs as wide as they will go.

"No one has been here except me," I hiss, plopping down next to him and shoving at his body. He obliges and scoots over, letting me fall next to him.

"Then why does it smell so…" He trails off, sighing. "The fancy magic dorm rooms are designed to make you feel like you're at home."

"Yes." I don't explain further, but I never need to worry about Dagan mincing words.

"This is what Shayde smells like." His words aren't full of judgment or anger. It's just a stated fact; one that, no matter how you feel about the subject matter, is true.

"It could be Jaymes's scent," I try to deny weakly.

"But it isn't." Dagan knows Jaymes's scent as well as I do because they hang out more often. Dagan has an in with the Gravediggers and uses that to his advantage; I don't care nearly as much about the prestigious group that rules over the campus.

"No. It isn't."

"Do you miss him?" Once again, there's no judgment in Dagan's tone, only pure curiosity. He doesn't seem to care that I'm shifting uncomfortably, or that I'm quiet for far too long.

"Every day." Even the ones where I see him in my dreams.

"Would you go back?"

"Good Grim, Dagan, could you not just show up out of nowhere and dissect my life choices like this? Why are you here, anyway? I thought you went home." I push myself up and off the bed, scowling as I stride over to the door. I don't want to leave, only to put distance between him and the burn on my cheeks.

"I like to dissect things," he says simply, pushing himself up onto his elbows. "*Especially* people."

"Well, isn't that nice and morbid?" I pace from one side of the door to the other, brushing my bangs back into place and tapping my nails on my thigh.

"Don't look so nervous, Azalea. I don't care what you do or how you feel. Who am I to dictate your emotions? I'm just a curious creature. *And* a morbid one." He grins, easing me entirely.

"I didn't think I would go back," I say eventually, pausing. "I—fuck, can't we play a drinking game if we are going to do this? Please tell me you brought alcohol."

"What kind of friend do you think I am?" He scoffs, unzipping the bag and pulling out two of his father's signature Dragon's Breath.

"The kind whose daddy owns a booze company." I grin and quickly stride over to snatch it away, popping the cap and taking a long swig.

"Truth or drink?" Dagan suggests as I sit back down, cackling when I nod my agreement.

"Do you want to go first?"

"I've already asked some invasive questions. Why don't you go? I'm an open book, Azalea." He pushes up to sit next to me, hand on my knee.

"Why did you come?" I think I know, but I want to hear it from him. Dagan hastily takes a drink, looking away. Quietly, I add, "I won't shoot the messenger."

"Ugh, fine. Jaymes was worried about you."

I figured as much. "He could have called." I take a swig even though I don't have to, grateful for the distraction from the shit show that is my life right now.

"Calls like that need to be planned." He waves his hand dismissively, cackling as he says, "He could have called while you were in the middle of an intimate moment with yourself, you know?"

"I'm sure he would have loved that."

"Oh, I would have, too." Dagan pauses, then sighs. "He's a good guy, you know?"

"I know."

"Why do you string him along, then?"

"Is that your question?" Dagan nods, and I groan, taking a long swig as I think about it. "I wasn't trying to. I just...I wanted a distraction from Shayde. Jaymes was there. He knew that I wasn't over it, and he didn't give me what I wanted because I wouldn't give him more than a slice of my heart. It was an equal trade."

"You are only supposed to drink when you don't answer," Dagan points out, then says, "That makes sense, I think. He just…pines over you in a way I've never seen anyone pine."

"Jaymes is intense," I say, because what else can I say?

"Only on every day that ends in y." Dagan cackles again.

"Are you in love with him?"

Dagan is in the middle of taking a drink when he chokes, sputters, and spits the sweet alcohol all over my black comforter. "Of course not." Another swig now to make up for the lost one.

"You just like him." I know it's true because I've seen the way he looks at Jaymes, seen the way they danced together in the summer.

"Sure, who wouldn't?" He tries to play it off, but I can sense the pain hiding behind the words.

"I think he likes you, too. I think he won't admit it because he's hung up on me."

"I think so, too." Dagan smiles sadly, squeezing my knee softly before letting his hand slip down between us. "The stupid, honorable man."

We fall into a comfortable silence before Dagan breaks it with another soul-searching question. "Does he scare you?" I don't ask which "he" is being referred to because I already know.

"Not in any meaningful way." I finish off the bottle, waving it up in the air and hoping Dagan has another to replace it with. "Mostly, what scares me is the way he makes me feel. The way I was head over heels before I knew anything about him. The way I should walk away and never look back, but somehow always turn around and take a few steps forward anyway. I thought I was a horrible person for still wanting him."

"And you don't anymore?" Dagan dutifully replaces my drink, and I hear more rattling around in that bag of his. He cracks open a second one, too, and lets out a tiny cackle as we take a swig together.

"No." I'm no more horrible than the good guys doing bad things for the sake of being good. The only difference between me and them is the labels they created for themselves; I have no qualms with being told it's wrong when I'm doing what feels right in my heart.

"I don't think you are horrible, either, if that means anything to you."

"It does," I say truthfully. I've liked Dagan from the moment I met him, oddities and all. I think it's because he reminds me of Demi. I quickly ask another question, not wanting to even *think* her name right now. "How'd you get that limp?"

"You noticed?" He seems surprised, his body stiffening. Ah, it seems I've found something he's sensitive about. Serves him right for digging into *my* private business.

"A few times. You hide it well."

"I don't think you'll understand; it's a morbid situation." It's a quiet admission, one that leaves a chill running down my spine.

"I don't have to understand to sympathize," I say plainly, turning to face him completely.

He tilts his head back, orange, blond, and black hair falling with his movement. "I did it to myself, and everyone I've ever told gets weird after I tell them."

"I've done lots of things to myself I shouldn't have. Consumed alcohol and drugs, thrown myself into dangerous situations where I knew I would get hurt, put myself in a position where I could die just to make my heart race. Most of this was before I could feel what I do now, and now what I feel makes me regret ever doing those things for the sake of feeling this shitty."

"Maybe you're just as crazy as me," he cackles, unperturbed by this supposedly morbid story.

"Who better to open up to?" I scoff back, watching him carefully. He doesn't look at me when he begins to speak, his eyes stuck firmly on the ceiling as though he doesn't want to watch my reaction.

"I cut off my leg," he says quite plainly, his familiar cackle following. Only, it sounds a little lackluster this time. Forced.

"Why?" I watch as he rolls up his pant leg, showing off a scar just above his knee that stretches around his leg.

"Because I could. Because I'm powerful. Because I hold power over death, and I needed to practice."

I blink, processing the information much slower than a sober mind would need. "So…you cut it off and used your powers to reattach it?"

"Yes."

"How does that work? I thought you Necromancers just reanimated the dead." I wave my hand at him, eyebrow raised. I told him I wouldn't react badly, and I won't. Of course, it is still…weird. Extremely so.

"Sure, we do that. But the most powerful of us can stop death from happening entirely. Of course, I wasn't given many opportunities to practice this particular ability growing up. Schools give us dead people to reanimate, not people close to death. I've never been sent out into battle, never even been to a hospital to test any theories. It's all seen as ghastly experimentation, and no one would have let me try. It's too taboo, even for the Charmed."

"How did you know you would be able to fix it?" That seems like a big risk to take for someone who had never practiced before.

"I didn't." He looks over at me now with a grin, twisted laughter under his breath. "But I've always known I was powerful. I can sense death from miles away, can smell Reapers as though they are right next to me when they are actually hiding in the trees. I don't *just* reanimate the dead like so many of my kind do; I pull their corpses from the ground and give them life."

"So you suspected," I conclude, blinking in astonishment. He's told me about some of these things before, but I've never met a Necromancer. I didn't realize that most can *only* reanimate the dead.

"I suspected," he agrees, grin falling.

"The leg is a big place to start."

"No one said I started with my leg."

"Good Grim, Dagan, please don't tell me you did this to all of your body parts." I scrunch my nose, imagining the pain he must have inflicted on himself.

"Not all my parts," he's cackling again, flopping backward onto the bed. "One is too precious to just chop off."

"Ew, Dagan, I don't want to hear about what's between your legs. Leave that kind of talk to Jaymes, please."

Dagan laughs again, holding up his wrists. "Want to see my scars?"

"Only if you want me to."

"You're precious, Azalea Jinx. Has anyone ever told you that?"

"Not a soul," I say truthfully, smiling. "And, for the record, I'm not going to act weird about this. I think it was kind of selfless what you did. Deranged? Most definitely. But selfless."

"No one's ever said that before. Not even my dad." His voice is quiet, his face open and vulnerable.

"You hacked yourself up so that, one day, you would be able to give someone else the chance to live. You practiced on yourself because you knew you needed to know how, and you didn't know a better way to do it. You're going to be a hero to a lot of people one day, Dagan." I reach over and grab his hand, noticing for the first time the perfect bands around the base of each finger. Scars.

"My dad thinks it made me a psychopath."

"We're all a little psychopathic, aren't we? It's the way of the world."

"I hope you do save the world, Azalea Jinx, because I don't think anyone else can." Dagan's voice is small and broken, a side of him exposed that I've never been witness to before. A weak, sad side that he hides deep inside. How many scars does he have? Is his leg the only thing that was different after his experiments? Do his fingers ache, his wrists creak, his ankles roll? I have so many questions, but I won't ask a single one of them.

"I'll either save them, or I'll doom them all to hell."

CHAPTER 29

"Scythe Partners can also transport, which, surprisingly, does not take much Charm Levels from them. So, even after they've depleted enough levels to no longer be able to form shields, they can still transport themselves to safety. They are not strong enough to take Conjurers with them, and usually will not leave their chosen partner unless told to do so. They would rather die than live without their partner."

—*You and Your Scythe*, written by Shifter Marcellus Stone in 1998 A.G.

After spending three days with Dagan, I know that I'm not going to be able to search Draxmere anymore. He's been attached to my hip like a parasite, snipping in my ear and dragging me into precarious situations just for the hell of it. Yesterday, he dared me to close my eyes and zap a tree with Light, which wouldn't have been so bad if he didn't want us standing on two opposite sides to see who it would hit once it fell.

I did it, of course. I'm not a fucking coward.

Turns out, I have shitty luck. Dagan barely managed to use a Hover Charm to stop it from hitting me, cackling all the while.

"What's the point of being alive if you aren't even living, Azalea?" he said, choking on the words as more cackling followed. To this, I replied, "What's the point of living if I'm just trying to die?" That was a little too philosophical for him, I think, because he quickly changed the subject, and we went on to the next, not-so-scary task of eating dinner.

Tonight, he seems a little bored and a lot on edge, and he can't seem to make up his mind about what crazy activity he wants to commit to.

"We should jump off the roof," he declares suddenly, waving a black fingernail around in the air dramatically.

"Wow, what a brilliant idea, Dagan. I know I told you I don't want to be a savior, but I don't think—"

"I'll cast the Hover Charm before you hit the ground." He waves his hand dismissively, scoffing.

"No, thanks. It's not that I don't trust you with my life, but…Actually, I don't trust you with my life."

"Buzzkill." He pouts, falling next to me on my bed. He doesn't have a shirt on today, and I'm fairly certain his shorts are just fancy boxers.

"Sorry, but I've had enough near-death experiences the past few months. I could go the rest of my life without another, actually. Figure out something else to do." I reach my hand into the bowl of popcorn he managed to secure from the cafeteria, missing television for the first time since I've been at Draxmere. At least if he was distracted by that, he wouldn't be trying to con me into almost dying.

"Let's call Jaymes!" He flops up again, hands already working the spell.

The square has already been formed when I say, "What if I don't want to…"

Dagan flourishes his hands, and a wavy bubble appears in the air, probably the size of my head. The inside is all misty and unclear, but a few colors poke through: white, tan, and blue.

I glance over, rolling my eyes as I say, "I don't think—" Dagan slaps a hand over my mouth, his own wide open. I turn back to the bubble, a small sound of surprise leaving my mouth despite the hand trying to hold it in.

Jaymes has his back to us, tan skin entirely on display and dripping wet. We can see every muscle in his back, the flexing of his shoulders, and the curves of his perky ass. We should definitely announce our presence, but it feels wrong now. And Dagan looks so satisfied…I'm not sure I could ruin this moment for him. But something must alert him to our presence, because he lets out a very, very long sigh and reaches off somewhere in the distance.

"You two get a good look, or should I stand like this a little longer?"

"A little longer," Dagan says seriously, unperturbed by the ice in Jaymes's tone.

I shove his hand off my mouth, saying, "Dagan wants you to do a spin, actually."

He cackles, nodding enthusiastically. "Yes, do that!"

Jaymes pulls a towel into frame, wrapping it around his waist quickly and efficiently. He turns around, a blush rising from his neck to his cheeks, and says, "Is this important or were you hoping to get a peek?"

"*I* was hoping—"

"Dagan, you've embarrassed him," I say, grinning.

"I'm not…"

"He's not…"

The two pause, exchanging a long glance I don't think I should be privy to. "Sure, sure. You're looking sexy as always, Jaymes." It's an attempt to break the ice, but I'm not sure it works.

"So? You two going to tell me why you called?"

Dagan takes me and pushes me back onto the bed, flopping down on his back beside me. The bubble floats above us, capturing most of our bodies and showing off my friend's shirtless form. *Show off.*

"Dagan's bored." I barely manage the words out as I funnel more food into my mouth. He was the one who wanted to call, so I'll let him do the talking.

"Ah, he wanted a sexy time call, did he?" Jaymes has a smaller towel now, rubbing it across his head.

"Of course I did." Dagan isn't shy about his attraction to Jaymes, and his confidence is endearing.

"Sorry, sweetheart, I'm not on call tonight."

"Boo." He grabs popcorn and throws it at the bubble, but it passes right through. I don't miss the red creeping up Dagan's neck, though.

I see a little black form move across the counter, the slinky tail whipping around like a rattlesnake. "Is that…is that my cat?" Why does my cat like to hang out with everyone who isn't *me*?

"Maybe." Jaymes glances at me slyly, trying to hide the smile creeping up on his lips.

"Why do you have my cat? *How* do you have my cat?"

Dagan cackles next to me, wheezing afterward.

"I don't know. He just showed up this morning."

"I haven't seen him in over a week!" Grimsly comes and goes as he pleases, which doesn't bother me. It *does* bother me seeing him next to my friend when he's supposed to be nearby, protecting me.

"Well, now you have." Jaymes picks him up into his arms, shoving him in front of his face so we can clearly see him. Grimsly howls, swiping his front paws at the bubble ferociously. "See? Nice and feisty as always."

"Little fucker," I hiss at the treacherous cat, throwing popcorn. "Booooo!"

"That's not nice, Azalea Jinx." Jaymes sighs and puts down the black cat, slapping the bubble so that he's out of frame. When he pops back into frame, he has changed into a pair of black sweatpants and a maroon t-shirt, the words "Gravedigger 4 Ever" sloppily painted on. He's strutting outside now, moving to sit on the swinging bench on the front porch.

"Arlo make that for you?" I snicker, gesturing to his shirt.

"Unfortunately, and he gets very offended if I don't wear it."

"How would he know?" Dagan asks, adding on, "And when do I get one?"

"You don't. And I don't know, but he always does."

"Tracking Charm is my guess," Dagan mutters, frowning. "Is that nonnegotiable?"

"Yes." It isn't rude or angry coming from Jaymes, just blunt and honest. I see Grimsly taking off toward the woods in the background, a tiny black dot in the already dark night. I can only see him because of the full moon illuminating the ground.

"Where is he going now?" I scowl, frowning. "Can he teleport or something? Is that how he just pops up? I really should do some more research on Scythe Partners."

"Yeah, you should." Dagan glances over at me, rolling his eyes. "That's basic knowledge, Azzie. Of course they can teleport."

"Don't call me that." I don't mean to say it so viciously, but Dagan recoils immediately as a result.

"Sorry, I didn't mean to ups—"

"What's that?" I squint toward the distance, sure something larger than Grimsly is back there moving.

"What is what?" Jaymes turns his head over his shoulder, wet hair flopping across his forehead with the movement. He jerks up so suddenly that the bubble wavers for a few precious seconds, righting itself just in time for us to see Reapers stepping out of the tree line. No, not Reapers. Just one.

Demi.

"Jaymes!" I shout, panic filling my lungs as I shoot upright. "Don't kill her!"

"She's a Reaper, Azalea," he hisses, Light flaring in his hands.

"Please," I beg, tears springing to my eyes. "Don't kill her. Shayde said we could save her. I know how. Kind of. Just don't kill her. I'm *begging* you!"

"Who is that?" Dagan whispers, panic in his eyes. He sits up now, and we glance at each other with dread and fear. We aren't Shadow Walkers; we can't make it to Jaymes.

"My best friend," I whisper back, the tears burning my eyes from being held in. I let out a weak sob, covering my mouth to try and hide it. But there is no hiding the screech that leaves my lips, or the tears that slip free from their weak barrier, when Jaymes sends out a warning blast.

"Shit."

"Yeah, *shit*." I take a shaky breath, shouting desperately, "Stop it, Jaymes! Stop it!"

"I'll stop when she's dead." His voice is cold and unattached, only a fraction of the man I know.

"You can't," I sob, helpless to do anything but watch.

Dagan wraps me in his arms, tucking my hair behind my ears and saying, "Don't be mad at him. He's only doing what he thinks is right."

"But it's not right! Shayde told me—"

"I can't believe you still trust him," Jaymes spits, chancing a glance over his shoulder to glare at me. "That you think he wouldn't do anything, *say* anything, to get you back."

"You trusted him when I didn't," I hiss back, angrier than ever.

"Things changed, Azalea."

"What changed? Because, from where I'm standing, you just woke up one day and decided it was over between you. That the love you felt doesn't matter anymore."

"I can't let my blindness to the people I fall in love with get in the way of my judgment anymore." It's a slap to the face, a knife's sharp edge stabbed directly in my heart.

"You mean me."

"You're part of that exclusive group, sure." I can hear him gritting his teeth, can hear the intake of breath as something else moves in the shadows.

"What is it? Who is…" I stop, seeing the giant antlers emerging from the treeline. "Oh, shit. Oh shit, oh shit, oh shit."

"That's a Grim." Dagan is shaking now, so fearful for Jaymes that he's immobile.

"It's *my* Grim," I say, hoping I'm right when I add on, "He won't hurt Jaymes."

We watch as the Grim form transforms into a Charmed one, Shayde bending down at the waist to scoop something up before striding forward. Grimsly. The cat is comfortable in Shayde's arms, and I can practically hear him purring despite the distance. I can feel it, I think, in my chest. He's happy to see Shayde.

"Shayde," I moan, dropping my face into my hands, "What are you doing?"

"Hello, Jaymes Bloodgood." Shayde's voice is rough and deep, his tone more sinister than it should be. Fuck. This is the other half of him, isn't it? The Grim that's trying to take over.

"Get out of here, Shayde, before I kill you and your pet." Jaymes gestures toward Demi, who still hasn't moved, but I can't see his face to determine how truthful that statement is.

"I'm not here to fight, Jay." Shayde shakes his head, grinning maniacally. "I'm here to talk."

"I have nothing to say to you."

He tilts his head, staring at the bubble where we watch curiously. "Hello, little flower."

"Don't hurt him, Shayde," I shout, wishing I could just reach through the bubble and grab Jaymes.

"Oooh, no, darling. I would never dream of it." Grimsly blinks up at the bubble, and I swear he winks at me. *What. The. Fuck?*

"What do you want, Shayde?" Jaymes's voice is a low growl, light popping around him nefariously.

"Do you know where it is?"

"I'm going to say no, since I have no clue what you're talking about."

"I wouldn't be so quick to answer."

"Then, please, enlighten me, Grim."

"The Grimoire." Shayde glances at me now, and I see the real him hiding inside the monster that's trying to take over.

"Why would I tell you if I did?" Jaymes doesn't sound confused or lost; he sounds *bored*.

"You knew," I whisper, hand over my mouth. "You knew and you didn't tell me?"

"I don't know when you talked to him or what he promised you, but none of it is true. The Grimoire is an old, unintelligible book that holds no worth."

"You don't know that!" I shake with a fury so strong that Dagan leaps away. Shadows and Light erupt around the room in a dazzling show of power.

"You trust him over me?" Jaymes turns to look at me now, rage boiling on the surface.

"I…" I pause, unable to finish the sentence. Because the horrible truth is *yes*. Yes, I do.

Shayde's smile in the back is beautiful and terrifying all at once. "Don't ask questions you don't want the answers to."

"Azalea, you can't be serious," Dagan hisses, taking Jaymes's side. "That's a fucking Grim!"

"He's more than that," I argue, glancing between the bubble and Dagan. "*He's Shayde.*"

"Not anymore, no." Jaymes is firm as he turns back to Shayde, Light suddenly steady as he aims his hands toward his best friend.

"But it could be! It could be if you just give us the Grimoire—"

"Us?" Jaymes lets out a bitter laugh, hissing, "Unbelievable. No wonder my mom tortured you, Azalea. You *have* been working with the Grim."

"How dare you say that to me?" I whisper, bottom lip shaking as I try to keep my control.

"Are you saying it isn't true? That you aren't meeting him somewhere and forming plans?" Jaymes sounds paranoid and unsure, as though trusting me is *hard*.

"I haven't been meeting him anywhere. I haven't been making plans with anyone but myself. I work for what's in *my* best interest, not a Grim's."

"And what is in your best interest, Azalea? And if you say Shayde…"

"Demi." The one word slams into Jaymes like a missile, rocking him on his feet. He turns to look at her in the background, her snarls echoing in the night.

"You want to save her."

"*Of course I do!*" I huff out my own laugh, furiously wiping my eyes. I hate feeling like this. I hate feeling so hurt, so betrayed, so *lonely*. How can I feel this lonely when I'm supposedly surrounded by friends? "She's my best friend." So much emotion in one simple sentence. So many things I can't say, but want him to feel.

Jaymes drops his hands, tilting his head back and sighing. "I wanted to save my best friend once, too. And then I realized he wasn't worth saving."

Shayde watches on with feigned interest, clapping his hands slowly as Grimsly crawls up to curl around his neck. "Drop the woe-is-me act, Jaymes. It doesn't suit you. You're just as twisted as I am."

"Fuck you," he spits back, head snapping back down. He blasts a beam of Light so fast that I don't see it leave his hands, so strong that it makes a horrific noise as it whips through the air. And Shayde just laughs.

"Your cat," Dagan says, blinking at the image.

"I know." I swallow, seeing the shield protecting Shayde. "He does that sometimes."

"Don't you know why?" Jaymes asks bitterly, refusing to look at me.

"No."

"Because you love him." Dagan is the one who responds, voice resigned. "You're in love with the Grim, so your Scythe Partner is duty-bound to protect him."

"That...it can't be..." Of course I love Shayde. I've never stopped. But to admit that openly, to share it with my closest friends; I wasn't ready for that.

"It's inconvenient," Jaymes says simply, cracking his neck with a sigh. "Would it help if I told you two that I don't know where the Grimoire is?"

"But you've seen it," Shayde says, pushing.

"Sure. My mom used to have it in her office at home. She had it in this case protected by a ton of Charms, none of which I'm privy to. I don't know if it's still there; I haven't been home in years."

"Thank you, Jaymes," I say, relief flooding me. Maybe finding the Grimoire isn't hopeless after all.

"Don't thank me," he whispers, turning his back to Shayde fully now. "I haven't given you a location."

My eyes wide with excitement, I say, "No, but you gave me an idea."

I glance over to see Shayde and Demi slinking away, apparently satisfied with the little intel they gathered. Maybe he knows I'm smart enough to understand the hidden message in Jaymes's words. He said that she *used* to have it in her office at home, meaning he believes it's no longer there. And if it isn't in her home office any longer, then what other office would she keep it in?

One she uses every day, protected inside a school filled with hundreds of highly trained Conjurers. One I slipped inside without her, or their, knowledge a couple of months back.

CHAPTER 30

"Be wary of the beast inside,
be wary of a friend who lied.
Don't query the Grim who hides,
don't query the friend who chooses sides.
Don't bury the secrets that died,
don't bury the truth you find."
—Recovered prophecy recorded in Seer Azalea Jinx's prophetic
journal, 2025 A.G.

"You fucking treacherous snake," I hiss to Grimsly when he shows up a week later, his belly drooping lower than I remember. "You left me to go protect *him*? What if I died while you were gone? Huh? What would you have done then?"

Grimsly only blinks at me as though bored, curling up on my bed and closing his eyes without a care in the world. "I worry about you," I add on, frowning. "You know that? You disappear for weeks at a time and expect me to be cool with that? What do you even *do*?"

His eyes slide back open, and he looks at me as though I'm stupid, and maybe I am. Because, clearly, he's been sneaking off to go visit someone he shouldn't—to protect a Grim—and he's been doing it the whole time I've owned him, probably from the moment Shayde picked him for me. Hating Shayde has never worked, and it's a painfully obvious fact that Grimsly has proved. The question is: What has Shayde been doing that warrants protection from my Scythe Partner?

"Never mind, actually. Take a nap, Grimsly. I don't want to know *any* of the things you and Shayde get up to in his free time."

Grimsly lets out a small huff and his eyes shut again, as though he's exhausted and can't bother to listen anymore. Maybe he is exhausted. He has to be getting to Shayde somehow, so he must be using a lot of energy to do so. I really need to do some research on Scythe Partners, don't I? Everybody seems to know more about them than me, and I'm the only person I know of with one.

I sigh and give him a weak smile, slipping out of my room and into the hall as quietly as I can. Ginny is already there waiting for me, just as I requested. "Hi, babe," she says with a grin, wrapping me in her arms. "How was your break?"

"Boring until Dagan showed up."

She frowns, hissing, "I knew you were going to be lonely. I told you I would stay if…"

I wave my hand dismissively. "I had things to do. Dagan was only in my way."

"And are those things why you called me here?" She raises a perfect auburn brow, flipping her long curls over her shoulder.

I sigh, smoothing down the invisible wrinkles in my school-is-sued skirt as I say, "Maybe. But if I tell you these things, you have to swear to keep them secret. I'm going to make the same offer to the Thatcher triplets. You'll be in the loop, but I can't let you bring anybody else into it. If you do, it could ruin everything. We won't be able to save…" I pause, clenching my teeth.

"Who? Who are you trying to save?" Ginny glances around us, her voice barely audible.

I match her tone and whisper, "Demi."

"What?" She practically screams the words, drawing the attention of everyone in the hallway.

"Shush, Ginny! Good Grim!" I tug on her arm, dragging her to the staircase where, blessedly, no students linger.

"How can you save her, Azalea? She's a Reaper! And dead, I thought."

"I can't give you details." I swallow, leaning in and whispering harshly, "But if you want to help her, too, then you'll agree to keep my secrets."

"I would have done it just for you, Azalea. You don't have to threaten me with Demi's life just because we were friends longer." Ginny seems sad, as though my not understanding that is painful for her.

"I…" I drop her arm, my voice broken and rough. "I wasn't sure anymore. Not after…" Not after I got her punished. Not after I put a target on her back. Not after she was forced to carry my beaten, bloody body into the school. Not after she realized I was a risk she shouldn't consider taking.

"You're my friend, Azalea. Nothing you say or do can change that fact."

"Don't be so sure." It's a dark vow, one I try to emphasize as I stare into her brown eyes.

"You don't scare me, Azalea Jinx." Her voice doesn't waver or crack. That sharp, beautiful face doesn't quiver. She only stares, angry and disbelieving.

"I should."

"Demi told me about the prophecies," she says after a long beat of silence, pausing as someone opens the door and passes us on the stairway. "She told me you would either be her savior or her doom."

"Yeah? Then you should realize how dangerous it is to love me." I don't look at her; I can't.

"You're going to be her savior, Azalea. I know it. She knew it. The Seers just didn't know because they can't see things clearly around you. But whatever plan you're forming? Whatever knowledge you're hiding? If you really think it will save her, then you're exactly what she knew you would be. What *I* know you are. I'll follow you anywhere, Azalea Jinx. You may not be *the* savior, but you will be hers. I'm confident in that."

A tear slips down my cheek, a sob leaving my throat unwillingly. "I hate emotions," I cry out, furiously swiping at my cheeks. "I hate that I love you, Genevieve Brady."

"You hate loving anybody, Azalea Jinx. I'm not special." She smiles, pulling me into her arms and letting my head rest on her shoulder. "Now, what's the plan?"

"I can't tell you here; it's too dangerous."

Ginny groans, face pinching. "Of course it is. We can't just have an easy, fun plan, can we?"

"Alright, smart ass. Just meet me in my room on Saturday at noon, okay? I have to gather a few more people, and I want to ask the triplets separately. I don't want them agreeing just because their sisters do; I want them to agree because they want to help.

And with a new Specialty class on my plate…" I pause to run a hand through my hair, patting my bangs down and sighing. The red is vibrant today, gleaming like blood. Whatever that hairstylist used hasn't needed any touchups, hasn't faded a bit. Some days it seems brighter. The extravagant cost seems worth it now.

"I forgot about that. Tell me how it goes at dinner, okay? And if the teachers keep trying to punish you…" She frowns, brows furrowing. "Well, then, I'll be in contact with a Grim." It's basically her way of saying she's going to talk to a manager, and it has my sad tears turning into joyous ones as I laugh.

"Yeah, Ginny. You do that."

We smile at each other, a new kind of trust forming. I had tried to push Ginny away for so long, and the triplets, too, but I can't do that anymore. I can't save Demi by myself, and I can't keep feeling lonely when I'm surrounded by friends.

I have to tell them the truth. What they decide to do after that is on them.

Charms is as miserable as always. It used to be my favorite class, but Professor Canmore has it out for me now. She can't punish me with penalties anymore, but she *can* punish me by giving me low grades and low self-esteem. She made me read a section from the textbook out loud, berating me if I mispronounced any word or if my slight southern accent came out at any point to make the words sound different. Then, she asked me to perform a Charm that most people here have learned by the time they're teenagers. It was a simple unlocking Charm, called a Delock Charm, but I didn't know how to do it. She'd smiled maliciously and marked something down in the book on her desk, pointedly asking someone else to show me the simple movement. Their hands formed a triangle, then broke it in one harsh movement, their fingers folding down toward the ground. I memorized it, cheeks blazing, and succeeded on my first attempt.

I stormed off to Combat Training afterward, refusing to acknowledge Ginny's small protests about Canmore's behavior. The problem is, Canmore is right to call me out. I didn't earn my spot here at Draxmere; I was born into it. And that fact infuriates me more than the shitty behavior of my professor.

Class starts okay. Professor Donovan won't look me in the eyes, but it's okay because I don't want to look at him, either. He allowed them to punish me, even if he never actively decided to do so. By not speaking out, he was complacent. Catrina Gordo is still hanging around him, apparently, because they watch us silently. They don't say a word to any of the students, not until I step onto the training mat.

"Your form is off," they say blatantly, waving a manicured hand at me impatiently. "Fix your feet."

"This is always how I—"

"Then it's always been wrong." Their tone is no-nonsense, and Donovan only sends me a sideways glance.

I grumble a few choice words under my breath and adjust my footing, holding my fists up. "Better?"

"Slightly." There's a punching bag in front of me, one I'm supposed to repeat a pattern of rapid-fire punches on before blasting with my power. I've done this process a million times before, and Donovan has always liked the results. "Hit it."

I do the jabs and blocks that are burned into my memory, then blast it with a ball of Light so intense it burns a hole in the fabric. I move to step off the mat, allowing the next Conjurer to step up.

"No, no. Come back, Azalea Jinx. I won't accept anything less than perfect from our *savior*." Their smile is poisonous, their evil infectious.

Anger bubbles up so fast that I can't stop it, Light and Shadow dripping from my fingers. "That wasn't good enough for you?"

"No. It wasn't."

I stomp back over to the bag, raising my fists and punching harder than ever before. Then, I release everything within me into the final hit. Light and Shadow slam into the bag, forcing it off its stand as it flies to the other side of the room upon impact. I give them a faux smile and a mock curtsy, saying, "A perfect hit, courtesy of your savior." Then I tap my chin, frowning as I add on, "Well, maybe not *yours*."

They don't like that, and open their mouth to tell me so, but I stomp off before they can. I rip the tape off my hands, heading to the locker room. I hear Donovan saying behind me, "Cat, that was unnecessary."

I can't hear all of their reply, but I'm pretty sure it went something like: "You're too soft on the girl. Everyone is. If she's going to do what needs to be done, then she has to sharpen up. Her moves are sloppy and weak. Sloppy and weak won't win us this war."

No, but their faction believes surrendering will.

Getting through the Light and Shadow Specialty classes took so much willpower that I was sure I wouldn't have enough to make it to my first Seer class, which had been rescheduled from early this morning to late afternoon for some reason. Jaymes wasn't in the Light class, and I ended up sitting with my back to a tree during both classes and watching my professors ignore me for two hours straight. It was horrible and humiliating, as usual.

I know these classes aren't as miserable as they were before the break—I'm not getting punished or tortured for made-up crimes—but my tolerance is subliminally lower. I don't want to sit here and pretend I care about these people or their rules. I want to learn, and I want to be good at Conjuring, but the environment I'm learning in is too hostile. Until Dean Bloodgood is gone, I won't be safe here. But I'm going to go through the motions. I'm going to keep excelling, despite Bloodgood trying really hard to make sure that doesn't happen.

And the second I find that Grimoire, I'm getting out of Dodge.

I straighten my spine, forcing myself to take step after step until I'm walking into the Seer room on the first floor. It's in one of the many rooms Dean Delarosa didn't show me when she gave me a tour of Draxmere, near the siren's Olympic-sized pool. When I walk in, I'm instantly smothered in a thick red smoke, the blood-like color matching the strands in my hair oddly well. I cough and wave at the air, jumping when someone begins screeching, "Shut the door!"

I'm barely through before it's slammed shut, the wind kicking up more smoke into my face. I cough and sputter, choking out, "What the fuck?"

"Azalea Jinx!" The voice is bright and ecstatic, but I can't tell where it's coming from. "Welcome, welcome! Oh, you have no idea how excited we are to have you here!"

I make a noise of surprise when a young face pops up in front of me, Light escaping from my hands before I can stop it. The woman only laughs, her strawberry blond bob swaying. She has a multicolored headband in it, pushing the hair out of her oval face to display pretty hazel eyes. She isn't dressed like most professors in their all-black Conjuring gear, choosing instead to don a light blue maxi skirt and a white crop top. Her light skin is hardly visible underneath all the smoke, her lithe body covered in gorgeous brown freckles.

"You must be Professor Frost." I glance around the room, only seeing vague objects in the gloom of the dark room.

"Call me Meadow, dear. Come, come!" She grabs me by the wrist, tugging and pulling me into the red mist.

"Um, sure. You're gripping kind of hard. Can you—" Her other hand abruptly slams on my mouth, stopping me mid-sentence. My eyes are wide as I'm forced to follow her deeper into the room, all the way to a desk somewhere in the back. She forces me into the seat, finally releasing my mouth.

"This is your assigned seat, Azalea. The pen and notebook here are for your journal. Whatever you hear or see, you write it down. The more details, the better. And when you're given a prophecy, you make sure you memorize every word. Eventually, you'll be practiced enough to jot down notes while you're still in the vision."

"Right. Okay, well—Grimsly?" The damn cat is sitting on top of my notebook, his eyes glowing in the darkness.

"Ooh, yes! Your little Scythe Partner is such a sweetie, aren't you? Yes, you are," she coos, petting the white dot under his chin affectionately.

"How often does he come here?" I mutter bitterly, glaring at him. The cat has a whole secret life that I'm not privy to, apparently. I really need to pay more attention to his comings and goings.

"Usually just on Tuesdays," she says solemnly, as though Tuesdays are bad. "That's when my students need the most comfort. He likes the pets."

"Right…and Tuesdays we need comfort because…?"

"Because of the bad news." She blinks at me as though I'm the one being confusing. "You know, Tuesdays are boo days?"

"No," I say bluntly, staring right back. "Care to elaborate?"

"No." She shudders, tilting her head to the side. "You'll learn."

She moves to walk away, but I call out, "What's with the red smoke? What am I supposed to do?"

"It's an aphrodisiac." She grins, wafting the stuff into her nose. "It opens our minds to the in-between. You, my dear, need to sit and prepare. Typically, the visions hit after about fifteen minutes."

"What do you mean they hit? Does this stuff cause the visions?"

She laughs, skirt flowing as she fades into the red. "No, my dear. You do that. We only help your mind adjust."

"That's nice." I put my book bag down, sitting and reaching out for Grimsly. He curls up into my chest and purrs so hard that it vibrates my entire upper half, his tail coming up to curl around my neck. "Can you quit doing all of this secret shit behind my back? You're supposed to be *my* cat, remember?"

Grimsly makes a little hissing noise but continues to curl up on me, his tail rattle snaking to show his annoyance. I open my mouth to keep berating him, but my head starts to split open, and every thought flees. I groan and tip forward, barely feeling it when my head hits the desk. Grimsly makes a noise of distress and claws his way out from under me, and I feel his tongue on my cheek like rough sandpaper.

I thought Professor—I mean, Meadow, said it would be fifteen minutes before I felt anything?

My vision fades to black so suddenly that I let out a surprised gasp, my ears ringing as I desperately try to stay aware of my surroundings. I don't see anything at first, the darkness all-consuming. It's terrifying and exhilarating; a rush runs through me as I wait for that petrifying voice to tell me the things it thinks I need to know.

The silence is consuming, the darkness surrounding me discombobulating. But then I see Jaymes wearing a white suit. His face is set in stone as he stares at me, or past me, I guess. I don't bother trying to call to him; I only watch. He lifts his arm, tapping on his wrist with a grim expression. His head turns slightly, blond hair ruffling on an invisible wind. His body glitches, his head seeming to turn over and over and over. Then, it's as though the whole thing is resetting, and I watch him lift that same arm and tap again.

"I don't understand what that means," I finally say after the third loop, growing increasingly frustrated. I can feel the desk underneath my cheek, can feel Grimsly rubbing up on my side. But I can't jerk myself out of this endless loop, can't force the vision to stop.

With a sudden ferocity, the familiar, aging voice booms out, "Be wary of the beast inside, be wary of a friend who lied. Don't query the Grim who hides, don't query the friend who chooses sides. Don't bury the secrets that died, don't bury the truth you find."

My head pounds with the new knowledge, albeit much more tolerable than the first time. I whimper, clutching onto my head as I say, "You told me that already."

Again, it says, "Be wary of the beast inside, be wary of a friend who lied. Don't query the Grim who hides, don't query the friend who chooses sides. Don't bury the secrets that died, don't bury the truth you find."

"I still don't understand what it means," I whimper, groaning as the pain increases. Then I remember what I had to do last time, and I repeat the words back. Again. Again. Again. And when that voice is finally satisfied, when the image of Jaymes has finally stopped looping, my eyes flutter open.

Grimsly is hissing on the desk just above my head, back arched and hair stretching upward. He's facing Meadow, warning her away. Her eyes look sad and worried, but Grimsly doesn't seem to care. She is cooing at him, trying to console him, but he only continues to bare his teeth. At least, until I groan.

His back falls, his body spinning, and his head rubs up against mine. I slowly force myself back up into a sitting position, blinking through the fuzziness and the intensity of the red mist around us. "It's okay, my Scythe," I whisper to him, shaky fingers reaching out to rub his soft ears.

"Azalea, dear!" Meadow takes the chance to leap forward, crouching down next to my desk and examining my head with nimble fingers. "You have quite an egg here." I wince when her fingers graze over the sensitive area of my forehead, groaning outright when she presses. She pulls her hand away when Grimsly begins to hiss again, wary eyes watching him tentatively.

"Write it down," she urges, pushing the pen and notebook forward.

I shake my head, glancing from the notebook to her, confidently stating, "I don't need to."

"You do. You risk forgetting it. We must instill the need to write down prophecies with the stude—"

"I've heard it before." My stomach squeezes at the thought of it, of the image it brought me before of Jaymes and Shayde fighting.

"No…no, you couldn't have. You must be mistaken." She shakes her head with a gentle smile, patting my arm placatingly. "I understand that it's overwhelming being here, that the methods in this class are unorthodox, and you didn't quite know what to expect, but we don't get repeated prophecies. Your mind is probably revisiting that first prophecy, but you mustn't worry! If it were important, the prophecy would have been repeated several times, and you wouldn't have forgotten. If you want, we can go over the vision and—"

"It was repeated. The first time I heard it was on that stage a few weeks ago. The voice repeated it and I did, too. Trust me, mellow Meadow, I have had this one memorized for weeks."

She flushes, mouth opening and closing. With a sigh, she pushes herself up and whispers so low I barely hear it, "Write it down, Azalea Jinx. Don't tell anyone else that your prophecy was repeated. If they find out…"

"What? Why is this so weird?" Why does everything I do and experience have to be special? Why can't I just have normal shit happen for once?

"Repeated prophecies mean trouble, Azalea. They're dire warnings. Is this one personal or worldly?" She watches me carefully, still entirely too quiet for my liking.

"Personal, I think."

"You think, or you're sure?" Her hands move to clasp together nervously, her body swaying.

I purse my lips, hesitant as I murmur decidedly, "Personal."

"Then this is an important message, Azalea. Our ability to prophesize is not the ability of some unknown being, you know? It comes from within. Our minds intuitively grasp onto threads of the future and present them to us in codes only we may understand. Others will study and form their own conclusions, but it's ultimately up to us to determine the meaning. So this message? This warning? It's up to you to interpret its meaning. And I hope for your sake you figure it out before it's too late."

"And if I don't?" The throbbing in my head has lessened, but I think I'm going to have to grab a vial of vampire blood to heal the giant goose egg I earned.

"Then you face the consequences."

She moves to walk away, but I frantically call out, "I didn't think the future could be changed? Isn't that a thing everyone says? That the future is set in stone and there is no changing fate?"

"Only fools sit around and let their destinies pass them by," she says simply, lips tilting up into a small smile as I begin copying down the prophecy into my notebook. "And I don't think you're a fool."

CHAPTER 31

"The price we pay for being this powerful is a steep one: our minds. I was willingly turned into this creature, willingly chose to pay whatever price being a Grim would make me pay. I'm learning now that the cost is my sanity, and I'm okay with that. You must be, too. It'll feel strange and discombobulating, but it'll be worth it. And if it isn't…there is a safeguard in place to stop the Grim process. I'll list it in detail, but I must stress that this cannot happen unless the situation is *dire*."

—*The Grimoire*, written by the first, unnamed Grim, 1 A.G.

Ginny only knocks once before I'm tugging her into my room, a small noise of surprise leaving her lips. "Azalea, what—"

"Shut up," I say harshly, slamming the door behind me.

"Um, okay, I know abrasiveness is your thing, but you don't have to be so—"

"Ginny, I'm being so serious right now. *Shut. Up.*"

Her lips purse, but she obeys, hearing the sincerity in my voice. I crack the door open again, peering out and waiting for my next guest. Dagan happens to be the next one at my door, her small cry of surprise swallowed by my hand as I tug her in and cover her mouth. "I'm going to tell you the same thing I told sweet Ginny here: Shut up."

Dagan glances over at Ginny, who's now perched on the edge of my bed, promptly rolling her eyes and shrugging before patting the space beside her. Dagan pouts but plops down next to her anyway, watching me with a curious gleam. I don't say anything until the triplets arrive, who I am just as quick to tell to shut up before going back to the door.

"There's more?" Willow mutters under her breath, cozying up next to Ginny.

"What did I say?" I snarl, sending shadows to tug on her hair. She yelps, batting away the strands with a whimper. She looks like she wants to say more but does the smart thing and waits.

The heavy bangs that come nearly ten minutes later scare the five girls, but they only fill me with relief. I usher the remaining Gravediggers into my room, pausing before I shut the door to glance around. There are a few stragglers out in the hallway, but I don't see any of them looking my way.

With a huff, I close the door, hands on my hips as I look over each of my guests.

"Why weren't they told to shut up?" Dagan remarks, frowning deeply and menacingly.

"Yeah, that's totally sexist of you, Azalea," Reese adds, nodding encouragingly to Dagan.

"Shut up," I say again, turning my attention to Jaymes. "Is there some kind of Charm that will make sure no one hears us?"

"Sure." He blinks down at me, running a hand through his fluffy blond hair. "The Soundless Charm. It'll make the walls sound-proof."

"Do that." I wave my hands at him, biting my lip apprehensively. To his credit, he does what I ask without question. He makes a 'z' with one hand, starting at the top, while the other hand simultaneously does the movement in the opposite direction. They end up in opposite positions where he then slams them down together, one palm on the top of the other. When he's done, the scarce footsteps and chatter we could hear before is entirely gone.

"Why did Jaymes have to do that?" Arlo questions, bushy red brows furrowed.

"Because if any of his mom's little Black Cloaks overheard us, we'd all be brought down to the torture chamber." The room goes eerily silent, so quiet I could probably hear a pin drop.

"Isn't that just lovely?" Reese says finally, glancing over at Nox when she adds, "Not that it isn't already torture to be in a room with all of you." We all sense the lie, but it's a nice way to break the tension.

"Why don't you just tell us what's going on, Azalea?" Ginny sighs, leaning back on her hands and raising a perfectly arched auburn brow.

"What I say cannot leave this room," I say solemnly, looking into the eyes of each friend I summoned. "We all swear an oath to each other that we don't talk about this unless it's with each other."

"What kind of oath?" Nox raises a brow, glancing over at Jaymes and Arlo.

"Ooh, she definitely means a blood oath," Arlo says on a nod, grinning. "Don't you, Z?"

"I don't care what kind of oath it is; I just want to be assured the oath will be kept."

"Blood oaths don't work, doofus." Dagan scoffs, cackling as she adds, "I've tried."

"I'll swear anything to you, Azalea," Jaymes says quietly, eyes only on me. "You know that."

"You don't even want to know what it's about?" I whisper, swallowing hard.

"Don't need to."

"Well that's fucking intense," Arlo mutters, glowering at Jaymes. "Save some of those romantic notions for the rest of us, won't you?"

"It isn't like that," he says, finally tearing his gaze away from me to pin Arlo down with a deathly glare.

"Hung up on Shayde, remember?" I add, feeling a blush creeping up on me. "I'm serious, though. If anyone isn't prepared to break a lot of rules and lie about doing it, then I need you to leave." No one moves.

"We're your friends, Azalea," Ginny says, breaking the silence. "How many times do we need to prove that to you?"

"I've never had friends," I admit, guilt clawing its way up my throat. "I don't know how this works."

Dagan stands, strutting toward me and poking long fingers into my chest. "Then let me tell you. You say jump, we jump. It's that simple. We trust you. And not because you're our savior or some bullshit like that. We trust you because you are *you*. None of us have known you very long, but we all know what's in your heart. We've all seen you broken at the hands of our corrupt government. So, if you tell us that you've got some kind of plan that the government won't like? Fuck yes, we are on board. You didn't even need to ask."

Nods ensue around the room, and my heart palpitates at the sweet gesture. "Then repeat after me." I swallow, taking a deep breath before declaring, "I swear on my life that I won't repeat anything said in this room. I swear I won't talk about the plans we make with anyone outside of this room. I swear I won't betray my friends."

Ginny gawks, surprised. "You really don't trust us? You really need us to prove you should?"

"That's the problem, Ginny. I do trust you. Every. Single. One. Of. You. But I've had a prophecy warn me twice about a friend who will betray me…" I shiver, wrapping my arms around myself. "I can't risk it right now. This is too important. It may not mean much to you guys, and there may not be any punishment for you breaking this oath, but this is important. It's a sign of faith for me. A sign that I can trust you with my life and the life of the people I love."

"I swear on my life that I won't repeat anything said in this room. I swear I won't talk about the plans we make with anyone outside of this room. I swear I won't betray my friends." Jaymes is calm as he says it, but his eyes flash with worry as he watches me shake.

One by one, my friends repeat the words, and Nox is the final Conjurer to take the oath. It relieves me to no end, and I'm finally able to slump onto the bed with the other girls. My legs are weak and wobbly, my body still shaking as I try to form the words to explain the plan.

"I'm going to sneak into Dean Bloodgood's office, and I need your help doing it."

Chaos erupts.

Jaymes is stalking over to me, his face set in hard stone. Ginny jumps up, squeaking out words of surprise and bewilderment. The Thatcher sisters all look at each other and burst into outrage, glares sent to each other and me. Dagan jumps in front of Jaymes, jabbing a finger into his chest and shouting something about supporting me. Arlo and Nox turn to speak to each other, which somehow ends up with the two on the ground rolling around. I can hardly stare at one person, and I certainly can't bring myself to look into anyone's eyes.

"Shut up!" Ginny shouts after a few minutes, her voice stern and demanding. When no one listens, we find ourselves submerged so deep underwater that the pressure clogs our heads. My lungs burn as I try to push toward the surface, a choked noise leaving me as I realize I'll never be able to make it to the top. I'll never be able to…

I gasp as I'm thrown back into reality, as my feet land hard on the ground, and I stumble into the wall. "What the fuck was that?" I croak, coughing and holding my chest. The echo of that burn still sits there, as though waiting for me to acknowledge it again.

"A glamour," she says simply, wiggling her fingers at me. "An illusion."

"I didn't know you were that strong, Brady," Arlo remarks, impressed. He, too, is holding his chest as though still struggling to breathe. The three sirens aren't as affected as the rest of us, but they, too, are shaken by the inability to swim in a body of water.

"That was scary," Willow says shyly, blinking at Ginny in as much surprise as the others. "Water is where we belong. It's where we are the most comfortable. But you took that away."

"I'm sorry." To her credit, she does look incredibly regretful.

"It's okay," Willow murmurs, flushing as she adds, "It was kind of hot."

"Glamourists are just as powerful as Shifters," she says with a shrug, grinning sheepishly. "The rest of the world just likes to look down on us."

"I won't anymore," Arlo says in awe, groaning as he sits on my floor. He pushes his back against the bed, tilting his head back and letting his curly red hair tip back onto the mattress. "Go ahead, Genevieve. You have our attention."

"Don't any of you want to hear why Azalea is going to break into the Dean's office? The place that our dean has suddenly warded against students as of late? And I say *is*, not *wants to*, because we all know she's going to do it with or without us. So we might as well hear her out." With that, she sits back down, arms crossed across her chest as her eyes meet mine.

"Exactly," Dagan says as she jabs Jaymes again. "That's exactly what I said! Jaymes knows why. I know why. And I think it's a good idea. I'll help you, Azalea. I don't need to know anything else to agree. But I'm going to sit here and listen to you explain, and I'm going to bite anyone who tries to interrupt."

"Bite?" Arlo whimpers, looking over at her with wide, terrified eyes. "*Bite?*"

"Yes, and you'll be lucky if I don't take a chunk of skin with me," she snarls, taking her seat by Ginny once more.

"Thanks, Dagan. I appreciate your…I don't even know what to call that." I run my hands through my hair, placing them on the sides of my neck and sighing.

"My commitment to the cause?" she answers helpfully, grinning.

"Sure, that." I swallow, dropping my hands and stepping forward. "Jaymes, quit looking at me like that."

"Like what?" His words are clipped and harsh, his deep green eyes blazing.

"Like I've just betrayed your trust! Like I've just punched you in the gut and walked away!"

"That's exactly what you've done, isn't it?" He takes a step forward and I take a step back, shaking my head vehemently.

"No. No, *you* told me that—"

"I told you that my mom used to keep the Grimoire in her office at home, not that she'd move it to her office here!" He's snarling now, taking another long stride toward me. I take another step back, and another, until my back is to the wall and he's looming over me. "I didn't tell you because I wanted you to go looking for it, I told you so that you would move on, so that you would realize it was hopeless."

"It isn't hopeless," I hiss back, tilting my chin up and staring into his eyes. "If I can find the Grimoire, it's not only Demi's life I could be saving. Don't you see that? Anyone who ever turned into a Reaper could come back."

"I'm sorry, what?" Reese blinks over at us in shock, her sisters stiff and immobile.

"I'm searching for a book," I say, not daring to turn away from Jaymes. "A book that I'm going to give to Shayde so he can tell me how to turn Reapers back into people."

"And you think he's just going to do that without a price?" Jaymes asks, scoffing.

"I already know what his price is, and I've already accepted it."

"You can't be serious!" He's shouting again, bending down to my height to stress the importance of this. "Once Shayde has his hands on you, he isn't going to let you go."

"He has before." I don't move, my body shaking from the effort.

Jaymes keeps his mouth shut, his lips pursed, because he has no argument against that. Shayde did bring me back last time, but only because I begged him not to keep me. I'm not going to tell Jaymes that I won't be begging for anything this time.

"What's his price?" Dagan asks quietly, watching as Jaymes turns away from me and strides to the opposite corner to put distance between us.

"It doesn't matter." I take a deep breath and step back toward the middle of the room, looking from friend to friend. "I've already decided to pay it." It's less of a price and more of a prize, truthfully. Shayde is what I want; *who* I want. He always has been. It's always been him.

"Azalea…"

"Don't, Jaymes," I snap, refusing to let him ensnare me with those enraged eyes again. "This is my decision. And everyone here decided to stay and hear me out."

"She's got you there." Dagan cackles, leaning back on her hands. "Tell them the good stuff, sweetheart."

"The book we need is called The Grimoire. It was a…diary of sorts from the first Grim. Shayde thinks it holds many secrets, one of which is how to turn Reapers back into Conjurers." I don't tell them about the other secret, the one that would make him feel normal again. They don't need to know that his mind isn't all there right now.

"You said you could save Demi, but she's dead," Wren says slowly, the information slowly sinking in. "At least, that's what you said…"

"Shayde lied," Jaymes says, growling softly. "Like he always does."

"Stop that," I snap, adding softly to Wren and her sisters, "Demi is alive, and Shayde's keeping her close to him."

"Oh, Azalea," she whispers, a tear slipping down her cheek. "He's using you to get that book. Who knows what horrible things are inside it? You can't just give him that."

"No one but a Grim can read it," I say, though I'm not entirely sure it's true. "Jaymes has seen it and said no one was able to read it. It has to go to Shayde."

Nox says solemnly, nodding toward the siren, "Wren is right, Azalea. We don't know what's inside that book. We could be handing our enemy the biggest weapon to destroy us."

"Shayde is…" I pause, struggling to explain this to these people who don't understand who Shayde is—what he's become and what he no longer wants to be. "He's done some bad things. I know he has. I'm not condoning it, but you need to understand that the Grim does things to him. It warps his mind. He needs this book as much as we do. If he wants to heal himself, then this is how he's going to do it."

"He's going to stop being a Grim?" Ginny questions, brow furrowed. "He can just do that?"

"That was *my* price," I say to try and make them understand.

"We can get Shayde back?" Arlo's question is quiet, but I still hear it.

"He never left," I whisper in answer.

"You guys believe this bullshit?" Jaymes scoffs, shaking his head.

"Knock it off, man." Arlo scowls, turning to Dagan. "Aren't you going to bite him now?"

"I would love to," Dagan opens her mouth and licks her front teeth, eyes dancing in delight.

"Now's not the time, but you can come talk to me about where to put your mouth later," Jaymes deadpans, not bothering to look at her. It does its intended job and throws Dagan completely off balance.

Pointing at the door, I snarl, "If you don't want to help, then get out. If you're going to keep walking around with your head up your ass, then we don't need you here."

Jaymes opens his mouth as though to argue, but he glances around at our friends before he says, "I'm not going anywhere."

"Then it's settled." I square my shoulders, turning to Arlo. "You're the strongest on a full moon, right?"

"Uh, yeah?" He scratches the top of his head, looking at me wearily.

"And when is the next one?"

"In three weeks." His answer is prompt and courteous.

"Perfect. So, this is the plan…"

CHAPTER 32

"A book of secrets, a girl who lies,
a Grim who forces her to change the tides.
A book of forgiveness, a girl who dies,
a man she loves who chooses to change sides."
—Prophecy found inside Seer Kelvin Melendez's prophetic journals, 1983 A.G.

It only takes one week for us to find the best time to visit Blood-good's office, considering she's never there. It takes another week to discover what kinds of Charms are on the room and how to get through them. I have to give the dean credit: she's careful. The dean's office is supposed to be a place open to the public, but she's managed to make sure it's only open to the people she wants to let in. To be fair, it is *my* fault that it's become such a secretive place. I suppose she didn't like the way I let myself in and made myself comfortable last time.

Jaymes accidentally set off her alarms on the first day after making our plans, to which he promptly lied his ass off about wanting to visit her. I'm not sure what was said during *that* meeting, but he came out grumpier than usual.

By the time the full moon rolls around, we are as ready as we will ever be. "You remember the plan?" I question Dagan as I buckle a Shadow bomb onto my belt, glancing over at her expectantly. The four of us are standing around in my room, helping one another get ready for the break-in.

She scoffs, helping Reese push her tits up higher in the extremely tight dress she's donning. "Of course I do. I'm with the guard dog."

"He's more wolf than dog," I mutter, straightening. "You three look…" I whistle, glancing over the three sisters appreciatively. They are pretty girls, if not leaning toward the average, but dressed up like this? They look every bit the sultry sirens I expected them to be. "*Stunning*."

Willow giggles, pressing her hands down the sides of the sky-blue silky dress. "Don't we?" The three almost seem color coded, with Wren in a blush pink and Reese in a sage green. Each wears matching jewelry, pretty diamonds dangling from their necks and silver hoops hanging from their ears. Slits rise to their upper thighs, showing off bare skin and missing underwear.

"Those guards are going to pass out." Dagan cackles, glancing over at me with a twinkle in her eye. Like me, she's dressed in all black Conjuring gear. We decided to send the sisters in as the guards' distractions because they know more than anyone the sick fantasies men often have about having them all at once. If they walk up to the pair of men, seemingly willing to participate in some drunken fun…well, from what we've gathered over the last three weeks, they aren't the type to turn an offer like that down.

"Let me hear your drunk giggle," I say, gesturing for them to make the familiar, high-pitched noise.

"I'll do you one better." Reese grins, snapping over at her sisters. Together they do a few drunken stumbles that end with them clutching onto each other or the wall for support, bubbling laughter escaping their throats as they send sultry looks under their lashes our way.

"Wow." Dagan blinks at them in awe, mouth popped open. "That's scary good."

"It really is," Ginny says from the doorway, surprising us all.

"Knock, Ginny! For Grim's sake," Wren shouts, her sisters echoing their agreement.

"Sorry, my bad." She holds up her hands placatingly, grinning sheepishly. She matches me and Dagan, dressed to blend into shadows and darkness. I catch her eyeing Willow for longer than necessary, her pupils so large they swallow her irises entirely.

"The boys are going to meet us there," I say, checking my belt one last time. I don't think I'll use any of these daggers or bombs, I don't expect the guards to come back and check on us, but I'd rather be safe than sorry. I won't be kidnapped and tortured a second time.

We all fall quiet for long seconds before Dagan says, "Well, let's go bitches!"

I lead the way out of my room, guiding my friends down the hall and to the staircase. When we reach the last step down, Dagan, Ginny, and I hide behind the door. I nod to the sisters, telling them to go forward. Willow sends Ginny a small, hesitant smile before throwing open the door.

"Good Grim," she shouts, laughing and stumbling as she tumbles out of the door. Her sisters howl in laughter behind her, reaching to grab her under the armpits. When the door shuts, the three of us move to look out the small window in the door, our eyes barely over the lip.

"Willow!" Reese shouts as her sister drags her down, and the three girls fall into a pile on the ground. They still giggle and cackle, slipping as they try to stand.

"Do you girls need some help?" The first guard appears from around the corner, leaving his station near the front doors of the school. His dark hair is shaved around the sides, leaving a mess of curls on top. I can see his surprised expression, his slow smile spreading from one large ear to the other.

"No, no," Wren says with a wave of her hand, screeching as one of her sisters slings her off the top of the pile of bodies. She groans when she lands, holding her hip and biting her quivering lip. "We are *totally* fine."

The guard raises an eyebrow, lifting his hand to his mouth and whistling for his partner. It doesn't take long for the second one to appear, a buzz cut blond with a nose so large it takes up half his face. "Ladies, have you been drinking?" The blond is grinning now, too.

"Of course not," Willow gasps, giggling and throwing her head back. Her brown hair sweeps over her shoulder, the long strands dangling behind her now.

"We would never," Reese adds, twirling a lock of Willow's hair around her finger.

"Not in our wildest dreams," Wren finishes, and the three burst into more outrageous giggles.

"We might have to turn you in to the dean," the black-haired one says, rubbing his chin thoughtfully.

"What?" Wren screeches.

"No!" Willow cries.

"We'll do anything," Reese begs.

"Anything?" the two guards echo, glancing toward each other with matching smirks.

"Anything," Wren agrees, kicking off her heels. She pushes herself to her feet, swaying toward the blond. She places a hand on his chest, bottom lip stuck out in a pout. "Come on. You guys don't really want to turn us in, do you?"

"Maybe they just need the right motivation," Reese adds, biting her lip as she follows her sister's lead. She stands and struts over to the black-haired one, pressing her body against him. He looks down at her, eyes going directly to the chest Dagan spent so long adjusting earlier.

"We can prove that we're good girls," Willow says, and I wonder if she tastes bile like I do when she says it. She crawls over to the couples, moving to stand between them. She puts a hand on each of the men's shoulders, looking up at them under her lashes.

"A tempting offer," Big Ears murmurs, placing a hand on Reese's waist. He glances over to Big Nose, nodding with a grin. "I'm sure we can take a small break."

"Only a small one?" Reese prods, giggling when he grabs her by the waist and pulls her into his chest.

"Or a long one," Big Nose says, gesturing with his head toward a room in the distance. He pulls on Willow's long hair, grinning. "Come on, we know a place to go."

"Eww." Dagan wrinkles her nose, adding on, "That is exactly why I don't wear my extensions all the time."

Willow meets my eyes through the window, sending a wink and a soft, reassuring smile. When everyone turns to leave, I see the vial with vampire's blood tainted with a heavy sedative gripped behind her back. I trust the girls to find a way to get the men to take the blood, and if they don't, I know they'll have no qualms with shoving it down their throats.

"Damn, they're good." Dagan whistles softly, waiting until they are gone and a few minutes more before moving. "Come on, let's go find our boys."

We slip out of the door, glancing around the long hall and giant entryway to check for any lingering students. It is two in the morning, but you never know with Conjurers. We could run into a Seer trying to visit the prophecy room, a siren going for a midnight swim, or a vampire looking for a midnight snack. That's why we've assigned guards, though.

"Alright, I think we are good. Send the signal." I nod toward Ginny, who proceeds to close her eyes in concentration. I watch in awe as a glamoured crow flies down the hallway, disappearing around the corner as it searches for the Gravediggers. "Have I mentioned your ability is badass?"

"Only every day for the past three weeks." Ginny rolls her eyes, murmuring under her breath, "It's not my fault none of you have bothered to watch me use them before."

"Yeah, yeah. We're terrible friends; I get it." I roll my eyes, smiling softly as I turn away from her.

"Finally," Dagan murmurs as two figures appear from around the corner. "Wait…where's Jaymes?" Arlo and Nox stride forward in the same all black Conjuring gear, stoic looks painted on their faces.

"Where's Jaymes?" I repeat the question when they get closer, brows drawn down.

"He didn't show," Nox says, glancing in the direction the three sisters went off to. "Are they...? Is Reese...?"

"They're fine," I answer his unasked question, smiling gently. "They should have those clowns locked in a closet any second now. She's fine; I promise."

"I can't believe Jaymes bailed," Dagan says with a scowl, fists curling up at her side. "He told me..." She turns away, her cheeks flushed.

"He's told me lots of things, too. Promised a bit more," I murmur bitterly. "I'm beginning to think he isn't always truthful."

"Almost never." Arlo grins playfully, jerking his head toward the dean's door. "Let's get this show on the road, ladies."

"I'm not a—" Arlo snaps his sharp teeth playfully at Nox to quiet him.

"Okay, we're down a Conjurer, so we are going to need to be extra careful," I say into the darkness as we step lightly toward the office. "Jaymes was supposed to undo the Charms, so Nox, I think you're the most qualified to take over his position." Nox's role before was as a guard, but also as an amplifier, just in case things went south. He's good in a battle, and his ability is damn useful. So, having him do this extra step shouldn't put a wrench in the plans.

"Yeah, alright." He nods, already moving his hands. There are five Charms on the door, each more complex than the last. The Counter Charms are complicated, more complicated than I have any right fooling with. Jaymes called one of the Charms a Veiling Charm, another a Hiatus Charm, and I think there was also one called a Glamorifying Charm. All tricky to complete, all complicated to undo. And if Nox does the wrong Counter Charm, this whole place will sound with alarms.

"Help!" Reese's hiss of desperation comes from down the hall, and we all turn to see two sisters dragging the body of another. Willow's arms are draped around Reese and Wren's necks, her head sagging and her feet dragging behind her.

"What the fuck happened?" I whisper, rushing over to help. Arlo replaces Wren, helping Reese by taking most of Willow's weight. Dagan tries to take over for Reese, but she refuses, glaring at her for even daring to try.

"One of those goons forced the blood down her throat," Reese murmurs angrily, trying to be as quiet as possible. "We had convinced them to take the blood with us to get high, but they wanted us to take it first. So Willow did. She was just going to take a sip, but one of them tipped up the vial and forced her to swallow the whole thing. He laughed like it was a fucking joke, but the jokes on him now, isn't it? He's the one passed out in a broom closet, naked, with his buddy."

"You stripped them down?" Arlo snorts, barely holding in his laughter.

"Of course I did." Reese sniffs, adding on, "He had a small dick, in case you were curious."

Arlo coughs and wheezes, choking as he tries to contain it. Even Nox is fighting a laugh, his body shaking as he carefully moves his arms. Dagan cackles, nodding enthusiastically. "They deserve it."

"Alright, punishments aside, we need to put Willow somewhere safe." I nod my head toward the siren pool, knowing that's the best place for her to be while she recovers. "Are there chairs in there to lie out on?"

"Yeah, a few. Come on, Arlo. Let's go dump her in one." Wren follows Reese and Arlo, her worried eyes wide.

"How's it going, Nox?" I glance outside at the moon, chewing on my bottom lip.

"One more," he grunts, and I see sweat forming on his forehead. I've never seen Charms work so hard against a Conjurer's body. And if Jaymes hadn't discovered exactly what Charms were placed here…I shudder, not wanting to think about what a disaster that would have been.

"I want to tell him to hurry, but I don't want to risk it." Dagan rubs at one of her hot pink nails, grinning.

"Don't," Nox growls under his breath, arms straining.

"I hate this," Ginny groans, pacing in front of me. "I feel like…like a *delinquent.*"

"You'll feel dead if we get caught," I say bluntly, putting a hand on her shoulder to stop her. "It'll be okay, Ginny. In and out, remember?"

"Yes." Her shoulders slump, worried eyes flickering toward Arlo, Wren, and Reese as they approach.

"He isn't done yet?" Arlo frowns, watching Nox carefully.

"I am." Nox's arms drop, his entire body shaking now. Only, it's not from laughter anymore. Reese rushes over to whisper something into his ear, rubbing his back comfortingly.

"Okay." I swallow, turning to my friends. "Let's go over the plan one last time. Arlo, Reese, and Dagan, you're with me. Wren, Nox, and Ginny, you're the guards. Ginny, if you see anyone you make them see an empty hallway. If that doesn't work, use your siren scream, Wren, to make them pass out. If all else fails, brute strength and your enhancing abilities, Nox."

Ginny smiles reassuringly. "We know, Azalea. We've got your back."

"Alrighty, then." I swallow, sending a hesitant smile to the others. "Follow me."

CHAPTER 33

"It is rumored that the Grim was created from a Charm gone wrong, but I think otherwise. I think the Charm was mutilated, twisted by a pair of Conjurers who wanted more power than any Charmed should hold. I think it was entirely purposeful. And, in my heart of hearts, I believe that they chose the cursed land Draxmere lives on for a reason. A reason that has nothing to do with beauty and everything to do with something hiding within."
—*Draxmere: A Tale as Old as the Grim*, written by Enhancer Kelvin Delaney in 1977 A.G.

The door creaks as we swing it open, the sound making me flinch. The inside of Bloodgood's office is dark, but I don't dare light one of the torches on the walls. If anyone outside saw this window illuminated, it could raise suspicions. So, I lift my hand and let some of my Light guide us.

I glance around, breathing harshly through my nose. "Arlo, the smell you're searching for is going to be old. It will be something dark and wrong." This is why I wanted him here on the full moon; not only is his physical strength at its peak, but so are his senses. I'm sure he can probably see in the dark right now. "Dagan, you can sense death lingering, so I'm hoping you'll be able to sense this."

"I feel…" She wrinkles her nose, my Light barely illuminating the action. "I feel something."

"I smell something," Arlo agrees, head whipping around. "It's somewhere in here."

I move to Bloodgood's desk first, rifling through papers and drawers. Only one is locked, but I am able to pop it open with a bobby pin. It isn't protected by any Charms, and I understand why as soon as I open it to find photos of Jaymes inside. It is like a scrapbook, just…in a drawer.

"That's depressing," Dagan remarks, looking down at it. Then she turns and begins rifling through one of the filing cabinets, shaking her head in disappointment when she gets through the last drawer without finding anything. It takes thirty minutes to search the entire room, and the three of us have empty hands by the end of it.

"We're running out of time," Arlo says, tilting his chin up and sniffing the air. "I swear I can smell it…"

"Try the floorboards. The stones in the wall. Anything." I swallow back my fear, my anxiety, as I fall to my hands and knees. I sweep under the desk, next to the window sill, past the filing cabinets.

"Here," Dagan says suddenly, her hand on a single stone in the wall below a hung portrait of Haiden Bloodgood herself. "It's here."

I leap to my feet, heart pounding. I hurry to put my hand on the stone, and the moment I do, my head is swarmed with a vision.

The pain makes me cry out involuntarily, my hands flying up to my ears as this static screech echoes in my brain.

I see myself, tied up and crying. I see the Grimoire at my feet, opened with pages blowing in the wind. I can hear the roar of a crowd in the background, barely audible over the loud, screeching static.

"Please," I beg, tears streaming down my face. "Please, not right now."

"Be wary of the beast inside, be wary of a friend who lied. Don't query the Grim who hides, don't query the friend who chooses sides. Don't bury the secrets that died, don't bury the truth you find."

"Not again," I beg it, my mind swimming as the vision flickers in and out of existence. I see Jaymes beside me now, his expression hard and fixed on something in the distance. "Okay, okay. I get it! Jaymes lied, right? He didn't show up? Is that it? Is that—"

"Be wary of the beast inside, be wary of a friend who lied. Don't query the Grim who hides, don't query the friend who chooses sides. Don't bury the secrets that died, don't bury the truth you find."

"Fuck you!" I scream, and I hear my words echoing. "Fuck you, fuck you, *fuck you!*"

With a harshness I've never experienced, I'm slammed back into reality, my body collapsing onto the cold ground with a vengeance. I'm still sobbing from the pain, my body curling into itself. My tears are pooling up underneath me, the sounds of my hiccupping gasps filling the silence.

"Azalea!" Dagan is next to me in an instant, her eyes wide and full of concern.

"Tear down the wall if you have to," I manage out, trying to stop the sobs. "Get the book."

Dagan nods solemnly, standing and tilting her head toward Arlo. He sends me an apologetic wince as he steps over my body, fist rising as he punches the wall fast and hard. It cracks and splinters quickly, caving in when he sends in a second punch. He doesn't dare use a Charm; that would raise an alarm. So, he keeps punching. He punches until his fist is bloody and raw, until the caving hole is a gaping one.

I push myself to my knees, grabbing Dagan's hand and using it to pull myself up. "The Grimoire." I laugh in disbelief, the tears on my face finally drying.

"You grab it, Azalea. This was all because of you, after all."

I nod, my hand shaking as I reach forward and grab the aging black book. I pull it out, staring down at the Grimoire. It's old and dusty, its pages worn and dry. I flip the book open, swallowing down my disappointment when I see that Jaymes was right about it being unreadable. I can feel this…this dark aura radiating from it. I almost want to drop it and never touch it again. But I need it. Demi needs it. So, instead of dropping it, I pull it into my chest and hold on tight.

"I can't believe we did it," I whisper, amazed. Then I glance at the hole we left, wincing. "She'll know it was stolen, but she won't be able to prove it was us."

"Yeah, there isn't much I can do—" Arlo is interrupted when a loud scream echoes in the hall. A siren scream.

"Shit." Dagan's head whips toward the closed door, her body tense. "I smell death."

I rush to throw the door open, Light and Shadow already dripping from my fingers. The door swings open, exposing us to the horrific sight waiting for us. Nox, on his knees, bloody and bruised. His hands are behind his back, wrapped by an invisible force. A dagger is at his neck, a small line of blood visible just underneath. Willow has been dragged into the hall, her body still limp, but her hands now behind her back. Wren is crying over a body, one with a head full of auburn hair. She's on her knees, head bowed over as she screams. But her scream is wrong, twisted and corrupt. Like she's trying to use her power but can't.

"We've been waiting on you, Azalea Jinx." Dean Bloodgood steps forward, a tight-lipped smile on her face.

"What did you do?" I stare down at Ginny's body, numb from the shock. Ginny can't be…

"What had to be done," she snarls, snapping her fingers. More Conjurers step out of the darkness, all wielding daggers in our direction. "If you don't want more of your friends to die, then you will come with us."

"I…" My chin quivers, my eyes unable to lift from Ginny.

"No." Dagan answers, her own chin rising in defiance. "I don't think we *will* be doing that."

"What are you going to do, Necromancer? Raise the body of your dead friend? Mutilate it in an attempt to free yourself?" Bloodgood scoffs, shaking her head harshly.

"There are other ways to get dead bodies," Dagan snarls, a dagger flipping from her hand so fast even I don't see it. It lands in one of the Conjurer's nearest us, buried to the hilt in her chest. The others shout and race forward, but Bloodgood holds a hand up. Her perfect blond eyebrow rises, as though challenging Dagan. Dagan doesn't take to that kindly, her power ripping through the air with an electric charge I can taste. Then the Conjurer is moving, leaping toward Bloodgood with a ferocity no dead person should have. This isn't the same as a skeleton being dragged from underneath the dirt; this is a strong, able body. Bloodgood realizes too late how powerful Dagan is.

"Now, Arlo!" Nox shouts, and Arlo rips into his werewolf form. He leaps for the Conjurer holding his best friend, claws ripping through his chest in a single, easy motion.

"Shit, shit, shit," I hiss, letting my shadows drip around the room. They encircle legs and wrists, pulling and tugging and tripping. I blast my Light into chests, refusing to let the tears threatening to fall come down. I see Dagan raise another dead body, one mangled and bloody with guts pouring out. But the body rises and attacks Bloodgood, who now has two people on her. I can't pull out my Shadow bomb without putting my friends at a disadvantage.

I turn away from the bloody fight beside me, trying to focus. But I see more Conjurers coming from the distance, replacements for the ones who have fallen. "Fuck!" I shout, still clutching onto the Grimoire with one arm. "Guys, there are a shit ton of Conjurers coming!"

"You won't win," Bloodgood shouts from somewhere nearby, her snarls sharp and penetrating through the chaos.

I ignore her, shaking as I keep sending out my power. I start forming balls of Shadow and Light, slinging them left and right and throwing Conjurers into each other. They fly across the room, slamming into more behind them like a bowling ball hitting pins. But it's not enough; it's not enough to stop someone from leaping on my back and forcing me to the ground.

I scream, trying to army crawl out from underneath the heavy body. But the body on top of me isn't a normal one, it's a werewolf. The tips of claws plunge into my shoulders, pulling a pained scream out of my lips. Someone in front of me grabs my hair, yanks my head up, and dumps something into my mouth. Before I can spit it out, they force my mouth closed, shoving my chin up so harshly that my teeth clang together. The hand that was in my hair now pinches my nose, giving me no choice but to swallow.

I feel it so quickly, the absence of my power. My hands are ripped behind my back, the invisible cuffs that the others wear now on me, too. It feels tight and painful, and the second I jerk against them, they tighten even more. I hear a wolf's cry of pain nearby, and my heart sinks. I know it must be Arlo, and I know the cussing screeches coming from Dagan in the distance aren't good, either.

"I told you, Azalea Jinx: you can't win." The claws are ripped out of me, my body jerked up by the arms. The Grimoire had been underneath me, and now Bloodgood bends down to pick it up. She grins so brilliantly, so evilly, that I can't stop myself from spitting on her.

"Fuck you."

She sighs, wiping the spittle off her cheek. "Take them to the dungeons. They can sit there and think about what they did until the morning when we hold their trials."

"What's the point? Kill me already and be done with it," I hiss, angry and terrified. I don't want to be taken to the dungeons. I don't want to be tortured and locked away. Not again. *Never again.*

"Oh, no, Azalea. You're too precious to kill." That smile stays put, her beautiful face so unbearably terrible.

"What does that mean?" I'm dragged back, my feet tripping over each other as I fight against the restraints to get back to her. *"What does that mean?"*

"It means you're valuable. Your friends, on the other hand…" She shrugs, flipping her hand at the others dismissively. "Well, the trials will determine their fates."

"Ginny!" I shout, clenching my jaw hard to keep my tears in. I won't let her see it: my fear, my pain, my horror. "Heal her!"

"I'm afraid your Glamourist friend has already faced her trial." Bloodgood kicks Ginny's body with a sigh, and not a noise of pain leaves my friend's lips. "Good luck, Azalea Jinx. You'll need it."

"No! NO!" I scream, thrashing and kicking and falling. I'm picked up and slung over a shoulder, Ginny's body fading into the distance as I'm taken away.

Not again. Not again. Not again. Not again. Not again.

CHAPTER 34

"A new friend you must make,
a formed bond you cannot shake.
With the jinx, a friendship will bloom,
with the jinx you will meet your savior or your doom."
—Repeated prophecy spoken to Demi Lockwood by Seer Shiloh
Bar in 2023 A.G.

DEMI

I watch from a distance as they push the ferocious one onto the stage, shoving her to her knees in front of the giant crowd. I can see her clearly from the top of this building, can see the numbness in her eyes. I don't recognize the girl who fought the master's offspring all those months ago; she's disappeared entirely. In her place stands a girl with torn clothes, no protective gear in sight. In her place stands someone who has given up.

I can feel the power in this place, the Charm Levels excruciatingly enticing. But I have strict orders, and if I disobey the master's offspring again…I shudder, remembering my punishment for the last time I disobeyed. I may get full now, but he will ensure I don't feel full ever again. So, I sit and I wait as the ferocious one's captor begins to speak.

"We have a traitor here at Draxmere!" Whispers ripple through the air, distrust and weariness settled within every Conjurer gathered in the courtyard. The blonde jabs her finger at the girl, crying out, "Delarosa lied to you when she claimed Azalea Jinx was to be your savior. The prophecies she chose to show everyone were carefully chosen prophecies that didn't reveal the entire truth."

I watch with little interest as she pulls a small notebook from her pocket, clearing her throat and announcing, "I will read some of the true prophecies about our supposed savior." And oh, does she. She recites prophecy after prophecy, all twisting the girl into some sort of villain. And at the end, she leans toward someone else and grabs a book from their hands before wielding it above her head.

"Azalea Jinx broke into my office last night with her group of treacherous friends and stole this book!" There are no more whispers, no more quiet disagreements, only silence and disbelief. "This book belongs to the Grim and has been protected by the Light Faction leaders for generations. This is what Azalea and her friends were trying to steal. Do you care to enlighten us as to why, Azalea?"

The ferocious one stays silent, her eyes glazed over and distant. She's not here anymore, the girl. She's gone somewhere else.

"Maybe you can explain it to your friends, then? Tell them the truth?"

More people are brought onto the stage, brought to their knees before the crowd to be judged. They all smell so good, so powerful…

"But, if you won't do it, I have someone who will." Gasps echo as someone new steps onto the stage, another blond who smells so *good*.

"Jaymes, what are you…?" A male asks this, his red-tinted hair visible from even this height. I sniff the air, wishing I could get a taste of him. Something about that smell is so enticing, so *deliciously* fragrant.

"She lied to you all," Jaymes says, and the ferocious one snaps her head over to him. Yes, I remember him now. The one who tried to burn me.

The ferocious one still doesn't speak, but her eyes aren't as empty as before. They look…sad. I wonder what that's like.

"Be wary of a friend who lied," she says, so quietly it's hard for even me to hear.

Jaymes's face cracks and settles, the movement hardly visible. "She isn't trying to save Demi. At least, she isn't *just* trying to save her." He clasps his hands behind his back, walking between his friends until he reaches her. "She's giving the Grimoire to Shayde because she wants him to kill his dad and take over as the only Grim. So they can be together without another force interfering."

"That is *not*—" the ferocious one snarls, body jerking forward toward the man.

"Azalea?" The wild-haired one asks, her eyes wide and confused. "Azalea, is that true?"

"That is not the entire truth, and you know it, Jaymes," the ferocious one spits, ignoring the other. "That isn't what—"

"You aren't even denying it," one of the girls who smells like the sea cries out, her voice shaking. "Ginny died for this, and you can't even deny it?"

"I…" The ferocious one pauses, hanging her head. "I *did* want to save Demi. Is it so bad that I wanted to kill a Grim while I was at it?"

"It is if you're only killing one to put the other in power!"

The ferocious one's eyes flare, her red and brown hair whipping around in the snowy wind violently. "That isn't what I'm doing."

"You aren't a very good liar, dear." The blonde woman sighs, snapping her fingers. "Come here, Son."

Jaymes goes back over to the woman, unflinching and stoic. "Of course, Mother."

"My son did a wonderful job last night when he came to me about these traitors. And with this new development, we know there will be confusion and unease. My son and many others are now questioning their loyalties. So, we held an emergency faction meeting last night and want to bring you good news during these troubling trials." She pauses, placing her hands on Jaymes's shoulders. "As many of you know, you can switch factions now. My son Jaymes here is the first to make that switch. He is joining me in the Light Faction, and I encourage the rest of you to consider this, too. If the Shadow Faction condones behavior like this, can we trust them to take our safety seriously? Can we trust them not to side with the Grim when their members are doing so themselves?"

The ferocious one tilts her head back and laughs. She laughs so loud, so wickedly, that even I wince. It's a sound that bounces around in the silence, and will haunt these Conjurers for a long time to come. And when the ferocious one opens her mouth and speaks, I grin. "The Grim will come for me. And when he does, I hope you're the first one he kills."

Voices erupt around the courtyard, fear and anxiety filling the air. I shift on my feet, sniffing to try and douse the rising hunger in my heart. But they smell so good, and I'm always so, so *hungry*.

"I thought you wanted me to save her for you, little flower?" The master's offspring struts through the crowd, Conjurers leaping away from him and his cape of shadows like he's poisonous to touch.

Everyone on stage is still; quiet and hesitant. The blonde female says, "Leave, Grim, before we make you."

"Will you, though? You made a deal with my daddy, didn't you?"

"With *him*, not you." She clenches her teeth, Light flaring at her hands.

"It's all the same," the offspring says while sighing, eyes stuck on the ferocious one he's obsessed with. The one he's risking his life for. "Hurt me, and he won't ever accept your deal. Let me take Azalea, and he won't have to know about this. You can still make your sacrifice in a few months."

The blonde doesn't look happy, and Jaymes looks even angrier. But, despite the long pause and the hilarious anger, she says, "Fine. Take her, then. We don't need traitors in our midst."

"And that," he snaps his fingers, and the book she is holding flies into his hands, "belongs to me."

"You can't!" she shouts, stepping forward. But Jaymes holds out an arm, shaking his head and stopping her from going forward. He knows more than anyone how dangerous the offspring is.

"Don't, Mother. He's right. We can't sacrifice the deal they made with us. If we truly want a ceasefire…" I can see his Adam's apple bobbing, as though it was hard to admit.

The offspring's head tilts, his eyes blazing as he stares at Jaymes and points at the one with the wild hair. "The Necromancer's coming with us, too."

"I will *not*," the wild one growls, snarling angrily.

At the same time, Jaymes grinds out, "You cannot—"

"She's collateral. The injured one in the infirmary? Ginny? If she dies, so does the Necromancer. If she lives, so does the collateral. It's a simple process, Jaymes." Azalea's eyes are wide now, as are the others on the stage. The blonde one said she was dead. How despicable. How malicious. How utterly *delightful*. I would love to eat that one, I think. She would taste so wickedly chaotic.

"Fine." The blonde waves her hand, and the offspring scoops the ferocious one into his arms. The same way he dropped her off all those months ago, he's now carrying her out. "Just-just leave. We don't want to jeopardize the original deal your father has graciously offered."

The offspring grins, the sight malicious and scary. "Oh, but you already have, dear."

And then he's disappearing, stealing her away into the light of the new morning with the Necromancer bound in shadows floating behind them. I sigh in disappointment, crawling off the roof and leaping toward the ground to race into the woods at the rendezvous point. I had so hoped things weren't going to be so peaceful.

I really needed a good meal.

CHAPTER 35

"A love barely formed between hearts already torn.
A future hiding in the shadows, waiting to be foretold.
A power so vast that not only love will form.
A destiny so heavy that only their hands are strong enough to hold."
—Prophecy recorded in Seer Shayde Glover's prophetic journal,
2025 A.G.

*A*live.

Ginny is alive and waiting in the infirmary, alive and now assured to be healed. She isn't dead, she isn't dead, she isn't dead.

"I can't believe you, Azalea Jinx," Dagan growls behind us, her voice bitter and angry.

"This isn't her fault," Shayde whispers, one hand brushing away a tear I hadn't realized escaped. He's holding me bridal style, my hands still tied behind me and unavailable for use.

"Of course it is; she's the one who fell in love with a fucking Grim."

My eyes blaze, and I lean up to look over Shayde's shoulder. "And you cut all your limbs off and fused them back together. Which is the worse offense?"

Dagan is quiet for a few long moments before saying, "Fine. You win. But you better hope Ginny survives because I swear I'm going to haunt you for the rest of your Grim damned life if I die as a prisoner of a Grim."

"If you don't run away, we won't have to keep you prisoner," Shayde says cheerfully, his light green eyes falling to meet mine.

"Why would I willingly stay?" Dagan scoffs, scowling. "*I'm* not in love with you."

"I have a job for you, Necromancer. One I don't think you'll be able to turn down. Your curiosity won't let you."

I can practically see Dagan's ears tilting up, her eyes already wide with fascination as she says coyly, "Is that so?"

"I want you to heal a Reaper." I whip my head back toward Shayde, staring up at him with a hope that I haven't dared let myself feel in the past few months.

"Isn't that what your little book is supposed to be for?" Dagan drawls, eyebrows raised. I can barely see her head above the winding shadows around her body, her feet dangling out from below her as she floats.

"It's an instruction manual," Shayde explains, twisting sharply toward the right, "not a final product." Dagan opens her mouth to respond, but a Reaper forces a startled noise from her lips.

"Demi," I breathe, relieved.

"I don't let her out of my sight. The two of us have moved locations quite a few times together," Shayde whispers, gently lowering me to the ground. He begins to move his hands, performing an unknown Charm. I start to ask what he's doing, because it certainly isn't a portal he's creating, when the earth beneath us begins to shake.

I scream when we drop, Dagan's wicked cackle behind me annoying and terrifying all at once. The fall isn't long or fast. It's like a shift from the ground above to the ground below, the giant hole we toppled from closing in on itself quickly and efficiently. We land without so much as a bounce, Shayde jostling as though he had just gone from one step to another below him.

We're now encased in a concrete basement, one filled with barred cells running along its walls. I count at least ten cages, the largest directly in front of us. I can see bones and blood inside, and I feel sick looking at the nest of human hair in the corner.

"Please tell me that's not what I'm thinking it is." Dagan gags, her previously blank face finally cracking. She's cut off her own limbs, but this bothers her?

"Okay," Shayde says simply, shrugging. I push myself to a sitting position, struggling with my hands still bound.

"Have you…have you been killing people for her?" I hiss, my eyes flickering over to the thing standing behind Dagan that used to be my best friend.

"Of course not, Azalea. But I had to feed her, and I couldn't give her enough of my power to be satisfied." Shayde…Shayde had been feeding her with his own power? Sacrificing *his* Charm Levels? "The bodies were dead already. Casualties from one thing or another. I just brought them here to keep her satisfied. She was the one who mutilated them." He wrinkles his nose as though the sight disgusts him, too.

If I didn't love him before, I certainly do now. "Thank you," I whisper, tears springing to my eyes. "Thank you for taking care of her for me. For finding a way to save her."

"I'd do anything for you, little flower." His eyes shine with something fierce as he stares down at me, the intensity burning deep inside my gut.

"Can you guys do the gooey eye thing later?" Dagan remarks, her own gaze stuck on Demi. "I really would like to be out of the encumbering shadows and the power-restricting cuffs."

Shayde snaps his head toward her, questioning lightly, "Your answer?"

"I…" She pauses, glancing over at me before saying, "I don't know. I need some time to—"

Shayde waves a hand at her, and she goes flying into the large cage full of blood and bones, her scream of outrage echoing in the empty area. Demi follows her dutifully when Shayde snaps his fingers, the barred door slamming shut behind them. Shock, outrage, and relief all flood through me in a barrage I can't process.

"Then maybe you can sit in here and think about it a bit?"

"With the Reaper?" Dagan cries, backing herself into a corner. "Fuck, no! I'll do it, okay? I'll do it! Just get me out of here!"

With another snap of his fingers, the door swings back open, Dagan flying out just as easily. The shadows fall from her body, and after another quick Charm, the cuffs fall, too. "If you leave this building, I'll know. My Reapers will have a delicious meal out of you before you make it more than a mile out."

"Shayde." I grind out, wanting to defend Dagan. But, if she *can* save Demi…

"Relax, Azalea. I get it. I'd be threatening myself, too. Don't worry about it, Grim. I won't leave. You were right: my curiosity won't let me leave. Or my ego." She gives me a stony look, as though I'm not understanding the situation at all.

"Demi, show her to the empty room on the top level."

They start to leave, but I can't stop myself from calling out. "Why?" She can't just be doing this because we are friends. She can't be turning her back on everything she's ever known for *me*.

Dagan pauses, turning her head and cackling softly. "I may be cut from a different cloth, Azalea, but we're both being used in the same pattern." She turns back to Demi, gesturing for her to continue. I don't miss the increased limp in her leg, and I certainly don't miss her flinch when Demi sends her a crude smile that reaches both ears. *Don't query the friend who chooses sides.* Could that…could that be referring to Dagan? To the piece of my pattern that I hadn't known I was missing?

As the two ascend the stairs at the front of the basement, I shove those thoughts aside to raise a brow and ask, "Aren't you going to take off *my* cuffs now?" They haven't been digging into me anymore, and I have a suspicion Shayde loosened them before he ever revealed himself to the crowd. But sitting on the hard ground, staring up at him and waiting for him to relieve me from the discomfort, isn't something I plan on doing much longer.

"No, I don't think I will." His eyes blaze with need, and the fluttering butterflies in my stomach turn to liquid heat.

"Which Shayde are you today?" I ask softly, but I already know the answer to the question. I've seen it in his crazed eyes the past thirty minutes, heard it in the callous way he spoke to Dagan.

"Every version of me belongs to you," he says, his voice low and dangerous as he stalks toward me. He rips me up by the arms, pressing his body flush against mine. "You've burned a brand into my heart, and I won't ever be able to get rid of it."

"Do you want to?" I say as Shayde reaches out and fingers the necklace around my neck, pulling the ring out of my shirt and letting his fingers run over its sharp edges. The bracelet he gave me for my birthday is sitting in my room at Draxmere, still hidden inside the drawer full of socks and underwear.

"Fuck no." His lips cover mine, slow and delicate. He doesn't devour me, he doesn't rush as though there isn't any time left in the world. He is deliberate with each move of his lips, with each stroke of his tongue, and I've come undone before it's ever begun.

I whisper against his lips hesitantly as his hands roam to my waist, "I've missed you so much, but I was too scared to admit it."

He swallows, pressing his head against mine. "I hurt you. And I can't promise I won't do it again." I can see him hiding there, waiting for me to pull him out, *my* Shayde.

"I've hurt you, too." Physically. Mentally. Irrevocably.

"You can keep hurting me. You can turn around and betray me right now, right in this moment. You can stab me again and again and again, you can break me over and over and over, and each time I would come crawling back. Begging. Craving. I'll never let you go. *Never.*"

"That sounds a little intense." I gasp into his mouth as a hand slides under my shirt, thumb rising to glide against the underside of my breast.

"Would you have me any other way?" His head jerks back, a low groan leaving his lips. His body stiffens, his thumb halting, and a painful hiss echoes across my lips. And then his eyes flash open, and I see him again, see the man I came to find, the one who's been forced into hiding by a side of himself that's too powerful to overcome.

"Shayde." His name on my lips is an invocation, his hand under my shirt an invitation. With one arm around my waist, he lifts me, and I wrap my legs around his waist and kiss him the way I've been dreaming of for months. It's harsh and abrupt, bruising and rough, and I don't even notice as we flicker in and out of existence.

"I'm so…" He can't get out words as we appear in a room that smells just like him. It's small and void, a queen-sized bed with a single dresser, but I know it's his from the clothes draped across the floor alone. From the books and maps strewn across the place, from the black cat purring on the red duvet. "I'm so indebted to you, Azalea Jinx."

"I like that," I breathe, grinning as he drops me on my ass next to Grimsly. I lean back on my hands, arching my back subtly. "Indebted. What would it take to settle your debts, I wonder?"

"You can't take anything you don't already have." He grins, nimble fingers popping buttons off his black shirt. "My life. My heart. My soul. All of it is already in your hands."

"I'm a very rich girl," I purr, glancing over at the cat.

Shayde notices and swats at him, muttering, "Go on, Grimmy. Go bug Dagan for a while." And just like that, he's getting up and strutting off, snake-like tail sneaking out of the open door just before it slams shut.

"Why was he here?" Why was he here when he should have been with me? I needed him. I needed him to keep me safe, and he was here, with a Grim, not doing his job protecting me.

"He came to get me when he saw what happened." Shayde pauses his movements briefly, tucking a strand of dark hair behind my ear. "He couldn't stop all of the Conjurers from attacking with his shields. He knew that, and so did you."

"Can you…how do you communicate with him?"

"The Grim is an animal of sorts." He slips his shirt off, baring his tanned, tattooed chest to me. "We can't speak with one another, but we can understand instincts."

"Right." My mouth dries seeing him like this, my heart racing as he crouches down before me. I watch in silence as he slips my boots off first, carefully untying each lace and running fingers down my skin in tantalizingly slow movements.

"I've dreamed of this moment," he growls, looking up at me as he pops open the button of my pants, and I lift my hips as he tugs them down. We don't have to worry about the belt I had on yesterday when I was captured: Bloodgood confiscated that rather quickly. Along with every bit of my Conjuring gear. They forced me to change into someone else's too-small clothes as a precaution. "I've been waiting to worship you for months."

"I've been waiting to be worshiped my entire life."

His lips leave a trail of heat as they start at my ankles, moving up to my thighs. I groan and shift as he presses a kiss against the outside of my underwear, then hiss when he moves away.

"I would have started a war over you." His eyes blaze as he stares up at me, one hand splayed across my stomach as he presses me back lightly. I lean back and put my weight on my restricted hands, already too far gone to care about the pinch of pain.

"I'm glad you didn't."

"If you hadn't told me you wanted to go back…if you hadn't willingly agreed to walk onto that campus…I would have destroyed the whole Grim damned place. I would have figured out a way to break those wards, would have sent in a thousand Reapers to avenge you. If I hadn't been able to find you, if I hadn't been able to save you…" He clenches his jaw, teeth grinding as though just the thought of it is painful. "I would have crossed a line I would have never been able to come back from."

"I'm glad you didn't," I say again, because what else can I say? What else can I do but submit to him, prove how much I trust him?

"Don't ask me to go faster," he says abruptly, reaching up to rip open my shirt. Those heated kisses trail up my stomach, and he rises with them, kissing over the swell of my breasts before coming up to plant a kiss on my lips. It's slow and intimate, but it leaves me shaking with need. "We've always gone fast, and today that isn't what you're going to get."

"Why not? What if it's what I want? What I need?" I'm panting as his hands slip under my bra, my back arching fully as he pinches my nipples.

"This isn't about you." Those enchanting green eyes clash with brown as I stare up at him, his firmness turning me to liquid jelly.

Breathlessly, I say, "I thought you were going to worship me?"

He grins, chuckling maliciously. "Oh, darling. When someone sacrifices themselves at your feet, you're supposed to accept whatever gifts they offer you. I *am* going to worship you—if you accept my offering." I melt fully then, practically turning into a puddle on this bed.

Shayde's lips move to my neck, his hands pinching and pulling at my breasts as he begins biting and sucking. He's slow, just as he promised, ensuring he leaves a trail of marks as he descends. And when that mouth finally moves down my stomach, below my belly button, I'm crying out before he ever slips the underwear off. Before his fingers even slide over my clit, before his tongue ever laps over me. Shayde takes his time exploring me, takes his time tasting and teasing. I'm arching up into him, begging him for more, more, more. But I don't ask him to go faster, just like he asked. My lack of control in this situation turns me on more than I want to admit, the ache from my tied hands a reminder that the savior has submitted fully to the villain. And *oh*, how I love it.

Finally, finally, he gives me what I want. I shiver when he unbuttons his pants, whimpering and pleading and whispering his name over, over, over. Shayde sits beside me, pulling me into his lap and pushing his body against mine. He holds me by the waist, helping me onto my knees and guiding himself to my entrance. And when he pushes in slowly, oh so slowly, I begin to cry.

Shayde wipes away my tears with his thumb as he pushes all the way in, whispering, "I know, little flower. I know." It's so intense, so pure, so *good*, that I can't stop myself from coming in only minutes. Shayde doesn't let it affect his pace, though. He keeps fucking me in a slow, deliberate way that has me bouncing over, over, and over again as I try to get him to do more. But I still don't have access to my hands and can only do so much to influence his decisions. Shayde grips my waist harder at my antics, shoving my hips down and groaning. His body shakes with the control it takes not to move the way we both want him to.

"*Please*," I whisper, moaning all the while.

"I don't want to…" He pauses his movements, taking in a shuddering breath. "I want this to last."

"Please," I say again, desperate. Shayde growls, something inside him changing. He pulls out of me so quickly I don't have time to complain, flipping me over and pulling my ass toward him. Then he's doing exactly what I want, what I need, and I'm falling over the edge of a cliff that I always seem to be standing on with him.

Only this time, we fall together.

CHAPTER 36

"I am writing this process down only because I know what it is like to lose someone you love, and I know what it feels like for your mind to obsess over that someone. I know what it's like to turn the person you love into a monster that cannot love you back. I didn't mean to do it, and it took me a full year to figure it out, but I have done it. My best friend, my lover, my partner in crime…I turned them into a Reaper. And now, I'm about to turn them back."
—*The Grimoire*, written by the first, unnamed Grim, 1 A.G.

Waking up next to Shayde three days in a row is surreal. We've never just…existed like that together. I've stayed overnight with him a few times, but it's never been so…real. Raw. Vulnerable. As familiar as I am with Shayde, with his body, with his smell; I'm unfamiliar with this side of him. Probably because I refused to look at it.

The three days aren't spent in bed, lounging around and being lazy, though. Shayde spends every waking moment with the Grimoire, focused on the pages that involve Reapers, and now he's finally decoded the entire Charm that will bring Demi back to us.

I've stayed as close to Demi as I dared, searching for her inside the Reaper. But I haven't seen any sign of my friend in the monster. This version of Demi is a snarling, howling creature who knows no mercy. A creature ruled by its hunger, barely containing itself in my and Dagan's presence. Shayde had to lock her up yesterday because she finally snapped, attacking Dagan just before dawn while he slept. Dagan managed to sling her off and came racing for our room, cursing and throwing insults at the Reaper all the way.

I'm grateful he doesn't have the capability to kill her.

"Okay, I've got it all written down." Shayde pulls a pencil from his mouth, his long hair tied back, but black strands still dangle over his face. He has his reading glasses on again today, entirely focused on the book in front of him.

He hasn't once looked at pages that mention a cure for him, and sometimes the surge of guilt overwhelms the surge of relief, knowing that I'm getting my best friend back. I'm so fucking selfish it's pathetic.

"And that's going to help me…how?" Dagan gripes, leaning back against the kitchen counter. It's a sleek room, every surface shiny and clean. It wasn't what I expected to come back to. Not that I thought Shayde would be living in squalor, but well, his mental state doesn't leave room for simple things like cleaning.

"You're going to read it, and you're going to practice. It'll probably take thirty minutes to perform the entire Charm, so you need to get every single move perfect."

"That's…a long ass Charm." I place my face into my hands, sighing. So many things could go wrong in thirty minutes, especially with these complex moves that have to go just right.

"He can do it." Shayde finally looks up from the Grimoire, his lips pursed as he stares at Dagan. He caught on pretty quickly to Dagan's pronoun changes, and like me, he can recognize the difference not through expression but through Dagan's mannerisms.

"I can do it," Dagan confirms, not turning away. "Even if it's tedious."

"Okay, then. Let's not waste any time."

Shayde lifts his glasses, propping them on the top of his head as he begins to show Dagan each move, one by one. The first is simple, forming a triangle with his thumbs and forefingers. The second breaks the triangle, one going down, one going up. The third, his hands stretch as though pulling back a tight band. The fourth, his hands go flying apart and spinning around clockwise. After that, they become a little weirder and a lot more complex. I lose track after the tenth move, when his flattened hands roll over and over and over before crossing in this zigzag pattern that leaves my head spinning. So, I leave the room. I go straight to Demi, sitting across from her cage.

"It should have been me," I tell her, my voice barely a whisper. "And I'm sorry it wasn't." Her answering snarls and cruel smile are all I need to know that she isn't sorry at all. I sigh, getting comfy as I press my back against the wall opposite her cage and close my eyes, knowing there is only one thing left to do.

Wait.

"I'm ready," Dagan declares as he descends the stairs three hours later, displaying more confidence than I feel. I wish Shayde could be the one to do this, but he says it can't be a Grim. He wanted Dagan to do it because Reapers are the closest to dying you can be without actually being dead. Since Dagan is one of the most powerful Necromancers alive right now, he's the most qualified for the job. It's not that I'm not confident in him, necessarily, it's just…I'm not confident in the Grimoire, I think. I won't be until I see proof that it isn't just some words written down in a notebook to trick future generations into thinking they have a chance at changing the future.

"Demi," Shayde calls, his voice loud and domineering, like a master giving instructions to its dog. "Do not move."

Demi screeches in outrage, howling at the orders. Her eyes are wide and panicked, as though she understands exactly what's about to happen. Maybe she does. Shayde's never explained a Reaper's mind to me before. I've always assumed they are brainless and driven purely by hunger, but maybe…maybe she's still in there after all.

I don't move as Shayde comes to sit next to me, our eyes trained on Dagan as he begins. I watch the triangle form and break, watch his hands throw out and spin. It takes less than a minute to get through five moves, and I can't begin to comprehend how he already has the whole thing memorized.

"Has she been…" I pause, inhaling deeply. I've been scared to ask about her, scared to know what she's been suffering through in this foreign body. It's clear from the evidence on her cage floor that she has changed, but how much? "Has she been listening to all of your commands?"

"Yes, my father ordered her to."

"Oh. Since he created her, technically…"

"Yeah, but he gifted her to me. I told him I had plans for her, to use her. Which wasn't a lie. I have."

I watch his Adam's apple bob before I ask the question I've been too scared to hear the answer to, "Why was Grimsly here so often? What has he been protecting you from?"

"He and I have been traveling the world," he says softly, leaning his head back and smiling.

"And that's been dangerous?" My brows rise, a choked scoff escaping my lips.

"I have many enemies, Azalea Jinx, especially now that I have revealed myself to the world. Anyone who recognized me attacked, anyone who sensed what I was tried to kill me. Animal, Conjurer, Reaper…you name it, and I was attacked by it."

"Reapers attacked you?" I gape at him, shocked. Why would they attack their master's son?

"First and foremost, I am a Conjurer. I'm not fully Grim. Not yet. Not all Reapers can sense that side of me, but they all smell my Charm Levels. It's too enticing to pass up, even if it risks death. Reapers were the only real threats to my life, but Grimsly always knew exactly when I would need him. And with him at my side, I was at least safe from being harmed. I'm not impervious to attack; I bleed like everyone else."

"You just don't die like everyone else," I say softly, reaching out and taking his hand in mine.

"No. I suppose I don't."

"What does kill you, then?" I've never asked before, if only because I would have used the information against him.

"I…" He pauses, glancing at Dagan. He still doesn't trust my friend, and I can't blame him. "I can't tell you right now."

"I can't believe Jaymes betrayed m—us like that." I've been trying so hard to forget about it, to keep it out of my mind. It's been hard with Shayde so busy, and with Dagan separating himself from us. He's kept himself holed up in his room, only coming out to eat and ask for updates on the decoding of the Grimoire. At night, when Shayde is so tired he can't see straight anymore, he doesn't need me bringing up the knife in my back, and his.

"I can." He turns to me and smiles, my eyes falling to the subtle tilt in his lips.

"Why did he do it? He hates his mom!" I force the tears away, force the pain from my mind. I've dealt with enough heartache, enough betrayal, for a lifetime already.

"I think…" He pauses, considering briefly, and says, "I think your denial hurt him more than you thought. I think my lies were piled too high. He knew you were choosing me over him, and he couldn't fathom why. Right and wrong, kill or be killed: It's all the Conjurers know. If something falls in the gray zone, it's wrong. You fell into the gray zone. He knew that loving me, that loving you, had clouded his judgment. I think he decided the only thing that could uncloud it was going against us. I'm not angry with him for his choice."

"I am," I hiss, angrily wiping the tear that slipped free despite my best efforts. "I'm so angry that I could choke him."

"You can, if you want to. I won't stop you." The wicked grin that follows is and isn't Shayde, and I can't tell if it's a joke or if he's deadly serious.

"I will," Dagan calls, not breaking a single movement.

"He betrayed you, too. He turned us all in. I should choke you, too, for taking his side." I'm all bark and no bite, though, and Dagan knows it. He doesn't say anything else, only continues to move his body to perform the Charm.

"I think he was tired of coming last," Shayde says quietly enough that Dagan can't hear. "I think he was tired of doing the right thing only for it to blow up in his face."

"So he joined the dark side." I pull my knees up into my chest, leaning my head down into them to hide the tears that won't fucking stop. "I-I understand it. I think. I just wish it didn't hurt so damn bad."

"Jaymes will come around eventually." He sounds so sure, so confident, that I don't question it. He's a Seer, too, after all.

With the thought in my mind, I ask, "Why can we see each other in prophecies when Seers aren't supposed to be able to do that?"

"I don't have an answer to that, Azalea. I wish I did. It would make this a whole lot easier. But I don't know. I suspect there is something else that ties us together, something more than the threads of fate. But I've never heard of anything like this happening. I don't know if it should be happening at all."

I nod, accepting his answer for now. We can find the truth later; we have a world to save first. "You seem pretty sane for someone who has a screw loose." I hear Dagan choke on a laugh, and Shayde curses and threatens him under his breath.

"It's your presence," he admits after a long silence. "I've never felt saner."

"I…*my* presence?" Love can do a lot of things, but it can't stop a mind from slipping into the unknown. Even *I* know that.

Shayde turns to meet my eyes, vulnerable and open. "Is that so surprising? I have been obsessed with bringing you back to my side from the moment I left you, and now you are here. I am at peace for once. *You* bring me peace."

"Or maybe it's the thing beyond the threads of fate you mentioned." I keep my head tucked in my knees to hide my blush, my entire body hot and bothered.

"One more…" Dagan pants from in front of us, and I forget hiding the blush as I jump to my feet. The last movement ends with hands slamming down onto an invisible force, and the Charm rocks through the room like an earthquake. I let out a noise of surprise as I try to catch my balance, the ground beneath us quaking.

"What's happening?" I hiss, clutching onto Shayde's strong arm to keep myself from falling. Demi seems unaffected so far, her withered, creepy body entirely still like she was instructed.

"I don't know. Maybe Dagan got something wrong?"

"I didn't!" Dagan shouts, turning over his shoulder to glare at Shayde. "And if you think you can do better, *Grim*, then—"

Demi wails inside her cell, her body curling in on itself. I race to the bars and watch with wide eyes as shadows encase her body.

The last thing to disappear is her face, her too-wide smile already receding.

"It's working," I breathe, amazed. "It's really working!"

"Don't get too excited," Dagan pants, rolling his shoulders and groaning as he collapses to the ground. "That took a lot of power."

"Power? I thought you were just performing a Charm. Charms don't…" I crawl over to him, mouth popping open when I notice that he didn't *just* collapse. He passed out.

"Fuck," Shayde groans, pushing himself to his feet.

"Yeah, fuck! If it takes that much power to reverse the Reaper process, then how are we going to convince the Conjurers…"

"A-Azz—"

I whip my head toward the cage, quickly leaving the unconscious Dagan behind; there's nothing I can do for him right now. I struggle not to fall in my rush to stand, stumbling into the bars as I stare at my best friend.

"Demi," I breathe, grinning. Her skin is still off, more gray than any living person should be. The rainbow braids in her dark hair are still pale, but there's more color than she ever had as a Reaper. It's *her*. I can see the tiny pinpricks of her canines poking out from her mouth, can see the words trying to form there.

"Azzie," she says, holding her head. "W-Where…?" She groans, eyes still closed.

"You're safe," I say, unsure how to explain. "You're here, with me." I rip open the door, launching myself into her.

"H-Hungr—"

I wrap my arms around her, crying into her shoulder. "I missed you so much. You have no idea how much I mi—" I screech as her teeth bury into my neck, but pleasure quickly overrides the pain.

"Azalea!" Shayde's shadows wrap around me, pulling me free from Demi's weak grip with ease. I'm pulled out of the cage and into his warm body, my blood heated and my mind spinning.

"Why'd you do that?" I giggle and slump into him, turning my head back to Demi. "It's okay, you can drink…"

"No, she can't," Shayde growls, glaring at her.

"I'm so sorry. I don't know why I did that." Demi covers her bloody mouth with her hands, eyes wide. Those eyes…they aren't the chocolate brown I remember. They're black now, rimmed in a plum purple.

"You haven't fed in a long time," Shayde murmurs, holding me tight.

I laugh, shaking my weightless head. "Oh, she fed, alright."

"I don't…Where am I?" Demi looks around, shrieking when she spots the hair nest among the blood and bones. She runs out of the cage like her life depends on it, turning to vomit when she reaches us. "That's disgusting!"

"Ugh, I know. I don't know how you slept on that!" I sigh, moving to reach for her again. "Want some more?"

"Azalea, now is not the time for this." Shayde rubs his eyes, not letting me move.

"What does she mean? What does that mean?" Demi cries, a panicked look overcoming her pretty heart-shaped face. "Wait…No. No, this isn't right. This…I was at graduation. There was an attack. *You* attacked!"

Demi bares her fangs and leaps at Shayde, forcing him to drop me. She hisses and snarls in his face, almost managing to bite him before he throws her off. She's weak and unstable, but determined.

The sight sobers me up, and reality jars me so hard that I almost vomit, too. "No, Demi!"

"You cannot be defending him," Demi hisses, readying herself to leap again.

I jump in front of Shayde, holding my arms out. "Just listen, Demi! Please. I-I know you're upset with him. I was, too. But let us explain, okay? Graduation was around ten months ago. A lot has happened since then."

"Ten months ago?" The horrified look she gives me crushes my heart, and the tears keep rolling. "How…how do I not remember that? Wh-what happened to me?"

"I wish I didn't have to tell you," I whisper, taking a few steps toward her. "I wish it had never happened at all. I feel like I failed you. I don't want you to hate me."

"I could never hate you, Azalea Jinx." Her soft smile sends me flying back into her arms, my sobs louder and harder than before.

"Okay, well, I guess I'll start back at graduation…"

CHAPTER 37

"Something went wrong. She isn't herself anymore, but she isn't a Reaper anymore either. She attacked me, bit me, even though she's only a Dimineer. And when she bit into me…parts of me began to disappear. I don't know if this is a blessing or a curse. I don't know if this will heal me or save me. *I don't know, I don't know, I don't know—*"

—*The Grimoire*, written by the first, unnamed Grim, 1 A.G.

"I don't know whether to kill you or thank you," Demi says to Shayde at the end of the story, whispering, "but I think I'm going to vomit again." And she does. She vomits until there's nothing left, until it's just her dry heaving and gasping for air.

"I'm sorry for my part in this," Shayde says, truly looking sorrowful. "I-I've been so lost for the past few months. I can't always remember who I am or who I'm supposed to be. And after spending all those months away from Draxmere, I only knew what the Grim inside me wanted me to believe. I knew that I needed to show my dad I could be a good heir, and I knew I needed Azalea. That was it. I didn't care about anything else. But having you here helped. In those moments where I was me again, you…you reminded me what was at stake. And now that Azalea's here, I feel better than I have in almost a year." Since he was forced to leave me, he means.

Demi looks up, tears in her eyes and a scowl on her lips. "You made me do horrible things."

"Do you…Do you remember any of it?" I ask quietly, hoping beyond anything that she doesn't.

"No, I don't…I don't think so. But I'm so hungry." She groans, fangs on full display now. "I don't want to hurt any of you, but I really need to eat."

"Drink from me," Shayde offers, holding out his wrist.

"I don't want Grim blood," Demi spits, eyes flickering over to me and then to Dagan, still unconscious on the floor. "Is that guy dead?"

"Not yet." Shayde shrugs, dropping his wrist. "But you can't drink from him. He hasn't given permission."

"Oh, you care about that now, do you?" Demi snaps her teeth angrily, whimpering suddenly and clenching her stomach.

"Use me, Demi. Please. I insist." I hold out my wrist now, begging her to take it. She looks weary, but after releasing a loud groan of disapproval, she brings it to her mouth. The high of a vampire bite is quick to take over, my mind lost so rapidly that I almost collapse from how sudden it seems to be.

"Not too much," Shayde warns, but his glowering figure wavers in and out of my blurry vision. I open my mouth to speak, to tell him it's okay and that this feels *amazing*, but nothing will come out.

A figure moves in the distance, approaching quickly. It's a black shape, one with four legs and…oh. Oh, it's Grimsly. I try to call for him, to introduce him to Demi, but my mouth still won't open.

And before I can tell her who's coming, he's leaping onto my chest and forming an explosive shield that rips Demi from my wrist. I moan in pain from the ripping sensation, tumbling back and into Shayde's arms. He's warm and comforting, his blurry face taking up all of my vision.

"Azalea?" I think I hear him say, worried and panicked. I try to reassure him, to tell him I'm fine, but my damn mouth still won't move. "Azalea? What did you do? What did you do to her, Demi?"

"I didn't…I don't know. I've drunk from her before, and that's never—" Her sentences stop abruptly, but I can see her mouth still moving. Shayde's, too, I think. I frown, eyes flickering between the two.

Demi's in front of me now, waving a hand in front of my face and shouting. I think she's shouting. I can't tell. I can't tell what she's saying, what she's doing, where she's going. I don't know where up is or down. I don't know where—

"Fucking Grim," I moan, holding on to my pounding head. It feels as though my head is being torn in two, or maybe into threes. It hurts so bad that I lean over and vomit, the sound of my gagging alerting someone nearby.

"Azalea?" It's Shayde, his shadows encircling me and pulling my hair out of my face.

"She's awake," Demi breathes next to him, relieved. "I'm so sorry, Azzie! I didn't know that I was…" She stops, and when I look up at her, she's gnawing on her bottom lip.

"What was that?" I moan, pushing myself back into what I recognize as a bed. Shayde's bed. Our bed.

"I'll let Demi explain." Shayde's voice is tinged with a numbness I don't recognize, a disappointment that he can't hide.

"Wait!" I stop him from exiting the room, breathing deeply as I ask, "Dagan?"

"He's fine. He's in his room upstairs, recovering. He woke up once to introduce himself to Demi, cackled when she thanked him, and passed back out. I suspect it'll take a few more days of rest before he's feeling like himself again." And with that, he exits the room, my hair falling back down past my ears as his shadows retreat with him.

"I like the red. And the short cut," Demi says softly, performing a quick Scouring Charm to get rid of the vomit before she crawls onto the bed. She's careful as she crawls over my body, falling into the pillows beside me on her back.

"I needed a change. The purple reminded me of you, and I couldn't…" I pause, sucking in a deep breath, "I couldn't look at it anymore." I couldn't take care of it, couldn't cut my bangs, couldn't even curl my hair without thinking about her; something I avoided at all costs.

Her bottom lip quivers as she says, "The things you had to see, the things you had to endure…"

"Yes," I say, because I don't know what else to do.

"And you did it all alone." A tear slips down her cheek, and I notice the once white patches in her skin have darkened to a light shade of gray. Maybe soon she will look like herself again, and none of her will be gray anymore. Maybe it just takes time.

"At first," I admit, the back of my throat hard and dry. "I drank and I snorted drugs and I used pills to make myself sleep. Anything not to see you turn into a Reaper when I closed my eyes, anything not to watch Shayde leave as a Grim. And then Jaymes knocked some sense into me, and the hatred took over the self-pity."

"What changed?" she asks quietly.

"Shayde was so persistent." I choke out a laugh, wiping away her tears. I avoid looking at that plum purple ring around her eyes, avoid noticing the muted colors in her once bright hair. "I told him that if I couldn't love him, then I would hate him instead. And I was very serious about it, you know? Because how else would I get over it? But Shayde…Shayde followed me everywhere I went. And soon I discovered there are things worse than being in love with a Grim."

"Shayde told me they hurt you. The school, I mean."

"Yes, they did." I don't want to think about it, don't want to remember the pain and the fear that comes with being tied up and beaten. "And Shayde saved me. A *Grim* saved me from the very people I'm supposed to be saving. That's what changed, I think. I realized that there isn't a rule book for being a savior, and that the easiest way isn't always the right way. So, I stopped doing the easy thing. I stopped wanting to kill Shayde for what he did and started wanting to save you from what his dad did. And I put all of our friends in danger. Ginny was hurt badly. Not dead, thank the

Grim, but unconscious, the last I heard. I haven't thought about her much. I feel too guilty for what I did to her and the others."

"She'll forgive you once she sees what I am now. They all will." Demi takes my hand in hers, smiling softly.

"And what are you?" I ask quietly, turning so I don't have to look her in the eyes.

"Azalea…"

"Just tell me, Demi. Just tell me we didn't completely heal you and get it over with." My heart clenches so tightly that I'm sure it's going to stop entirely.

"I'm not completely healed," she says, and my heart beats so violently that I lurch up, clutching onto it.

"Did you…" I can't say what I suspect, can't voice it aloud.

"When I drank from you, I took some of your Charm Levels, too." Her voice is numb and disappointed like Shayde's. "I don't know if I will be able to feed without taking Charm Levels. And I was so hungry that…" She was starving, and she took too much because of it.

"That won't always happen," I reassure her, turning to her with wild eyes. Charm Levels replenish if you don't take them all at once. Mine have probably already been replenished, honestly. But if Demi can't survive without Charm Levels…"You can work on that. You won't take that much every time. You won't."

"Azalea…" She puts her hands on my cheeks, holding me still as she says slowly, "I'm always going to be starving. I'm always going to be craving something I can't have. I'm always going to be hungry. So, so hungry."

"The hunger stays," I whisper, body shaking as the sobbing begins. "The lust for power stays."

"It does," she confirms, her own tears pooling down. "But I can control it, I think. For now. But if there ever comes a time when I can't, I'm asking you now to kill me. Don't get me wrong, I'm grateful that I'm here with you right now, but you should have…" She chokes on her words, shaking her head furiously and dropping her hands into her lap.

"I should have killed you?" I shout, a distressed noise leaving my lips. "How could I have? I thought about it, I really did. And then Shayde told me once you were dead. And that…that was so much worse than knowing you were still here, just not yourself. So when I found out you weren't, and that there was hope to save you, I knew, no matter what you had done or would do, I couldn't kill you. I could never kill you."

"You must!" she cries out, desperate and angry. "If I cannot control myself, you must kill me. There is no more saving me, Azalea. You brought me back, and I will forever be grateful for it. But we both know that I'm not just a vampire anymore. I'm still a Reaper. And being a Reaper does not bode well for me. Just promise me, Azalea. Promise me that if I am ever lost within myself, you will kill me. I trust you, and only you, to do this. *Please, Azzie*. This is how you save me." She dips her head down onto my shoulder, arms wrapping around me tightly as she weeps.

I wrap my arms around her, tucking her tightly into my body, hissing through my teeth, "I promise."

I was never attached to the whole savior complex Delarosa had thrust on me from my very first day at Draxmere, but I *was* attached to the idea of being Demi's savior. I was confident that I wouldn't be able to save the world, but I was even more confident that I could save her. It was my only purpose after everything that happened, my only motivation, and now…now what is left? Am I supposed to want to save a world that doesn't want to be saved?

Demi is still a Reaper. I'm still not a savior. I'm still in love with a Grim.

The next step is obviously to help Shayde. I'll make sure that, at least, works. I love him too much to give up, just like I loved Demi too much to let her stay a Reaper. I won't fail this time. I can't. And the rest of the Charmed world…they can wait until Shayde is healed.

If it takes time to heal Shayde from his Grim, then so be it. The Conjurers made their choice when they stifled my powers, brought me onto a stage, and shoved me onto my knees in front of everyone. They made their choice when they looked at me in disgust as Bloodgood read off every single prophecy that claimed I may not be the savior they all desperately wanted me to be. And maybe I'm not. I've thought long and hard about what I really am, and the answer is simple:

I am a Grim fucker, and that's all I ever want to be.

Acknowledgements

I started this book four separate times, and each one was difficult because of the emotional turmoil I put myself through trying to see this world from Azalea's point of view. It was hard, and heart-crushing, and I wouldn't have been able to do it without the help of the many people who brought this book together. I want to say thank you to my beta readers, who helped correct Azalea's path. I want to say thank you to Jessica, who is always honest and uplifting and beyond supportive of my work. I want to say thank you to my wonderful editor Sage, who made a huge impact on the quality of this work and who made me smile with her comments. I want to say thank you to my wonderful street team for helping me make my dreams come true, and to the arc readers who took a chance on my work. And last, but not least, I want to say thank you to my readers for continuing this journey with me.

See you in book three!

About the Author

M.N. Lash, despite having a bachelors degree in biology and minors in chemistry/psychology, is a stay-at-home mom from Alabama. When she isn't reading or writing you can find her crocheting or attending to her many pets. Cruelly Divine is her third book, and she is readying to publish her fourth novel, an installment in the Draxmere Academy of Conjuring Series. You can also find her on Instagram for updates on future works @m.n._lash

ALSO BY

The Draxmere Academy of Conjuring Series
Conjuring A Grim
Charming A Grim
Unreleased Third Book (2026)

The Kiss Me Series
Kiss Me And Die (November 18th, 2025)
Unreleased Second Book (2026)

The Divine Providence Series
Royally Divine
Cruelly Divine